A departure from the conventional...
read.' Caroline Crofts, Rights Manager

"Tense and **darkly playful**, *Dead Gone* is a cleverly constructed début thriller that explores the twisted potential for psychological experimentation. Murphy and Rossi are a **fresh** and intriguing detective partnership and Luca Veste casts a fascinating new light on the Scouse sensibility." **Chris Ewan – Bestselling Author of** *Safe House*

"Luca Veste hits the ground running with a gripping and **shocking** crime début, that will make the hairs on the back of your neck stand up." **Mark Edwards – Bestselling Author of** *The Magpies*

"A fresh, original voice with Northern warmth and inter-weaving plot-lines that kept me turning the pages quickly. Using an **innovative** psychology angle, Veste has created a story that builds up **suspense** fully towards its climactic outcome. I can't wait to read more of Murphy and Rossi." **Mel Sherratt – Bestselling Author of** *Taunting the Dead* **and** *The Estate series*

"A **gripping** descent into the **darkest corners** of the human mind." **Neil White – Author of** *Beyond Evil*

"Gripping, **unpredictable**, genuinely shocking and impossible to put down, *Dead Gone* is a remarkable début." **Steve Mosby - Dagger Award Winning Author of** *The 50/50 Killer*, *Black Flowers,* **and** *Dark Room*

"Luca Veste is an innovative and powerful new voice in crime fiction. His début novel *Dead Gone* is a truly original and **chilling** book that will stay with you long after you've finished reading it. *Dead Gone* is a story so startling, disturbing and twisted, I wish I'd thought of it. You might not want to read this one before bedtime." **Howard Linskey – Author of the David Blake novels,** *The Drop, The Damage* **and** *The Dead*

"Gripping and well-paced, this is a superior piece of crime fiction. Murphy & Rossi are a **cracking double act** sure to find plenty of fans." Emlyn Rees – International Bestselling Author of *Hunted*

"Luca Veste takes the serial killer novel into new and **unexplored territory**. This is an original and terrifying book, plunging into the black waters of psychological experimentation, drugs, and mind control. Assured, confident, never exploitative, this is the kind of book that makes you think. With a début as **distinctive** as this, you can only wait with bated breath for the next instalment." Stav Sherez – Critically Acclaimed Author of the Award Nominated *A Dark Redemption* and *Eleven Days*

"Dark, tense and terrifying, *Dead Gone* is a remarkable début. It lives and breathes Liverpool. Luca Veste is a name destined for great things." Helen FitzGerald - Author of *The Devil's Staircase, The Donor* and *The Cry*

"*Dead Gone* is one of the most **accomplished** débuts I've read in a long time. Veste has combined the **sleek prose** and deft plotting of the police procedural with an interrogation of the human spirit usually only seen in the best kind of psychological thrillers to produce a serial killer novel which stands head and shoulders above the competition, and in the process announces himself as a major new talent on the crime scene." Eva Dolan – Author of *Long Way Home*

"Dark, dangerous and complex, *Dead Gone* is that rare thing – an intelligent serial killer novel that's both entertaining and **thought-provoking**." Nick Quantrill – Author of the Joe Geraghty Trilogy

DEAD GONE

Luca Veste is a writer of Italian and Scouse heritage, currently living on the wrong side of the River Mersey. He is married with two young daughters, and is himself one of nine children.

He is currently a mature student, studying Psychology and Criminology in Liverpool.

He is the editor of the Spinetingler Award nominated charity anthology series *Off The Record*, which raises money for children's literacy charities. He also has short stories in numerous publications.

A former civil servant, actor, and musician, he now divides his time between home life, University work and writing.

To find out more about Luca visit his website www.lucaveste.com or find him on both Facebook and Twitter @lucaveste.

LUCA VESTE

Dead Gone

AVON

AVON
A division of HarperCollins*Publishers*
1 London Bridge Street
London SE1 9GF

www.harpercollins.co.uk

A Paperback Original 2014

First published in Great Britain by
HarperCollins*Publishers* 2014

A catalogue record for this book is
available from the British Library

ISBN-13: 978-0-00-752557-7

Set in Sabon LT Std by Palimpsest Book Production Limited,
Falkirk, Stirlingshire

Printed by CPI Group (UK) Ltd, Croydon CR0 4YY

MIX
Paper from
responsible sources
FSC
www.fsc.org   FSC® C007454

Without the support of so many, this book would not have been possible. I owe my eternal gratitude and thanks to the following people.

To Eva, Nick, and Helen, who where always just an email or phone call away, and consistently provided excellent advice and guidance. Similarly, Steve, Stav, and Neil, who inspired much of what appears between these pages. Charlie Williams, who dared me to write a story and then told me to keep going. To early readers Vicky Newham and Linda Moore, who afforded their time to me and where a great help.

Thank you to my agent Philip Patterson, who changed my life (and this book) with one conversation, and has continued to give unwavering support since then. Also to Isabella and Luke at Marjacq for all their hard work. My incredible editor at Avon, Sammia Rafique, who has gone above and beyond my wildest expectations with her drive and tenacity for the book. Thanks also to Keshini Naidoo, and everyone at Avon and HarperCollins.

To SallyAnn and John and Gina Kirkham, for all the policing advice. All mistakes are my own, and probably intentional.

My family, who have constantly been a source of both support and inspiration. My parents Alan and Tracy Veste, Sue Kirkham and John Brisk, and Carole and Alan Woodland (it was a group effort). My grandparents, and all eight of my brothers and sisters (I'll name you all in the next book!). Perry and Cath Hale, Mike and Jemma, Peter and Izzybella Veste.

Finally to my wife Emma, who is ridiculously supportive of me, *ti amo bella,* and to Abigail and Megan, who put up with daddy's grumpy moods in the morning, following late night writing.

For Emma, Abs and Migs - It came true.

PART ONE

Life is pleasant. Death is peaceful. It's the transition
that's troublesome.

Isaac Asimov

*We are taught from an early age to fear death, that
unknowable force we are all moving towards, simply
by existing. However, this aspect of human life is not
one discussed easily amongst those in western society.
Death is not an easy topic to discuss openly, without
the fear of perhaps upsetting or insulting. This one
aspect that binds us all together, touches us all, irrespec-
tive of race, gender, or orientation; the one thing we all
have in common, yet so often it is considered a 'dark'
subject. Talking about one's own mortality is considered
morbid and morose.*

*One truth remains however. We all die. Every single
living organism experiences death. Indeed, according to
Dr. Sigmund Freud, 'It is the aim of all life.' We live
to die. Homo sapiens as a species have shown great
technological advances over the past few centuries. Yet
one thing we have not, and will arguably never achieve,
is to create a way of dealing with death in a uniform*

manner as a population. We grieve differently, we die differently.

Death touches us all. Should we fear death, try to actively repel it, through attempts to prolong our lives? If technology moved to such a point that death could be avoided, endless life became a possibility, would we ever be able to really live?

Without being able to investigate death and the repercussions for the deceased, is it possible to study death in any meaningful way, without being able to experience it?

Taken from 'Life, Death, and Grief', published in Psychological Society Review, 2008, issue 72.

Experiment Two

She hadn't been afraid of the dark.

Not before.

Not before it entered her life without her knowing, enveloping her like a second skin, becoming a part of her.

She hadn't been claustrophobic, petrified the walls were closing in around her. Crushed to death without knowing they'd even moved. Not scared of things that crawled around her toes. Wasn't afraid to sit alone in a darkened room and wonder if something was touching her face, or if it was just her imagination.

Nope. She wasn't scared before.

She was now.

It took time to become afraid of those things, and time was all she had, stretching out in front of her without end.

She blamed herself. Blamed her friends. Blamed him. She shouldn't be there, and someone was to blame for that.

Had to be.

She'd become a responsible adult. The right thing, supposedly. Gone were the days she'd spent going into town, two, sometimes three times a week. Karaoke on a Friday, pulling on a Saturday – if there were any decent lads out – quiet

3

one on a Sunday. Now she was always the first one to leave, early on in the night, when everyone else was just getting started.

She didn't like the feeling of being drunk. That loss of control, of sensibility. She'd been hungover so many times. She'd decided it wasn't what responsible adults did. Her mum had drummed that into her one night, holding back her hair as two bottles of white wine and god knows how many vodka and lemonades decided they wanted out.

She'd rather be at home now, watching TV after a day's work, especially if it meant he was sitting close to her. She didn't even mind that he always had the laptop on, playing that stupid football management game. Just being there with him was enough.

She still enjoyed a drink at the end of a work day, a glass of wine with a meal and the occasional full bottle at the weekend. But the binging had stopped. That was for certain.

When a Cheeky Vimto cocktail had been forced into her hand by one of the girls who told her she'd love it she didn't say no. Port and WKD. Who thought of these things? She didn't care. It tasted bloody great.

One more led to four more, and before she knew it, she was in an eighties-themed nightclub, dancing her heart out to Chesney Hawkes. Two a.m. hit, and she was saying her goodbyes. She loved them all. Her girls. Always left wondering why they didn't see her more often.

'Don't go yet, we'll all share a taxi later. Club doesn't shut for another hour.'

'It's alright, I'll be fine. I'm knackered, want my bed. Need to get back . . . No, it's okay I'll walk up to the tunnel stretch by the museum if I can't get one.'

Voice going hoarse from shouting over the music. Promises to do it all again soon. To give them a text when she'd arrived home.

Finally she was out of the club, the bouncer helping her down the final step. Fresh air hit her, along with the realisation she was as drunk as she'd been in a long time. She began searching through her handbag for her phone, eventually finding it in the same pocket it was always in, wanting to call a taxi to pick her up.

'For fuck's sake.'

Too loud. Not in the club any longer, but her voice hadn't caught onto that fact yet. A couple stared as they passed by, as she continued her argument with the stupid battery-sucking smart phone. The decision to wear comfortable shoes becoming the best idea she'd ever had. She set off for the taxi ranks at the end of Matthew Street, hoping it wouldn't be too long a wait. She walked past the old Cavern Club, the sound of some shitty band murdering old hits wafting out of the doors, as a few tourists spilled out onto the street.

She couldn't find a taxi, queues of people down North John Street. She walked away from the lights of the clubs in the city centre, hoping to get one coming out of the tunnel. When she was younger it had been easier, as there was always enough of them to be safe getting the night bus home. Now she had money in her pocket she wouldn't have to sit on a full bus, the stink of kebabs and vodka shots seeping into her clothes. The lads who were either squaring up to each other, or trying it on with any girl with a pulse. No thank you, she could pay the eight quid and get home without any of that.

She stood on the corner near the museum, waiting for a hackney with its light on to pass her. She wrapped her arms around herself, cold air beginning to bite as she stopped walking and leant against the St John's Gardens wall, the museum over to her right. The entrance and exit to Birkenhead tunnel directly opposite her. Swaying to silent music.

She was cold, wishing she'd picked a warmer coat when

she'd left the house earlier. She'd picked the right shoes, that was supposed to be enough. Ten minutes went by, then fifteen, before a hackney finally came towards her, slowing down before passing her.

'Hey!'

It went up towards town, then did a U-turn and headed back her way, coming to a stop in front of her. She opened the door, barely registering the driver at all, just shouted her address at him, and settled back in the seat. She was glad to be in the warmth of the car.

As they drove through the city centre, she began to feel just a little uncomfortable, the driver looking straight ahead, barely acknowledging her presence. He'd not said a word since she'd entered. Must be one of the new foreign drivers that were coming over from Eastern Europe or wherever. Her mum would know. She should ring her mum tomorrow, she thought. She hadn't been in touch much lately, and she wanted to catch up.

She yawned a few times in succession, the blurred buildings going past becoming hypnotic as the cab wound its way out of the city centre towards home. She battled her tiredness and lost, as her eyes closed and stayed that way.

That was her mistake.

She woke when the cab came to a stop and looked up to see the driver getting out of the cab. Through bleary eyes, confused by the sudden absence of movement, she sat fully upright.

'I'm awake, it's okay,' she called out, but he was already walking around the cab, past her door and out of her sight.

Panic didn't set in straight away. Confusion was first.

'Where are we?' The windows inside had misted over, and she swiped her hand over the pane. To one side she saw trees lining a gravel driveway. She tried opening the door, but the handle wouldn't budge. She moved across the seat, and tried that door handle. Same result. She swiped her hand over the window again, seeing a house to the other side. A strange house. Not her house. Oh shit, not her house.

'What's going on?' She could hear the man's shoes crunching through the gravel behind the car and then her window darkened. She jumped in her seat. He was crouched level with the window, his face obscured by a black balaclava.

Panic started then.

His voice came through the window. Slow, precise.

'We're in the middle of nowhere. So if you scream, no one will hear you. More importantly, if you do scream, I'm going to break the fingers on your right hand. Scream again, and I'll cut them off. You understand me?' There was no trace of an accent, yet there was something odd about his voice.

She started to move across the back seat to the opposite door. Adrenaline kicked in. The need to get away, to get out of there, overtaking everything else.

He was quicker though. The door opened behind her and a hand grabbed her by the shoulder. He was strong.

Fight back, fight for her life, fight back.

Without screaming.

She used her fists against the opposite window, pulling on the door handle with all her weight, as the man attempted to drag her out.

He got a firm grip of her dress, and placed his arm around her neck, turning her around. She kicked out at him, but felt herself being lifted from the car. He dragged her all the way inside the house, his grip around her throat choking the air out of her lungs. Her eyes drifted downwards and then around. Stone steps with marble pillars to the sides marked the entrance, but she had no time to look at them as she was pulled along a darkened corridor. She needed to breathe properly. Watched as one of her comfortable shoes slipped

7

off and became lost in the darkness. She kicked at the ground, scratched at his arm, used her fingers to try and prise her way out of his hands, but nothing worked. She was being dragged along on her heels.

He stopped, shifted his grip so she was now in a headlock. She could breathe a little. They went through an opening, before she bounced downwards. A staircase, she guessed. She couldn't tell. It was too dark.

They came to a stop. He took his arm from around her head, and before she had a chance to move, he pushed her with two hands. She fell backwards, landing hard.

She heard, rather than saw a door close. She sprang up, the pain from the fall lost in the midst of heavy breathing and adrenaline.

'Let me out of here you bastard! Open this door, open it now.'

She was in darkness and grasped at the door, trying to find a handle or anything that would open the door. She used her fists, banging on the door with all her strength. 'Please, don't leave me here.'

She continued to bang on the door until her hand started to ache.

She switched hands.

It came then. A voice through the walls, an audible static over it. She stopped, cocking her head to listen.

'You will be fed. You will have water. There is a hatch opening on the door which can only be opened from the outside, through which this will be provided. On some days your food will have an extra ingredient, in order for me to clean up. You will not know when this is. If you're good, I won't have to kill you.'

The voice was silent then. She stood still, straining to hear any other noise, backing away from the door carefully. She put her hands out in front of her, her eyes trying to adjust.

There was no sound, other than her own breathing, panting in and out. She spread her arms around, jumping a little as her hand brushed against a flat surface.

She took a large breath in, struggling to keep the panic in. She couldn't see the walls around her, yet she could already feel them. Closing in on her.

She was alone, in the darkness.

1

Sunday 27th January 2013 – Day One

Frosty, brisk air swirled around Sefton Park and its surrounding area, the early morning mist only just beginning to lift above the tree line. Detached houses, set back from the main road, lined the street on one side, where flashing lights from multiple vehicles had drawn out bleary eyed gawkers. They stood on the pavements shifting on cold feet in the early morning light. Mostly, they wouldn't say two words to each other, but the early morning excitement had driven them out, even caused conversation to break out. At one time the houses had contained whole families, now most were converted apartments, selling for six-figure sums.

Detective Inspector David Murphy turned his attention back to the park over the road; not your small, family friendly, swings and slide type of park. Instead, acres of greenery, beautiful old trees, and enough space to see something new each time you walk through there.

And the odd dead body turning up unannounced.

It was usually suicides. Hanging from a tree or a bunch of pills in the middle of a field. Hoping no one finds them before they go.

But at times it was something else.

He saw the lights in the distance. Blue, red, shifting from left to right. The constant pattern having a seemingly hypnotic effect on those straining to see further into the park beyond. Murphy was sitting in his car, the engine settling as he summoned up the energy to get out and make his way over. The lights of the marked cars parked in front of his Citroen reflected off the dark interior inside, a strobe effect bouncing off the dashboard.

Murphy shook his seatbelt off and leaned forward, attempting to see past the lights and people milling around the park. He slumped back in the seat when it became clear he wouldn't see anything.

He scratched his beard, the trim he'd performed the previous night giving it a coiffed edge, which he decided said 'distinguished' rather than 'hiding a double chin'. He stifled a yawn and opened the car door, stretching his long legs out, the tight feeling in his calves telling him he'd maybe overdone it on the cross trainer the previous evening, trying to shift those last few pounds of weight.

He'd been awake no more than fifteen minutes when his DCI had called. That made it less than an hour into the day for him, and he was walking towards the body of a dead girl.

Not how Murphy usually liked to start off a day . . . especially a Sunday. A phone call from work before he'd even had chance to drink his coffee. Have a slice of toast. Put a fresh suit on.

Death could be incredibly selfish.

'Murphy,' he'd answered once he'd finally located the phone hiding in his jeans pocket on the bedroom floor. Stabbed at the screen, trying to answer the stupid thing.

'David?'

Murphy's shoulders slumped. DCI Stephens. Which, outside of normal hours, usually signified nothing good. 'What's happened?'

'A body. Suspicious circumstances. Found in Sefton Park.'

'Shit. Bad?'

'Not sure of all the details at the moment.'

'I'm wanted?'

'Why else would I be calling you David? I'm not your bloody alarm clock.'

'It's been a while, that's all. Was starting to wonder if I'd be stuck on break-ins for another six months.'

'Well you've got something else now.'

'Who's with me?'

'Rossi or Tony Brannon. Your decision.'

'Great. Not exactly Sophie's fucking Choice.'

'Language. Weren't you taught never to swear in front of a lady? And anyway, beggars can't be choosers. How long until you can get down there?'

Murphy crooked his phone between his shoulder and ear. Grabbed his trousers from where they had been lying next to his jeans. 'Which end?'

'Which end of what?'

'The park.' Jesus wept.

'Oh, Aigburth Drive. Just look for the lights. Sounds like half the bloody force is there.'

Murphy zipped up his trousers and gave the previous day's shirt a sniff. 'I'll be there in twenty minutes.'

He left the house five minutes later reversing out the driveway, and onto the road. Decided twenty minutes was probably a little optimistic. It'd probably be double that this time of the morning, even without the usual weekday traffic through the tunnel. He shook his head, tugged on his bottom lip with his teeth, and turned right out of the small winding road which surrounded the small estate, lamenting the fact he was already going to be playing catch up when he got there.

The commute may have been bad, but at least it gave him

a chance to wake up. Within five minutes he was on the motorway heading for the Wallasey tunnel, which separated the Wirral and Liverpool. The Wirral is a small peninsula, only separated from Liverpool by the River Mersey, and connected by a mile-long tunnel underneath the seabed.

The Wirral hadn't always been home. In fact, he'd only been able to call it that for the previous few months. The differences between the two places was closing in recent years. The Wirral was historically known as simultaneously living in Liverpool's shadow, whilst also enjoying much more wealth than most of Liverpool. These days, the link was closer. Whilst the wealth was still strong in the west of the Wirral, with the likes of West Kirby and Heswall, the destruction of the shipping trade at Cammell Laird's on the east side meant that the Wirral now had its own pockets of deprivation. Even the kids spoke in a Scouse accent these days, albeit a bastardised version of it. Murphy was comfortable living there, even if the subtle differences became more apparent every day, needling at him.

He loved the city of Liverpool. The people, the buildings, the history. He just needed to time away. Working there was enough for now.

He used his fast tag when he arrived at the Wallasey tunnel booths, and broke the forty mile an hour limit going under the River Mersey, but it was still forty minutes after the phone call by the time he'd pulled the car to a stop.

He walked out into the damp and cold January morning, zipping his coat up as he walked towards the railings which lined the path, hastily strung-up crime scene tape strewn across them. The wide main road was shadowed by high trees on both sides, which masked most of the view. A couple of uniforms stood guard at the park entrance – a quick flash of his warrant card and he was able to pass through.

He could see the hive of activity a couple of hundred

yards or so up ahead, near a stone path which cut through the grass on either side, leading from the entrance into the distance. The main activity seemed to be concentrated on a grass verge which went up into the treeline. Murphy dropped his head as the wind picked up, and began walking towards it.

'Sir!' Detective Constable Laura Rossi, second generation Italian. Five and a half foot tall, dark long hair. Strong looking, from the broad shoulders which made her look stocky, to the roman nose which complimented her features. Most of the single, and quite a few of the married, lads at the station had tried and failed with her. Murphy wasn't one of them. She came bounding towards Murphy and brushed her hair away from her face, tucking strands behind her ear. 'You all right?'

'What have we got?' Murphy said as she reached him.

'Morning to you too sir.'

Murphy looked down at her, Rossi being at least eight inches smaller, and about half his weight. He smiled as she looked up to him, before realising where they were and adopting a stoic face once more. He was glad she was there. In a weird way, and completely without context given he had no kids of his own, he wanted to look after her; be a father figure of some sort. She was inexperienced, he supposed. Needed some guidance. Which, if this was a bona fide murder case, he could definitely do without. Especially considering his last effort. 'Let's get on with it. And stop calling me sir, how many times do I have to tell you.'

'Course. Sorry sir. Young female, found by a corpse sniffer around six a.m. Fully clothed. Nothing around the body, just laid out beneath a tree.'

Murphy looked around and spotted the man she was referring to, talking to some uniforms. An older guy, probably in his mid-sixties, his dog sitting next to him, silent on his lead.

'He have anything to say?' Murphy said.

'Not much, dog ran off into the trees, he went looking for it and found the girl.'

'Is nobhead here?'

Rossi looked confused. 'Who's a nobhead?'

Murphy smiled, still finding it amusing that the Scouse accent didn't match the Mediterranean looks. 'Brannon. Is he around?'

Rossi attempted to hold back a laugh behind a hand. Murphy noticed her fingernails, bitten down rather than manicured. 'Yeah, he's off on the hunt for clues. His words, not mine.'

'Good.' Murphy replied. 'Fat bastard could do with some exercise. SOCOs here yet?'

'About twenty minutes before you.'

'Any other witnesses?'

'Not at the moment.'

'Okay. You looked at the body yet?'

Rossi shook her head.

'Well then. Let's not keep her waiting.'

Murphy snapped on his gloves, extra-large, and began walking towards the scene. He could see the Palm House, a large dome building which was the centrepiece of the park, in the distance, past the trees. The great glass windows which gave it the appearance of a huge greenhouse looked dull and lifeless in the muggy morning light.

Murphy and Rossi entered the tent which was being erected around the body. The treeline was thicker there, the ground, still not completely unfrozen from the previous harsh winter, crunching underneath his feet.

The click and whirr of photographs being taken was the only soundtrack to the scene. Murphy let his eyes be drawn to the girl. Early twenties he figured. Plain looking, dressed conservatively in black trousers and a red v-necked jumper. One earring, which meant either one was missing or was now a souvenir.

His money, as always, was on the latter. Always to the morbid thought first. To be fair, he was usually right.

Murphy side-stepped around the edge, carefully avoiding anything that looked important, and stood at the foot of the body, taking it in. She had the distinctive pallor of the dead; pale, the colour drained out of her as the blood stopped flowing. The clothes looked new, unworn, the creases on the jumper looking like they were from packaging, rather than wear.

She was spread-eagled, her arms outstretched in a V, her legs doing the same. Carefully placed in the position. It looked unnatural, posed, which was probably the intention, Murphy thought. Her face was what drew his gaze. Half-lidded eyes, staring right through him. Blue, glazed, the last image they'd captured that of whoever had left her here. Her mouth was slightly parted, the top row of her teeth on show in a final grimace. Ugly, red marks over her bare neck.

Dr Stuart Houghton, Stu to his friends, was crouched next to the girl. He'd been the lead pathologist in the city for as long as Murphy had been working. His grey hair was thinning, his posture looking soft as he stood up from his haunches. His short, squat stature only enhanced by the ever-growing paunch he was cultivating around his middle. He turned to look at Murphy.

'Dr Houghton, what have we got?'

'Took your time Dave.'

Murphy shot his hands to his mouth. 'Calling me Dave when you know I don't like it? You never fail to shock. And it was only because I knew you'd be here already. What can you tell me?'

'Are you running this one?' Houghton said.

Murphy gazed at the pathologist and shrugged his shoulders. 'I just do as I'm told.'

Houghton pursed his lips at him. 'Well then, can't tell you much at the moment,' he said, gesturing towards the young woman. 'This is how she was found, her arms and legs outstretched like she's doing a star jump, only lying down. There's no evidence around the body as far as we can tell so far, and she's been dead around twelve hours. No ID, handbag, purse, nothing. Other than that you'll have to wait for the post mortem for me to tell you more. We're moving her out now.'

'Why suspicious then?' Murphy asked, knowing the answer but wanting to piss off the doc a little more.

Houghton muttered something under his breath before continuing. 'As you can no doubt already see, there's bruises around her neck which indicate asphyxiation. First paramedic on the scene noticed them, and, in my opinion correctly, assumed it was better to call in the big boys.'

Murphy looked closer at the girl. Large bruises under her chin, turning darker as time moved on. A large birthmark, or mole, the colour of strong coffee on the lower left side of her neck.

'Did she die here?'

'Not certain yet, but I'm almost positive she wasn't. No signs of struggle around the area. The grass is flattened only in the immediate vicinity of the body.'

'Any other distinguishing features aside from the mole, I need to know about straight away. And let us know when the post mortem is.'

Houghton nodded, and went back to work.

Murphy left the tent, Rossi trailing behind him. 'We'll take a statement from the witness and then we should try and find out who she is.'

17

Rossi nodded and set off towards the witness. Murphy began the process of removing his gloves and looking around the area, seeing a few familiar faces from older crime scenes about the place. He nodded and exchanged greetings with some of them.

No one stopped to talk to him.

He wasn't surprised. He gave one last look at the finished tent, the uniforms walking around the area, looking under the bushes and scouring the ground.

Back to it.

2

Sunday 27th January 2013 – Day One

'This is Eddie Bishop,' Rossi said as she led the dog walker towards Murphy. He was a grey-haired man with a stooped posture, a little Jack Russell padding alongside him. Yellow, stained teeth grimaced back at Murphy, the man's wrinkled hands gripping the lead tighter, as he kept the dog close by.

'Just a couple of questions, Mr Bishop.'

'Eddie is fine.'

'Okay Eddie.' Murphy replied, noting the softness of the infamous Scouse accent. Softness which you only really heard from the older inhabitants of the city nowadays. 'Do you walk this way often?' he continued.

'Twice a day, first thing in the morning, again in the evening.'

Murphy watched as Rossi wrote down the conversation in her notepad. 'And the dog found the victim.'

Eddie's face grew serious as he explained how he'd found the dog stood over the young woman. 'Terrible shame. Will take me a long time to get over this, I'll tell you that for nothing.'

'And you didn't notice anything out of the ordinary this morning. Anything at all?' Murphy asked.

Eddie shook his head. 'Same as always, just me and Floyd.' he replied, gesturing at the dog.

Murphy finished up with Eddie, explaining the need for a formal statement and promising to keep him informed, knowing that would be highly unlikely.

'Anything else?' Murphy asked Rossi, as she finished writing the conversation down in her notepad.

'There's someone who keeps telling uniforms at the gate that he heard something. Might be an idea to check that out.'

'Okay. We'll do that now.'

Murphy stopped to take in the place. The park was big enough to get lost in, vast areas of green and small wooded areas surrounding it.

'In the dark, you could become invisible in a place like this,' Murphy said to Rossi as they neared the gates.

'True. Perfect places for this type of thing. In and out, probably without being seen in the early hours,' Rossi replied, stepping underneath the crime scene tape. 'I'll be coming to interview this witness with you, yeah? I mean, I guess I'm getting to partner up with you on this one?'

Murphy paused. 'Let me see. We've worked together on and off for about two years, right?'

Rossi nodded her head up and down slowly.

'Ever known me to choose to work with Brannon?'

She smiled and mocked a salute. 'I'll just go and get a new notepad from the car.'

Murphy watched as she walked towards her car parked over the road, her posture straight and assured. The trouser suit looked new.

'Sir. Sir!'

Murphy stopped and turned. Sighed for effect. 'What do you want Brannon?'

DS Brannon stopped jogging and bent down with his

hands on his knees, panting. 'I . . . sorry . . .' He brought himself up again. 'I just wondered if there was anything I can do?'

'Haven't you already got something to do?'

'I just thought you might have something more interesting. I'm being wasted walking around looking through the mud.'

'Rossi is assisting me on this one Brannon. Maybe next time. For now, I want witness statements from everyone who lives in these houses which face the park entrance. Start organising it.'

'But . . .'

Murphy smiled inwardly and turned back towards the road outside the park. Brannon wasn't all that bad really. He was annoying rather than incompetent. He wasn't even all that fat, but first impressions stick.

The uniforms were already being harassed by local residents eager to discover what was occurring near their homes. Murphy pushed through, ignoring the questions being directed towards him from a particular wild-haired older man, adorned only in a dressing gown and slippers.

Murphy took the uniformed constable who'd been trying to placate the man to one side. 'Which one says he heard something?'

'The loud-mouthed one.'

Typical, Murphy thought. 'Okay, where does he live?' The constable pointed to his house, which was exactly opposite the entrance. 'Take him back in. We'll be there in a minute.'

The first thought that struck Murphy as they approached the house, was that it seemed a little big for just one man.

As he entered, the second thought was that it wasn't big enough for one man and the amount of stuff he seemed to own.

Newspapers were stacked up along the hallway in bundles,

at least four feet in height, held together with what looked like old twine. A staircase with no carpet ran up the other side, which was similarly stacked with paper, but magazines instead of newspapers. As Murphy walked towards the first door which led off the hallway, he became aware of a sour milk smell which assailed his nostrils, making him thankful for the lack of breakfast that morning. Rossi was a few steps behind him. Murphy turned to see if it had reached her yet. From the look on her face, he knew it had.

'In and out?'

'Definitely, or I'm going now.' Rossi replied, covering her mouth with her hand.

They turned into a large living room, Rossi almost bumping into the back of Murphy as he stopped in his tracks.

'Jesus.'

The room was full. The only visible space to stand was that which Murphy was occupying. Small portable televisions teetered precariously on top of microwaves with missing doors. Stacks of crockery were piled onto an old mantelpiece a door missing its glass leaning against it.

It was the world's biggest game of Jenga, only using household goods instead of wooden bricks.

'Who's there?'

The voice seemed to come from within the mass of what Murphy could only think of as every item a person could acquire in their life, without ever throwing anything away.

'Hello? I'm Detective Inspector Murphy, this is Detective Constable Rossi.' Murphy turned to introduce Rossi, but there was an empty space behind him.

Great.

'I have a lot of work to do. Are you going to get on with it?'

Murphy ducked a little, trying to find the source of the

22

voice. He saw a flash of brown through a small gap in the structure. 'Can you tell me your name?'

A loud sigh. 'Arthur Reeves.'

'Right. And you live here alone?'

'Do you see anyone else here?'

'I can't even see you Mr Reeves.'

A small chuckle. 'I guess that's right. Let's cut to the chase. I heard a car last night. It kept going up and down the road, disturbed my sleep. I got up out of bed and looked out the window. I couldn't see very well, there's not many streetlights up this way. It stopped at the entrance to the park. I assumed they'd been trying to find a parking space. Then it drove on again, right into the park.'

Murphy stood back up. 'Did you see notice anything about the car? Colour, model, reg plate?'

'Not really. It was dark, as I said. Could have been dark blue, or dark red. Looked like a normal car. Or a van. A small van.'

'Okay. And what time was this?'

'About four a.m. I think. Maybe five or three, or in between. I thought it might be important, considering.'

Not exactly the early break Murphy had been looking for. 'Anything else?'

'Sorry. I went back to bed. It wasn't until I saw all the police cars turn up that I even gave it a second thought.'

'Well, thank you Mr Reeves,' Murphy said, patting his thigh, 'that's a great help.'

'Is that it?'

'Yeah. An officer will come and take a formal statement soon. But for now, you can get back to work.'

Murphy turned out of the room, almost coming face to face with Rossi. 'There you are.'

'Found the smell.' Rossi whispered. 'In the kitchen. There's about two thousand empty milk bottles in there. Estimating of course. Think he got bored of rinsing them out.'

23

'Let's get out of here.'

They left the house, Murphy filling Rossi in on his conversation. 'What was his deal do you reckon?' he said as he finished.

'One of those hoarders I think. We should call environmental health. Can't be safe living like that.'

Murphy murmured an agreement. 'Nearest CCTV to here?'

'At the top junction which leads onto Ullet Road. Almost a mile up the road. Will get onto that.'

'What about from the other end?'

Rossi clicked her tongue. 'A lot of roads up that way. If our guy came from there, it could be any number of places. All CCTV in the area then?'

Murphy nodded. 'Best to check everything.'

'What now?'

They'd reached the entrance to the park again. The early morning mist had cleared, winter sun threatening to break through the remaining clouds. Murphy could still see faint traces of breath as he exhaled. 'We need to find out who she is. Back to the station, check the system for any missing persons who match the description.'

'Okay, will meet you there.'

Murphy reversed around a corner of a small cul de sac, and pointed the car back towards the station. Sefton Park is about four miles out of the centre of Liverpool, away from the hustle of town, into a leafier suburb. Once Murphy had turned into Ullet Road and then further onto the A roads which led towards the station, the contrast was complete. Half completed buildings appeared in the distance, scaffolding and cranes became the landscape. The River Mersey was off to his left, but was masked by warehouses and housing estates. Toxteth on the opposite side, still struggling to recover from the events of twenty years earlier.

A city of contrast. Light and dark. Rich footballers and child poverty. Derelict housing and glass-fronted office buildings.

Murphy lived it all. Took it all home with him, and attempted to make sense of it. How one city could have so many nuances to the lives of its inhabitants. Then he'd realise that every major city has the same issues. Feel slightly better about it all. It wasn't just Liverpool, they weren't a special case.

Then he'd wake up and begin a murder investigation of a young woman, and the old feelings of resignation returned. A thread in the tapestry of his life coming loose. Frayed and torn. Threatening to be destroyed completely. A feeling in the pit of his stomach. Not a nervous feeling, something a little different. Something harder to ignore.

Fear.

3

Saturday 18th February 2012
Eleven Months Earlier
Rob

Rob Barker was nothing if not average. Average height, average build, average wage earner, average Sunday League player.

No one called him special. He didn't win trophies or certificates.

He lived in an average-sized house, with an average-sized garden. His car was an average-priced model.

When magazines or newspapers talk about the 'average twenty-five to forty-year-old male', that was him. He ticked all those boxes.

It wasn't accidental. He desperately strived to go unnoticed, to not do anything special as he'd grown older and reached that pivotal moment of his early thirties. Bad things don't happen to normal, average people. That fact had been drummed into his head from an early age.

Don't get cocky. Don't strive for more than you can handle.

Bad things happen to those who put themselves out there, raise their head above the parapet and ask life to take pot shots at them. Much better to fly under the radar, coast through life, happy and content.

Yet there was one area of his life he couldn't control.

Who he would fall in love with.

Intelligent, witty, beautiful. Jemma was all that and more. So much more. She was bright, quick witted, and the worst cook Rob had ever known. She put a whole packet of noodles in a microwave once. Might have been okay if she'd taken them out of the packet and added water first.

She was gone.

And it was his fault.

Rob woke that morning to the sound of a Scottish ex-footballer complaining about a red card in a football match he hadn't seen. The joys of talkSPORT. He steadily came around, listening to the radio as he began to wake. A split second when he wondered where he was before normality came in. It always took him some time to wake up – he was a deep sleeper, as Jemma would constantly remind him. With a radio show on, especially one discussing football, he was more likely to be up and ready for work a lot quicker.

She'd texted him before midnight to say she was having a late one. Rob had pretended it was fine, no big deal. Inside, he was shaking. How would she get home? Anything could happen to her at that time of night. Did she care?

He didn't trust her. He couldn't remember a time when he had. Everything was too good. Too nice. They barely argued. It didn't feel real. Relationships weren't perfect.

She wasn't in the bed next to him. He wasn't surprised. He'd been prepared for that.

'Downstairs. She'll be downstairs.' His voice sounded alien, scared. He knew then that she wouldn't be, but he wanted to kid himself everything was still normal. An alarm bell at the back of his mind clanged against his skull with every thought of her being home and safe. That wasn't the case, and he wouldn't let himself believe it.

He sat up in bed, swung his legs to the side and slipped

on the clothes he'd discarded the night before. Blue tracksuit bottoms and a footy shirt. Red.

The house was too settled, no sounds of light snoring coming from downstairs. When Jemma had been drinking she had a tendency to snore a bit. Rob didn't hear any snoring. He'd hoped to turn into the living room and find Jemma lying there, sleeping off a heavy night.

He wasn't surprised to hear silence.

Panic started to permeate inside him, a churning feeling. He began rubbing at his stomach, wondered if they still had any Rennies left.

How does Mr Average react to his girlfriend not coming home from a night out? Does he ring the police straight away? Her friends . . . her mum? He was sweating, nervous energy running through him. He needed to think.

What had he done?

'Relax,' he whispered to himself. 'Calm down.'

Rob boiled the kettle and had a cup of coffee. Two and a half sugars. A dash of milk. The early morning sunlight came through the window in the empty kitchen, reflecting off the microwave he barely used. The kitchen was exactly as he'd left it the night before. Nothing disturbed. Everything in its place.

She'd barely been on a night out since they'd moved in the house. Rob had never stopped her, she just preferred staying at home, watching a film or some crap on TV whilst he messed around on the laptop next to her. She never seemed unhappy.

He believed she was. Why else would she stay out late?

It was true that he'd pushed her to go out with her friends. Told her she needed to have a night out, let her hair down, dance to shit music and have a few drinks. He wouldn't stop her enjoying herself. She just needed to stay safe. That's all. Not put herself in danger.

28

She hadn't listened to him. Obviously. She never fucking did. That was the problem. If she'd just listened, they'd be sharing breakfast now.

They never listened to him.

Four years they'd been together. She'd even started dropping hints about marriage, kids. They weren't getting any younger.

He couldn't see it. One day, she would have realised she was wasting her life with him. Left, and found someone as special as her.

He should ring around. Check her mates out. Do something.

'Phone.'

He checked his pockets, coming up empty. Took the stairs two at a time as he remembered where he'd left it. Entering the bedroom he was struck by her absence again, the unslept-upon side of her bed. Always the left side, even though that had been his side of the bed when he was single. She got her way about that, as she'd continued to do throughout their relationship, Rob happy to give way on just about everything.

He reached over the bed to find his phone, having left it on the bedside table the previous night. He looked at the screen to check there were no missed calls, or texts waiting for him; a blank screen flickered back at him. He clicked on the phone button, Jemma's number the first one on the list of recent calls.

'Hi, this is Jemma. Can't get to the phone right now . . .'

It was right that he tried her first. He had to think things through properly. He ended the call without leaving a message. Started flicking through the contacts on the phone to find her best friend's number. Pressed the green call button and waited.

'Hello.' Carla's husband. The woollyback with the fake Scouse accent. Rob bit his lip.

'Andy? It's Rob. Is Carla home?'

'Yeah mate. She's in bed. Left her phone down here. What's going on – it's a bit early isn't it?'

'Is Jemma there?'

'Erm, no. Should she be?'

'She hasn't come home. Can you see if Carla knows anything? Starting to panic a bit here.'

'Course Rob.'

Rob heard him walking, a muffled conversation, before he came back on the phone. 'Carla said she got off early. Said she was getting a taxi home,' Andy said.

Rob swore under his breath, 'Didn't anyone go with her, make sure she got off okay?' Rob said, his voice rising. He needed to know whether anyone left with her; to know that she left the club alone, as anything could have happened in that time.

'I've no idea mate.' Andy replied. 'Jemma's a big girl though, she can look after herself. I wouldn't worry about it yet. She could have gone on to somewhere else or something.'

'Who with Andy? She said she was going home. Get Carla up for me. I need to speak to her.'

'Come on Rob, she didn't get in 'til late. She deserves a lie-in, she hasn't been out since the baby was born.'

'For fuck's sake Andy, Jemma hasn't come home. Tell Carla to get on the fucking phone. I want to speak to her.' His own anger didn't surprise him. People not listening to him. Always a trigger. He needed to calm down. If he carried on, alarm bells would start ringing with the stupid dickhead on the end of the phone. Rob softened his voice. 'She could be anywhere.'

'I understand mate, but it's only early, you need to calm down a bit. Don't start worrying just yet. Give it a couple of hours and see if she turns up. Have you tried ringing her mum yet? She might have gone there for all you know.'

Rob sighed. Strike two. 'No. I'll try now.'

'Cool. Look, I've got to get on with giving Leah her feed. Let me know when she turns up, okay?'

'Okay.' He ended the call and tried ringing Jemma again. He had to leave a voicemail this time. Could be important. 'Jemma, it's Rob. Ring me.'

He sent a text message.

Babe, I'm worried. Where are you? x

He rang the number for Jemma's mum from memory. When they'd first started seeing each other they spoke on the phone a lot. Her mum used to go mad at her for tying up the line.

Jemma's mum answered on the third ring. '2461.'

'Hi Helen, it's Rob. Is Jemma at your house?'

'No. Should she be?' Rob heard her stifle a yawn.

'I don't know. She went out with Carla and the others last night. I've woke up this morning and she's not here. Just thought I'd check to see if she'd ended up at yours instead.'

'I haven't heard from her for a while. Are you saying she's missing?'

'I don't know. It's just not like her to not get in touch.'

'Have you spoken to her friends? Maybe they know something.'

'Yeah, spoke to Carla, well, Carla's husband Andy anyway. She left earlier than the others and went for a taxi.'

'This doesn't sound good Rob. Should I come over?'

'No, you don't have to. I'm sure it'll be fine.'

'Well, I suppose I best stay here just in case she comes here. Ring me the second she turns up.'

'Will do.'

Rob pressed the red end call button and stared at his phone. He stood next to the bed, and dropped down when he'd ended the call. He tried to think of where else she might have been. Who else he should call before the police.

What was he supposed to do? What was the right course of action?

Carla and her mum, they were the only people he knew Jemma spoke to regularly. He glanced at the alarm clock.

'Shit.' He should have been leaving the house now, going in to work at the university for overtime. He wasn't going anywhere though. He walked back downstairs, going through to the living room and looking outside, hoping to see Jemma passed out on the doorstep. Nothing again. Outside, only socks on his feet, looking around the front of his house, the pavement, the side alley near the bins. Still the expected nothingness. Rob shivered, looking around the quiet street, looking for any curtains twitching. Anyone walking past or peeking out of their windows from the houses surrounding him would have seen a confused looking, average bloke, searching for someone. That was right.

He went back into the living room, ran a hand through his hair, still messed up from sleeping. Dropped his hand across his face and the intentional three-day stubble. Stood near the window, opening the blinds and began drumming his fingers on the windowsill.

It had finally happened.

She was gone, and now he had to deal with the consequences.

4

Sunday 27th January 2013 – Day One

There are two tunnels running underneath the River Mersey
and into the Wirral Peninsula. Only separated by a mile and
a half of water, the tunnels provide the only way into
Liverpool from the Wirral which doesn't involve a ninety
mile round trip down the motorway and through Runcorn.
Murphy could see a connection becoming closer each day,
the sheer amount of traffic coming from the tunnels telling
their own story. If you filled in the Mersey with concrete,
most would barely recognise the difference. Coming from
the city centre, the first tunnel you hit is Birkenhead tunnel.
Carry on further, down a wide A road, Byrom Street, which
runs directly from the city centre, pull into the left hand side,
and a curved road takes you around to Wallasey tunnel. Stay
on the right hand side and within minutes you're on Scotland
Road. Turn off onto Hunter Street and behind one of the
four universities in the city is St Anne Street running parallel
to the tunnel approach. Halfway down, over a dip in the
road, amidst abandoned warehouses, coverted offices and a
car-wash on one side, a small housing estate on the other,
was the police station which served Liverpool North
division.

Murphy pulled up in the car park behind the station, and sat for a moment amongst the police vans, unmarked cars, and personal vehicles. The dirty red brick building, which loomed over the street five floors high, looked as ominous as ever. An old-style office building, repatriated as the hub of a policing section which served seven areas of Liverpool.

Scratch that, Murphy thought, it was eight now. Cuts meant they'd inherited part of Liverpool South. He sighed to himself. If that hadn't been the case, the dead girl in Sefton Park would be someone else's problem.

He ran through the last couple of hours in his head. He still hadn't eaten. Probably a blessing in disguise. Even after almost twenty years he still felt a jolt at seeing someone with the life sucked out of them. He'd run on adrenaline until then, but he needed to eat. Plus, of course, if you let adrenaline take over this early, it could lead to mistakes.

He could do without any of them.

Murphy pushed his way into the major incident room, people bustling back and forth as the events of the morning took precedence over other cases. He spotted DCI Stephens barking orders at a number of DCs.

Rossi had beaten him back there. Hunched over her computer screen, A4 sheets of paper strewn over her desk, one pen in her hand, another behind her ear.

'Anything?'

Rossi turned in her chair to face him. 'Nothing yet. There's been a number of missing women reported in the last month. Trying to narrow it down now.'

'Good. I'm going to run Reeves through the system. Make sure he's not a murderer and we've already screwed up.'

He moved over to his desk, noticed a post-it note stuck to his computer monitor.

CALL HOUGHTON

He picked up the phone on his desk and called the

pathologist. He'd be at the hospital morgue, tucking the body away for the post-mortem later in the day.

'We found something on the body when we removed her clothing. A letter. I think you'll want to come see it.'

'Right,' Murphy replied, pleased the pathologist was getting straight to the point. 'Anything interesting?'

'I think it's best you see it for yourself.'

EXPERIMENT THREE

To Whom It May Concern,

I don't know you yet, but I will. The same applies both ways I suppose. You'll be trying to find out my name. My reasons. Everything will become clearer over time. Just know, I do it all for a good cause. We need to be clear about that.

The young girl you have found isn't the first experiment I've carried out.

She won't be the last.

When the American government was experimenting on an unsuspecting public, we didn't accuse them in the same manner you will be accusing me. They were the beginning of the end I feel. The last of my kind, willing to go to any lengths in order to study mankind.

What you have with this girl is a modern interpretation of one such experiment.

Part of the MK Ultra programme, Operation Midnight Climax was the first scientific exploration into the effects of LSD on unwitting humans. For example, men, on the pretext they were enjoying a private visit with a prostitute, were given LSD without their knowledge and studied. They experimented on their own men, federal marshals, employees within the CIA . . .

It went much further than that.

The results are astounding. What this girl was willing to do when dosed with the drug was way beyond my expectations. She became a different person.

Giving her more and more of the drug compounded her state of mind. An endless trip.

She wanted to die. She begged for an end. Not because she was in pain, or through fear. She believed she could see the afterlife.

I'm not one for silly fairytales, so it was probably the drugs talking. Possibly. That's part of the experimentation. To find answers to these questions.

Her last dose ended fatally, unfortunately for her.

Throughout history, man has attempted to understand the complexities of life. Why are we here? What is our purpose? I am attempting to prove my answer to those questions.

We are here only to die.

Think of every funeral you've ever been to. The grief people exude from themselves. It becomes one with the atmosphere, an almost physical feeling in the air. Death is natural, yet people somehow make it *unnatural. They say things such as 'it wasn't his time' or 'taken too soon' as if that bears any relation to the fact that whether it be one year or a hundred, the result is still the same.*

Death is inevitable, yet people are always surprised when it happens.

What do we experience at the moment of death? How can we ever know that feeling? Without research, without experimentation, we are no nearer an answer to these questions.

So enjoy it.

This is just the beginning of my work. To discover more about life . . . through death.

'Great. We need to find him fast.' Murphy said as he'd finished reading the letter.

'He?' Houghton replied.

'Just a guess. Could be her or they I suppose. This is my copy, yes?'

Houghton nodded, waved his hand away. 'Yeah, original has gone to forensics. What is it then?'

'You didn't read it?' Murphy said. 'Thought you'd have had your nose right into this by now. Well, apart from some screwed-up talk about death, there's something about the effects of LSD on humans, and some shite about something called MK Ultra and Operation Midnight Climax. Sounds like I've stumbled across a screenplay of the new James Bond film.' Murphy said.

'I've heard of Operation Midnight Climax.' Houghton replied. 'It was a CIA thing. Linked with the whole MK Ultra deal. You must have heard about it.'

Murphy stared at Houghton, who looked as though he was trying to keep his round face straight. A trace of a smile threatened to break out, the lines on his face creasing further.

'No I haven't smartarse, what is it?' Murphy said.

'Touchy, aren't you? You could just bow to my superior knowledge you know.'

'Consider me bowed. Now explain.'

Murphy moved aside as Houghton scanned what he'd been reading. 'From what I remember, Operation Midnight Climax was a psychology experiment to show the effects of LSD on people. They would give people doses of acid without their knowledge and then watch the effects of the drug on them through two-way mirrors. They filmed ordinary men with prostitutes in an attempt to see if anything could be used in conjunction with possible mind control efforts. All very secret and clandestine. It was shut down in the sixties, but some people think the US government still does this sort of thing.'

Murphy tried to take it all in. 'So the government was giving acid to people without their knowledge, and then filmed them with prostitutes?' Murphy said. 'Seems pretty pointless.'

'Yeah, all it did really was add to the growing acid usage in the sixties.' Houghton replied.

'What does this have to do with the girl though?'

'Well, that's for you to find out, you're the detective.'

'Okay, so we have a letter taped to a dead girl, about the government giving LSD to people in the sixties. It also talks about death and the way people react to it being unnatural.'

'That about sums it up.'

'We don't know how she died yet.'

'The PM will be done later on.' Houghton said. 'We'll know more then.'

Murphy walked around the table, becoming aware of a pain growing behind his eyes. Another headache coming on probably.

'So, she's got strangulation marks around her neck, but this letter says she died of too much acid?'

'I'm willing to bet that we find a large amount of LSD in the girl's system, but it will have to be a ridiculously large amount to be the cause of death. Any luck with identifying her yet?'

'Laura's looking into it now. I should get back and help out.'

'Okay, will one of you be coming for the show?'

Murphy gave him a sneer. 'Show? Such class.'

'Okay, sorry. The post-mortem.' Houghton used his fingers to make quotation marks around his last two words, which made Murphy smile a little.

'I'm sure I'll draw the short straw of having to subject myself to being in your company for a lengthy amount of time.'

Murphy left Houghton's office, once again thankful that no matter the pitfalls of life in the police, at least his office wasn't located in a hospital. His energy began to return. His stomach still gurgled and growled, but it barely bothered him. Purpose. He had purpose again.

Righting wrongs, doing good – that kind of thing was why he'd joined the police twelve years earlier. Applied for CID as soon as he was allowed. Breaking up fights in town and dealing with domestic violence got tiring within months. It wasn't for him. Murphy wanted to be Sherlock Holmes, not the local bobby.

Took him about three minutes on his first day in CID to realise no bugger there was Sherlock. Mostly, it was menial work, small things. Domestic cases, in the main. Of course, it wasn't always as soft as all that. Some cases, they still stuck with him, forever marked in his mind. He bore the scars well for the most part. Sometimes he boiled over, but surely that was to be expected. That's why this case was so important. He had much to make up for.

In the past, when his line of work was discussed at parties or barbeques, he had to dampen the expectations of the normals. With murder, it was almost always someone the victim knew. Much of the time, it was a partner, or ex. Domestic violence they call it. Carried out by vile little men, who are useless for anything other than using their power over women.

That's why the letter didn't bother him. He wanted to play the odds. Whoever had killed the girl was probably someone close to her. Someone she knew. The letter was probably some kind of distraction technique. Left to throw them off the scent.

Murphy had seen this kind of thing before.

Which meant that what was most important, was finding out who she was.

5

Sunday 27th January 2013 – Day One

Another dead end.

Not literally, which was a good thing she supposed, but she wished it was easier to identify someone when you had next to nothing to go on.

Everyone should be tagged. Like a pet. No . . . that was too weird. Too Orwellian.

'*Mannagia alla miseria.*'

Rossi's voice was quiet amongst the racket of the room as she expressed her frustration in Italian at the lack of answers from the computer. Her mind kept flashing back to the lifeless face of the young woman they'd found that morning.

It wasn't her first murder case. In the two years she'd been a detective constable, she'd been part of four murder investigations. Three of them were domestic cases. Two women in their forties and fifties. A sixty-three-year-old man. The other, a stabbing outside a nightclub in Concert Square; a fight over someone's girlfriend going too far. The lad with the knife had been sentenced a few weeks earlier. Twelve years. He'd be out before he was thirty. She shook her head . . . worthless.

She loved the job. That was the main thing. Growing up, she hadn't been one of those kids who reeled off a list of things they wanted to be when they were older. She'd shrug her shoulders when asked. Went to uni, studied Sociology, and when she left and realised jobs with that degree were pretty limited, fell into policing.

She'd grown up pretty quick after that. Twenty-one years old and splitting up fights between blokes twice her size in town. She'd got her head down and worked through it, before she was fast-tracked into CID. It was then she realised this was what she was born to do, even if her parents didn't agree. To them she was still the baby of the family.

She loved her job. But this was the first time she'd seen herself in the victim. She was a few years older than the dead girl, but close enough in age that she could remember being her not too long ago. She wasn't supposed to feel that way, to put herself in the victim's position. Distance was supposedly key. That's what they'd drummed into her in training.

She pushed her hair behind her ear, away from her face, and knocked the pen that had been balancing there onto the floor. She bent down to pick it up.

'While you're down there.'

Rossi looked up, sitting up quickly as she saw Brannon standing next to her desk, wearing one of those ridiculous false grins he always seemed to wear. She rolled her eyes. 'What do you want?'

'Just seeing how you are getting on. Could be a big case, this. Just want to make sure you know my expertise is available if you run into any trouble.'

She could almost taste the morning sweat emanating from him, mixing with the cheap bodyspray he wore to try and hide it.

42

'I'm fine.'

'Well,' Brannon replied, shifting some of the paper on her desk so he could sink his large arse onto the edge, 'I just want you to know I'm here.' He leaned over her, one hand on the desk, the other hanging loosely near her right shoulder. 'And I'll be waiting for you to fuck up. I'll be right in there. Got it?'

'*Vaffanculo* Brannon.'

He sat back, a question mark on his moisture-ridden face. 'What's that mean?'

Rossi smiled, 'An old Italian phrase. Now get off my desk before I let the boss know you're the one who used her cup last week.'

Rossi flinched in spite of herself as Brannon leaned forward, his hand on the arm of her chair. His face was only a few inches away from hers as he smiled, 'Listen. Don't think I don't know what you're doing. Flashing a bit of leg, smiling at the right people. Well, it's not going to work. Just because our famous nutty DI wants you to partner him on what'll be his latest, and hopefully last, fuck-up, don't think it makes you better than me. You'll be sussed out soon enough and then we can ship you out to where you belong.'

Rossi met his gaze. 'You finished, or do I have to get my magnifying glass out, find your dick, and rip the fucking thing off you *pezzo de merda*?'

Brannon shaped as if to say something, then plastered the grin back on. 'Yeah, well. We speak English here. You just remember what I said.'

'Yeah, yeah.' Rossi replied, waving him away with the back of her hand. She picked up one of the print-outs of a missing person and pretended to read it, waiting for him to leave.

Bastard. She should introduce him to her mum. Mamma

Rossi would have him begging for forgiveness within three seconds.

Her dad would just kill him. Probably.

Not important. She had work to do. She wanted to find a name before Murphy returned. Prove herself. Make their partnership more permanent.

Most importantly . . . not make any mistakes.

Murphy wiped his mouth free of crumbs from the sandwich he'd picked up on the way back from the hospital, shoved the napkin in his pocket as he stepped out of the lift and walked down the short corridor towards the incident room. He steeled himself, and pushed open the doors.

The noise from earlier on had died down to an acceptable level. Murphy headed straight to his desk, not for the first time wishing he wasn't six foot four and instantly filling a room. He wanted to lie low for a while; at least until they had a name. Maybe check on some CCTV if any had been delivered. Basically keep his head down and hope no one noticed he wanted to be anywhere else but there right then. He knew all eyes would be on him, remembering the last time he'd been in charge of a murder investigation. Sure, it wasn't completely his fault how screwed up that had gone, but mud sticks. He couldn't mess this one up.

'Sir.'

Rossi had snuck up on him whilst he was keeping his head down over his desk. Typical. 'Got a name?' he asked her.

'Not yet. Just checking on whether one of the names on the missing list had a tattoo or something. What did Houghton have to say?'

Murphy filled her in on what had been discovered on the victim. He tried to play it off as being a red herring, but he saw her eyes light up as he explained the content, giving her a copy of the letter, which she quickly began scanning.

'MK Ultra. What's that?' Rossi said, as Murphy leaned back in his chair. 'Sounds familiar.'

'Some weird psychology thing according to Houghton.' Murphy replied. 'The CIA were involved . . . I don't know, it's all very confusing. You went to university, you should know about that sort of thing.'

'I did Sociology, not Psychology.'

'What's the difference?'

'Well, Sociology is like Psychology, but without the rules.' Rossi replied.

'What's that mean?'

'It's supposed to be an insult to Sociology students, but to be honest, it's probably true.'

Murphy shook his head and turned back to the letter. He'd read it over and over now, without really getting any more information than the first time he'd read it. His attention began wandering, his desk now becoming his main focus. Would be nice to have an office. That had gone recently. They needed the space, apparently. Now he had a desk and a small filing cabinet of his own. He'd managed to fill both within a week. Murphy always meant to tidy it up, but never seemed to find the time. Besides, he enjoyed the clutter. Box files took up half the desk, his barely used computer, the other.

'So what do we think then?' Rossi said.

'I think it's a hoax, but we're not discounting it. Likelihood is, it's something to throw us off. The PM is happening soon, couple of hours probably. Houghton has put a rush on it, so hopefully he'll have made a mistake.'

'You want me to go?'

'Not if you don't want to Laura. I know you're not the biggest fan of them,' Murphy said.

45

'I'm surprised you're still willing, you know . . . after that whole . . . thing.'

'My parents died Laura, it's not a thing. You can say it.'

'I know. I just don't like bringing it up.' Rossi replied.

Murphy noticed her shifting on her feet, plainly uncomfortable with the conversation. It'd been the same since it happened. Everyone waiting for him to show weakness. He'd become adept at the whole stiff upper lip deal though, not showing or sharing anything. It was better that way, he'd decided. Move on and forget.

It was becoming harder to forget though. And the dreams came more often.

His phone beeped in his pocket, 'You go Laura. It'll be good to get some more experience under your belt. You'll get used to it at some point,' Murphy said, giving her a supportive pat on her shoulder as he took his phone out.

Rossi's shoulders slumped a little but she began to nod her head. 'Okay, okay I'll go. I've left the possible missing persons on my desk. I'll bring them over before I leave.'

'Good.' Murphy said looking at his phone. 'You best get a move on, it starts at twelve.' He waved the phone at her. Rossi trudged off towards her desk.

Murphy began going through the messages on his answer machine, deleting the ones he deemed not needed. Rossi dropped a file containing some papers on his desk, whilst simultaneously pointing at Murphy's computer and mouthing 'use that' to him. Murphy gave her a two-fingered salute as Rossi smiled and walked away.

Nothing of importance on his voicemail as usual, so he opened the file of missing persons. He pictured the victim in his mind; short, around five foot four inches, brunette, average build, not skinny or fat, just normal. She'd been wearing a red jumper and black trousers. She had a mole on her neck he remembered. Not overly large, but noticeable.

And dead, he thought – let's not forget that.

It'd been a while since Murphy had been in contact with a dead victim. He'd been dealing with teenagers mostly. Serious assaults, drugs, teenage boys always seeming to be involved. Lives wasted before they'd even begun. The sneers on their faces matching the dogs they always had on short leads. It reminded him of life on the council estate he'd grown up on. The kids he'd knocked around with then would probably not be in the same lofty position he occupied now. More likely to come across them during an investigation than any other way.

It was something Murphy thought of often. The different paths life can take. He was no different to those lads at that age, doing stupid things, getting into trouble. Nothing that serious though. Few fights here and there. He'd been over six foot tall from the age of thirteen, which made him stand out. He'd been to the local boxing club for a while but gave up when he realised spending time with his mates and girls was more enjoyable to him. His parents had been a constant presence however. Always trying to lead him into a better way of living. He pushed back at first, tried to defy everything they attempted to instil in him. As he got older, more mature, he calmed down. Met his first wife at twenty, divorced at twenty-one. Married too young, but it gave focus to his life.

It had led to him doing a job he loved. But it wasn't without its dark moments.

Some so dark and personal, he had trouble letting them go. Kept him awake at night, dead eyes staring down at him in the darkness.

Murphy tried to clear his head. He needed to focus and find a name for the girl. He started reading the names of the missing. They had DCs doing the same work in the room, yet Murphy would share the load. There wasn't much else he could do at the moment. No CCTV to look at, witnesses to interview. Finding the name of the victim was the most important thing they could do right now.

An hour later, it came.

'I've got it. Donna McMahon.' Murphy looked up from his computer screen at the DC standing over him. DC Harris. Murphy was sure this time.

'Positive, Harris?' Murphy replied, hoping he was right.

'Pretty much.' DC Harris replied, smiling briefly, before quickly becoming serious-faced again.

At least he remembered some names, Murphy thought.

'What do you mean "pretty much"?'

'It was the mole that did it. The only distinguishing feature we had to go on really. Matches the description we have, just getting a picture now.'

'Who is she then, where's she from?' Murphy said.

'Twenty years old, from Leicester originally. She's a student at the City of Liverpool University. Her housemates reported her missing six days ago. Her parents still live in Leicester, but they've been staying up here the last few days. We'll contact them to confirm the ID.'

'Good work Harris.' Murphy said. 'Rossi is at the PM now, get the picture sent to her phone just to check it.'

'Okay sir.' DC Harris scuttled off. Murphy watched him go back to his desk. They had a name. And parents who had to be told their daughter was dead. The thought of informing them began to filter through to Murphy's mind, sending a shudder through him. That was a conversation he really didn't want to have. Nerves jangling again. Voice in his head repeating itself.

'Don't screw up again . . . don't screw up again . . .'

A student. Has to be a boyfriend then. All that psychology talk in the letter pointed to a fellow student.

Talk to her friends, find out she was seeing someone. Murphy would bet good money there'd been arguments.

Case would be closed within a couple of days. Tops.

He sat back in his chair, his mind wandering. Tiredness washed over him, his eyes threatening to close, the sounds of the busy office becoming muffled as he lost himself in his own thoughts.

What if he was wrong?

6

Early evening. Late spring turning into a summer which would see more rain than sun. Night was drawing in, the fading light turning the world outside grey.

The text message that had been sent to him, drawing him here had been simple, yet effective.

WHEN WAS THE LAST TIME YOU CHECKED ON YOUR LOVED ONES DAVID?

He'd opened the door using the key usually kept under the fake rock in the front garden.

The rock had been moved. The key tossed to one side. A red smear on the fob. He'd held the key carefully, trying not to disturb the mark. Knowing what it was, refusing to believe it meant anything.

He entered the house, his movements slow and methodical, an overbearing silence greeting him. A smell in the air that was familiar, yet his conscious wouldn't place what it was. He moved through the hallway, the living room door to his left, closed. Something drew him towards the door at the end of the hallway which led to the kitchen. He moved slowly along, his senses heightened. He could almost track the progress of every hair as it began to creep up on the back of his neck, his heart hammering against his chest.

He reached out to push the kitchen door open, noticing his hand was shaking.

It was empty. No one there. Nothing out of place. The sun, low in the sky, was shining through the window which overlooked the garden, creating an orange tinge to the light inside. He turned and left the kitchen, going back down the hallway towards the closed living room door, knowing that was where he was supposed to have gone first. Being drawn to the kitchen was his mind trying to keep him from entering, drawing him to the safe place.

He stood at the closed door, somehow knowing what lay behind it. Not wanting to see, knowing he had to. His hand moved of its own accord – in his head he was screaming at himself to stop, not to see, not to feel.

The door opened, and all was red.

7

Sunday 27th January 2013

Mid-afternoon on the first day. Rain battered the windows, as the weather turned to its usual Northern charm. Murphy sat forward in his chair, grinding the palms of his hands against his eyes.

'It's on Radio City and Merseyside, but that's it. No nationals yet.'

Murphy took his hands away from his face, his eyes unfocused for a split second, turning everything into a blurred mess around him. DS Brannon stood by his desk, running a bloated tongue along his bottom lip.

'That's good. Anything else?'

'Just . . . you know I'm here right? To pick up any slack, that sort of thing.'

'Yeah. Course. Did you get around the houses near the scene?'

Brannon straightened up. 'Yes. Everyone was asleep. No one saw anything. Except that nutty bloke you spoke to. I organised the uniforms into teams, got it done quicker. Time is of the essence and all that.'

Like a child with a painting of nothing more than a blob of colour, brought home from nursery, expecting a parade to be thrown in his honour. Murphy just nodded at his work. Let him squirm.

'Right. I'll go chase up that CCTV then?'

'Okay.'

Brannon left Murphy. The atmosphere around his desk becoming less polluted as a result.

He checked his phone again, waiting on a response from Rossi. He'd messaged her twenty minutes previously to let her know they had a name. His phone was still blank.

Murphy had updated HOLMES himself, internally complaining about having to use the computer to do so. Every piece of information on an investigation was stored on the HOLMES system, leaving no chance for a piece of evidence to be overlooked. Just more admin for him to sort out.

The TV shows get at least one thing right. The first forty-eight hours are crucial. The longer time goes on, the less likely someone is to remember something they may have witnessed, or that an offender will still be in the area. Yet Murphy was stuck on his arse, transferring information from one place to another.

At that point he had a name, and from the look on the face of the young DS making her way to Murphy's desk, a partner who was struggling to hold down whatever food she'd been able to grab that day.

Murphy smiled, sitting back in his chair and lacing his hands together across his stomach.

'Fun?' Murphy said, as Rossi stopped next to him.

'You know. Could be worse I suppose. Death was caused by asphyxiation.'

Murphy smiled. 'I knew the letter was bollocks. Bet it's an ex.'

Rossi noticed something under a fingernail and used another one to scrape underneath it. 'Not necessarily. Houghton has a theory. In the letter he doesn't specifically state she'd actually died from the overdose, only that the last dose was fatal. Houghton said it's unlikely any human could die from an LSD overdose. Well . . . he actually said near impossible at first, but changed his mind. The level needed to OD on LSD is far too large to be ingested at one time. Plus by the time they're able to take more, the last dose is beginning to wear off. He's sent samples off to the lab though and expects there to be a large amount in her system. But cause of death was asphyxiation, nonetheless.'

'Interesting. I still think it's bollocks though.'

'How so?' Rossi said, perching herself on the edge of Murphy's desk.

'The letter wants us to believe she died as the result of some weird experiment.' Murphy said, pulling a copy of the letter out from underneath a coffee cup. 'When really he's just distancing himself from the fact he killed her with his own hands. He sees himself as something he's not. Possibly thinks he's better than any other murderer, when in fact he's strangled some poor girl. My money is still on a boyfriend. He's just created this thing to tone down his own guilt.'

'What if it's real?'

Murphy paused. Experiment Three, the letter had said. That would mean two others and a pattern. And he really didn't want to start thinking about what that would mean.

'We cross that bridge if we come to a river of evidence.'

Rossi nodded slowly. 'At least we have a name now.'

'Yeah. Harris got it. Donna McMahon. She's a student at the university.'

Are the parents on the way? Houghton is waiting for them to ID her.'

'Harris is sorting it out.'

'Time for something to eat?'

54

Murphy raised his eyebrows in mock surprise. 'Feeling better already? Usually it takes a while for you to be feeling okay after a PM.'

'I'm getting better at it sir.'

'Good. And how many times do I have to tell you? Stop calling me sir. There's barely five or six years between us.'

'Sorry. Habit.'

Murphy sighed, rising up from his chair. 'We've got nothing from canvassing the surrounding area. CCTV will be here soon. Brannon is chasing it up.'

Murphy smiled as Rossi snorted at the mention of Brannon's name. 'He causing you problems?'

'Nothing I can't handle. To be honest, nothing a five year old couldn't handle. He's not exactly quick with the insults.'

'Yeah, well. If he crosses a line let me know. I'd love an excuse to tear him a new one.'

They walked side by side towards the lift. Rossi's shorter legs moving quicker as she tried to keep pace with Murphy. He allowed her to move ahead of them as the lift doors opened, pressed the button on the lift as they both entered.

'It's been a while since we've dealt with a suspicious. Even then it's usually the husband or wife.' Rossi said as the lift doors closed.

'True. What was that one last year we worked together? Wife did her husband in with the spud peeler he'd bought her for her birthday?'

Rossi laughed, the sound bouncing off the walls of the small lift. 'That's right. That was a good one. Stuck him right in the neck with it. Blood everywhere. Do you remember what she said in the interview?'

Murphy smiled remembering. 'He got my birthday wrong. It's not for another three months.'

Rossi tried to stifle her laughter. Failed.

Murphy sniggered quietly along with her, remembering

the DCI's face when they'd gone into her office after the interview.

Murphy snorted. 'We've got a proper case here, and you're with me all the way. Hopefully it's open and shut, and we have a closed one for your record. We just have to make sure there's no cock-ups, and we catch the bastard.'

'We will. He's given us a lot to go on.'

Murphy sighed, leaning against the back of the lift compartment. 'Yeah. You're probably right. It was the mole you know, that got us the name. All these advances in technology and it's a bloody birthmark that gives us the lead.'

'The mole eh? Always good to have a distinguishing feature. It's why I've got the tattoo.'

'Of course that's why. Nothing to do with being young and foolish I'm sure.'

Rossi turned away, suddenly finding the lift display interesting.

Murphy smiled to himself. The smile disappearing as the images of that morning entered his mind again.

Not as easy. Not as easy as it used to be.

Cold. It was always cold down there. No matter how many times he was told it was normal room temperature in the corridors away from the rooms where post mortems were held, Murphy had to stop himself from shivering when he was there.

It had been a while.

Heels smacking against hard floors, echoing around a colourless corridor. Houghton's assistant came to a stop near their group of four. Two detectives, two parents. One of them silent as the other rambled on.

'I apologise. We've never had any dealings with the police before. Hoped we never would, to be quite frank.'

The assistant pathologist entered the room behind them.

Murphy was distracted by the sight of her wheeling a bed up to the window, waiting for the cue to pull back the sheet.

'We're really sorry, but we need you to confirm this is your daughter,' Rossi said, directing Donna McMahon's parents closer to the window separating them from their daughter.

They'd introduced themselves in plummy voices, a world away from the accents you would hear on most Liverpool streets. John McMahon looked half broken. Tall, lean, with a shock of grey hair which was slicked back, wearing a suit that looked like it had been tailor made for him. Professional. Moneyed. Donna was obviously a daddy's girl. Carole was holding back tears, trying to keep a stiff upper lip. She was shorter than her husband but not by much. Her skin was tanned and leathery looking. She fiddled with a large beaded necklace which was worn with a smart trouser suit.

Murphy noticed John's hands were shaking as he turned to face him. Murphy cued the assistant through the window to pull back the cover and Carole turned away, burying her face in her husband's shoulder. Murphy watched as the realisation hit Carole as she moved her face away from John's shoulder.

John could see what she was doing through his hands and pulled her back. 'Don't Carole, it's . . . it's her.' He said.

'No. No it can't be. John, don't say that. She's halfway through her degree, she can't be . . . be gone.' Huge, racking sobs suddenly filled the corridor.

John put his arms around her, clutching her in a desperate embrace.

The temperature increased. Gone was the chill he always felt. Murphy could feel the heat in the place, seeping out of the drab, beige walls. Memories flooded in, crowding his mind. One minute the girl's parents were stood there, the next, him.

Her.

Murphy looked down at his hands, wringing themselves together. Began shifting on his feet, wanting to be anywhere else. Wanting the cold to come back.

Rossi glanced his way and frowned at him. Turning back to the McMahons, she remained stoic. 'Mr and Mrs McMahon, I know this is difficult. Are you sure that's Donna?' he said.

'I know my daughter, officer.' John said.

Murphy had an overwhelming temptation to correct his terming of Rossi's rank, but bit back on it. He wasn't thinking straight. Why were they still crying? It was too hot to cry. He needed to get out of there. He was burning up, his chest tightening.

This was the moment it changed for him. When it became real.

Murphy felt eyes on him, realised the father was looking at him. He averted his eyes, not wanting to speak. He was still crying and Murphy couldn't look at him like that. He needed to leave. 'You got this Laura? I'll erm . . . I'll go update the team,' he said.

'Er . . . yeah, okay.' Rossi replied.

Turning towards the parents, Murphy muttered, 'I'm sorry for your loss' and left, eyes to the floor, watching as his trousers bounced carefree up and down against his polished black shoes.

He walked briskly towards the toilets. Once inside he went straight for the sinks, and began to run the tap. Murphy splashed his face a few times, trying to cool down. He caught his reflection in the mirror, noting the roughness of his face. He looked pale, tired. Breathed in and out slowly. The tightness in his chest began to subside.

What was wrong with him, was it the grief? It must be. He couldn't handle those parents crying about their loss. That was it. Of course it would take time.

Or maybe he was just ill. A virus or something. That'd be it. He splashed his face a few more times, the coolness of the water bringing his temperature down. He turned the tap off, took some paper towels from the dispenser, and wiped his face dry.

Was this it? Was this the one? An investigation he could lose himself within. Screw up his career for good. Let Sarah go for good. He rubbed the bare patch on his ring finger with his right hand.

How long could he really go on like this?

He shoved his still-damp hand in his pocket and left the bathroom, almost running into Rossi as he walked out the door.

'Sir, you okay?' she said, the concerned look on her face seeming sincere to Murphy.

'I'm fine Laura. I must be coming down with something, that's all.'

'Okay, you want me to take you home?'

'No, I'll be okay. We need to get cracking now we have a positive ID. Speak to her roommates, track her movements.'

'Yeah. Look, the parents are distraught; I got hold of that victim support officer, before coming to find you. She'll be here soon.'

'Good, good. Let's get on.'

'If you're sure sir?'

'I'm fine. Leave it alone. I'll write up what we've got so far, you get names of the roommates.'

Rossi shrugged and walked away. After a moment, Murphy followed, feeling more like himself with every step.

More like the person he'd become in the last few months.

8

Saturday 18th February 2012
11 Months Earlier

Rob paced the living room, back and forth, almost always missing the coffee table as he walked. Shadows shifted across the room, the day darkening as the afternoon came and went.

Had he called them too soon, too early . . . he didn't know.

No matter. They'd barely listened. Over eighteen, not even twenty-four hours since she'd gone, call us back if she doesn't come home tomorrow, blah, blah, blah.

He'd called Carla again, who was becoming a little more concerned , but not all that much.

Her mum hadn't called.

He walked out of the living room, walking up the stairs and entering the bedroom.

He kicked at the bed, swearing out loud when pain shot through his foot. He slumped down on the bed, facing the door, that side of the bed smelling faintly of her. The scent of the red berry shampoo she used, emanating from the pillow.

He looked at her bedside table and frowned.

He picked up the small charm bracelet, turning it over in his hand. He remembered buying the bracelet for their first

Christmas together, promising he'd fill it with more charms to add to the three already placed there. Each one meaning something to both of them.

He rolled one charm in the shape of a dolphin between his fingers. Jemma was obsessed with dolphins. They'd gone to Orlando in Florida a year or so before, and she'd swum with them for half an hour. The uncontrolled joy on her face for weeks afterwards was an incredible sight and Rob didn't mind the pictures and trinkets they'd had dotted around the house. It made her happy, which in turn made him happy.

He turned over the charm in his hand.

RB ♥ JB

Their surnames began with the same letter. It meant if they got married, it'd still work.

Fate.

Tiny inscription, which he'd paid a lot for. Intricate work, he'd been told.

He'd bought her the charm on their fourth anniversary. She'd cried when he handed her the box. But then, she cried any time she was happy.

Was it an act? Did it really mean as much to her as it did to him?

His heart was pounding in his chest, his hands began to shake, and he struggled back to standing.

He slammed the bracelet back down on the bedside table and left the bedroom, jogging down the stairs. He grabbed his car keys, wallet and checked his pocket for his phone and opened the front door.

He'd forgotten somewhere he was supposed to go. Something he was supposed to do.

He wasn't doing the right things. He needed to make a list.

He pulled the car out, waiting for Jemma's mum to answer the phone.

'Helen, it's Rob, I need you to get around to the house.'

'Rob slow down. Has she turned up?'

Rob turned the corner at the bottom of the road with one hand on the wheel. 'No. I'm going to look for her.'

'I don't understand Rob. Maybe we should talk.'

'We'll talk later. Just please go to the house just in case. I can't sit there any more.'

'Fine. I'll call in half an hour. But ring me if you hear anything.'

He threw the phone in the passenger seat, driving towards the town centre. Someone needed to be at the house. He shouldn't leave it empty.

Ten minutes later he drove past Matthew Street, parked the car on double yellow lines, and got out. He walked down North John Street, the top of Liverpool One shopping centre behind, past various takeaways and newsagents. He slowed as he passed the Hard Day's Night hotel, the Beatles-themed place which was always busy. Up towards Castle Street and back down again. People milled around, sometimes sidestepping him as he walked slowly, purposefully.

He had to be noticed. The place would be crawling with cameras. If he was seen here, it'd seem like he'd gone looking for her at least.

That's what he was doing.

He walked down Matthew Street, the various bars on either side of the walkway already filling up. A few tourists milling around outside the Cavern Club, getting their pictures taken with the John Lennon statue. For a Saturday evening it was still pretty quiet. The grey paved street not filled with wandering drunks just yet.

He walked further down, towards the club Carla had told him they'd ended the night in. Grim, faceless. Just a garish neon sign outside. The club wasn't open, so he rapped on the door.

Rob rocked on his heels as he waited. A minute or so went by and he was about to knock again, when the door opened.

'Yeah?'

A thick necked, shaven-headed beast of a man stood in the open doorway. Rob took a step back. 'Hi, were you working here last night?'

'What's it to you?'

'My girlfriend has gone missing, I was just wondering if you'd seen anything.'

The bouncer looked around. 'Yeah, I was here last night. But a lot of people come in and out of here, I probably won't be able to help you. You should ring the police or something.'

Rob took out his wallet, removing the small picture he had of Jemma inside. 'Do you remember her?'

The bouncer looked at the photo, his brow furrowed. 'I think I do as it happens. She left on her own, about two. She was on her phone. She walked off towards the top.' He gestured towards the top of Matthew Street.

'Did you hear her talking at all, where she might have been going?'

He shook his head in reply. 'Sorry I can't be any more help. I hope you find her.'

Rob thanked him and wandered back to his car. He couldn't think of anything else to do. He needed that list. He walked back to the car and started driving towards home. He called Helen at the house, glad to find she'd gone there as he'd asked. He turned the radio on, looking for some music to try and clear his mind of the images which were threatening to enter. He found the local radio station, but it played that shite dance music and Rob quickly scanned past it. He settled on easy listening.

Focus. That's what he needed to do. Decide on a plan of action and start doing something.

He started at the beginning. Jemma had been out with her friend Carla. So start there. He turned right instead of left on the road out of the town centre, and drove towards her house.

Carla had married Andy the previous year, in what Rob had described as a fuck of an expensive party, much to Jemma's distaste. She'd loved the whole spectacle of it.

Should have noticed that. All her friends were married. She always seemed happy, but why hadn't he wanted to make things more permanent?

He pulled up outside Carla's house around ten minutes later. He checked the dashboard clock, almost eight in the evening. A quick pang of hunger hit him as he got out the car. He hadn't eaten since earlier in the day, when he'd made a sandwich and taken two bites of it before throwing it out. Too nervous. The thought of eating anything at that moment was enough to start his stomach churning again. Rob tried to shake the feeling off as he approached the door of the terraced house on the quiet street. They'd moved there recently. New baby, new house. Always the way.

As he reached for the doorbell, he stopped and knocked softly, mindful of their newborn. Thirty seconds later and he knocked again, a little louder. Andy opened the door, a tea towel over his shoulder, his hands still wet.

'Rob. Come on in mate. I was just washing some dishes.' Rob wiped his feet on the doormat and closed the door after himself. He followed Andy into the living room, where Carla was sitting with her feet underneath her on a leather sofa, watching some reality show on TV. She wasn't stunning, but Carla was nice looking in an understated way. Smaller than Jemma, brunette instead of blonde. Small in stature, but big on confidence. Sometimes that can go a long way. Sometimes, only on the odd occasion he needed something a bit different to fantasise about, Rob had pictured her face in the dark as he and Jemma made love. He looked away from her as the thought entered his head.

Their newborn daughter was in a small Moses basket next to her. Sleeping. From what Jemma had said, that was a rare occurrence.

'Hi Rob,' Carla said. 'Any news?'

'Nothing.' Rob replied. 'You don't seem too worried.'

Carla leaned over to check on the baby. 'I am, of course. But I'm sure she'll come home when she's ready.'

Andy shifted beside Rob. 'You want a drink or something?' he said.

'No thanks.' Rob replied, shaking his head. He sat down on the sofa opposite Carla. Andy looked over at her, and she nodded slightly. 'I'll get back to doing the dishes then.' As he left the room, Carla leaned back, her hands coming to a rest across her stomach. Rolled her eyes at the door.

'What's going on?'

She shifted her feet and stretched out her legs in front of her. 'Look Rob . . . she told me what was going on between you. Are you that surprised that she's gone away for a bit?'

'What are you talking about?' Rob said.

'You know . . . you and Jemma haven't been getting on lately. She was talking about leaving.'

How to react. Surprise? Acceptance? Fear? The first one. 'This is news to me. When did she say this?'

'Last night. She said she was fed up with the arguments and wanted to go away for a bit. This isn't the first time she's done something like this, just disappeared for a few days or longer when she wants to clear her head. So no. No, I'm not worried.'

'Are you serious?' Rob said, unable to keep his voice from rising slightly.

'Shh, you'll wake Leah. Look, I know it's a shock, but you

65

must have known she wasn't happy. You did know, didn't you?'

Rob sat back on the sofa, ran his hands through his hair and down onto his face. He wanted to say something then. Confess it was his fault. And it wasn't the first time. Instead, he kept going. 'No. I had no idea. She always seemed so happy. We never argued over anything big, just stupid stuff really. Whose turn it was to wash up, why couldn't I pick my socks up. You know, small insignificant bollocks like that. Nothing major. She wasn't happy?'

Carla placed her hands either side of her and lifted off the sofa slowly. She came across to him, settling down to his right, placing a hand on his shoulder tentatively. 'Look Rob,' she said. 'Sometimes we don't always see what's right in front of us. I'm sure she's just gone somewhere to clear her head.'

That wasn't supposed to happen. No touching. Calm. He needed to stay calm. 'You said it's not the first time she's done something like this. What did you mean?'

'Has she never said anything to you?'

He shook his head in response.

'Well, Jemma was seeing someone, a few years before you. She didn't know how to leave him, so she just left one night. She was gone for a few months, turned out she'd planned it well before that night. Had a friend down south who she stayed with. Even worked for a bit down there.'

Rob lifted his eyes from the carpet. Looked across at the flickering quiet images coming from the TV. 'We were fine Carla. I don't understand any of this. If she had problems, why didn't she say anything?'

Carla began to move her hand down his arm, before resting her hand in his.

'Sometimes, she doesn't know a good thing when it's right in front of her. That was always a problem for her.'

Rob looked down at her hand, moved his eyes upwards

and held her gaze for a few seconds. She opened her mouth a little as if to say something, but nothing came out. A voice from over her shoulder broke the silence.

'Everything okay in here?' Andy said.

Carla jumped up off the sofa at the sound of his voice. 'Fine babe. Rob just needed to hear some things he didn't know about Jemma.'

Andy came fully into the room, stood behind Carla and placed his hands on her shoulders. 'I best be getting back.' Rob said.

Carla took a step forward. 'I'll see you out.'

At the door, Rob turned around to face Carla. She put her arms around him before he had a chance to resist. 'She'll be okay Rob. Just don't let yourself be played with. You're much better than that.'

He stepped back and she unwrapped her arms from around him. 'I'll be in touch if I hear anything,' he said and stepped off the door step.

Rob heard the door shut behind him, standing still for a moment.

'What the fuck was that about?' He heard Andy's voice from outside. Then a door slamming. Through the blinds in the window he could see Carla rushing to the moses basket and picking up Leah. And then her eyes locked with his.

Looked like someone else was having problems. At least they were both there to sort them out.

Rob turned and walked back to the car. What Carla had told him had knocked him back somewhat. Donna just leaves sometimes, pisses off to the other end of the country like a petulant child.

He didn't really know her at all. She wasn't some perfect woman. She wasn't right.

Some of the guilt lifted.

But he still needed to keep going. Keep the show going.

Her mum next. Then . . . he couldn't think of the next step.

What was he supposed to do next?

9

Monday 28th January 2013 – Day Two

Murphy stood in his kitchen, waiting for the kettle to boil so he could fill the large mug that was sitting on the counter. Coffee and a little milk already added. He yawned, the previous night's lack of sleep catching up on him. The events of the previous day conspiring to keep his mind ticking over into the late hours, the ache in his neck telling him falling asleep on the couch was probably a mistake. Yet again, he'd drifted off to the sounds of canned laughter, from the endless re-runs of American sitcoms he watched late at night.

And then there was the small fact of still not feeling at home.

Murphy had one proper friend. Jess. Twenty years they'd known each other. Never a hint of romance. Jess had tried to help in the previous couple of months. Trips to Ikea, that sort of thing. He appreciated it, knowing she was probably hating every second of the experience.

She didn't like change. Wait . . . not quite right. She didn't like other people changing. And so much had changed in the last few months.

'You've bought a house?'

'Yeah, I needed somewhere to live.'

'But it's a little soon don't you think? It's not been that long. Where is it?'

'The Millhouse Estate in Moreton.'

'Over-the-water Moreton? Why would you do that? That's at least a half hour drive for me. You couldn't have moved around here?'

'Sorry Jess, that wasn't really my concern.'

'You prick. You're just trying to get rid of me.'

'Jess, I've been trying to get rid of you for twenty years. It hasn't worked so far. You're still technically my best friend.'

'Don't say that. That's depressing. And anyway, I'm your only friend.'

'Honest, I wouldn't know what I'd do without you.'

'Oh, grow a pair will you Bear. Start living up to your name for once.'

Bear. The same nickname she'd used since they'd met over twenty years ago. She'd become used to his new place within weeks, still preferring to drive over to his house rather than eat alone. Must cost her a fortune in tunnel tolls.

'Shit.'

Murphy paused in his coffee-making and jumped as the alarm on his new phone went off again. He fished it out of his pocket and pressed some icons in an effort to stop the noise.

It had woken him at the correct time. Although it being in his trouser pocket had confused him at first. He shut it off, the noise threatening to wake the entire cul de sac. Apparently there was a difference between turning off and sleep mode.

A quick look at his watch told him it was coming up to half seven, an hour before he usually got in to the station.

Time enough for a quick wake-up call.

'Bear, it's too fucking early. What have I told you? Don't bother me before at least lunchtime.'

'Morning Jess. Did I wake you?'

'No, I'm up. Peter is at his dad's and I had to make sure the little bastard is up for school. Can't rely on that lazy twat he calls a father, and he'd bunk off given half the chance. Fucking teenagers. What do you want?'

Murphy took a bite of his toast. 'Got a murder yesterday.'

'Shit. The girl in Sefton Park. Seriously? They gave it to you?'

'Yeah. First one in months.'

'How is it?'

'Interesting.' Murphy put the half-eaten toast back on the sideboard and opened the fridge with his free hand, taking out a bottle of water. 'Killer left a letter. Victim is a student. Usual nutcase stuff. You'll probably end up defending him in court.'

He heard a snort on the other end of the line. 'Well . . . congrats I suppose. I know you wanted to get back into it quicker than this.'

'But . . .'

A large sigh. 'Just . . . well . . . don't let it get to you. I worry, you know.'

'I'm fine.' Murphy replied, his attention more on trying to unscrew the top off the water bottle with one hand. 'You gracing me with your presence soon?'

'We'll see. I'm going back to sleep.'

The line went dead, and Murphy smiled as he put the phone away.

Until the previous day, it had been a quiet couple of months for the team he worked on – E Division, headed by DCI Stephens. Lately they'd been tasked with investigating the increase in gang activity around the city centre, but that was proving to be long,t difficult work. No one wanted to talk, there were no high-profile murders of youngsters to shake up the city. Just a lot of illegal activity that everyone would rather turn a blind eye to.

It beat murder though. He took another bite out of the slice of his toast. Nice balanced breakfast. Always important.

Murphy had been a DI for over five years, so he'd seen more than his fair share of murders and manslaughter charges. Most of the time, solving a case came down to one thing.

Luck.

The psychology of it wasn't something which interested him really. He'd seen the newcomers come into the force, mostly university graduates thinking they could apply some of their attained knowledge to police work. Sure, sometimes they could come up with a fresh angle on some things. But mostly, Murphy stuck to what he knew. Investigate everything, and if nothing turned up, hope to get lucky.

Murphy finished eating and switched off the radio, the Chi Lites snapping into silence mid-song. Good old-fashioned songs, from the sixties, like his mum used to play. There was even a radio station dedicated to playing that era of music now. Jess had bought him a digital radio at Christmas, and he'd not switched off the station since.

Bear. Jess still refusing to let that nickname die a death. His groomed beard was beginning to show some grey, and his short hair, that matched his beard length, receding backwards. He was washing more and more of his face every day. He wore his nickname well, his size being the main reason for it. It fit. Never caught on at work though.

He locked the house up and got into his three-year-old Citreon C5. Red. Extravagant really for what he actually needed. He'd grown up on a council estate in south Liverpool, but got out as soon as he could. Working and living over there as a PC, in Speke where he'd lived most of his life, had caused a few problems. So he'd lived out in Dingle, until recently. His parents hadn't moved though. Worked all their lives, been together since school. Thatcher had enabled them to buy their council house in the eighties, although their opinion on her didn't change because of that, saved for a long happy retirement together, with no money worries and plenty of day trips on coaches.

And they were both dead at fifty-eight years old.

Murphy was an only child, so everything went to him. Which meant he had a nice sum of money in the bank, no mortgage, no kids, no worries.

And no excitement away from the occasional bad marriage or tough case.

Apart from the occasional holiday he planned and never took, he had no idea how to spend it. His dad had been frugal, always saving for a rainy day, and Murphy guessed he'd picked up the same habits. . He smiled as he started the car, remembering his dad explaining to him that he could do without a new iron, as the old one still heated up occasionally.

Murphy checked his watch, waiting for the apartment door to open. Looked around and raised an eyebrow at Rossi, who shrugged in reply. Bass heavy music came from behind another door in the corridor.

'Taking their time.'

'Students for you.'

The door opened a few seconds later, revealing a couple seemingly clinging to each for dear life.

Murphy cleared his throat. 'I'm Detective Inspector David Murphy, this is DS Laura Rossi. I'm told you knew we were coming?'

'Yes,' the woman answered from behind a damp tissue. She was frighteningly young to Murphy's eyes. Dainty features, small in stature, with just socks covering her feet. The long cardigan she was wearing looked like it was at least two sizes too big for her, the sleeves balled up in her hands. 'Do you want to come in?'

Murphy shifted on the balls of his feet. Rossi took over. 'It looks like it could get a bit crowded if we're all inside. Is there somewhere else we can go, somewhere a little private?'

'There's a communal kitchen downstairs that no one really uses. We could go there?'

'Perfect.' Murphy replied.

Five minutes later, they were led down to the kitchen. The young woman had introduced herself as Rebecca and her boyfriend as Will. A small breakfast bar with three stools took up most of the space, with Murphy electing to stand to the side as Rossi sat opposite the couple.

'So when was the last time you saw Donna?'

Rebecca had gained controlled of her sobbing. 'Last Monday evening, around six. We had a Maccies and then she said she needed to go up to uni to do some revision. She's done all-nighters before, so I wasn't too bothered when she wasn't back when I went to bed.'

'Where does she usually go to study?' Rossi said, her eyes not lifting from her notepad.

'The library. It's open twenty-four hours, so she usually goes there. I think it was probably to get out of the flat, bit more space and that.'

Murphy studied the boyfriend, looking for any sign that he knew more than his silence was letting on. Tried boring a hole into his head using just his eyes. Got nowhere other than a sharp pain in his head from overstraining.

'Okay.' Rossi continued. 'So what happened next?'

'Well, the next morning she still hadn't come home, so I texted her. Usually she replies really quickly, but I didn't get anything back. I was worried, but thought she'd just crashed out somewhere. I went up to uni and checked the library to see if she was still there, but she wasn't. I left it a few hours longer, and then started ringing around. No one had heard from her. I tried ringing and texting all day but got nowhere. So, I called the police that evening. We've been waiting for news for almost a week.'

'We're sorry it wasn't better news,' Rossi replied. 'Was Donna worried about anything? Concerned about someone following her perhaps?'

Rebecca shook her head. 'She was just normal. Stressed a bit because of her exams, but nothing out of the ordinary.'

Murphy shifted forward. 'Where were you that night Will?'

Will lifted his head at the sound of Murphy's voice. 'I was out with mates, and got back to the flat around twelve. Wasn't I Bec?'

Murphy watched as Will turned to Rebecca, something flitting across her eyes, which was followed by a quiet nod. 'I'm going to need the names of your mates.'

Will turned back to Murphy. 'You don't think I had anything to do with this, do you?'

'Not saying anything yet,' Murphy replied, keeping eye contact with him. 'I'm just covering all bases. Nothing to worry about I'd imagine.'

Will seemed to accept this with a nod. He gave Rossi a few names and took out his phone to provide her with numbers.

Murphy turned his attention to Rebecca. 'What was Donna studying?'

Rebecca had watched the exchange between Murphy and her boyfriend open-mouthed, and took a few seconds to respond. Murphy tapped his foot, waiting. 'History,' she said eventually.

'We'll need a list of anyone else she was friends with, anyone she had arguments with, or fallen out with lately. Don't leave anyone out. Understand?'

Rebecca nodded, before breaking down and crying once more.

Murphy rolled his eyes

'Don't you think that was a little harsh?'

Murphy grunted at Rossi in reply. Bloody students, he thought, which was about as far as his sympathy went for the couple they'd just left. He was driving back to the station, his foot not really lifting much off the accelerator. He wanted to get back and start making some headway. Time was passing them by.

'I mean, they seemed pretty upset,' Rossi continued. 'They're only students you know. Just felt a little over the top.'

'Laura, if I want advice, I'll ask for it. Now instead of wondering about those two dipshit students and their feelings, let's work out what's next.'

Rossi sighed. 'Okay. I'm guessing we start at the university? Start interviewing?'

'Yes. We check in first and get the team working. There's a lot of work to do. I want that boyfriend checking out. Something's off with him. I think you should talk to the girl on her own.'

'Really, you think so? Seemed okay to me.'

Murphy snorted. 'Always look for the easiest explanation. This letter has us all thinking too broadly. It'll probably end up being someone she's turned down or something. I want him checking.'

'Okay. I went to that uni, you know. Maybe I should get in contact with some of my old tutors. Might get us somewhere a bit quicker.'

Murphy went back to grunting.

Experiment Two

She'd been asleep.

Lying on the mattress, or at least what she hoped was a mattress, sleep had taken her without her welcoming it. She'd been crying, she remembered that. And then she was floating into nothingness. As random thoughts and words faded away, she couldn't recall at what point the room disappeared around her.

She'd been dreaming. Lost on a whisper of consciousness, gone forever.

She rubbed at her eyes with greasy palms. At least she wasn't crying anymore, that was a bonus. One-nil to the petrified girl in the pitch black room.

She took her palms away. Her eyes fighting to become accustomed to the dark once more. She could make out some shapes, but nothing concrete.

She laughed, the sound of it echoing back from the walls. It made her recoil, it didn't sound like her.

Everything surrounding her was concrete. The walls, the floor. But from touch alone, she guessed the door was something a little different.

She stood, found the wall next to the mattress. Placed her

left palm against it, and walked slowly, tracing her way around the room. She stopped as she got to the corner, turned to her right and carried on. She passed her fingers over the ridges of the door, into the next corner. Turned right and walked forward.

Her foot struck porcelain. She felt around the top of the cistern and then downwards, finding the seat. She placed it down and turned around.

After she relieved herself, she instinctively reached for toilet roll. She was surprised to find some there, thinking it would be another home comfort she would have to do without. She flushed, and started the process again. Placing her fingers against the wall above the toilet and moving back towards the mattress in the corner of the same wall. Her feet bumped against something and she stopped. Crouching down, she moved her hand down and began feeling around. More smooth surface. She knocked on it, the sound created sounding similar to the toilet she'd discovered earlier. She grasped both sides of the porcelain, feeling with her palms as she stood up. As she reached the top, it became wider, before dipping down dramatically on the other side.

She felt the outline of something metallic, a hole at one end, fixed to a smooth surface.

A sink.

She tried the tap, twisting it. Water came out, cold. She ran her hands underneath. She cupped her hands together and splashed her face.

This was good. A place she could wash and feel refreshed at any time. 'Things are looking up,' she said aloud, the sarcasm echoing back at her.

Great, talk to yourself out loud. That'll stop you going crazy, she thought.

She turned the tap off, and moved her hands around,

trying to feel for a plug. She couldn't find one. It'll do though, she decided.

She wiped her hands dry on the front of her top, then moved back toward the mattress and stood next to it. She could feel the frustration bubbling up inside her again, her hands gripping the ends of her t-shirt and twisting it around and around. Nobody had the right to do this to her, nobody. She wanted to do something, anything, to release it.

'Can you hear me? I'm talking to you. Can you hear me? Let me out now. People will be looking for me, people you don't want to meet. You best let me go now, you bastard.' Her hands were shaking. Not just through anger and frustration.

It was fear. She needed to control herself, push down the dread which was swarming over her. She was stuck there. In the darkness with no escape.

'Let me out, please. Just let me go.'

Silence was her reward. She listened closely for anything else.

There was something, she couldn't place what it was though. She moved alongside the mattress again, trying to pinpoint the noise. In the next corner she stopped and listened.

A light humming noise from above her. She looked up but couldn't see anything. Just darkness.

She reached up towards the sound, but her small stature betrayed her. Her arms slumped back to her sides. She needed something to occupy her, to stop the terror bubbling inside her from increasing. She placed her back to the wall, the mattress to her right, and counted off paces to the next wall.

'One, Two, Three, Four, Five, Six . . .'

Her foot hit the wall. The door was to her left. She placed her back to it and walked towards the toilet.

'One, Two, Three, Four, Five, Six, Seven . . .'

One the seventh pace she slipped her foot past the toilet bowl and hit wall.

Six by seven. Almost as big as the box room at her home.

A noise by the door, a lock turning. She turned towards it and something clanged down. The hatch. Something was pushed through, clattered to the floor. The hatch closed again. Jemma stayed still for a moment.

No sound.

She went towards the door, pausing as her feet brushed against something. She bent down and felt around. A plastic bag, something squishing inside as she squeezed the content. Her mouth salivated as she realised what it was. From the shape and texture she thought it was some kind of sandwich. She moved her hand around and found something else. It was wrapped, long, rectangular. Chocolate bar she guessed.

She was hungry, but stopped herself from tearing open the food and devouring it. Anything could be in there. She didn't want to lose any more control than she already had.

'I'm not eating this, you hear me? Someone's coming for me. I don't need this.'

She threw the bag containing the sandwiches against the door. Lifted herself up and moved back to the mattress.

'Someone's coming for me. You hear that you fucking shit, you best hear me. You're screwed, you hear that. There'll be nothing left of you.'

She heard a whirring noise. It came to her then, what it was.

'You're filming me? You sick twisted animal. Film this.'

She stuck two fingers up towards the corner she thought the camera was placed.

Lights blared out. She shielded her eyes. Bright light from the ceiling illuminated the room. She'd been in darkness so long it took a while for her to remove her arm from her eyes. She squinted against the brightness. The walls were dark, her eyes adjusting constantly against the sudden light. All around her, written on the wall. Words and words. Blood red, daubed across, surrounding her, causing her to flinch back. She moved towards the writing, reaching out her hand and tracing a fingertip over the words.

Alone, friendless, abandoned, deserted, forsaken, solitary. Isolated.

Over and over. Written on the walls. She pulled her fingers back, looking at the tips of them as she did. Red stains.

She looked around and saw the sandwiches near the door, the Crunchie bar lying close by.

'No one is coming. Eat, don't eat. Nothing changes that simple fact. You're alone here.'

The voice seeped from the walls, like blood running down the concrete. The words in red becoming larger, pulsating, alive. She blinked, and they went back to normal.

'You fucking . . . I'll kill you. I'll tear you apart, you sick bastard.'

A low chuckling sound was her response.

Then, the lights went out. The darkness returned.

That was day one.

81

10

Monday 28th January 2013 – Day Two

Almost thirty-six hours after the body of Donna McMahon was found in Sefton Park, Murphy and Rossi parked up near the City of Liverpool University.

Liverpool is the home of four universities within its city. One near the city centre, which could be seen from the windows of the police station where Murphy worked. Two more further out from the waterfront, one to the North near Ormskirk, one to the south, Childwall University.

City University lay just beyond the outskirts of the main hub of Liverpool. In another of Liverpool's little paradoxes, the city centre isn't actually in the centre of the city, but to the left of centre as you look at it from above, built out of the port at Albert Dock. Being a former major worldwide port, that was where the money came from, the shipping merchants of the eighteenth and nineteenth centuries building their big houses just outside the centre. Murphy had a book somewhere, which detailed the whole history of it, but couldn't remember where he'd left it now. Probably lost in one house move or another.

Murphy looked around the campus, the vastness of the area taking him aback. There were walkways linking the different buildings, with the students guild building smack bang in the middle. Directly opposite was a bookshop which seemed to only stock large textbooks, which Murphy imagined students would need a wheelbarrow to cart around.

'We need to walk down to the old library, and there's a building near there that houses the history department,' Rossi said, a folded map in her hand. 'It's moved since I was here.'

'I don't see a library.'

'It's straight ahead. About ten minutes' walk.'

Murphy stopped. 'Exactly how big is this place? I thought this was it.'

Rossi turned, but didn't stop. 'Big.'

Murphy moved, shaking his head. 'No wonder they had to increase the fees. The council tax alone must be bankrupting.'

'I doubt they pay . . .'

'I know, I know,' Murphy interrupted, 'I just didn't realise it was so big.'

They continued to walk in silence. A few minutes later, a walk across a busy main road, a shortcut across a small grassed park area, and they were at the bottom of the steps which led to the history building. Grand stone steps led upwards to a bulky door, old brass door knocker and number on the front. In the window to the side, a poster hung, asking for solidarity against university cuts. Murphy rolled his eyes and pushed open the door, holding it open for Rossi.

'What's the advisor's name again?' Murphy asked, as they ascended the stairs inside the building.

'Lynn Ripley. She was here when I was studying. Don't know her though.'

They stopped outside the office on the first floor, the staircase continuing upwards to more floors than Murphy could count. He reached out and knocked. A voice from within told them to enter.

The office was neat, tidy, efficient. The window faced out onto the green they'd crossed earlier. Lynn Ripley sat back in her large office chair, smiling tightly. Her hands were clasped together on the lap of her long skirt. White blouse, buttons closed all the way up over her ample chest, to her neck.

They introduced themselves, and Murphy allowed Rossi to take the lead as he scanned the office. Everything had its place, tucked away, maximising space. Clearly labelled. Nothing would be lost in this office.

'We're all in a state of shock in the department,' Murphy heard Lynn say as he tuned back in, 'she was well thought of by the staff. She would have gone far.'

Murphy waited for the tears to fall, but she composed herself. 'What can you tell us about Donna?' he asked after a few moments of silence.

'She was well liked. Seemed to always have someone to talk to, many friends.'

'Anyone special?'

'Not that I know of. We don't usually get involved in that side of things unless there's a problem.'

Murphy scratched at his beard. 'What about teachers, lecturers, anyone take a special interest?'

Ripley took a moment to think and then answered him, 'No, it was all strictly professional with her lecturers as far as I was aware.'

'Any problems with other students? Anyone who hung around when he wasn't wanted, that type of thing?' Murphy leaned forward, leaning on a filing cabinet for support.

'She lived with a girl . . . I forget her name . . .'

'Rebecca,' Rossi said.

'That's right. She has a boyfriend. Little stocky thing, shaved head. Short man syndrome.'

Murphy nodded, waiting.

'I saw them arguing a couple of weeks back. In the library. Only caught a bit of the conversation, but it was definitely heated.'

'What did you hear?' Murphy asked, the wheels turning.

'Donna was saying she was going to tell her. I don't know what that meant.'

Murphy breathed out. 'I think I have a pretty good idea.'

They walked briskly back to the car, Murphy talking a mile a minute as he laid out his theory to Rossi. 'So, Donna finds out Will is doing the dirty or worse, behind Rebecca's back. She threatens to tell Rebecca everything, Will loses his mind, and kills her.'

'Hmm,' Rossi replied, looking off into the distance.

'What? It wouldn't be the first time something like this has happened.'

'I know. There's just something missing.'

Murphy stopped. 'We're picking him up. See if he can massage your worries away.'

'It's . . . just . . . I don't know.'

'Spit it out, Laura.'

They were standing face to face outside the book shop in the main university square. Rossi was scanning around, not wanting to look him in the eye. 'I just didn't get the impression that lad had the capacity to write that letter, and come up with that kind of cover story. That's all.'

'Oh. Is that it? He could have got that idea anywhere Laura.'

'I suppose.'

'Look,' Murphy said, softening his tone, 'we'll pick him up and see what he has to say.'

'What do you study Will?'

He wasn't under arrest, Murphy made sure he was aware

of that fact. He could see how nervous he was however, clammy hands clasped, making a wet sound as they came together. The touches he gave to his ear every ten seconds or so.

'Music.'

'Oh, you want to be a musician? What do you play?'

'Violin.'

'Really? You don't look the type.'

Will crossed his arms in front of him. 'Looks can be deceiving you know.'

Murphy leaned back, catching Rossi's eye. 'I'm sure. Do you know why we wanted to talk to you?'

'You think I've got something to do with Donna being . . . well, you know.'

'We're not suggesting anything. We just have a few questions.'

Murphy had relented to Rossi's suggestion that they speak to Will Ryder at his flat. He'd wanted to bring him down to the station, get him in an interview room, and question him there. They were sitting in the small living room, trying to ignore the abundance of takeaway cartons strewn about, and the smell of weed in the air.

'Okay,' Will said, 'fire away.'

'Did you and Donna get along?'

'Didn't really know her all that well. She was just Bec's flatmate. Didn't have much to do with her.'

'Did you talk much?'

Will fidgeted with his earlobe. 'Not really.'

'No arguments or anything?'

Will stopped fidgeting. A look passed across his face which Murphy couldn't be sure was guilt or confusion.

'Not that I remember. Maybe once or twice if we made too much noise.'

'How about in the library at uni a couple of weeks ago?'

That got his attention. His eyes darted about, looking for an exit. Murphy tried to keep a smile from breaking out. This was going the way he wanted. Nice easy solution.

'Yeah, we had a little conversation about something.'

'What was that about then?'

Long pause. Will began pulling at a thread on his grey joggers. Ran a hand over his shaved head.

'If I tell you something, you won't say anything to Bec will you?'

Murphy's hand wavered in the air. Maybe, maybe not.

Will sighed, looked to the ceiling. 'Okay, it was a one-off. I don't want you thinking I do this sort of thing all the time. I was out in town a few weeks back. Got absolutely wrecked, and kissed some random girl. Donna saw it happen. Didn't even know she was there. Pulled me up about it and I had to practically beg her to not say anything.'

'And she didn't?'

Will smirked. 'Do you think I'd still be here if she had? Bec would have thrown me out on my arse. Doesn't like cheaters.'

Murphy looked over at Rossi. Couldn't read her expression. 'So you just left it at that then?'

'Yeah. Thought she was going to say something eventually, but just hoped she'd listened to me. I told her how upset Bec would be if she found out, played that emotional stuff, you know. Promised it was a slip, just the drink, never happen again. She seemed to accept that. Doesn't matter now of course.'

'Are you sure that's all? You never saw her there again, argued?'

'Yeah,' Will replied, sitting forward off the settee, 'that's it. Look, I've got nothing to do with what happened to her. You've got to believe that.'

Murphy sighed, checked his watch. 'That'll be all for now. We'll probably want to speak to you again, okay?'

Will looked relieved, which pissed off Murphy more than the state of the room. 'Yeah, no problem.'

He showed them out, leaving Murphy and Rossi to walk down the stairs towards the exit of the building. Murphy tried to make sense of his thoughts. He was so sure he'd got his man, but the performance of the young lad had been too convincing. He was scared, not of being caught, but of being questioned. Being thought of as anything less.

Murphy didn't know what to think. Only that he was pissed off he wasn't arresting the cheating scrote. Open and shut case, to keep the wolves at bay. A murder case at that.

'Well?' Rossi eventually said as they sat in the car.

Murphy gripped the steering wheel a bit tighter than he already was. 'I'm not convinced. I want you to speak to the girlfriend. On your own. I think you'll get somewhere.'

'Okay.'

They drove back to the station in silence.

Murphy sighed and leaned back in his chair. The day was coming to an end, an endless round of interviews with various possible witnesses and students getting them nowhere.

'Anything from DC Harris yet?'

'Not yet. He's the last one.' Rossi replied from her desk opposite.

'We might not have got anything from those interviews, but I think we need to keep focus on the university. If it's not Will, it's someone there.'

Rossi pursed her lips, seemingly thinking of something to say in rebuttal, before thinking better of it and saying nothing. She was learning quickly. Murphy liked that.

There was something more bothering Murphy though. He kept coming back to the letter, the words seeming to mock him personally. He'd attempted to dismiss them as the ramblings of a spurned student, trying to put them off track.

Yet he kept coming back to the passage about death, unable to stop thinking about it. The words burned onto his memory.

Death is inevitable, yet people are always surprised when it happens.

He shook his head. He needed to go home, eat, sleep, shower.

Murphy stood up, taking his jacket from the back of his chair. 'I'm getting off Laura. Nothing more we can do right now. Get some sleep, okay?'

'Oh, okay sir. Meet you here at eight?'

'Yeah, fine.' Murphy replied. He turned and headed out, entering the lift which was thankfully already at his floor.

Murphy leaned against the back of the lift, closing his eyes. The pain was back, rocketing across his head behind his eyes. Brilliant flashes of stinging light.

Stop thinking about her. Stop it. He repeated the mantra softly to himself for the entire lift journey, only stopping when the doors opened again.

The image of the dead girl, Donna McMahon, lying pale and peaceful, laid out on a bed made from damp earth, stuck in his mind. The image flickering across his conscious, soft, sharp, in focus, blurred.

The pain became worse. The image didn't fade.

Murphy had to sit in his car for fifteen minutes, eyes closed, before he felt well enough to drive.

The pain subsided. The image didn't. The way it always was. The pain was good in a way. At least it dampened down the worst of the flashbacks. The images of red flashing across his eyes, the pounding of his heartbeat as his breath shortened and became shallow.

They were always there. Ready for him. He just wanted to be normal again. Not some clichéd version of himself.

Donna's face blurred and became others. It wasn't supposed to be like this.

He was haunted. The past, the present, forever blighted by his life. He couldn't see any end to it.

This was just him now.

Rossi watched Murphy leave, entering the lift and resting his head against the back wall, his eyes closed.

Merda. He was losing it already. Great.

She could see Brannon watching her from his desk, a dirty smirk on his face. He could see it too. All she needed.

She checked the time; just before half past seven on day two. She pulled the letter from her desk and read it again.

It was too neat, too academic. Non emotional. If it was someone the victim knew, wouldn't there be more there? Could someone who killed her, strangled her to death with his own hands, then put this together so sufficiently?

No. She didn't think so.

She was using pop psychology. 101. Garnered from her first year at uni, when she'd taken a module just to see if it was of interest. It wasn't for her. After the interesting bits had been and gone, she'd been left with a bunch of long words, which didn't mean anything really. She was happier with sociology, learning about the world around her, how capitalism works, theories, and all that sort of thing. How social policy affected all their lives.

And she'd still ended up in the police. At least the degree had meant she moved out of uniform quicker.

She couldn't put it off any longer. She had to leave. Pay her dues.

Be the good daughter.

Alessandro and Isabella Rossi lived in a small terraced house in West Derby. A fifteen-minute drive from the station, a straight run on West Derby Road to the town, and then down a few side streets until she hit their road.

They'd lived there the past forty years, ever since they'd been talked into coming into the country with promises of endless work and riches. Salvatore ended up on various building sites, and then on the docks later in life. He got caught up in the docker's strikes of 1995 and now existed on their meagre pensions, bringing in just enough to buy the food that was always needed, and keep Papa Rossi in his Sky Sports and Lambert & Butler cigarettes.

They loved life, and each other. It was plainly obvious to anyone who met them. Always well liked in the quiet street of semi-detached houses, more middle class than the estates, but still maintaining the sense of community.

Laura Rossi was their youngest, and she was reminded of the fact constantly. The baby of the family, and only girl of seven. Six older brothers. She hadn't been able to bring a man to visit until she'd been twenty-five. The first family dinner had sent him running for the hills.

Literally. He was backpacking somewhere in Africa, last she'd heard. Wanted to climb Kilimanjaro or something equally ridiculous.

Rossi sat in her Astra, letting the engine cool as she braced herself for entry. When she couldn't put it off any longer, she walked up the small path and knocked.

Mamma Rossi opened the door, mocked fake surprise and ushered her in. '*Bambina*, we haven't seen you in so long. Sal, look who has returned to us!'

It had been five days since her last visit. Typical.

'*Ciao Mamma, come stai?*'

'Come in, I have some *polpette* left over, you'll eat.'

'Yes Mamma.'

She walked behind her mother, who went directly through into the kitchen at the end of the hallway. Rossi hung her coat on the banister and went into the living room. Her Dad was sat in his usual spot, the leather armchair facing the TV.

'*Ciao Papa.*'

'Hello beautiful. How are you?'

The accent still rolled from his tongue. He still looked good for his age, almost seventy, but his tanned skin and full head of grey, slicked-back hair made him look at least ten or fifteen years younger. Thick, dark-haired forearms on show, his shirtsleeves rolled up to the elbow. He removed a cigarette from a packet and turned the TV down.

'Good. Got a new one yesterday, so I've been busy.'

'The girl in Sefton Park? Nasty business. It's been on Radio Merseyside all day.' He crossed himself with his free hand, and then lit his cigarette, waving smoke away from where Laura was sitting near him on the end of the settee.

'Yes.' Hoping that would be the end of the conversation. Papa Rossi peered at her over his cigarette and seemed to make his mind up about carrying on further.

'*Oggi in figura, domani in sepoltura,*' he said finally.

'Today in person, tomorrow in a grave.' Rossi repeated in English.

Her mamma appeared then with a mountainous plate of meatballs and spaghetti, topped with parmesan cheese. It was worth the feeling of guilt for not visiting as often, for the food she knew would be waiting for her.

Later, once she'd cleared her plate and decided that would be enough food to last her the rest of the week, the three sat in almost silence, only the gentle murmur of the TV providing a soundtrack. Mamma was stroking Laura's hair, just as she had when she was a child. She could feel her eyes growing heavy, as the rush of the previous couple of days caught up to her.

Peaceful.

No dead girls threatening to ruin her tranquillity.

Murphy was right. It was a simple case, a fake letter, and definitely someone close to the victim. She let her mind wander to Murphy. She knew of his recent past, the horror of it, the pain. She felt drawn to him, not in a romantic sense, but as a pupil. She knew of his success, his power and tenacity. She wanted to learn from him, get close and hopefully always be his first choice. Make a real push forwards in her career, breaking free of the shadow that was her family, becoming her own person. She just needed Murphy to get back to his normal self.

She let herself close her eyes and sleep in her mother's arms.

Rossi woke to the sound of her phone ringing. Her mother had covered her with a blanket and left her on the settee. She answered wearily, her voice croaking a greeting.

And then . . . everything changed.

11

Saturday 18th February 2012
11 Months Earlier

Rob pulled up outside his house ten minutes after leaving Carla's. The car settled as he looked through the window at the semi-detached house. He remembered the first time they'd seen it together. He and Jemma must have looked at maybe fifty houses before deciding it was the one for them. Three bedrooms, one for them, one for the future, and one for an office that neither had ever used. Needed some work doing to it when they'd first moved in, but one loan from the bank later, and they had the money to do it. They'd worked hard making it just right. This was supposed to be it. Their first home.

Rob stepped into the house, slipping his coat off after closing the door behind him. He paused as he began to hang it up, placing his free left hand on the black woollen coat he'd bought Jemma for Christmas.

'Helen?' he called.

'Through here.'

Rob hung up his coat and turned to enter the living room. Helen was in the doorway. Her eyes were tinged with red, slight mascara stains underneath.

'Anything?'

Rob shook his head, then collapsed to a sitting position on the staircase, his head in his hands. Too much, it was too much. He wanted to scream out. Didn't think he could.

Helen stood over him, placing a hand on his shoulder. The second woman that night to do so. 'It's okay. Rob, she's okay.'

He looked up, his eyes trying to find hers. She wouldn't meet his gaze though.

'You think?'

'Carla just called. She told me you'd just been around.'

'Yeah. But you can't think the same as her, can you?'

'Look. Jemma has always been her own woman. Even as a young girl, I couldn't get her to do anything. I remember once, she'd have been about eight at the time, sitting for two hours at the dinner table waiting for her to finish her mash. I gave up before she did. Jemma had eaten them twice a week for years, but one day just decided she didn't want them anymore. She's headstrong, knows her own mind. Always has.' Helen took her hand away, and turned towards the kitchen. 'Carla said you didn't know that she's done this before.'

Rob stood up too quickly, a sudden swirling feeling in his head. 'She never said anything. Are you telling me you think she's just left, in the middle of the night, without saying a word?'

'She was happy before you, you know, with, erm . . . whatever his name was. It didn't stop her leaving. This is what she does.'

'But just leaving like that, she'd do that?' Rob knew the answer before it came.

'She's done worse. You may have been with Jemma a long time, but there's a lot you don't know about her.'

'I know her now. She's not like that, not with me.'

'Come on, come and sit down. I'll make us a cup of tea.'

Helen turned and walked up the hallway towards the

kitchen. Rob sighed and followed her into the kitchen. As he walked up the hallway, he paused in front of the collage of photographs that took up the centre of the wall. Jemma had spent days, weeks maybe, putting together snapshots of their lives together. Friends, nights out, the day at Aintree races, him suited and booted, her in a long cream-coloured dress. The holidays they'd taken, Tenerife, Rome, and Florida. He traced his fingers across the photographs. Watched as they blurred into one. Became a final image. The bare bulb which hung in the hallway illuminating the frame, placing a glare across the top third.

He could hear Helen taking cups out of the cupboards, the kettle steaming up and boiling. He took his hand away and looked up at the ceiling. Breathed out and followed Helen through into the kitchen.

He pulled one of the chairs back at the small dining table that was never used. Too small to eat at really. They'd talked about throwing it out a few times, but never got around to it. Helen was pouring milk into the cups. 'Two sugars, right?' she said, still not facing him.

'Yeah.'

Helen finished stirring and brought the tea over, placing the cup down and sitting across from him.

'Thanks.'

'That's okay.'

Rob took a sip without thinking, the hot tea burning his mouth a little. He bit back on a yawn, the feeling of exhaustion creeping up on him. He set the cup back down on the table. He needed to smoke. Something he hadn't felt in a long time. 'When Jemma's dad died, she took it hard,' Helen began, her eyes on a coaster she was fiddling with on the table. 'She was fifteen, in her final year of school. She had plans to go on and do her A-levels, then uni. But her dad died, and she shut down. They were close, a proper pair. He

96

got her a season ticket when she was six, and she went to the match with him every time they were at home. I wouldn't let him take her to away matches, too tribal. He never called her Jemma, it was always LP. Little Princess. She was at school when he died. Massive heart attack; he was dead by the time he hit the floor the doctors told me. She never got to say goodbye. At the funeral, she didn't cry. She stood there with a confused look on her face, as if she didn't know where she was or why. I didn't want her to go the cemetery, but my sister talked me into it. Said it would be good for her. Not sure I'd agree with her now. Anyway, after that, Jemma wasn't the same. I caught her sneaking money out my purse, she'd be out all hours, coming home smelling of drink. I tried talking to her, but it was pointless. Her exams were a wash out. She never did her A-levels.' She dropped the coaster and picked up the cup. She brought it up to her lips, blew on the tea softly before taking a sip. Rob watched her, the clock ticking in the background the only sound.

'The first time she left, she was gone three days,' Helen continued, 'she was only sixteen. She left a note saying she was going away for a while and not to worry.' She snorted quietly. 'Being a parent, that's your main job, to worry about your kids. Anyway, the police weren't really interested, said she'd turn up when she ran out of money. I was sick with worry, had my sister's husband driving me all round Liverpool trying to find her. Then, three days later, she walked through the door like nothing had happened. You can't imagine how I felt those three days. I was lost, imagining everything that could have been happening to her.' She shuddered as the memories came back to her. Rob sat in silence, taking in the very different version of the woman he'd shared his life with.

'I screamed at her, called her for everything, but she didn't listen. She wouldn't even tell me where she'd been. For the next few years, she'd take off every month or so. Sometimes

97

a couple of days, sometimes weeks. When she met Mark, I thought she was settled. She was happy again, her old self.' Helen shrugged her shoulders. 'But it didn't last. She'd tell me about the arguments they would have, that kind of thing. And then she left. Six months she was gone. Not a phone call, email, nothing. After a month or so, I started to worry. Phoned everyone in the family, her friends, no one knew where she was. I called the police, but she was twenty, she could do what she liked. They put her on a list, questioned Mark a little, but nothing came of it.'

She paused, tracing a finger over the rim of her cup. 'She'd been at my sisters. She lives in Boston. Over on the east coast.'

'In America?' Rob asked, surprised Jemma had never mentioned it.

'No, it's in this country. Funny, I know. It's nice over there, but we don't talk much, me and my sister. Especially since then. Not once did she tell me Jemma was there. The worst thing was what my sister said when Jemma came home and told me where she'd been. Said she'd do it again if Jemma asked.' Helen muttered something under her breath which Rob thought sounded a lot like 'Stuck-up bitch.'

Rob finished his tea, took the cup over to the sink. 'It's different this time Helen.'

'It's not though Rob. You know that. You've been arguing a lot, she told me. She wasn't happy.'

Again, surprise. He'd had no idea she'd been talking about their relationship behind his back. Play with it. 'This again? We were fine, we didn't argue. I don't know what she was telling you but it's wrong.'

'Rob. This is what she does. Why would she lie about you two arguing? Maybe you just didn't think it was that big a deal.'

Rob slammed the cup down into the sink, breaking the

handle. The crash made Helen jump. 'Sorry. I just . . . I just don't understand any of this.' Rob's voice was loud in the silent kitchen.

Helen stood up. 'You don't get it Rob.'

Was this his out? Dampen the guilt he was feeling? 'What don't I get?'

She smiled softly. 'She's run away again. That's it. You need to accept that.' She glanced at the gold-plated watch on her arm. Jemma had bought her it for her birthday.

'Look, I best be going, Danny will be wondering where I am.' Rob moved aside as Helen placed her cup in the sink.

'Helen . . .'

'Don't, Rob. I'm going home. Make sure you eat.'

Helen walked out of the kitchen and Rob watched through the doorway as she put her coat on and let herself out the door. Rob pulled his phone out of his pocket, searched for Jemma's number and called it.

He hadn't tried for a few hours. That wouldn't look right.

Voicemail again.

'Jemma, it's me. Look, I don't care what's happened, or if you're worried about coming back. I just want you home. Please come home. I love you.'

Rob slumped back into the chair.

His head fell into his hands, and for the first time since he'd woken up alone that morning, he let the full weight of what had happened fall on him.

His face grew damp rapidly as the tears fell from his eyes.

He wasn't just going through the motions, even though he'd dealt with this before.

It was different.

He was different this time.

He made a list.

He had to get it right this time.

He didn't title it WHAT A NORMAL BOYFRIEND WOULD DO IF HIS GIRLFRIEND WENT MISSING.

That would have been too much.

He wrote down what he'd done so far. Began adding items.

He had to go to Boston and visit the aunt. That was first.

Chase up the police. Make them aware he was worried about her safety. See if that got them moving.

Missing posters? Contact the media? Convince people she hadn't run away. Get them thinking.

Good. He was on track.

Rob mindlessly flicked through channels on the TV, unable to concentrate on any programme for longer than a minute or so. His head was spinning, lack of sleep and food causing his thoughts to be in disarray. Around three a.m. his stomach growling became too hard to ignore and he got some food from the kitchen. By the time he'd sat back down with ham on two slices of wholewheat bread, and a packet of crisps, his stomach began to churn. He didn't make it past two bites, the crisps sitting on the coffee table, unopened.

It was almost dawn when he finally drifted off, unable to keep his eyes open any longer. A dreamless sleep, enveloped in darkness, unaware of his slumber.

He woke slowly a few hours later, aware of the low hum from the TV which was still tuned to the last channel he'd been watching. For a second he forgot why he was asleep on the sofa, before reality came back to him. The weight of it on his chest, heartbeat increasing by the second as the panic set in, his mind racing with images. He remembered arguments. One in particular. Where the sense of foreboding had began. When he knew it was only a matter of time. A couple of weeks before Christmas, when the university had finished for the first semester.

He'd gone the pub after work one night, had phoned Jemma to tell her he'd be late in, promised to be home within an hour. He'd had one drink, then another, chatting to his mate Dan, who was bending his ear about students and the lecturer's life.

He'd been in the pub for three hours when he realised what time it was. He'd quickly checked his phone, discovered he'd missed quite a few calls from Jemma. He'd finished his drink and gone home straight away, trying to call her the whole time, but she wasn't answering. He'd got a taxi home and steeled himself for a bit of a telling-off, then a takeaway and a cuddle more than likely.

Instead they'd argued for most of the rest of the night. It'd turned out Jemma had decided to cook a romantic meal for them, a meal which was cold by the time he'd walked through the door almost three hours later than she'd expected him to. It was a big deal really. Rob took on most of the cooking, so it was a big deal when she made the effort. The only remnants of her labour, dirty pans and melted candle wax pooled on the surface of old saucers.

He apologised, but after a barrage of *woe is me* and *why don't you understand*, and *why don't you listen to me*, and *me, me, me*, he'd grown weary. He was feeling brave with four pints in him, and he'd begun to argue back, making the point that maybe if she cooked more often it wouldn't be such a big deal if he missed a meal she'd prepared every four years or so. Plus the pork looked overcooked, and the sauce had stuck to the bottom of the pan. Another Jemma special. It escalated. A plate or three was thrown. Rob thought he may have been responsible for at least one of them. Within minutes she'd stormed upstairs, calling him a boring, selfish bastard and slamming the bedroom door on her way. It was at that point Rob had started to feel guilty. He'd followed her, found her lying face down on the bed, and started to apologise profusely for the next hour. They'd fallen into an uneasy truce, ordering pizza, and going to bed soon after, with only the TV providing noise.

He made his way to the bathroom, yawning as he lifted the seat. Jemma's toiletries overwhelmed what surface space there was in there. She seemed to have creams or lotions for any possible event. Rob looked around whilst relieving himself, noticing for the first time that this room was the only one that still retained the scent of her.

Not true.

He finished up and went through to the bedroom and sat on her side of the bed. Lay down and buried his face in her pillow. He'd seen it being done in films, the one left behind searching for the scent of the other.

All he could smell was fabric softener.

Everything started to swim in front of him. He turned and threw a straight right fist into the wall above the bed, then grabbed the first drawer out of the bedside cabinet, flinging it across the room, spraying its contents across the floor. Adrenaline was pumping through him like water through an open dam. He was aware of what he was doing on one level but felt powerless to stop himself on any other. He upended the mattress on the bed, before turning over the small dressing table, sending the surface contents scattering.

He was conscious enough of what he was doing to stop himself breaking the full length mirror which was propped against the wall, pausing before it, seeing his reflection. He was blowing hard, red in the face, tears falling slowly down his cheeks. His usually coiffed hair looked bedraggled, the last twenty-four hours conspiring to leave him close to breaking point. He wanted to lose it completely, smash the reflection of himself, destroy himself.

No. He couldn't do that.

Everything could be mended. Broken to unbroken in a matter of minutes.

Almost everything.

He wiped tears from his eyes, not knowing when he'd begun to cry. Let a quiet chuckle pass his lips, and began picking through the bits of bedside table drawer, finding an address book and snapping back into reality. He picked it up and, giving one last look around the mess, went down to the kitchen and filled the kettle. He placed the book down on the small table and waited for the kettle to boil.

Leafing through the book he recognised most of the names; old friends, new friends, doctors, dentists.

Item one on the list. Go visit the aunt.

He mentally added, *fix the bedroom*, to the list.

He went back to beginning of the address book, praying she'd listed the aunty in there. Rob didn't have a name for her, just a place name, and he really didn't want to involve Helen in this. It needed to be of his own accord.

It would look better. More proactive.

He found it near the end, Aunty Susan, an address in Boston, no phone number.

He placed the open book down on the table, picking his coffee up and draining half the cup in one gulp. He stood and emptied the rest into the sink, standing at the window, looking out over the garden. Jemma had been gently mithering him to sort out the overgrowing grassy patch which took up most of the space for months.

Now, there was no one nagging at him over the small, insignificant things that just didn't matter. A constant droning, which had only become worse over time.

He wasn't sure if he preferred the silence.

Rob pulled his trainers over his feet in the hall and grabbed his car keys.

It was time to go through the list.

Experiment Four

He'd shocked himself with his capacity for anger. He'd never have believed he was capable of the violence months before. He searched for a cause for it. An answer to why he'd lost it so completely.

When it came, it was simple.

The first one hadn't screamed as much.

This useless lump of skin and bones had almost brought the ceiling down with the level of her cries. And then, with her mouth wide open, her teeth had almost made contact with his face.

The nerve of her.

'Mmmf, mmmf.'

She was still going on. Even behind the gag he'd now secured across her filthy mouth. Her naked body already showing red marks rising up from where he'd had to placate her.

'I had plans for you,' he said, pacing back and forth in front of her. 'So many plans. You could have been so much more. There's a plan. A step-by-step guide. And you're ruining it.'

He knelt down in front of her, far enough away that her thrashing limbs did not touch him. Her face was marked with black streaks, as tears and sweat mingled to create a river of mascara cascading down her round cheeks.

'I was under the impression all you girls used that waterproof stuff these days. You look awful.'

He studied her some more, attempting to formulate a different sort of plan. One that would appease.

It was no use though, and he knew it. It was supposed to go a certain way, and he'd already failed. He'd marked her, spoiled her features.

It wasn't his fault. It was his mistake, but she had caused it.

'You stupid fucking bitch. Do you have any clue as to what I am doing here? I am changing things. This work is important. But you don't care, do you?'

He stepped forward, drawing his foot back, kicked the bottom of her outstretched left foot. The noise behind the gag grew louder.

He enjoyed that sound. He felt something shift inside him. More alive. More powerful.

'You're selfish, you know that?' He punctuated his words with more kicks. 'Your death could have been glorious. A work of art. They would have still been talking about you, long after we're all gone. Now, you're a worthless piece of excrement on my shoe. A hindrance, a burden on me. I would have shown you the courtesy of dulling the pain. Now . . . now you'll feel every last second of what I'm going to do.'

He crouched down again, taking in her sad form. He snorted. 'You are undeserving of this work. You're just a piece of waste to be taken care of.'

He reached into his back pocket, held up the knife into the light glaring from above.

She recoiled as he walked back towards her, breathing heavily as she attempted to break free of her chains. All the while, a muffled scream was the only noise in the room.

Then he moved quicker. Arm raised above him.

And then it went down towards her. Again and again.

The room turned red. He didn't stop until the exertion overtook him, leaving him panting for breath with his back against the wall.

She was lifeless. Unrecognisable from the woman he'd brought here.

He smiled. He knew how to rectify this mistake.

12

Monday 28th January 2013 – Day Two

The dashboard clock flicked over to eight-fifteen p.m as Murphy pulled the car up outside his house, his phone chirruping as he switched the engine off.

'Murphy.'

'Where are you?' Jess's shrill voice barked down the phone.

Murphy shook his head, smiling. 'Hello Jess.'

'Yeah, fuck that. Where are you? I've just driven all the way out to yours, and you're weren't even in.'

'I'm not sure if you're aware, but I'm working a murder at the moment. Long hours kinda come with the job.'

'You're still on that? Thought they'd have dropped you by now.'

Murphy sighed, getting out of the car, locking it behind him. 'Yes, thanks for the support.'

'That's no excuse. I have to go to my mum's for food now. You know how I feel about that.'

'I know, I'm sorry. Maybe ring ahead next time, make sure I'm in?' Murphy said, smiling.

'You wish. Listen, Sarah called me again today.'

Murphy sighed. 'What did she want?'

He heard Jess breathe heavily before continuing. 'She wants to see you.'

'Not going to happen.' Murphy extricated his keys and opened the door, entered his house in darkness.

'Think about it. You can't just ignore her forever.'

'Yeah, okay Jess. Listen I've got stuff to do, big case and all that. Give me a ring tomorrow.'

'Fine, whatever Bear. Just think about it, okay?'

Murphy closed the door behind him quietly. 'Okay.'

He walked up his small hallway, flipping the light switch and relaxing as he bathed in light. He removed his jacket, kicked off his size fourteen shoes and walked through to his living room, collapsing on the sofa. He reached for the TV remote, wanting to switch off for a few minutes at least.

Sarah. She wouldn't just give up. At least she'd stopped ringing him personally. Now she just went through his friends. Well, friend.

His stomach growled at him. He knew he'd forgotten something. He'd wanted to pick up a takeaway on the way home, but instead had driven in a daze. Distracted.

Twenty minutes and a trip to the kitchen later, Murphy was flicking through the TV recorder, trying to decide what to watch from the seemingly hundreds of programmes he'd saved over the last month or so. He settled on an episode of *The Sopranos* and sat back with his microwaved family-sized lasagne to watch. The meal was its usual disgusting fare, but Murphy carried on eating, dipping slices of dry bread into the lowering amount of sauce. He made a note to buy margarine at some point, knowing he'd forget within seconds.

He eyed the cross trainer in the corner, an extravagant purchase, for what was more or less running in mid-air. It had made him a little fitter though, made him feel less guilty for eating meals intended for more than one person. He turned his attention back to the TV.

The words from the letter found on the victim kept coming back to him, circling his mind, stirring up memories. He attempted to shut out the dominant thoughts but he was failing. Memories mingling with the present overpowering him.

Then there was Sarah, not letting him go. Forever trying to get back in.

Who was he kidding. She'd never left. A parasite in his head he couldn't shift. A tapeworm that wouldn't leave his gut.

Murphy winced at the imagery. Had it come to that? Was that all she meant to him now?

He thought back to the time when all was good. It was supposed to be that way forever. People would tell him how happy they seemed together, that they were made for each other. And it was like that at first. The love was different, strong. Just not strong enough, he guessed. The anger which had clouded him only months earlier was dissipating slowly over time.

She was still his wife.

He went back to eating his food, finishing the plate soon enough. He picked up the glass of coke he'd poured himself, deciding not to drink anything stronger in order to keep his mind clear for the next day.

It wasn't though, not by any stretch. It was on auto-play now, flicking through memories like a flip book.

Some good, mostly bad.

The day his dad had bought him his first car, a shitty little banger that barely lasted a year or so. His mum singing along to the radio as she cooked a Sunday roast. The night he came home to find Sarah crying in the bathroom, the baby she'd been carrying inside her for nine weeks gone.

Walking into the other house, a few days after consoling a devastated Sarah, finding nothing in the kitchen, and everything in the living room.

He screwed his eyes up, willing the images away. Stopped them before they all turned red, black, angry, hateful.

Dead.

He lost himself in the blinking images from the flat box in the corner, his eyes dropping as tiredness overtook.

He woke hours later, rubbed at his eyes and yawned, the tired feeling still not shaken. He could hear his mobile ringing, incessant noise drilling into his ear canal and rattling his sleep-muddled brain. He wanted to ignore it.

Did he even want this any more? He looked around his nicely decorated home, which always felt empty. No photographs on the walls, just the occasional piece of 'art' which he'd picked up from Homebase. It was all for show. A part of the façade he had built around him in the previous few months.

His phone had stopped ringing.

Murphy dragged himself upright, checking the arm of the sofa for his phone. It had slipped down the cushion and whilst he was digging it out, it began ringing once more. He grabbed it before it slipped right down into the frame, trying to answer it at the same time.

'Damn touch screen, useless piece of shite,' he said as he attempted to pick up the call, noticing it was Rossi calling as he did so.

'Murphy,' he said, finally answering.

'Sir.' Rossi was panting, out of breath. 'We've been trying to get hold of you. We've . . . we've got another one.'

'What?'

'We've got another body. Found earlier. Near the lake in Newsham Park. Same posing, and another letter. I'm just on my way there now.'

'I'll meet you there.' Murphy said, ending the call.

Another one. That couldn't be right. He'd felt so sure, so

110

convinced it wasn't going to be something like this. One murder, one victim; nice and easy. It had to be.

Or the first letter was real and he was already making mistakes.

'Focus, you need to focus.'

He needed this. He couldn't make any mistakes. People relied on him for answers, all looking up to him.

And Murphy didn't know if he could provide them.

It wasn't supposed to be like this.

She was posed like the first victim, but that was where the similarity ended.

In the late night darkness, the large lights erected around the body illuminated the area, casting shadows around. There was no mistake as to where the attention of the couple of dozen people scattered about the place lay. The body was entirely lit up, stark and bright. The lake was to the left of them, silent and still. There was a hush as bodies passed each other with barely a raised voice.

Newsham Park, just past Kensington, a mile or so from town. The West Derby Road leading a path straight to it. A flat green space with a large lake at the top, surrounded by trees. Invisible from the road.

Again. Same type of scene.

They say you get used to it. One victim becomes another. An endless array of body parts lit up, wounds, scars, blood. If you deal with death all the time, you develop a gallows humour, dark jokes passed around.

Murphy knew differently. When it was bad as this, there was no levity to be found. You got on with the job, and hoped to catch whoever did it before it happened again.

She was laid out with her arms and legs outstretched, the same as Donna McMahon, but as Murphy got nearer he winced as he saw what had been done to her.

Large gashes were open on each cheek. She was topless save for a black bra. Numerous slashes to her skin, stab wounds.

Murphy stopped counting them at eleven. One in particular would live with Murphy for a long time.

Her neck, opened up, deep.

It was difficult to see a patch of skin which was actual skin tone.

So different.

Her face was a mask of red. Dark, dull, almost brown. Her features were unrecognisable. Her nose was almost level with her face. Her mouth a grotesque open wound, stretching outwards towards her ears.

Once he'd brought her here, he was calm enough to lay her out, and disappear into the night.

Murphy stepped back allowing a SOCO to pass. 'Is this what he wanted to do, another experiment or something?'

Rossi looked from Murphy down to the body. He tried to work out what was happening behind Rossi's eyes, but failed.

'Second one in three days. Either someone is trying to cover his tracks from the Donna McMahon murder, or we have a serial,' Murphy said, moving out of the way. Putting distance between him and the body. 'Witnesses?'

'Just the one so far. Someone walking through the park on their way home from seeing her boyfriend. Young girl, seventeen. She's being treated for shock apparently. Doubt she'll be walking this way again any time soon.' Rossi replied, gesturing towards a path which led from the lake, a few hundred yards towards the main road. 'We can talk to her later if she's calmed down. Don't think we'll get much though.'

'Okay, we'll let the SOCOs work, check to see if CCTV covers any of the area. We'll wait for, let me guess, Houghton?' The look from Rossi confirmed it. Murphy rolled his eyes and continued. 'For now, we canvass the area, knock on doors.' Murphy looked at his watch. 'Wake people up.'

'This is nothing like the first one. This is . . . just unbelievable.' Rossi coughed, looked away before turning back to him. 'He must have dropped the victim here earlier though. She was found at just after two a.m. Maybe midnight, just after?'

Murphy pointed towards the main road. 'He could drive up that path from the road, and no one would think anything of it. The park is dead this time of night, no lights at this end. Wouldn't be much of an effort at all.'

Murphy looked around; the wind whistled through the trees, sending a chill through him.

'Haven't been here since I was a kid. Not changed much.' Rossi said, following Murphy's gaze.

'Only been here as a PC,' Murphy said. 'Cleared out the drunk teenagers at the weekends. Couple of bommy nights. We had the Venny when we were kids. Didn't need anything else.'

'The Venny?'

Murphy patted his pockets. 'Yeah, the Venny. Adventure playground in Speke. Was well good when we were kids. Not been there for a while though. Hope kids still go there.' Murphy found what he was looking for, popped a cough sweet in his mouth and offered the pack to Rossi.

'Sore throat?'

'No.' Murphy sighed, put his hands in his coat pockets. 'What the hell is going on here Laura?'

'Victim has been dead between eight and twelve hours. Not killed here. Again, she was moved here.'

Murphy watched as Dr Houghton shifted the victim onto her side. 'How long has she been here?'

'Hard to say. Lividity suggests she has been on her back

between six and twelve hours. However, if she's been moved, it'd be difficult to determine for how long she's been lying in this position.'

'Can you put a rush on the PM?'

Dr Houghton pushed out a sigh. 'Won't be until the morning of course. But we can move some around for you. As a favour.'

Murphy snorted. 'Thanks for that.'

Dr Houghton muttered something under his breath and Murphy took his cue to leave. They'd never got on. Worked together for years, but it had always been that way. There was something off about the good doctor that Murphy had never been able to figure out. Houghton's attitude towards him was that of general dismay, bordering on disgust. Obviously not old school enough for him.

He found Rossi talking to some uniforms and waited as she gave out instructions.

'Anything?' Rossi asked when she'd finished. She had dark circles under her eyes, but still seemed to exude energy, bouncing from one foot to the other.

'Not really. She'd been moved here, as we thought.'

'Post-mortem?'

'In the morning. Until then, let's try and find out who this girl was.'

He watched as they moved around his handiwork. Assured of their roles, of the tasks they had to do.

He had to hide a smile from the other gawping passersby who had stopped at the police cordon to see what had happened.

He knew.

The two officers in uniform, their big flak jackets beaming fluorescently in the dark night.

They knew.

114

But this was power. Standing here in plain sight. No one had the first idea it was him who had brought them all here.

His work.

He'd waited so long, and then two in the space of a few days. All that planning, now coming to fruition.

What one person can do to another. Fascinating.

The smaller of the two officers in bright uniform, a hard-nosed female, wearing no makeup, her hair hidden by her hat, was scanning the small crowd. The man with her seemed more interested in what was going on behind him in the park.

He'd wait a little longer and then leave. See if he could catch a glimpse of who was investigating.

Not too long though.

13

Tuesday 29th January 2013

Murphy's eyes stung as tiredness threatened to overwhelm him. The long night drifting into the early mist of a late winter morning.

The picture of the new victim, fresh in his mind, made him push forward and carry on.

So different to the first victim.

The thought of her grieving parents came back to Murphy, and he pushed it down. He couldn't deal with what came with those thoughts. His mind was racing, the coffee he'd been downing at regular intervals taking effect.

It had been bitterly cold out there at the scene. Murphy was glad to be in the relative warmth of the major incident room at the station. It was quiet, the early morning changeover hadn't kicked in yet. Rossi had been wearing the same smart trouser suit as the previous day and Murphy thought she'd probably ended up at her parents' the previous night. They hadn't worked together as much as others had, but he knew some of her habits.

He'd sent her home in the early hours for a few hours more sleep, but decided to stay on himself at the station waiting for a copy of the latest letter to arrive.

Murphy busied himself going through missing person reports, finding preliminary matches. He looked at the description Rossi had noted down of the woman again. The victim had been around twenty-five to thirty years old, five foot five inches, dirty blonde hair, dressed in black bra and jeggings. Whatever jeggings were. He sent a text message to Jess, his usual contact for anything modern he didn't understand.

'What in the name of fuck are Jeggings, Jess?'
Send.

He put his phone back in his pocket, and continued going through the list. Local reports first, discounting the long list of teenage reports instantly. They had south of fuck all to go on and her face wasn't going to help much in its present state. The rest didn't match any last descriptions of what women the same age had been wearing before going missing. He wondered if those who'd cared enough to report them missing would ever get resolution. A lot did; most missing persons turn up within seventy-two hours. Too many don't.

His phone vibrated in his pocket and Murphy took it out.

'Like leggings but they look like jeans, numb nuts.'

Murphy shook his head and left his phone on the desk, putting off the reply for later. Once he'd gone through some more possible names.

He reached over and turned his computer on as fresh faces arrived in the room, taking coats off, chatting animatedly with others. The room was shared across the whole of CID for Liverpool North. One whole floor of the building, most walls knocked through. At that moment, as well as the two murders which had occurred in the area, they were also dealing with a spate of armed robberies in off-licences in the area, various sexual assaults, and two stabbings, both victims thankfully on the mend in the Royal Hospital. Neither saw anything, meaning it'd be pretty difficult to get a conviction.

Murphy wished he was on those cases. At least they were alive.

'Have I missed anything?' Rossi said, appearing at his desk.

Murphy jumped a little when she appeared. 'Can't you wear a bell or something Laura, announce your arrival. Fuck's sake.'

She was carrying two cups of coffee in paper cups. Costa Coffee rather than canteen downstairs. Which meant they'd at least be palatable.

'Sorry.'

Murphy shook his head, taking the proffered cup from Rossi. 'We've got the PM at nine, so we best make a move.'

'I'll drive.'

It was the smell, as clichéd as that was, which always bothered him about these things. The cold, hard air which inhabited the room only conspired to make it worse. Sterile, absent of anything real. He had the same feeling about hospitals, but at least there was life in a ward or bay almost all of the time.

Here, there was only death.

They'd stood back as numerous photographs had been taken, every inch of the woman captured over and over.

Murphy watched as Dr Houghton gave way to his assistant, who was around Murphy's age but with a better tan. He was studious looking, stern, thin as a rake. Houghton introduced him quickly, Murphy only hearing his surname. Lawrence. Listened to Houghton's instructions carefully as they meticulously circled the body, taking fingernail scrapings and more. Much more.

Murphy turned away when it became more intimate.

'Hmm. Difficult one,' Dr Houghton said without looking up. 'No distinguishing features, birthmarks or tattoos. We've taken some scrapings which could be of interest. We'll send samples off to see if it's of any use. There are thirty-one stab wounds inflicted on the body, all with the same weapon.

118

Numerous bruises. Defensive wounds to both hands, but only bruising and what appears to be a fractured wrist. Nothing from the weapon used to the rest of the body.'

'That's interesting.' Murphy said, moving a few steps closer. 'He beat her up, and then what? She was unconscious and he stabbed her repeatedly?'

'Possibly. There are no head wounds consistent with a brain injury. It's more likely one of the stab wounds inflicted was incapacitating early on. My money is on the one to the neck.'

Murphy went to rub his beard, but thought better of it. 'Type of weapon?' he said instead.

'Looks like a standard knife wound. Could be a typical household implement. You find the knife David, I'll match it.'

Murphy nodded. 'We'll get right on that. We can take a copy of the letter with us?'

Dr Houghton looked up from the body. 'Leaving us so soon? You know you'll have to get over yourself at some point. It's just a dead body. You scared or something?'

Murphy smirked, not rising to the bait. 'I think we've got all we need for now. Laura, you need anything else?'

Murphy turned to Rossi, who was looking ten shades paler than when they'd entered the room. 'Let's go,' Rossi replied, already turning to head out.

EXPERIMENT FOUR

Detectives,
  Do we call you detectives in this country, or have I been watching too many American cop shows? Never mind, that's what I'll call you until I find out your names. I assume there's more than one of you, in fact I imagine there's a whole team. A whole team tripping over

themselves, trying to find any rhyme or reason for two young lives snuffed out.

Two now. In just a few days. Unfortunately, unlike the first body you found, I can offer no grand announcement to the nature of this one's death. No results to share, no past experiment improved upon, expounded research . . . nothing.

She just is.

I had plans for her of course. You may want to Google 'Unit 731'. The books are surprisingly light on the subject and I can't imagine you have a very sufficient library there (think Josef Mengele on a far eastern tour! Ha Ha!).

If you'd like a suggestion, the library at the City University has a vast selection of psychology books.

Alas, I couldn't do what I wanted to with this subject.

Far too much racket, screaming and yelling, she even tried to bite me. No respect for others these days. What has this country come to? Distressing to say the least. She had to be terminated I'm afraid to say.

I may have to revisit this experiment with a new victim at some point. I so want to find out how that would pan out.

Sorry for the brevity of this message, but there is not a great deal to tell. The experiment had to be terminated.

The blood was glorious though. All that blood, from one wound. I think I could

have severed her entire head given the
inclination.

Anyway, must dash. You see . . . I'm
already working on number five.

Unsigned again, handwritten in large sloping letters. Murphy had no doubt it was the same writer. He turned his head to see Rossi making a few notes. 'What are you writing?' Murphy said.

'Just the main bits. "Unit 731", what do you think that is?' Rossi replied.

'Balls if I know. Maybe we should do as he says, and Google it.'

'Okay, you know how to do it?'

Murphy snorted. 'Be my guest, but just because you've got a few years on me, doesn't mean I don't know how to work the internet Laura.'

'I didn't mean you couldn't, was just saying . . . you know.'

'Just do it. I'll do some proper work on finding out who she is. Was.'

Fingerprints had given them no match to anyone in the system, so Murphy went back to the missing person reports.

Hannah Reid – Dark Brunette. Not her.

Carrie Wearing – Aged forty. Strike two.

Another twenty minutes and Murphy had got precisely nowhere.

'How do we narrow this down?' Murphy said, looking over his screen towards Rossi.

Why don't you check if any missing person reports have come in for students?'

Shit. Why hadn't he thought of that? 'Good thinking. I was just going to suggest the same thing.'

Rossi hesitated and then thought better of saying anything. Good. He was the one in charge.

Within five minutes he had two names. One a bit younger than twenty-five, at twenty-two. The other, twenty-seven. Could be either one.

He walked across the room towards the corner where DCI Stephens was in her small office. Stephens spent most of her time in there, believing in a hands off approach to management, which suited Murphy fine. Two murders in a couple of days meant he had to keep her updated however.

Murphy rapped on the office door, causing heads of those close by to turn around.

'Come in.' Stephens' voice came through the closed door.

Murphy entered, taking stock of the layout. Everything in its place as usual, Stephens was an incredibly neat person, right down to the slicked-back dark hair, tied in a perfect bun. Immaculate suit, green eyes like lasers, which could spot something dodgy at fifty paces.

'Hello boss, just thought I'd give you an update.' Murphy said.

'Of course David.' Always the first name, the only person around the place who called him by it. To say it annoyed Murphy would be an understatement, even if she were his boss. Murphy brought the DCI up to speed on the night and morning's events, telling her about the contents of the letter.

'Do we have any possible names for the victim yet?' Stephens said.

'Two. Possibly. We're working on the theory it may be another student.'

'We need to be more proactive. You and Rossi pick one of them and go and visit the next of kin, or whoever reported her missing. Send Brannon to speak to the other one.'

'Okay.' Brannon going to see a relative of a missing person, possibly to tell them they'd been murdered. Murphy could see that going very badly.

'I want you at the press conference.' Stephens continued.

Shit. He'd forgotten about that. He was supposed to be sitting with Donna McMahon's parents asking for information in a few hours. Murphy hated doing the media thing, he always looked huge next to normal-sized people.

'Yes. Best spruce myself up a bit before that.' Keep it light. Nothing wrong with him at all.

'Don't worry, we'll have the parents do most of the talking.'

'Understood boss. I'll get right on it.'

'Good. And how are you feeling David, you finding this difficult at all?'

Murphy shifted uncomfortably in his seat. 'Not at all. You've been DCI here the whole time I've been a DI. You know I've worked murders before.'

'Not since what happened though David. And this is the first since the unfortunate incident last year.'

An awkward silence filled the room. 'Which *unfortunate incident* are you talking about?' He smirked as she shifted uncomfortably in her seat.

'That business with the Phillips girl.'

Murphy stopped smirking as he remembered. Flick. The image front and centre instantly. Nineteen years old. Her whole life ahead of her. Lying on her back, her face a mask of blood.

The man cuddled up to her, his dirty fingers stroking her hair.

'That won't happen again.'

Stephens smiled thinly. 'Look David. I know the past year has been tough on you, but you have to move forward. That's why you're leading this investigation. I want you to know my door is always open, if you have anything you need to get off your chest. I don't believe in bottling things up. But if you want to carry on in this job, you need to be able to handle everything that comes with it.'

Murphy bit back on his initial desire to snap. He

swallowed it down and instead went for a conciliatory tone. 'I can handle it boss. I appreciate your concern.'

'Very good.' Stephens replied. 'Anything else?'

Murphy shook his head and left the office. The aroma of the perfume Stephens wore religiously, still on his nostrils. The fresher air outside the office relaxed him slightly.

He made a beeline for Rossi, who still sat at her desk.

'Laura, get the address for one of these names,' Murphy told her, finding the two possible mispers on a sheet of paper. 'We're going to see them. Boss' orders. We're taking the photo Houghton gave us, hopefully they'll be able to recognise her from it.'

'Okay, any particular one?'

'Take your pick. Brannon can go see the other.'

'Right.' He noticed her wince slightly. Rossi pulled up the names, and wrote down the address for the first name on the list.

'Stephanie Dunning,' Murphy said. 'Let's go see what you've left behind.'

14

Saturday 18th February 2012
11 Months Earlier

He nursed his cup of cheap-tasting coffee, watching through the window of the cafe as two truck drivers smoked and chatted outside. Mused on whether the services on this motorway differed to any other.

He'd driven east on the M62, heading for Boston and Jemma's aunt who lived there. The radio tuned to talkSPORT, two ex-footballers arguing over a penalty which was either given or not given the previous day, Rob couldn't tell. He'd reached over and switched stations, settling on a soft rock music station as a compromise.

He didn't want silence in the car.

The Waterboys came on, their only recognisable song playing. Rob found himself tapping along to the music on the steering wheel. The song reminded him of his dad, who had been a proper muso. He'd had even played saxophone in a few bands in the seventies and eighties, just around the local pubs. One of his bands even built a bit of a following, touring around the north of England for a while.

Rob had tried to introduce some old music to Jemma once.

She'd pulled a face. Asked him how old he was. That music released ten years before she was born wasn't really what she wanted to listen to.

He looked down at the dashboard, his speed dropping below sixty m.p.h. He put his foot down, gripping the steering wheel tightly.

The sat nav instructed him to turn off at the next junction, with mostly A roads ahead. Rob relaxed as he let himself be guided along the rest of the journey. The windscreen became rain splattered as the clouds above him grew dark once more.

As the roads became less busy, the landscape changed around him. He looked from the car at the passing green fields, golf courses, and small farms. The area was a lot nicer than the bustling city he had left behind, the air cleaner, with fewer buildings cluttering up the view.

Rob was surprised to find he quite liked it. He and Jemma had always disagreed about moving out of the city one day, light heartedly he'd thought, with Jemma wanting to be somewhere nicer than the endless rows of houses in which they'd lived.

Was it that? Was he holding her back?

He shook the thought away.

The trip had been a pointless exercise. Just another item on his list to cross out. Something to show people in the future that he had tried to find her.

He'd left not long after arriving, the awkwardness of the encounter driving him away, pulling off near Leeds at a service station after another couple of hours of driving, wishing he'd accepted the offer of food from Jemma's aunt Alice. Paid well over the odds for a pasty and a coffee which could only have been made with dishwater.

He took out his phone. Back to the list.

'Hi Dan.'

'Rob, you okay?'

That voice. It betrayed Dan's auspicious upbringing. A world away from the council estate Rob had grown up on. Yet, somehow they'd clicked almost instantly when they'd met at work. Dan was a lecturer, Rob in a lowly admin job at the university. Not exactly well matched for friendship, but it turned out they just got on well. It helped that Dan was into sport, so they always had something to talk about. If they'd been at school, they'd be best friends. As it was, they were the blokes in their thirties version of best mates.

Really, Dan was the only friend Rob had.

'Jemma didn't come home on Friday night.' Rob could feel the emotion rising at the back of his throat. He composed himself, breathed in and out for a few seconds, then told him what had happened since.

'Rob, you need me and I'm there, okay?' Dan said when he'd finished talking.

'I know, thanks mate.'

'I'll pop around in the morning.'

Rob smiled. 'You don't need to, but I'd appreciate the support.'

'Not a problem. Get some rest if you can, I wish you'd have told me sooner.'

'Would you have listened on day one?'

He heard a chuckle over the line. 'You caught me out. Listen, I have to go now. If you need anything please call.'

Rob felt a little better for the phone call, relieved to share the burden. He forced the pasty down him, finishing the coffee off with a wince.

Now what? The little voice in his head said. What are you going to do now? It wouldn't be long before that little voice

127

grew louder, constantly telling him how fucking useless he was. How his life meant nothing without her.

And he would be forced to listen.

The police turned up the next day.

Jemma's mum had called him early that morning, decided she'd had a change of heart over the weekend and was starting to worry. She'd been to her local police station and pulled a few strings with an old friend so they'd take her seriously.

It was Monday morning and he should have been in work an hour earlier. By now they would have heard Jemma had gone from Dan. Would be best to let them know himself though, especially as he was expecting a knock at the door at any moment.

Rob finished the call and went through into the kitchen, deciding a cup of coffee and then a fresh plan of action was needed. The kettle had just clicked off the boil when his phone began to ring in the other room. His heart jumped a little.

He rushed through into the living room, snatching the phone up and frowning at the screen. 'Unavailable' was the caller's display name.

'Hello?' Rob answered.

'Hi, is that Robert Barker?' The voice on the other end replied.

'Yes.'

'It's Detective Constable Nick Ayris here, from Merseyside Police.'

Rob's heart was beating against his chest wall, his hand was shaking. He wiped away a sheen of sweat which had formed on his forehead.

'We need to speak to you concerning your recent report of your partner's disappearance. Would it be possible for myself and another officer to visit you soon?'

'Yes, of course,' Rob replied. 'When will you be round?'

'We're in the area, we'll be there in ten minutes.'

'Okay. Okay, good.'

Rob placed the phone back. His palms were sweaty as he ran them through his hair.

He just had to try and stay calm. He'd followed the list. Nobody could doubt him.

The knock on the door came a couple of minutes later. Rob rushed to the door, almost breaking the lock in his speed opening it. He'd expected the police, but instead Dan was standing there.

'Hey. How are you?'

Rob didn't say anything, turning around and going back to the living room. Dan followed him through.

'You want anything, drink or something?' Rob said, taking up the same position he'd taken up earlier, his back to the sofa, sat on the floor. He'd been willing the clock to move faster, get the thing over and done with. If it was bad news, he wanted it ripped off quick like a plaster. Not drawn out, destroying him bit by bit.

'No, I'm okay. Any word?'

'The police are on their way.' Rob's voice faltered. 'I think they may have found out something.'

Dan crossed the room, sitting on the sofa, his knees level with Rob's head. 'You don't know that yet Rob. It could be for any number of reasons.' He laid a protective hand on Rob's shoulder. 'Let us see what they have to say first before jumping to conclusions. Okay?'

Rob wiped his sleeve across his face. 'Thanks mate.'

'What are friends for? Athough I can't stay long. I'll be back later on though. We can go looking for her or something.'

There was a knock at the door once more. Rob breathed out silently, preparing himself. He pulled himself up, brushed himself down, noticing his jeans were looking a bit scruffy. He hadn't changed them since the morning he'd woken up alone for the first time. He was grateful for the quick shower he'd forced himself to have that morning.

Opening the door, Rob was greeted with the sight of Little and Large. A big bear of a man, with a nicely shaped dark haired beard, and a small wiry guy with a pointed nose.

'Hi, Rob is it?' The big bear had a deep voice to match his size. Rob had gotten into trouble with his short temper in the past, but he tended to choose his fights well. 'I'm Detective Inspector Murphy, and this is DC Ayris. Can we come in?'

Yeah, he wouldn't be choosing one any time soon.

'Of course.'

Rob showed them in, apologising for the mess, even though he was sure they'd seen worse. He introduced them to Dan, who shook each of their hands in turn. The little one was carrying a small folder, which Rob tried not to look at. His hands clasped together, his sweaty palms made a smacking sound. 'Can I get you a drink or anything?' Rob said.

'No, we're okay thanks.' The little one, Ayris, answered, before sitting down in the single chair that was to the right of the sofa. The big one, Murphy, was taking in the room, choosing to stand, by the looks of it. He seemed to be focussed on the pictures on the far wall. His eyes flitted about the place, possibly accusatory.

'I assume you've come about Jemma?'

'That's why we're here. Take a seat Mr Barker.' Ayris said, waiting to talk as Rob did as he was told.

'What happened to your hand?' Murphy said.

Rob looked at his hand, still cut and red from the previous day. 'I erm . . . I got a bit pissed off yesterday, punched a wall.' He said.

'You do that often?' Murphy said.

'No. It's been a tough couple of days that's all.'

'Hmm. Of course. It's just that you have a bit of history with keeping a lid on your temper, don't you?'

'What's that supposed to mean? I got into trouble when I was younger, yeah. But I'm past that now.' Rob could already see what path the conversation was taking. He was caught in a staring competition with Murphy though, and he wasn't about to back down.

'More recently as well,' Ayris said, looking at his notes, 'accusations of assault from a Melanie Parker. Your previous girlfriend.'

'I was never charged with anything. She took it all back, said she'd made it up. I don't lose my temper like that.'

'Until yesterday, of course.' Murphy said.

'Yes, until yesterday. But that was just frustration. Surely you know what that's like?'

'I usually don't take it out on walls. You and Jemma having any problems?'

'No. We were . . . are fine. She just . . . I don't know. She's been telling her mum and best friend that we were arguing.'

'And you haven't?' Murphy was frowning at Rob.

'No.' Rob replied, his raised voice echoing back to him. We were . . . fuck, *are* happy. We never argued really. A few crossed words about stupid stuff. Well . . . except for one time, but that was nothing.'

'Nothing?'

'Look, what's this got to do with anything? Is anyone doing anything more to find Jemma?' Change tack, anything to get away from this conversation. Rob could feel his anger rising. He didn't want them to see that.

'I can assure you we're doing everything we can Mr Barker.' Ayris said cutting in. Rob was still staring into the big detective's eyes. Rob looked away.

'Of course.' Rob said, moving his gaze across to the smaller man. 'I just don't know what to do. She's been gone three days.'

'I, we, understand.' Ayris, said, standing up. 'We just need to know the whole story. From the beginning. Let's start again.'

'Thanks I'd appreciate it.' Rob replied, before explaining everything that had happened over the previous few days.

Whilst he was talking, the big detective had excused himself from the room. No doubt to snoop around the house. Rob was fine about that. He wouldn't find anything.

'That's it. She wasn't with her aunt, I really don't know what else to do.'

'Leave it with us now. Get some rest, it looks like you've not slept well.'

'I'm sure you understand why,' Rob replied.

'Of course.' Ayris said, as Murphy entered the room again, sharing a quick look with him. 'Thank you for your time.' He exchanged nods with Dan, Murphy choosing to leave without a word.

Rob showed them to the door, the big detective turning once he was outside. 'Here's my card. If you have anything else you need to tell us, give me a ring.'

Rob took the card from the man, catching his eyes again. He didn't like the stare he got in return. 'Thanks, I will.'

With that, they left. Dan made his excuses and exited shortly afterwards, with a promise to be back later, leaving Rob to close the door behind them all. He could still smell the cheap aftershave the little one had been wearing lingering in the air. Rob walked through to the kitchen, bending down underneath the sink to find the air freshener. It wasn't at the front where it was usually kept, so he began moving things around, trying to find it. Old carrier bags, sponges, thrown out of the way, as Rob began to get frantic. He needed to be rid of the smell, he needed to get the house back the way it was.

Rob began emptying the cupboard faster, bottles of bleach flew across the room, until it was empty. The air freshener still not to hand.

Rob sat back, his head resting against the kitchen cupboard, bottles of cleaning products, dishcloths and carrier bags strewn around him.

'I can't even find the fucking air freshener.'

And if he couldn't even find something as simple as that, what hope did he have of doing anything?

Murphy shoved his hands in his coat pockets, shivering against the cold February air as they walked back to the car. He turned to see if a figure would appear in the window, watching them walk away, but all he saw was the net curtains unmoving.

'What do you think then?' Nick said as Murphy sat down beside him in the driver's seat.

'I think I need a new car. One with heated seats.' Murphy replied.

'I meant about him, in there,' he said, pointing back towards the house. 'You think he had something to do with his girlfriend going missing?'

'I don't know. The bloke has a record as a teenager, few scraps here and there. There's that complaint that was made against him by the ex, but that could be something or nothing. Maybe it's as her mum has said, she just disappears every now and again. There's something not right about the whole thing though.'

'Maybe. What now then?'

'I've been on all night and I was only doing this as favour because the mum knows the boss. I need to get home and have a kip. Going for a meal later with Sarah and the parents.'

'Anywhere nice?'

'No idea. Knowing them, it'll be the Italian in town. They love that place.'

Murphy turned the ignition and drove off. Allowed himself a small smile of satisfaction. He and Sarah were happy, already discussing the right time to start trying for a baby. His parents had accepted her, even knowing her past. Even work was going well for once.

Maybe he should book a surprise weekend away for them both. They could even use it as an excuse. If not start trying, at least get a bit of practise in.

Only a few weeks away from his world collapsing in on itself.

Experiment Two

It had been too long.

She'd been convinced he was going to try something. Violate her more than he already had. But there'd been nothing.

She'd gone back to looking for a way out. A crack, a loose bit of wall, or a defect in the door she could exploit. She'd done it so many times, and knew what she'd find, but she tried all the same. She spent so much time trying to force her way out of the solid door. Open the hatch from the inside so she could crawl out.

It was amounting to nothing. A perfect seal around her, keeping her locked away down there for days already.

Days. Weeks maybe. She didn't know. Time was a stranger in the room. Sleep came in bursts, the boredom taking over and sleep breaking it up.

The only interruption came when the hatch clattered down and food dropped through.

'What do you want from me?'

She'd said the words over and over, desperately hoping for a reply, a sign, anything that would suggest something was going to happen. Sometimes quietly, sometimes screaming it so loud, it began to hurt her throat. Then, she'd drink the water from the tap over the sink, the metallic taste making her gag at first, before the need to quench her thirst overtook it.

The room was beginning to smell of sweat and fear. Or how she thought fear would smell. It seeped into her pores, up through her nose, in through her mouth. She attempted to clean herself over the sink, but it wasn't helping.

She waited for the hatch to move. It happened after what seemed like hours, but could very well have been minutes for all she knew.

A glint of light appearing, and then seconds later being snuffed out.

A face. Featureless, imaginary. Looking in at her. She could hear his short breaths quiet in the darkness which had followed.

She counted.

One one thousand, two two thousand, three three thousand, four four thousand, five five thousand, si . . .

The hatch closed.

Five and a half seconds.

That's what separated her from the outside.

The dim face in the darkness and all that represented. Her mind worked overtime trying to place it, her memory of it fading within seconds. There was just nothing to hang onto, no prominent features she could place, compare to anything else.

Footsteps walking away, echoing back up the stairs, coming to a sudden stop. She imagined him turning, coming back and opening the door properly.

Her heart was racing. He could come in there and do whatever he liked to her. She barely had the strength to walk the length of the room, never mind fight him off.

She was helpless.

The footsteps began again. She strained her ears to work out in which direction they were heading. Realised she was holding her breath after ten seconds or so.

She waited for what she thought would be enough time and then moved.

She felt around the hatch again, knocking the food out the way as she reached the door. Where the hatch was built into the door, it felt different. Smoother than the heavy material surrounding it. She tapped her knuckles against it, a metallic clanging emanating from it. She felt around the ridges.

It was big enough. She'd have to be quick. And there was no telling what he'd do to her if she got it all wrong.

But she had to try.

Her stomach growled, the feeling of hunger she'd been experiencing on and off washing over her once more. She hadn't eaten a morsel in all the time she'd been down there. The hunger was like nothing she'd ever experienced. The lack of energy, the weight slowly falling away from her.

'How long have I been here? Let me out now.'

Her throat was hoarse, but still she screamed. She got no answer. The man hadn't spoke to her in a while.

She had to eat.

She tore off the wrapping, biting into the first half of the sandwich. She almost choked on the first swallow, her mouth dry and cracked. She spread her other hand across the floor, finding the bottle of water, and unscrewed the cap, not caring it wasn't sealed properly. She took a large swig, noting the metallic taste she'd experienced from the tap water wasn't there. She went back to the sandwich. She finished the first half quickly, moving onto the second half once she'd finished. It tasted like tuna mayo, with a watery cucumber as garnish.

She finished eating and drained the rest of the bottle of water. Her stomach seemed to balloon as if it was going to explode, sharp pains hitting her like she was being repeatedly stabbed in the stomach.

She sat back against the wall, head between her knees, breathing deeply to try and stave off the sickness she was feeling. She swallowed several times in an attempt to fight down the overwhelming urge to purge the food which had entered her body.

She needed to keep as much in her as possible.

She'd need her strength if she was going to attempt an escape.

He watched her on a small monitor as she ate. Looked at the clock on the wall, and marked the time.

Just over seventy-five hours it had taken for her to relent to her hunger. To give up that scrap of control.

He had to monitor this one carefully. Experiment two. Note everything down. Study her actions, her progress.

It was important.

There was a long way to go.

138

15

Tuesday 29th January 2013 – Day Three

Another student. Just like the first victim.

Stephanie Dunning. Twenty-seven years old. She'd gone back to further education the previous year, performing well in her access course, and landing a spot on a degree course at the university.

Now she was dead, lying in a morgue only a few hundred yards down the road in the Royal hospital.

Murphy sat across from her husband at their dining room table. Open plan room, St Francis Xavier's Church looming over the small house opposite. Only a few minutes drive from the station, just up the road near Browside Gardens. Two young children, both boys, sat in the living room in front of the TV. *Spongebob* was their distraction as Rossi took the photograph back from Nathan Dunning. He'd confirmed it within seconds. He knew his wife's features, even when they'd been so damaged. Murphy watched him closely as he'd shown him the picture, looking for some kind of reaction. His face had betrayed nothing, only his eyebrows shifting north indicated he'd even been surprised. Now, he looked between his two children, and the two detectives who had brought death to his house.

'Can I see her?'

Murphy looked to Rossi, raised an eyebrow. Suspicion was rising by the second. He'd given out bad news plenty of times, so recognised the subtle differences. There was no shock here. Not yet. Maybe he needed to see her body first, Murphy had seen that before also. Nothing was real until it was in front of them. Stark and unambiguous. Still, he made a mental note of his reaction in case other things didn't add up.

Rossi spoke up, 'Yes. Do you have someone who could come around and watch the children?'

He nodded and went through to the kitchen to use his phone.

'She'd been gone four days,' Murphy whispered as soon as he'd left. 'He keeps them somewhere.'

'We're looking at a double then?'

Murphy nodded. 'Both students at the same university. Both left with letters attached to them, talking about psychology. You know where this is leading.'

'The university.' Rossi replied, her attention moving from Murphy to the living room. He followed her eyes.

He didn't want to be around when they were told.

'Do the press thing and then go there?' Rossi said, closing the car door.

Murphy fastened his seatbelt. 'Sounds like a plan.'

'Maybe I should try the psychology department at the university. The experiments so far have had a psychological basis to them, probably best to go to the source, don't you think?'

'Yeah. Good idea.' Murphy replied. 'What subject did that Will study?'

Rossi paused then answered. 'Music.'

'Hmm. Still think there's something with that lad. I know

we've been sidetracked, but sort out a meeting with the girlfriend.'

'Okay.'

Within minutes they were back at the station, pulling into the car park. Rossi turned the engine off and turned to Murphy. 'Is everything okay?' Rossi said.

Murphy reached across to take his seatbelt off. 'I'm sound. I wish people would stop asking me if I'm okay, but other than that, I'm good.'

'Just concerned, that's all. You look a bit tired that's all?'

Murphy turned and gave Rossi a stare. 'Let's get upstairs yeah. If I need anything I'll ask. Okay?'

'Fine,' Rossi replied, getting out of the car. Murphy sat for a second or two, then followed her.

Fine. She'd said fine. Murphy knew what it meant when a woman said fine. Never anything good. He sighed, catching up to her quickly.

'Laura. Listen, you don't need to worry, okay. I'm in the right frame of mind for this. If I wasn't, I'd have Brannon instead of you working with me. Then we'd know I'd lost it.' He tried a smile.

Rossi returned it, looking reassured.

'Okay sir. We've got an hour before the press conference. I'm going to ring the university whilst you get ready, okay?'

Murphy agreed. Wondered if he had enough time to get changed before he made an appearance in front of the cameras. Silently prayed that nothing would go wrong.

'If anyone has any information, we urge them to speak. Tell someone what you know. It's our daughter today, but it may be yours tomorrow if you don't say anything.'

Murphy was impressed by the performance of Donna McMahon's parents in the face of the media. There was hope that their impassioned pleas would help with the investigation, but Murphy was pessimistic. They didn't have much to go on. She'd been missing days before she was found. He was also uncomfortable under the glare of the lights, wishing he was anywhere other than behind a long desk on a platform, staring down the lens of far too many cameras.

DCI Stephens spoke for a few minutes, before Murphy had to give them information on how the investigation was going.

'Coordinated searches were undertaken at the scene and the vicinity. We ask that anyone who may have seen a car or small van in the Aigburth Drive area of Sefton Park between the hours of two and five a.m. on Saturday morning, to please call the helpline.' Thank you the hoarder who witnessed a vehicle in the early hours of the morning. Thank you indeed Mr Reeves. That'll result in around four thousand calls, none of any use probably.

Murphy had been surprised when he stepped on the platform earlier. The news of Donna McMahon's death had gone national, with Sky News, BBC and ITV reporters dotted about. A few broadsheet journalists and the usual tabloid crew. Her background played no small part in bringing it to the fore. Middle-class, good upbringing, well spoken and well presented. Murphy wondered if the other victim would be similarly scrutinised, but doubted it. A mature student, with kids at home. He could already see the *Daily Mail* headline being written.

'Detective Inspector, do we have a serial killer in the city?'

'Should students be worried in particular?'

'Have you arrested anyone yet?'

'Will you be interviewing all the lecturers at the university?'

Murphy patted away the questions, long answers which essentially made the same point over and over as a subtext. *We don't know yet.*

He spotted a reporter he knew from one of the local papers. A rotund man, with thick dark glasses. Murphy had had run-ins with him before. And from the look on his red sweaty face, he was about to have another.

'Detective Inspector Murphy. Russell Graves from the *Liverpool News*. Do you think you're the best man to be heading up this investigation?'

Murphy was about to answer when DCI Stephens interrupted.

'DI Murphy has the full confidence of this force to investigate this murder.'

The large reporter pushed his large round glasses back up his greasy nose. Murphy attempted to gain eye contact with him, but he was busy looking at the notes he was holding. He could feel the sweat breaking out on his own forehead.

'With what happened in his recent past, don't you think a high-profile case such as this should be dealt with by someone other than him?'

'My past has no bearing on this case.' Murphy said, affecting confidence. 'My focus is only on giving Mr and Mrs McMahon justice for their daughter's murder.'

'Come on Detective Murphy,' the journalist cut in. 'Are you trying to tell us you're the best person to be dealing with a potential serial killer in our city, someone who can't even keep his own family safe?'

Murphy shot up off his seat. 'Listen nobhead, I've worked more cases than you've got stories correct in your shitty newspaper. Now unless you've got something worth answering to ask, will you kindly shut the fuck up.' The noise level increased in the room as Murphy's outburst was digested. He shook his head, knowing he'd made a mistake. Above the din, Murphy heard Graves ask the same question over and over.

'How does the Phillips family feel about Detective Murphy taking this case?'

The question was aimed at DCI Stephens, but Murphy wanted to answer.

'The . . .'

Murphy felt DCI Stephens' hand on his arm, pulling him back down.

DCI Stephens quietened the room. 'Past cases have no bearing on the present. DI Murphy has my full confidence. That concludes this press conference. I'd like to remind everyone of the serious situation which has occurred in the city, and also the fact two parents need answers and help to receive them. Thank you.'

Murphy heaved a sigh of relief, glad it was over. He knew he was in for a bollocking from the DCI though.

He stood up, trying to lock eyes with the reporter who had riled him. Murphy spotted him sharing a laugh with someone sat close to him. The man turned to Murphy and the smile disappeared from his face, as he winked at him. Murphy shook his head in response.

Murphy winced as the door slammed behind him. Yep. She was pissed off. He stayed in the chair as DCI Stephens moved past him and took up her station behind her desk. He looked down, hoping she'd take pity if he looked sorry enough.

She slammed her bag on the desk. 'What the hell was that David?'

He looked up, before averting his eyes to the floor again. 'Sorry. He was winding me up.'

'I don't care if he was tap dancing on your lap, you never rise to the bait. You know that. Graves is a pompous prick, but what do you think is going to be on the front of that rag tomorrow? Thankfully, I've pulled some strings, and TV news are going to cut that bit out of the appeal. But know this, you lose your temper, and we all look like idiots. Don't let it happen again. The last thing we need is the parents of a murdered girl going to the press by themselves, complaining about how a hot-headed DI had screwed up the investigation into their daughter's death. So, enough, okay? No more.'

Murphy nodded. 'No problem.'

She sighed. 'We should have known the Phillips girl would have come up.'

Murphy rubbed his eyes. Was he supposed to carry that around with him, along with all the rest of his shitty baggage as well now? It was nothing. Just a small mistake.

'You're going to have to get used to it, you know.'

Murphy said nothing.

'It was an error of judgement, but it's exactly what that lot out there will use against you.'

Murphy sighed, picked a piece of fluff from his trousers. 'Anything else?'

'Where are we, what's the latest?'

Murphy looked up; bollocking over. 'We're investigating a link to the university.' He brought the DCI up to date with the morning's occurrences.

'Okay, good,' DCI Stephens replied. 'Get down there, exploit Rossi's connections if need be. Just find something that we can use. I don't want a serial working in this city.'

'Understood.' Murphy watched as she tucked an unruly strand of dark hair behind her ears and then busied herself with paperwork. He left the office.

Rossi was on the phone at her desk when Murphy returned. He strode over, ignoring the sniggers from the officers milling about near the DCI's office, who had overheard his reprimanding.

He waited until Rossi had finished the call.

'Who was that?' He asked as Rossi finished the call.

'It's perfect. We've already got a psychology link to the killings, and the university link of course. No point in asking the boss to pay for a consult from a psychologist at this point, as we'll only get a *no, budget restraints* and all that bollocks. So, I called someone I knew from the uni in the Sociology department. They put me through to the psychology department.'

'And?' Murphy was becoming agitated by Rossi's enthusiasm.

'And . . . sorry, he's called Richard Garner,' Rossi said re-checking her notebook. 'Professor Richard Garner. He's the head of the psychology department. He was very accommodating and eager to help. Just doing his civic duty he said. Can you believe that? He sounds really posh.'

'Get to the point Rossi. My coffee is getting cold.'

'Right. Sorry. He's going to help us try and make a bit more sense of what's going on here. A professional opinion I guess. He has office hours this afternoon. He's expecting us.'

'Well we best not disappoint the professor then,' Murphy said.

16

Tuesday 29th January 2013 – Day Three

The psychology department was on the other side of the campus they'd visited a couple of days previously. It was a different place. Newer buildings mixed with old architecture. The amount of pubs rivalling Matthew Street or Concert Square in town.

'I spent most of my time on this side. Sociology and Psychology both have their departments at this end,' Laura said, as Murphy half listened. 'And there's another library just down there.' Rossi pointed towards the end of yet another side street.

She began pointing out different buildings as they passed them. Old Victorian buildings surrounded a small grassy area, and were now used to house different scholarly departments, instead of old merchants and bankers. Rossi pointed out the second library, a large glass-fronted building which had more in common with a modern office building than the libraries Murphy was used to. Overall, the place screamed wealth. No expense spared. A redbrick university where any middle-class parent with a child not going to Oxbridge would be happy to send their offspring. No matter that five minutes down the road was dilapidated housing and an unemployment rate a royal family would be proud of – you couldn't see the differences well enough from campus, so that was good enough for them. Murphy knew of so many places like that in the city. The haves and have-nots sitting side by side.

'You know who used to live in these buildings Laura?' Murphy said, interrupting her.

'Millionaires?'

'Not just millionaires. Merchants. From the shipping companies which built the port up from Albert Dock. Cotton, sugar, and tobacco. This city was built on the back of the slave trade you know?'

Rossi looked surprised. 'So you do know some stuff then?'

'I know about the history of my city.' Murphy replied. 'Have you seen pictures of Liverpool before the sixteen hundreds? Nothing but a fishing harbour. We start taking a bunch of people in Africa and enslaving them to work on tobacco and sugar plantations in America and the West Indies, and all of sudden we're a major city. Shouldn't forget that.'

Rossi nodded in response. 'We covered all that in uni. This city is just rich with history. I remember my dad going through a period where he just devoured every book going on Liverpool. He'd sit us down on a Sunday and lecture us on it.'

Murphy laughed. 'They seem like good people. How long have they been over now?'

'Over forty years.' Rossi replied. 'They still go back to Italy every now and again, but they consider this home now.'

'And you're the baby of the family?'

Rossi hit him playfully on the shoulder. 'Don't remind me. Six older brothers.'

'Probably explains why you're single.'

'Yeah. Most blokes don't hang around long after meeting the family. Intimidating I imagine.'

'They're just looking out for you.'

'I know.'

Rossi led them up to a smaller building which she informed

148

Murphy was named after a prominent women's rights campaigner. She seemed to be revelling in the tour guide role, so Murphy left her to it, occasionally tuning back in to the words, all the while feeling he didn't belong here, his working-class roots shining through. He knew it was ridiculous, that there were probably many students there with the same background as him, but he couldn't shake it off.

A quick flash of their ID at reception, and they were whisked through to the psychology department proper by a lecturer on his way up there.

'Tom, Tom Davies', he'd introduced himself as, shaking each of their hands in turn. He was younger than Murphy, casually dressed in baggy jeans and a t-shirt which seemed to have a cartoon on the front. Murphy looked down at his Burton's suit. Overdressed, even for an academic setting.

Rooms lined the corridors, different names attached to doors, doctors and professors side by side, behind closed doors.

'How many bloody doctors and professors work here?' Murphy grumbled.

'Psychology is a popular subject.' Tom replied. 'Always a large intake every year. Also it's a research-led university, so there's always something going on.'

Murphy huffed, 'complain about our pensions, should come and take a look at what's being spent here.'

They came to a door at the end of the corridor. 'Here we are. Just give him a knock. Good luck.' Tom turned away with a quick smile, leaving Murphy trying to work out if he was wishing him luck with the case or the professor.

Murphy stood back as Rossi knocked on the door. A small voice answered in response, and Rossi opened the door.

It was a mess. Books everywhere, loose papers strewn about the place. Not very large either. Murphy had to squeeze himself past an open filing cabinet to enter the room. At the centre of it sat a man who was seventy if he was a day. Bent over slightly, wiry strands of grey hair protruding from his head. He was as thin as a rake, wiry features, pointed nose and dark sunken eyes. His jaw came to a sharp point underneath slim blood-red lips. A walking stick balanced against the desk in front of him as he turned in his chair to face them. It was the smell that got up Murphy's nose though, an old musty smell, mixed with nicotine. He almost gagged as the man shook his hand, Murphy aware of the bony fingers being lost in his grip. He shook lightly, afraid of crushing the professor's hand.

'Professor Garner?'

'Hello,' the professor said in a raspy voice, which explained the nicotine smell. 'That'll be me. Pleased to meet you both.' Murphy exchanged a bemused look with Rossi, who gave a slight shrug in response.

'Don't worry, I'm not as old as I look. Not about to fall apart if that's what you're worried about.'

An uncomfortable silence followed which Rossi ended swiftly. 'It's a bit cramped in here, is there somewhere else we can go?'

'Yes, of course. We shall go to the conference room down the hall, it will be empty at the moment,' Garner said, slowly getting to his feet. Murphy spied his fingernails as they gripped the edge of the chair. Dirty.

Garner led them down a corridor to a small conference room, which was thankfully large enough to put some space between them. Murphy sat on a chair that seemed to have been made for a slightly smaller person than him. Rossi had her notebook at the ready, and Garner plonked himself down behind a table, interlocking his long fingers. 'How can I help this afternoon?' Garner said.

Rossi took the lead, Murphy allowing her, with it being more of her comfort zone. She explained the two murders and the possible link to the university, stopping short of revealing the existence of the two letters from the killer. They'd agreed before the meeting not to disclose exact details, and just ask questions. The media weren't being informed, it was best if no one else was. Especially as it was likely they'd be searching for suspects from the department.

'So we just have a few questions about the university and perhaps some questions about certain psychology links we may have to the case.' Rossi continued. 'And we were told you'd be the best person to speak to.'

'Well, I have been at the university for a long time.' Garner said with a

laugh. 'And head of the psychology department for the last few years. Please, I would be more than happy to help in any small way.'

'Did you know either of the two victims?'

Garner paused, looking up as if the answer would reveal itself to him from the ceiling. 'I don't know the first girl, sorry, but I was aware of Stephanie Dunning. I lecture to over one hundred and fifty students at a time. But I remember the name. She was a mature student, and they tend to be more forthcoming than the younger ones.'

Rossi spoke next, 'Do you remember if she was particularly close to anyone?'

Garner grimaced, showing red gums and those yellow stained teeth once again, 'No, I'm afraid not. Unless I have them in my advisory group, I don't have much contact with them outside of lectures. You should ask Colin.'

'Who's he?' Rossi asked.

'Works in the library. Nice man. Helps out the students quite a bit. Knows where most of the books in that library are kept, plus most of the subjects they cover. He always suggests the best books to get the highest grades. Invaluable.'

Rossi looked to Murphy, who took the cue. He shifted in his chair, worried it was going to break at any time, as he

151

thought how to broach the subject in the letters. 'What can you tell us about MK Ultra?' Murphy said.

'The psychology experiments?'

Murphy nodded in reply.

'Ah, the CIA and their nefarious activities. Not much is known, but they did some pretty unethical experiments. They were interested in mind control above all, using different types of drug to see if they could be used in interrogation. All very top secret. Most of what they did at the time will never be known, as many of the files were destroyed when it came to light.'

'And the LSD part of it?' Murphy said.

'There was some sort of experiment involving brothels . . .'

'Operation Midnight Climax?' Rossi cut in.

'That's the one. Yes, sounds ominous does it not?' Garner said with a toothy grin. 'They gave LSD to unwitting participants to see their reactions. Filmed and studied. Not ethical at all in today's world. What they did to those poor men doesn't bear thinking about. One family waited years to find out what happened to their father. He killed himself, according to them. Flung himself from a tenth floor hotel window. The CIA of course denied all responsibility, but questions remain.'

'What about Unit 731 . . . Does that mean anything to you?' Rossi said, her notebook open.

'Hmm. That's a tricky one. Not much evidence exists regarding what occurred there. It was a set of camps during the second world war, not unlike the concentration camps Nazi Germany operated during the same period, only in China. A section of the Japanese army had control of a state there.' Garner said, waving his hands away. 'They've been accused of experimenting on humans, performing vivisection whilst they were still alive, testing the effects of grenades on live subjects, the effects of blood loss on bomb victims. They used germ warfare, infecting people with syphilis and gonorrhoea to see the effects.' He paused, and as Murphy was about to speak Garner smacked a hand on the table. 'Fleas. That's it. They had plague fleas, encased in the bombs they dropped in China. Killed hundreds of thousands when the area became diseased with cholera and anthrax.'

Rossi was writing everything down whilst Murphy tried to keep track. 'What about death? Psychologically speaking what does death mean to you and your profession?'

Garner held Murphy's gaze, cocked his head slightly. 'We all deal with death differently, detective. I subscribe to Freud's view on it personally.' Garner said.

'And what's that?' Murphy replied.

Garner was silent for a few seconds, still holding Murphy's eyes. 'Well, it's quite simple really . . . it is the aim of all life.'

17

He watched them leave, looking out from his office window as they walked away from the building. He was searching for the word to describe how he was feeling. The one word which could sum up the sensation coursing through his veins. How he felt after what he'd done in the last few days.

Exhilarated.

Every fibre of his body was tingling with electricity. The hairs on the back of his neck stood on end, his hands shook when he lifted them up in front of his face. He wondered if the adrenaline pumping around his body would ever dissipate.

He'd barely slept since he'd started. Yet he didn't feel tired at all.

He had never felt as alive as he did in that moment.

And the secret was death.

He was death, come to life. That was his purpose. That was what he had learned to become. He brought death to all he touched, in turn bringing a reason to his own existence.

He knew what his purpose was, the point of his being as successful as he had been. Successfully born into wealth, education, being.

And now death.

His body shivered with excitement. Of what would be next.

Of who would be next.

He looked out across the campus, shaking his head. Turned and added ice cubes to a glass, poured himself a drink. The cracking of the ice breaking the silence surrounding him. It probably wouldn't be good to be seen drinking on the job, but he felt like celebrating.

They'd been here. And he was still free.

He couldn't fail.

He lifted the glass tumbler to his lips, the ice had melted a little, taking the edge off the sharpness of the whisky. The smoothness remained, warming his throat as it travelled down.

That last girl. Pitiful. All that planning gone to waste.

The previous one, almost perfect. Watching her, high as a bird, seeing things he couldn't imagine. Ending her life when it became time.

Almost.

Unit 731. The Asian Auschwitz. Not as famous as its inauspicious kin, yet the information was there if you wanted it.

And he had.

Fascinating.

They could only estimate at the amount of people who had died there, anything between three thousand and two hundred thousand. Incredible numbers.

A labour camp for military research in China, during the Second World War. They performed tests to see the effects of grenades at various distances, but then went much further. Limbs were removed, pregnant victims had children ripped from their wombs without anaesthetic.

But it was the blood loss experiments which had fascinated him.

Intermitting bloodletting. That had been his plan for the bitch. Until she made him change his mind.

He'd come back to that one. One for the future perhaps. And what a future he had in store.

He'd been shown the light. And the dark.

He was grateful for both.

He turned over a fresh page of his writing pad. And began to write.

Experiment Five
Bystander Theory

How long can a dead body go unnoticed in a public place?
Not so much unnoticed, maybe ignored.
Make it apparent the person is dead?
Location important . . . Liverpool One, Liver Buildings, Albert Dock . . . somewhere big, accessible, lot of foot traffic.

He looked over what he had written. He knew the place. It was just a case of picking the person who would take part.

He had the perfect specimen.

18

Tuesday 29th January 2013 – Day Three

Murphy and Rossi walked back to the car. Garner had been unable to help them any further, but his words had played on Murphy's mind since the short meeting. Death seemed to be circling around him, constricting him.

'What now?

Rossi was asking the pertinent question . . . what should they do?

'We need to get a track on the two victims' last movements,' Murphy replied.

Murphy counted pubs they passed as they went back to the car. Four. Bloody students.

'And I want a list of everyone who works in the psychology department. We start interviews with them all tomorrow.'

Rossi nodded in reply. She looked as tired as Murphy felt. 'We should go to the library now. See if that librarian is working?'

'Good thinking,' Murphy replied, 'may as well whilst we're here.'

They trudged off towards the library, the effort of it beginning to grate on Murphy. He was tired, having had little sleep the night before, and the long day was catching up to him. 'What did you make of the professor?' Rossi said, pulling out into the main road.

'No idea. Struck me as a bit strange, but then, aren't all those type of people.'

'What about what he said about death? The Freud view of it?'

Murphy sighed deeply, unsure of how to respond. 'I always thought Freud was all about wanting to shag your mother and that kind of weird stuff. Didn't realise he had a sideline in sad sayings about death. I've no idea though. I don't know if that's a healthy outlook to have on life to be honest. If all you're doing is waiting around to die, when do you actually live?'

Rossi turned to look at Murphy. 'That's a bit deep for you sir.'

'Yeah, well . . . I'm like an onion Laura. I have hidden layers.' Murphy replied.

'I guess so.'

The library was at the end of the side street Rossi had pointed out before their visit with Professor Garner. It stood proudly, sprawling over a large area. Glass fronted, lit up in the late afternoon dusk.

Colin Woodland was sitting proudly behind the front desk, smiling as they approached, then quickly becoming serious when they announced who they were.

He took them into a room off the vast open space of the ground floor, explaining the books were kept on separate floors. Various computers were dotted about the space, used for looking up certain books.

There were a few students about, but Colin explained it would be quiet for the next week or so.

He didn't stop talking. Murphy was getting even more exhausted just by listening to him. On the walk to the staff room, he'd more or less given them the entire layout for the university, and the university schedule. Rossi looked to be revelling in it, interjecting with questions every now and again.

They sat down on comfortable chairs in a small kitchenette area. A low coffee table separated Murphy and Rossi from Colin Woodland. He was a small man, late forties, Murphy guessed. The wisps of hair which had been missed when he'd shaved that morning, stood out on his little round face. A faint mix of Lynx bodyspray and sweat oozed off him.

'Would you like a drink or something?' Colin said, starting to stand up again.

They both said no, eager to move on. They explained why they were there, receiving a shocked gasp when they told him the name of the second victim.

'We take it you knew her then?'

Colin took his hands away from his face. 'Yes. She was a mature student. Used to do quite a bit of studying in the evenings when it was quiet. Nice woman. Intelligent too.'

'Do you remember seeing her last Thursday evening?'

Colin thought on that, his tongue sliding forward a licking his bottom lip. 'I think so. I was working that night.'

'Did you see anyone hanging around, anything suspicious?'

'No. I'd have called security if so. We have CCTV covering the entrance. I'll get you the tapes. Such a shame. And so soon after the other girl. What is going on?'

'We're looking into a number of possibilities Mr Woodland.' Rossi answered.

'Wait. There was something. A couple of nights before that Thursday. Stephanie was here studying, but she seemed distracted. She came down to the entrance a few times, looked out, but then went straight back up. Like she was waiting for someone.'

Rossi wrote the information down. 'Thanks. That could come in handy.'

'Such nice girls here. So fresh faced and pure. Cherries waiting to be picked.' He looked past their shoulders, god knows what images going through his mind.

Murphy looked towards Rossi, knowing the look he was going to get. He started talking before she had a chance to say anything. 'Well, that's . . . erm . . . an interesting way of putting it.' He stood, 'we'll leave you to it.'

Rossi started to say something, but Murphy shot her a look.

It was almost six p.m. when they made it back to the car. The day was turning to darkness. February was just around the corner; spring would be upon them before they knew it.

'I don't like him.' Rossi said, getting into the car and pulling the seat forward.

'Really?' Murphy said, sarcasm dripping from his tone.

'Yeah. Very creepy. The way he started talking about the students.'

Murphy went over the end of the conversation. What he'd listened to anyway. He'd tuned out most of the rest once they'd moved on. Probably a mistake, but he was glad Rossi was paying attention. 'We'll be having a meeting when we get back. We'll bring his name up, see if anyone can come up with anything on him.'

'If you don't mind me saying sir, you look a little tired. Maybe you should . . .'

'I'm fine.' Murphy snapped. 'Stop babying me Laura. I'm your superior remember. Keep going, and fat bastard will be walking next to me quicker than you can say fuck all.'

'Of course.' Rossi replied. An uncomfortable silence followed, which Rossi once again cut off. 'So, we go back the station then?'

'No. Let's get something to eat first. My treat.'

Rossi smiled, Murphy's snap at her forgotten, or so he hoped.

DCI Stephens held court in the meeting room, sitting at the only desk in there. Keeping an eye on Murphy, probably. She was looking more anxious by the hour, biting her manicured fingernails every now and again. Probably regretting her decision as this case grew into more of a mess, Murphy thought.

He was standing off to her side, bringing everyone up to date on what was happening on both murder cases. He listened as the other officers detailed their own work that day, the house-to-house enquiries coming to nothing. Various interviews with family members, possible witness sightings.

All nothing.

Next, the preliminary results of the phone calls which had been coming in since the TV appeal earlier that day. He delegated a few of the more interesting leads to the DCs who were coming on shift. Every now and again he'd pause, take a deep breath before carrying on. The pressure was increasing; he could feel it in every sideways look from his DCI, every whispered conversation between the other detectives.

He wrapped up the meeting within half an hour, sending home the team who had been working all day. Stephens then told him to do the same.

Murphy thanked his lucky stars and got the hell out of there.

Rossi remembered about the girlfriend five minutes after Murphy had left. Flatmate of the first victim, her boyfriend had argued with Donna McMahon but the girlfriend had given him an alibi.

Rossi didn't think that would stick. Something wasn't right and she had to make sure they weren't screwing up.

161

She scribbled down the mobile number they'd been given by Rebecca and tried calling it on her way out of the station. Switched off. She could swing by the flat on the way home. The packet of instant noodles could wait another half an hour or so.

Rossi thought about ringing Murphy and letting him know what she was doing, but decided against it. He needed the time away, even if it was just a few hours. She was fresher than he was. He could do with her showing a bit more ambition, relieving the pressure a little.

She drove the short distance through the city centre and arrived at the students' flat within minutes of leaving the station. She parked up on a quiet side street and tried to call Rebecca again. No answer.

Rossi reached the flat and pressed the buzzer for entry. Waited for thirty seconds and then tried again. She took a step back, peering upwards to see if she could work out which flat was Rebecca's. Most of the windows were in darkness. She tried the buzzer, pulling her phone out as she did so, waited another couple of minutes, and turned to leave.

The door opened behind her. A young girl, looking impossibly fresh faced and small in the large doorway appeared. Rossi took out her ID and introduced herself.

That was how she found herself on Matthew Street, music pounding in her ears, as she searched three different clubs for Rebecca. In for a penny, in for a pound as they say. Although it'd cost her six quid to get in the current one. The nightclub was on three levels, different types of music on each, although in Rossi's sober state, they all blended into one thumping bassline.

She found Rebecca on the second floor, ensconced in a corner booth, talking in another girl's ear. Rossi waited to be noticed, and Rebecca didn't disappoint. The look of surprise, which was then followed quickly by nervousness, set Rossi on alert.

She had to shout above the din. 'We need to talk,' she said and pointed to the stairway which led out of the main dance-floor. Rebecca gave a quick glance to the girl she was sitting with, but Rossi was already turning.

Once out in the relatively quieter area, Rossi made sure Rebecca positioned herself against the wall. 'Just wanted a quick chat,' Laura told her, getting in close so she could hear every word.

'Now . . . here?'

'No time like the present.'

'What's going on?'

Rossi moved slightly so someone could get past her. 'It's about your boyfriend. I want to know where he was that night.'

Rebecca's eyes shifted away. 'What night?'

Rossi gave her the best 'don't mess with me' look she could come up with. Wasn't sure if it came out right, but it seemed to have some effect.

'He was with me.'

'I think you're lying. This is serious Rebecca. If you're found to be covering for him, you're going to be in trouble as well you know.'

'I know . . .'

'So tell me.'

Rebecca sighed, still not meeting Rossi's eyes. 'I don't know.'

'You don't know what?'

Finally, she faced her. 'I don't know where he was. But he wouldn't hurt Donna. I know he wouldn't.'

'I should arrest you right now. You should have told us straight away.'

'I know, I know, but he told me you'd all think he did it.

163

I swear he didn't though. I didn't see him that night, but he left his mates in town around eleven. He was going home, he was really tired and he had some work to do for the next day. He was texting me the whole time, I promise. He's not like that at all.'

Rossi's phone vibrated in her pocket. She took it out, checking the display. Murphy. 'I've got to take this, stay right there.'

'I've got to go, you can't make me stay.'

Shit. 'Listen, I'm going to take a full statement from you tomorrow. Be at your flat at eleven. Okay?'

Rebecca nodded, and slipped away as Rossi answered the phone.

19

Tuesday 29th January 2013 – Day Three

Murphy didn't go back there very often, but sitting in his car outside the house sometimes set his mind at ease. Knowing she was there, just out of reach, gave him a strange sense of comfort. He looked at his watch, seeing it was almost midnight. A solitary light shining from behind the drawn curtains in the living room suggested someone was still awake.

The house which was once so familiar to him now seemed alien. Murphy looked from the side window towards the face of the house, trying to decide what to do. He wanted to walk up the path, open the front door as if nothing had ever happened. Murphy sighed to himself and shook his head.

He wanted to know what happened. How it had come to this point.

He asked aloud, the ticking down of the car as it cooled the only response.

He knew what had happened, the man's face appearing easily to him as it always did. It was burned on his memory like a brand on cattle, and just as painful. He closed his eyes, trying to shake it free, knowing it wouldn't go easily. The night stretched out in front of him, weariness bearing down on him.

She was only yards away. Murphy imagined getting out of the car, walking up the short path, the door opening and that warm welcome he'd receive. Or the slap in his face, maybe. Whichever it was, he wanted to feel it.

He wanted to feel anything other than the pain which had shadowed him for the past year.

Murphy looked back at the house once more, happier memories replacing the horror of *that* face which had preceded it. He didn't know which he preferred. Sadness or anger.

He turned the car back on, deciding to leave and not go any further.

He didn't see the curtain twitch in the house. Sarah, his wife, looking out of the window at him as he drove away.

Murphy arrived home, his stomach growling from hunger. It was late, the drive out of Liverpool done in complete darkness. He sat in his car for a few moments, his street quiet, a few houses with lights on. Not even ten p.m. and people were already going to bed.

He really was a long way from home. Almost middle class now. Over the water, as they say, referring to the Wirral. Separated from Liverpool by the River Mersey. Scousers were nothing if not imaginative.

He entered his house, hanging his keys on the board of hooks on the wall. A housewarming gift from Jess. He checked his phone for any messages from her. Nothing. Which probably meant she was going to turn up any second.

He felt uneasy. Had been for a few hours. It took a while before he realised what it was.

Guilt. For the way he'd spoken to Rossi earlier. Tiredness had affected the way he reacted to her concern and he'd overreacted. He needed her on his side. Especially now. He pulled out his phone and scrolled through his contacts.

'Laura?' There was loud music in the background, dance,

from the sound of the bass over the phone speaker. Murphy held the phone a little way from his ear. 'Can you hear me?'

'Hang on a sec sir.'

Murphy waited as Rossi moved away from the noise.

'Can you hear me now?'

'Yeah,' Murphy replied. 'Is it a bad time?'

'No. Not at all. What's happened?'

Murphy stroked his beard with his free hand, moving through to his living room. 'Nothing. I just wanted to say sorry about today. I shouldn't have snapped like that. You're doing a good job.'

'Oh. Thanks.'

'Listen, we need to start going through the list of people at the university tomorrow morning. So we should concentrate there,' Murphy continued.

Murphy could hear loud voices over the phone. 'Definitely sir.'

'Where are you Laura?'

'Nowhere. Listen, I've got to go. Speak to you later.'

Murphy stared at his phone, the call ending before he had chance to say anything more.

Strange.

He shook it off. He needed to eat, but couldn't be bothered to even go through the freezer. He grabbed a takeaway menu from kitchen and rang through. Sat in front of the TV as the minutes passed by.

His mind wouldn't shut off, a constant array of images mixing into each other. Possibilities, questions.

His thoughts were interrupted by the door bell.

'Hello Bear.'

'Oh, Jess. Wasn't expecting you.' Jess bounced on her heels, her bright auburn hair hanging loose on her shoulders.

'Thought you could do with some company. Plus you've got Sky and I haven't.'

She got on her tiptoes and threw her right arm around Murphy in a quick hug. Murphy let Jess past him, following in her path as she shed her hat, scarf, gloves and coat seemingly at once. She put her hands on the radiator in the living room, as Murphy hung up her coat and accessories properly. 'You know, you could at least attempt to be tidy,' Murphy said.

'Fuck off. It's freezing out there. Not that you'd notice with all that fat behind you. Can you at least turn the heating up a bit?'

Murphy sighed. 'It's not fat, I'm just naturally big,' and went to turn up the thermostat, trying to remember a time when Jess had called ahead before a visit, failing to recall one. He looked through to the living room, where she'd already made herself comfortable, kicking off her high heels and stretching out on the couch, her feet tucked underneath her. 'Where's your Peter?' he said, raising his voice so she could hear him from the kitchen.

'Staying at a mate's or something. I tell you, that kid is getting worse by the day.'

'That's teenagers for you. Remember what we were like?'

'God, I hope he's not that bad.'

No one understood their relationship. She was attractive in her own unique way. Her natural confidence shone. Bright auburn shoulder-length hair, which only Murphy knew came from a bottle. Just the right amount of curves, dark smooth skin.

And he'd never in almost twenty years of knowing her, wanted anything more than what they had. He knew she felt the same way.

She'd been a single parent for almost all of her son's life. Never really getting involved with anyone else. She'd told Murphy she just wasn't interested in making things more complicated, but he wasn't so sure it was just about that. Fear probably played as much a part of it as anything else.

'There you moaning bint,' Murphy said, walking back into the living room. 'What brings you anyway? I'd just ordered pizza.'

'Meat feast?'

'Yeah.'

'Good, I'm starving.'

The pizza arrived and Murphy was forcing a second slice down himself, his appetite not as strong as he'd thought.

'I've got this case this week, you won't believe it,' Jess said, taking the pepperoni from the box where Murphy had taken it off his slice. 'Some lad tried to rob a bookies. Went with a balaclava over his head, and pretended to have something under his jacket.'

'Go on,' Murphy said, taking a bite. Savouring it, trying to jump start his hunger.

'Well, as it happens, his mum worked at a bookies.'

'No way . . .'

Jess started laughing, 'yeah. He only tried to rob the same shop she works in. He gets to the counter, demands money, and she just goes "Our Mark, what are ya doin'". He just says "sorry Mum", and runs out. Ton of witnesses, and he pleads not guilty. And I get to defend him. Sometimes I wonder why I do this job.'

Jess had gone to university late, studied hard and become a lawyer at age thirty. Murphy had been at her graduation, proud as punch of his friend. They were two success stories from an estate which didn't have all that many.

'So why'd you come around?' he said between mouthfuls.

'Worried about you again.'

'I'm okay. Doing better.'

'How long have we known each other? Since we were sixteen, both hanging around Speke parade, getting pissed on cheap cider. I know you. You're not okay. You look

169

knackered. I bet you haven't been sleeping. Ever since the first murder.'

'Just getting back into the swing of things, that's all. It's been a while since the last one.'

'Since last year?'

Murphy stood up and went through to the kitchen, giving a quiet confirmatory nod to Jess on the way past. He pulled a glass from the cupboard and ran himself a glass of water.

'I heard about what happened today. With the press.'

Murphy grunted. 'Parasites.'

'The Phillips girl was mentioned I heard.'

'Yeah. I should probably get used to that.'

Jess pulled out her phone, checked it, then placed it on the arm of her chair. 'What happened there?'

'I already told you.'

'Not properly.' Jess had followed him into kitchen, sauce from the pizza smudging her chin. 'She was killed by her stalker wasn't she? What could you have done?'

Murphy drank half of the glass of the water in one go. 'I screwed up. I should have taken it all more seriously when she came down to the station.'

'You saw her?'

'Yeah. She turned up one day in bits. Crying like you wouldn't believe. I just happened to be there in reception. Told her I'd help. I didn't.'

Jess tapped a finger against her bottom lip. 'This was when, like, a few weeks after the funeral?'

'About that?'

'And she had a case ongoing anyway?'

'Of course.'

'Then I don't understand how you can blame yourself for that. How did that paper get your name involved anyway?'

Murphy shrugged. 'How they get anything these days. They ask the families, look for juicy angles to sell their papers.

170

I just happened to have been in the news only a few weeks before, so that was their connection.'

'You ever speak to anyone about things other than me?'

'Don't need to,' Murphy said, sliding past her to go back in the living room.

'Yes you do. Bear, you don't just get over something like what happened to you. You need help.'

'I'm fine.' Murphy picked up his half-eaten slice of pizza, taking a bite.

'Have you spoken to Sarah at all?' Jess said, moving back to the couch.

Murphy looked up at the only picture in the living room. The four of them, together. Smiling.

'No.' He replied. 'No plan to either.'

Jess shook her head. 'You're going to have to at some point. She deserves better than this.'

'Does she? You think?'

'It wasn't her fault.' Jess replied, swinging her legs out from underneath her. 'She didn't know.'

'Are you kidding me? You know her past. Tell me, is she using again?'

Jess stood up. 'You think I'd be pushing you into talking to her if she was?'

Murphy turned away from her stare. 'I don't know what to think. Why are you so close to her all of sudden?'

'Because she lost as well. And there's no one else helping her.'

Murphy sighed. 'I'll talk to her. I just need time, okay.'

Jess nodded. 'Good. Now about this case . . .'

'I'm fine.' Murphy interrupted.

'No, you're fucking not.' Jess said, her voice bouncing back off the walls. 'You're working a murder case, and your head's not right. It hasn't been right for over a year, which is understandable, considering.' Jess was still standing, her right hand on her hip, giving him the cold stare he'd become familiar with over the years.

Murphy swallowed the food, reached for the glass of water. 'I don't want to talk to some stranger about what happened.'

'You didn't talk to me about it.'

'What am I supposed to say, Jess?' Murphy said, his voice raising. 'My parents died, they were . . . they died, okay.'

'That's just it Bear. They didn't just die in their sleep. They were killed, murdered. And you found . . .'

Murphy stood up. 'Don't, I don't want to fucking talk about it. Understand?'

'You're going to have to, otherwise it'll eat you alive. I know you. You can't just shove this down inside yourself. It has to come out.'

'Not now.'

'Fine.' Jess replied, her hands slapping against her sides in frustration. 'If you don't want any help, I won't waste my time. Just remember, I was here after it happened, I've always been here. You shutting me out won't change that.' She left the room, appearing a minute later with her coat on.

'You don't have to go Jess,' Murphy said, moving towards her.

She shrunk back, turning her back to him. 'Yeah, yeah I do. Before I have to slap some sense into you. You know where I am.'

She left Murphy alone standing in his living room.

In the house paid for with his parents' blood. Lost in his own thoughts as he dropped onto the couch and stared at the wall, past the television.

Gone.

20

Sunday May 29th 2012
Eight Months Earlier

His hand pushed open the living room door, as if unconnected to his body. Everything about the situation called for him to stop. He knew what would lie behind it, yet he couldn't help himself.

All was red.

He took one step into the room. Across the wall were words but he didn't read them at that moment. Instead, his vision focused on what took up the main area of living room floor, where the coffee table was supposed to be.

His mum had prided herself on her home, spending hours making sure it looked just right, just so. Now it was disorder, chaos; the TV in the corner upended, the sofa cushions thrown to the side. The coffee table had one leg broken off, tipped over and in the opposite corner. Mum's ornaments from the mantelpiece lying smashed and broken on the fireplace.

He saw his dad first, his face a mask of blood, lying on his back, one arm off to the side, the other across his chest. His dad's white shirt was saturated, turning an odd muddy red colour. He could see holes where something had gone through the shirt, ripping into his stomach and chest.

He became aware of himself, of what he was seeing. His dad, who had made him sit and listen to old songs on an ancient record player, who would call him every few days to see how he was. Who would sit and watch old Marx Brothers movies with him for hours when he was younger. That man was gone and all he could do was stand there, frozen in shock, staring at the lifeless form of his father.

His mum was further into the room, near the French windows they'd installed to cut off the dining room. She was in a sitting position, her arms hanging to the sides, her head lolling forward. One shoe had fallen off her foot and was lying in a pool of blood near her legs. Strands of greying hair had fallen across her face, obscuring it from view. For a fleeting second he thought maybe it wasn't her, wasn't his mother. Yet he knew the truth.

He couldn't move, couldn't breathe. He became aware of his hands shaking uncontrollably. The sound of sirens approaching came through the windows. He turned his gaze to the wall opposite the fireplace above the sofa. Three words had been daubed onto the wall in his parents' blood. He could trace the trail from the bodies of his parents to the wall, across the carpet and the sofa, onto the wall itself. Three words.

She was mine.

Experiment Two

The soundtrack to her living nightmare had changed. In between her fitful attempts at sleep, the overbearing silences had been replaced.

All she could hear was screaming.

Ear splitting, bloodcurdling screams.

At first she thought it was her. Took a few seconds to realise her mouth was closed.

She could make out the words being shouted, but only just. It reinforced how thick the door was that separated her from the outside.

He'd brought someone else down there. She was sure of it. Maybe a replacement for her? She wasn't giving him what he wanted, perhaps?

She didn't know how long it had been now. Lost count of the times she had fallen asleep. Not that she wanted to sleep all that much any more. If they weren't dreams of the outside, normal life stuff, they were filled with darkness. It was a toss-up for which was worse.

She'd tried to talk to whoever was down there with her, but hadn't got a response. She'd given up quickly, not wanting to waste her energy.

Let someone else rot down here, she thought. She weighed it up, checked herself for any feelings of guilt. Not even close. She just wanted out. And if it meant someone taking her place, then so be it.

It didn't matter anyhow. It was almost time. She'd run through things in her mind over and over, until she had her whole plan in focus. She closed her eyes, picturing every instant of what she planned. Slowed it down in her head, so each moment played out in it's own singular frame. No room for error.

She became conscious of her hands rubbing together, her pulse beating in her fingers. Her heart banging against her chest. All nervous energy, coursing through her as she realised what she was about to attempt. If she made a mistake, she was dead. There was no doubt in her mind. Until then, she'd been the pliant captive. Locked away in her hole, eating and drinking like a good little prisoner. Now, she was going to change all that. She couldn't stand it any longer. Now was the time.

Footsteps. The clicking of a heel coming down into the basement. Each footfall punctuated by the screaming somehow increasing in volume. She moved towards the door, placed her ear against it.

The footsteps stopped just outside, a noise she couldn't place just away from her.

The screaming stopped. Cut off mid squeal. Silence returned, and she enjoyed the bliss for a few seconds.

She forced herself away from the door. Breathed in deeply, holding it for a few seconds, then releasing it.

She turned to face the door. Clenched her fists to stop them shaking. Then waited.

He approached the door, the room behind it holding his experiment. Allowed himself a smile. His experiment. He still felt a frisson of excitement at what he'd created. The key was patience. He was here for the long haul. He could never allow himself to forget that. He was still learning; always learning. Take the food to her, hope she eats it. Make sure everything was still in place so she couldn't escape from this place. Lower the hatch, allowing only a sliver of light to enter. Never engage her in conversation, or he'd have to start all over again.

From watching the monitor the effects of being isolated in the room had already began to tell on her. She talked to herself. Quite often. She slept more, fitful, disturbed and broken, but sleeping nonetheless.

Five days she'd been down there. A working week. No time at all.

He'd watched her as often as he could, waiting for a sliver of guilt to kick in, for what he was putting her through.

It still hadn't.

The experience would live with her forever, of that he had no doubt. It was the effect of that experience he was most interested in.

Would she always be afraid of the dark?

Would he ever let her go to find out?

He didn't know the entirety of the plan.

The importance of what he was doing. He had to concentrate on that.

He stopped as he reached the door. Took the key out of his pocket, and turned the lock on the hatch. The hatch would lower from the outside, big enough for him to observe her if needed; wide and tall enough for his head and shoulders to be in profile. He'd made the door himself, fashioning it from an old, heavy piece into something much different. He'd spent hours down in the basement before her arrival, making sure it was ready for its purpose.

He removed the key from the lock on the hatch front, pocketed it and lowered it. The atmosphere changed as the darkness from inside the room seeped out, bringing the smell of desperation and fear with it. He shuddered a little in spite of himself, imagining being inside there, alone, with nothing but his own mind to keep him sane.

He picked up the food parcel and bottle of water he'd left at his feet, breathed in and put his hand into the opening, preparing to drop the food.

Out of the darkness, a hand shot out and gripped his wrist. He squealed as fingernails dug into his wrist, his thumb pushed back as he tried to shake it free.

Pain shot through his arm as the sharp needles of long, uncut nails entered his flesh, drawing blood.

Within seconds, it had come from the darkness. Refusing to let go of him.

He knew the hatch had been too big.

The footsteps stopped outside the door. She tried to focus her eyes, but she was working on instinct alone, her sense of sight gone. She was just waiting for the sound.

Breathe in, breathe out. Breathe in, breathe out.

Five and a half seconds.

She watched as the hatch opened. She waited for the right moment, and then something she hadn't anticipated happened. Up close, there was more light. She could see a little. An arm holding something came into view.

She didn't think twice. She grabbed on and forced her way through.

'No. No.'

This wasn't supposed to happen. She'd slithered out of the hole like a snake, holding onto his arm as he jumped backwards.

She sprang up, arms outstretched, attempting to claw at him. He stepped back, driving a hand into her face.

178

'Stop,' he said as she fell backwards. 'This isn't going to help.'

'Fuck you,' she screamed, wiping a hand across her face. She went for him again.

He grabbed her arms as she reached him, pulling them back as he twisted her around. Shoved her down, her knees hitting the floor hard, taking the wind out of her. She gasped, trying to get her breath back, but he didn't let up, twisting her around again and forcing her down.

'Stop,' he said through gritted teeth. 'Stop this. You're going to come with me now, you're not supposed to do this. You're mine.'

She spat in his face, laughing as he recoiled in disgust. Disgusting. He could feel her saliva dripping down his face.

He snarled at her, wiping her excretion from his face with the back of his sleeve. 'You bitch. I'm going to kill you, you hear me? I'm going to kill you.'

He went for her again, but she was ready. As he came forward, about to land on her again, she breathed deeply then drove a knee into his midsection, catching him squarely in his most delicate of areas. Her scream of effort echoed around the basement.

He cried out, falling backwards, his head hitting the wall next to the open doorway to the room she'd been kept in.

His eyes began to droop, his vision darkening.

The last thing he saw before unconsciousness took him, was experiment two heading for the steps away from him.

'Help . . .'

She didn't pause. She got to her feet without pausing for breath, knees almost buckling, and bounded towards the steps, not caring where they led. She reached the top, not looking back to see if he was following her.

Not thinking about the fact that although she hadn't seen

his face, something about the man down there had been familiar.

She reached the door, turning the handle, suddenly sure it wouldn't be locked. The door opened and she fell over the threshold, the sudden change in light burning into her eyes.

She stood, slowly. She had to find her way out, escape.

She heard it coming from down below. What had been invading her room for the previous few hours.

Crying, pleas for help. They'd become louder. More pleading. She was stuck on the threshold of the doorway. The basement behind her, the house she'd been dragged through days earlier. Or was it weeks? She didn't know.

She couldn't move. She was frozen on the spot. Her breathing becoming shallow and quick, as the adrenaline began to fade.

She couldn't just leave her down there. By the time she got help, he could be long gone with her, or worse . . . killed her already.

She had to go back.

21

Wednesday 30th January 2013 – Day Four

Stuck in traffic at the tunnel entrance, Murphy listened as the early morning headlines on Radio City talked of nothing else but the two students found dead in the past few days. It was becoming big news, helped in no small way by the front page of the *Liverpool News* which was sitting on the passenger seat.

The stupid little shit Graves had run a story about him. About his outburst at the press conference the previous day. It might have been kept off the TV coverage, but Stephens hadn't been able to keep it from the front page of the rag.

Murphy didn't know who he was angrier with. The scumbag who was concentrating on his ability to head up a murder investigation, or himself for losing it so quickly.

That was a lie. He knew who he hated more.

He knew the *Liverpool Echo* wouldn't be running the same story. Bit more dignity over there. Same with the *Post*. He just hoped the rumours were true, that the *Liverpool News* had only months left in existence. Good riddance to shitty crap.

The cars ahead moved a few inches forward. He followed

suit in an automatic state, his hands and feet working on impulse. His mind working, independently.

Going through a mental checklist. Of what they'd done so far, trying to spot a mistake, something missed. Events were moving quickly, and they had little help. With Rossi and himself driving the investigation, the pressure was on.

A front page of the local rag, proclaiming him to be 'unstable', probably wasn't going to go down well with DCI Stephens in that case. Murphy felt guilty, as he knew she'd be backing him up to the Super.

Thirty minutes later, he finally made it to the station and was met at the door by Rossi.

'I went to see Rebecca last night,' she said. 'The girlfriend of Will Ryder. Admitted to the alibi being a lie.'

'Seriously? You didn't think that was a major development? You should have let me know instantly.'

'You still think he had something to do with this?'

Murphy thought on it for a few seconds. Weighed up the possibilities and made a decision. 'I think it deserves looking into more. I'll have a word with Brannon.'

Rossi rolled her eyes at him. 'What are we doing today then?'

Murphy went with point one on the to-do list. 'DC Harris has put together a list of all the employees at the university. We're working on students next. Everyone with a record of violence gets spoken to first. Then, anyone with just a record. Then, anyone who has had any contact with police, any complaints made against them, that sort of thing.'

'How many have we got helping?'

Murphy drained the last of his coffee. An internal shudder as the last caffeine hit his system. 'Just about to find out now. Meeting the boss in five minutes.'

* * *

The university had over four thousand employees, something Murphy thought was excessive, until he was told there were twenty-five thousand students attending.

'This is going to take us all day. All week in fact.' Murphy said, drinking his third cup of coffee of the day.

Rossi stretched in response.

Murphy had sent DS Brannon out to find out more about Will Ryder, which seemed to please the little prick no end. Probably thought he was being primed for a better position.

He needed to concentrate. He was inputting names into the system, seeing if they had a record, and splitting them into piles. He could have delegated out the menial task, but he wanted to keep himself occupied. Standing around, waiting for something to happen, was only going to lead to him becoming lost in his own head.

So far, they hadn't found anyone with a criminal record of any kind. He guessed the university had a policy of some sort, but didn't want to leave any stone unturned.

His phone rang on his desk. He put down the cup.

'Murphy.'

'Houghton here. Just got back results on your first victim.'

Murphy sat forward, grabbing a pen from the stack .

'Go on.'

'Positive for lysergic acid diethylamide. LSD. Not a lethal amount, but enough.'

'Right. So the letter was truthful in that sense.'

'Yeah. I suppose so. He lied about the method of death though. He said she'd died from the LSD, but asphyxiation was the cause of death.'

Murphy chewed on the end of his pen. 'True.'

'Listen, I've got to go. Just thought I'd let you know.'

'Cheers.'

Murphy replaced the handset. 'First victim had LSD in her system,' he said to Laura over the desk.

'Well, that kind of settles it then. The letters are real.'

Murphy sighed, ran fingers through his beard. 'Shit.'

'Indeed.'

Another hour passed. Murphy had been mulling over one name for a few minutes. Trying to place where he'd heard it before. Robert Barker. Worked in admin in the psychology department.

It rang a bell. The man only had a passing reference on the system. An ex-girlfriend had made an allegation but quickly retracted it.

But there was something about the name. He couldn't quite place it. It was gone. Too many names and faces over the years.

One of the DCs who had been procured for the trawl through the records came over, breathless with tangible excitement.

'Colin Woodland. History of complaints. Was given a conditional discharge for lewd behaviour. Only one that went to court.'

Rossi found the record and read off the screen. 'Ten years ago. He was accused of cornering a twenty year old in a nightclub and trying to kiss her. She resisted and he grabbed her arms, pushed her against a wall and proceeded to fondle her.' She sniggered, 'kneed him in the genital area and he went down. Bouncer saw it all and ejected him. Seems like she took it as far as she could. His defence was that he misconstrued the signals.'

'How long has he worked at the university?'

Rossi reached over for the file which contained the list, flicked through to the end where Woodland was listed. 'Six years.'

'Wouldn't have shown up then. A year had passed.'

'So Mr Woodland has a history of trying to force himself on women, manages to get himself a job where he's in contact

184

with young women on a daily basis. CRB checks are outstanding aren't they?'

'Both of the victims showed no signs of sexual assault though.'

'Hmm,' Murphy replied, tapping his pen against his chin. 'He did hold onto them for a few days though.'

'I'll call the university. See if he's in work today.'

Murphy went back to the computer, looking to see what else they had on file for Colin Woodland.

A few minutes later, Rossi finished her call. 'He was supposed to be in work at ten this morning. Hasn't shown up.' She looked at her watch, 'over an hour late.'

'Spooked by our meeting yesterday, you think? Let's go pay him a visit then.'

Colin Woodland's house was a small two-up, two-down, in a cul de sac near Stanley Park. Murphy rapped on the single-paned blue door, the crooked brass numbers on the front rattling as he knocked.

No answer.

Rossi was in the entry which ran behind the houses on the street. Murphy waited a few minutes, and tried knocking a few more times, almost putting his fist through the flimsy excuse for a door. Still nothing. He moved over to the front window, standing in long uncut grass, cupping his hands to get a look into the living room. The blinds were open slightly, revealing a seemingly normal room, no TV left on, things spilled as if he was in a hurry to leave. A coffee table in the middle, four remotes laid out on it.

Normal.

After five minutes, Rossi returned. 'Not here then.'

'Doesn't look like it.'

'Why would he go now, he was telling us how much he loved his job twenty-four hours ago. It's not right.'

'Can't argue with you.'

Murphy weighed up his options. 'Okay, we need a list of known relatives. See if we can found out where he might have gone.'

'Should we stick around, see if he turns up?'

Murphy checked his watch. Almost one in the afternoon. 'I'll stay here for now. Check with the neighbours. There's a butty shop round the corner. I'll have tuna mayo.'

Rossi rolled her eyes and began walking off.

Murphy looked back at the house. It looked sad, desolate. The drab net curtains at the upper two windows. The rotting windows.

He was giving houses characters now. He shook his head and started knocking on doors.

Experiment Five

It all happened so fast.

Colin Woodland was just walking home from work. Late shift at the library again.

Home. Empty house, empty bed. Empty life.

Work wasn't too bad though. Pretty girls on the first step into adulthood. Some carefree, some stressed out. Youthful and wide-eyed.

Sometimes they even talked to him. Asked for help. He enjoyed that part.

He thought about the detectives who had visited him that day. That was worrying. He worked hard, helped the girls when they needed him, sometimes when they didn't realise they needed him. He didn't want that taken away from him.

The campus was quiet, a few students dotted around the place. He plastered a smile on his face in case he bumped into anyone he knew. Keep up appearances.

As he turned onto a side street he began to speed up a bit. He didn't like this road, its lack of streetlights making him feel claustrophobic.

Maybe he should go into town, see if anyone he'd been

helping recently was out in the clubs or bars. Try to steal a kiss or two. They always liked that. Confidence.

He stepped past a short alleyway, pulling his coat up tighter as a sharp wind bit at his bare neck.

Movement came from his left, a sudden change in the atmosphere surrounding him. He found himself on one knee, a ringing in his ears. He looked around, confused. The world span, the buildings around him folded in on themselves.

He was more aware of the second hit. Coming from a figure standing directly in front of him. Then, an arm curled around his neck.

It all happened so fast.

He waited for his wallet to be taken from his back pocket. His bag to be lifted off his shoulder. Thoughts crashing against each other as he struggled to stay lucid.

It was a mugging, of course it was.

His vision grew dark, as it became harder and harder to breathe.

He came around in stages. Blinking away the headache which was pounding in his head.

He couldn't move. Something was binding his body to a hard surface. He felt as if he was floating in mid-air.

He tried to call out, but his mouth wouldn't open.

He remembered the feeling of passing out, and was expecting to wake up with his face in a puddle, minus the eight pounds and thirty pence he was carrying.

Not this. He hadn't expected this.

He was in a room of some sort. Tried to look around, but his body wouldn't respond. All he could do was stare upwards, at mottled brickwork.

And then the man appeared over him. He had to listen, unable to move his head away.

'Do you understand what you are a part of here? Selfish, that's what you are. You're important, probably for the first time in your life. And all you can do is cry and moan about it.'

Was he crying? He couldn't reach up and touch his face to check. Could he feel his face growing wet?

He sniffed, the smell of damp and bleach assailing him. He tried to speak, but his lips wouldn't move. He looked down as much as he could, seeing something plastic across the bottom of his face.

'Pathetic. What happens here tonight will be remembered forever. Your name will live well beyond our lifetimes. You're worthless to me. A means to an end.

A body.

Pliable. Useable. That's all you are.'

His face was becoming wet. He could definitely feel it now. There was other places he thought he may be wet too.

'So if you want to waste time crying, pissing yourself, fine, do it. But don't expect my sympathy. I'm giving you infamy, and you're throwing it back in my face.

You should be begging me to do this. To make you famous throughout the country. Isn't that what everyone wants these days, their fifteen minutes of fame? I'm giving you so much more.

And it could be so much worse for you. This will be relatively quick compared to what's happening in the other room. Can you hear her singing? She's a special project.

Aren't you feeling blessed?

You should be on your knees thanking me for finding you, including you in this. You're barely worthy of being here. Stop crying. It annoys me.

We're almost ready. Anything you'd like to say before we start?'

Colin attempted a pleading look, his screams kept silent behind his closed mouth. And all he could hear was Katy fucking Perry being sung at full volume and out of tune, and the breathing of a madman above him. The smells of bleach, of the washed away fluids which they masked, of dampness, darkness, crowding around him. The walls closing in, a droplet of sweat dripping down onto his nose from the man above.

'She's loud isn't she? Trying to get my attention, of course. Don't worry though, soon it won't matter to you.'

He removed the knife, ran his gloved index finger across the blade to the point.

His aim was off with the first thrust down into his chest. Missed the heart. Screams from behind the gag. He needed to get it right.

He tried again. Blood seeping through from the first wound he'd made, joined now by that from the second.

'Too high.'

He tried again. And again.

'At this rate I'll be able to see your heart anyway,' he said, laughing.

He kept going. Decided he wanted to see it.

Cut away the skin surrounding his left nipple. Kept digging around the area now surrounded by holes where his knife had entered. He used the knife as a saw, hacking away at the muscle, determined to find it.

'There it is.'

Inside the chest cavity he had created, much smaller than he had imagined. The heart, still beating, although slow and filling with blood.

The man on the table wasn't screaming any longer. Shock had taken over and he was on his way.

He watched. The beating slowed.

He raised the knife, then, drove it straight through the middle of the pulsating heart.

Later, the man who had taken Colin Woodland sat down at his computer. Found the best route to where he needed to go, and planned it all out.

It was a risk. But he was willing to take it.

This was his one. His idea come to life and death.

Experiment five.

Gone.

22

Thursday 31st January 2013 – Day Five

PC Hale grappled with the shaven-headed lad, simultaneously attempting to extricate his handcuffs. His heart was still threatening to burst out of his chest, his hands shaking as he got the cuffs on, quickly looking to his right to check his partner was doing the same to the girl.

'I didn't do nothin', honest officer. I was just walking past with me bird, and thought he looked a bit dodge, that's all. Hey, Shell, tell 'em will ya.'

'I'm arresting you on suspicion of murder . . .'

'Murder! We called you. Why would we call the bizzies if we'd done him in?'

The accent grated on PC Hale. He hated working in the city, but it was the only force taking on new recruits in the area so he had to put up with it. He continued with the caution, struggling to keep the tracksuit-wearing scally under control.

A police van arrived, navigating its way onto the paving stones which were usually only used for pedestrians and taxis picking up late-night drinkers from the dock's new trendy bars. PC Hale let out a breath as the lad sank to the floor.

'We'll sort it all out at the station mate.'

'I'm not your fuckin' mate,' the lad replied. PC Hale wiped away a globule of saliva which had flown out of the lad's mouth.

His hand reached for his baton, anger bubbling up inside him, before he stopped himself.

It was getting harder for him to stop.

Murphy exited the car, taking in the smell of the river front. He looked out over the water, seeing the Wirral in the distance. The ferry was on its way back, coming into dock on the Liverpool side. He imagined he could hear the song which was always played on board. *Ferry Cross The Mersey.*

One for the tourists.

The Pump House was behind him, the old building looming over the scene.

He approached the huddle of uniforms, stamping their feet and rubbing their hands together. He zipped up his coat as he reached them. 'How long has he been there?'

Murphy looked around waiting for an answer, blank expressions from the uniformed officers who were the first on the scene.

'We arrested a lad on the scene. He said he noticed him at two-thirty p.m. but he doesn't seem all that reliable sir.'

Murphy turned to face the PC speaking. 'Where is he now, PC . . .?'

'Hale, sir. He's in the van over there,' Hale replied, gesturing towards a marked van near the crime scene tape.

'He's a witness. Make sure nothing happens to him. Keep him happy.'

PC Hale looked as if he was about to disagree with Murphy, but thought better of it and instead nodded his head.

'Where's SOCO?'

Rossi appeared, putting her phone away. 'Just chased them up. They're on their way. You think he's been here long?'

193

Colin Woodland was laid out in the now-familiar way. Lying on the ground next to an old anchor, now a photo opportunity rather than a ship's tool. Murphy snapped on gloves. 'He's stiff. Reckon he's been laid out here at least all morning. How many people do you think walk down the Albert Dock on a Thursday morning Laura?'

'Hundreds,' Rossi replied, looking around. 'At least. Always busy down here.'

'First two have both been dumps at night. Any reason we should think this one would be any different?'

Rossi shook her head in reply. 'Too many people here earlier in the night. Bars don't shut until two. Then it's busy in the mornings.'

'Exactly. Which means it will have been late at night, around three or four in the morning.'

Murphy peeled back the jacket covering the victim, the shirt underneath falling away with it, exposing his chest. 'Fucking hell.'

Rossi peered over his shoulder as he turned away. 'What is that?'

'His heart, Laura. That would be his heart.'

Murphy looked away, his wrist covering his mouth as he bit on the urge to vomit. Looked across towards the river, the scenery of the docks paling into insignificance when you were feet away from death. The Liver Building in the distance, one of the birds looking down on them disapprovingly, the other turning its head in dismay.

'You think he's been here for over ten hours?' Rossi said, her eyes not returning to the body.

Murphy shook his head. Tried to dismiss the feeling.

'That's if it was last night.'

'We waited outside his house for hours. I wonder if he was taken the previous night?'

194

Murphy let Colin Woodland's coat fall back, as the inside pockets proved to be empty. The hole driven into his chest now hidden once again. 'Possibly. He was probably taken the night before. That'll be why we couldn't find him.'

'There are cameras which point towards the entrance and exit of the docks. Hopefully we'll catch something,' Rossi replied, looking back towards the main stretch.

'Yeah. I've got Brannon getting them now.'

'Sound.'

EXPERIMENT FIVE

Detective Murphy

Yes, I know your name now. Makes things a lot easier when being able to write a letter to someone personally. Takes away some of the formality, I'm sure you'll agree.

Let us talk about grief for a moment. It fascinates me so. They never move on you know, the parents in particular. They carry around the weight of having to bury their child forever. Why is that? Why is this society so obsessed with the idea that burying ones offspring is so out of the norm? They fetishise this type of death, seemingly unaware in other cultures it can be normal for this to happen.

Back to Experiment Five: The Bystander Effect

It's an interesting examination into the diffusion of responsibility. When an emergency situation is in progress, in a crowded area, how many people will stop to help? How long will it take for someone to step in and take control?

Interest arose in this area amongst psychologists after a particularly horrifying tale was told. In 1964, a young woman was attacked and stabbed multiple times.

She screamed for help, pleaded for her life.

The killer was disturbed by a passing neighbour. He took off.

He returned minutes later to finish the job.

It was reported thirty-eight witnesses heard the attack, yet did nothing to stop it. All hoping someone else would step in, take control.

And that's not the only occurrence . . .

Sergio Aguiar in 2008. Beat his two-year-old son to death in California whilst being watched by bystanders. Most reported they didn't step in because they were worried he was psychotic, and he might have had a weapon concealed on him.

Wang Yue in 2011, two years old. Hit by a van, in China. Eighteen people walked past her stricken body, some stepping around the blood gushing from her wounds. It took almost ten minutes for someone to help her. She died some days later.

Diffusion of responsibility. It's someone else's problem. Not mine, let someone else deal with it.

How long was this man here for? Laid out, arms and legs outstretched, in plain sight of all the visitors to our famous dock?

I'm leaving him there at three-thirty a.m. on the 31st January.

I've been reading up about you, David Murphy. A highly respected member of the police service. That is, until you married your second wife. The way in which you two met was frowned upon by your fellow officers. I'm sure they came around when the time came for you two to marry. But who's to say what was really said behind closed doors.

Then he was released. And he wasn't happy, was he David?

There's a lot about you in the papers, you were quite the local hero at one time. Rising through the ranks, a local council estate child done good. Then, it turned. Your parents were murdered. I read a lot about this, and your past was raked through in the media. Your marriage broke down, which is understandable given the circumstances, and nothing more was heard about you for a long time. That is, until I came onto the scene. Then there's the Phillips girl you didn't help. I'd love to know if her face still haunts you, detective.

Maybe we'll get the chance to discuss that one day . . . Would you like to be the subject of one of my little experiments perhaps?

I have focus now. Meaning. I know the man who is trying to stop me. I hadn't factored that into my analysis. An odd thought to be the subject of a manhunt.

I thought the piece on the front page of the Liverpool News was terribly overdone. Something should be done about that reporter. Say the word, detective, and he's gone.

It wasn't hard to find all this information on you, everything lasts forever on the internet. You know that of course. I'm sure you're aware of the videos that still exist of you outside your parents' house. Your anguished screams of grief, captured forever. Beautiful to watch.

So you know something about loss, grief, pain . . . death. It's apt that you will be spearheading the investigation into my activities. Because it's not going to stop now. I have learnt so much. It'll be exciting to see what is to come.

I'll be seeing you.

'Just under twelve hours then.'

Murphy nodded at Rossi in reply. A dead body lying in full view of passersby for almost twelve hours. The papers would have a field day with that information.

'Where does he keep them?' Murphy said, mindlessly doodling on a notepad.

'His house? I don't know. Seems to be planned out properly, so it'll be somewhere he feels secure.'

Murphy grunted under his breath. 'He'd have to be able

to keep them subdued for a period of time. He seems to keep them for at least twenty-four hours before killing them.'

'He seems to be focused on you now.'

Murphy smirked. 'Not the first time.'

It'd been two days since they'd spoken to Colin Woodland. One day on from them sitting outside his house near Stanley Park, Liverpool football club's stadium only a few streets away. 'We need help with the psychology angle of this. I don't think your sociology degree and my woodwork CSE is enough. I'll speak to the boss about getting someone in.'

Rossi nodded enthusiastically, bringing the nodding dog he used to have on the dashboard of his car to Murphy's mind. He bit back a smile. He was finding it more difficult to control his emotions.

Laughing one minute, despair the next.

'Where do we start then?' Rossi brought his attention back to the room.

'CCTV?'

As if on cue, Brannon puffed his way into the incident room, making a beeline for their desks.

'Got them, sir,' he said as he arrived, banging into the desk as he somehow misjudged the distance.

'Excellent. Start watching them. Make a list of all the vehicles that turn up between one a.m. and six a.m.'

'Great. I'll get right on that. '

Murphy watched as Brannon winked at Rossi and left.

Murphy picked the letter back up, the plastic evidence bag crinkling in his hands.

'We need to start again. From the beginning.'

23

Thursday 31st January 2013 – Day Five

'Donna McMahon, LSD experiments. Found in Sefton Park. Strangled to death. Julie Ward. The fighter. Found in Newsham Park, two days later. She has no experiment linked to her other than what he says he was planning to attempt. Died from stab wounds to the throat, with more to her chest and abdomen.' Murphy attached the last photograph to the white board. 'Today, Colin Woodland, bystander effect. Preliminary post-mortem report gives the cause of death as stab wound to the heart. Although, as you can see from the photos, there was significant damage done to that area.'

'He was trying to find the right place to hit the heart?' Rossi said.

'Maybe it started like that, but he destroyed that area of his chest, hacking away at it. A stab wound goes directly though his heart.'

'Jesus. Three in five days. I've never known anything like it.'

Murphy stepped back, looking at the map of the city. Attempting to see some kind of pattern. Nothing jumped out at him.

'Two in deserted parks at opposite ends of the inner city. One at the Albert Dock. Two women, one man. Different ages, all connected to the university. Two students, one librarian. The two students were studying different subjects, in different parts of the university.' Rossi paused, tucking her hair behind an ear. 'Where were they all taken from? That might be the key.'

Murphy snapped his fingers. 'Good thinking. We need to find that out. Where are we with looking at the CCTV?'

'Eight taxis, six private, two black hacks. Six cars we're running through the DVLA now.' DS Brannon had appeared beside Rossi, holding a packet of crisps, barely pausing between speaking and shoving them in his mouth. 'Already discounted the taxis, as they were in and out.'

'Anything else?' Murphy said, looking at Rossi, sensing her discomfort as Brannon got too close to her.

Brannon began to shake his head, but then stopped. 'There was something a bit weird. There was a guy stood right in front of the camera for about twenty minutes. He's standing there, then he takes out his phone, speaks for a bit, and then looks around. He just got off after that though.'

'What time was that?' Rossi asked, moving over to the map on the wall.

'Think it was about three-ish, Laura.' He said her name like it was foreign on his tongue, pronouncing it slowly. Murphy closed the distance between them,, facing Brannon. The smell of cheese and onion stuck in the back of Murphy's throat. 'Did we get a good look at him?'

'Enough that we can see him properly.' Brannon replied, placing a finger in his mouth dampening it, before removing the dregs of the crisp packet and sucking it off a fat sausagey finger.

Murphy turned away. 'Good. Laura, I'm going to take a look. You make a start on the cars from the DVLA.'

Murphy walked behind him, the bounce in Brannon's step becoming quickly annoying. Like they were off for a visit somewhere fun.

'It's really a good picture. I knew there was something off about him. As soon as I saw him I knew I had to tell you.'

Yeah, okay, that's why it was an afterthought nobhead. Murphy scolded himself. Brannon was just trying to please, and that sometimes brought results.

Murphy waited as Brannon rewound the footage to the moment the man appeared. The camera was set up to monitor the entrance to the road which led down to the Albert Dock's clubs and bars, which now attracted most of the visits there after dark. Come to see history in the day, make history at night. Not one of their better slogans. The man appeared in frame at five minutes to three, clearly waiting for something. He was looking up and down the road which ran along the outside of the Albert Dock; a wide main road, which ran most of the length of the seafront, up towards Bootle in the north and Parliament Street towards the south.

'There he is.'

Brannon paused the footage. 'Can you zoom in a bit?' Murphy asked. Brannon pressed a couple of buttons and the man's face became slightly larger, but also blurrier.

It didn't matter. Murphy knew who he was.

Murphy paced Stephens's office. 'His name is Robert Barker. Me and Nick Ayris interviewed him about a year ago after his girlfriend, Jemma, went missing. Nick is a DI in South Liverpool now. You know her mum. Helen Barnes?'

DCI Stephens steepled her fingers under her chin. 'Jemma. Known Helen for years, but we don't really keep in touch.'

'Yeah, well anyway, Robert Barker was the boyfriend who reported her missing. She's never been found. And now we have him on camera at the dumpsite for the latest murder.'

'Coincidence?'

'I don't think so. The reason I recognised him straight away and knew his name, was because I'd seen it recently.

He works at the university. Some admin job in the psychology department.'

'Ah, now I see why you're here.'

'Exactly. Enough?'

'Definitely.'

They sat at a table in the canteen, a couple of uniformed officers on the other side of the room for company. Murphy relaxed a little as he added three packets of sugar to his coffee, looking around for a spoon before shrugging his shoulders and using his finger.

'Asbestos hands, like my mum,' he said, flicking his finger dry, noticing Rossi shake her head.

'Of course. Nothing to do with laziness?' Rossi replied, reaching behind her to take a spoon off the next table.

'No. You should see the walking I'm doing on that treadmill. Miles every night. Don't even need to leave the house.'

Rossi laughed. 'There's me thinking it would just gather dust in the corner. Good to hear you're actually using the thing.'

'Yeah, well, I've got to do something with my evenings.'

'Still haven't spoken to her?' Rossi said, finding her cup overly interesting at the same time.

'No. And don't give me down the banks about it. Jess already had a go the other night.'

'She's your wife. You need to speak to her at some point. It's been almost a year.'

'I know Laura. It's . . . just hard, you know.'

Murphy looked away as Rossi lifted her head.

'I was a PC when you got together. I remember what was said, even nicked her a couple of times myself.'

Murphy shook his head. He hadn't known that. 'And?'

'So, I knew you were taking a chance. Heard what everyone

was saying, but I had my eye on DS at that point and knew I'd probably end up under you. So I kept my mouth shut.'

Murphy turned his head as Rossi took a sip from her coffee.

'She wasn't a proper druggie you know,' Murphy said. 'She might have hung around with smackheads, but she wasn't like them. She'd take speed sometimes, bit of coke here and there. But she was different from all of them. She still had life in her eyes, a spark. And he was taking that away from her.'

'So why can't you sort it out?'

Murphy bit on his bottom lip, holding back what he wanted to say. 'Shit happened. It wasn't her fault, but I can't forget it.'

'What about forgive?'

'I don't know.'

Rossi shook her head.

'I know it doesn't make sense, but that's how it is.' Murphy said, finishing off his coffee, wincing at the heat.

Rossi stood up. 'All I know is that she's waited around for you, still is. Are you going to wait another year before either ending it, or sorting it out . . . sir?'

Murphy smirked. 'We'll see. Anyway, drink up. We're going to get Barker.'

PART TWO

You do not understand even life. How can you understand death?

Confuscious

Grief is perhaps the one aspect of death which can be examined. However, even this comes with its own issues of experimentation. There are many different reactions to death, with a seemingly vast array of diverse responses towards it. A death of a loved one can lead to many issues for the person left behind. Dr Kubler-Ross forwarded the theory of the five stages of grief, namely denial, anger, bargaining, depression, and acceptance. However, this arguably compartmentalises a strong set of emotions which cannot be streamlined into a set of ideals. Simply; death and the response to it, is anything but universal.

We all deal with death according to our own emotional set up. How we live our lives, our past and present, informs how we grieve.

We should also be aware that grief is arguably a social construct. It has been created by man to instruct us how we should act when someone dies. We mirror each other's reactions, learning how we must react to death.

There is no correct way to act. When we grieve, we do so in a way that has been designed for us by the society in which we live.

However, we are not all the same. We all feel differently, react differently to events than each other. Inwardly, we struggle to define ourselves by those social ideals, causing psychological issues as we deal with our own grief.

Grief isn't a real, tangible object. The way in which we use it is.

Taken from 'Life, Death, and Grief.' Published in
Psychological Society Review, 2008, issue 72.

Experiment Two

She stood at the top of the stairs, trying to catch her breath, the sound of it hitching in and out reassuring her that she had made it this far. Only a few feet from the safety of an outside world.

It was a really bad idea. Going back was a really stupid idea.

In fact, in a list of bad ideas, this was probably the worst one she'd had. She should run. As fast as she could in the opposite direction. Never stopping.

But she couldn't leave the other girl down there. She could hear the screams looping around and around, the same cries and pleas. She couldn't exactly leave her there, run for her life and hope she got help quick enough to save her.

It wasn't her fault if something happened to the woman locked away down there, in the room opposite where she herself had been kept. No one would blame her for leaving her there.

She battled with her conscience.

If it was the other way around, wouldn't she hope someone came back for her?

It came down to a simple fact. She couldn't live with herself knowing she'd left someone else in that position.

She listened to the quiet, trying to hear if there was any movement from the bottom of the steps. She couldn't see anything properly, just outlines of form, the silence giving shape to invisible obstacles.

She stepped down, not wanting to move too fast in case she disturbed the unconscious man she hoped was still where she had left him. She tried to muffle the sound of her bare feet slapping on the stairs.

Two steps away from the bottom, she finally saw him. Still in a crumpled heap against the wall. There was a thin shaft of light coming from somewhere behind him, further down past the doors.

He was around six feet away from the door which she needed to open. She reached the bottom of the steps and kept moving, reaching the door within a few strides. Her right knee throbbed, and she could feel dampness leaking down her shin.

The door was locked.

She'd known it would be, but she still tried to open it again. Searched for a bolt or something which would be easy to slide back and open it up.

She looked back at her own door, the bolt across the middle, the hatch still open.

But she found nothing like that. Just smooth wood and a keyhole, with no key.

The girl behind the door screamed out again, making her jump. She looked over at the man.

Unmoving.

She breathed in deeply, letting it out in a low whistle.

She wanted to get out of there. There was a little more light now her eyes had become used to the darkness outside of her room. Not enough to see more than a few feet in

208

front of her, but it was nowhere near as tar black as the darkness which lay within her room. The basement was small, but seemed to grow in size as she stood in front of the door. She could see what she needed near the bended legs of her captor.

Captor. A strange word. Not one she was used to saying, or thinking, but it had just popped into her head. Why would that be?

What the hell was she doing focusing on her choice of words?

Concentrate.

She stepped lightly over him, his shallow breaths lifting his chest up and down softly. She moved quietly, but quickly. Grabbing the keyring from the floor, she noticed it held three keys. She wondered what the third one was for. Almost smacked her own head when she remembered the door leading to the basement. What a fool.

She berated herself again. Focus.

She turned back the way she came, her eyes constantly shifting between where she was stepping and the man slumped on the floor, his head tucked into his chest. The smell of blood filled the air, fresh. How did she know what blood smelled like?

She wished those breaths would stop. Then she wouldn't be shaking so much.

She tried the first key on the ring, sliding it in the lock. Turned it, but nothing happened.

Of course it wasn't the first one. This was her horror film, and at any second the scary man was going to grab her ankle and pull her to the floor. She held her breath, checking he was still unconscious, the few feet in length that lay between them contracting, seeming both longer and shorter in distance.

Snap out of it. Try the second one. It won't be the second

209

one. It's always the last one. She decided to just try that one instead then.

She moved past the second key and tried the third key instead.

The lock turned. She swung the door inwards and took a step sideways, expecting the girl to come rushing out. Not wanting to be knocked over by a screaming banshee.

She waited a few seconds, but no one came out of the room. She stepped back into the open doorway, the dim light from the basement offering her a little sight.

She stood, open mouthed, in the entrance.

It was empty.

She jumped back as the screams started again. Louder now, with the door open and with her standing close to it.

From the walls. The sounds were coming from the walls.

She opened and closed her mouth, suddenly dry. Stepped back until she was clear of the basement. Confused.

It wasn't real.

She turned to go back up the stairs, when she heard a shuffling from behind her.

'You fucking bitch.'

She turned quickly, seeing him start to rise to his feet. 'No . . .'

She moved quickly, towards the stairs, her injured knee sending a wave of pain through her body as she twisted. She cried out in pain, but kept moving.

'Come back here. I haven't finished with you yet.'

She reached the stairs, not willing to risk looking over her shoulder. She took them two at a time at first, before the pain became too much. She could hear him shuffling forward behind her.

She stumbled as she reached the top.

There was a moment when she thought she would regain

her balance, become upright and stable, reach the door, run for safety.

Why did she go back? What an idiot. Always thinking of others. She should have just run. Why didn't she just run?

She wanted it more than ever.

To sleep in her own bed. Eat hot food, lie in a bath. Go for a run.

See daylight. Sit and watch TV, or go for a walk down the front. Look over the Mersey and see the ferry.

Instead, she found herself falling backwards.

Laughter came from behind her as she fell down the steps, her shoulder taking the first impact, before she rolled over and her legs took over.

It was over in an instant. She threw her arms out to try and stop herself falling, every joint seemingly on fire with pain. As she crashed to the floor, her hands took most of the weight, her body thrown around with no control.

She was on her back, her surroundings seeming to pulsate. Her eyelids felt heavy. She could hear screaming but didn't know if it was coming from her, or the walls.

The walls. A failsafe. Played on her compassion, so she couldn't escape.

She had been so close. Freedom, escape, only mere moments away. Now she was gone.

Why did she go back down?

The air around her changed. She moved her head to the right, seeing the man loom above her.

She could swear she heard him smile, actually hear his lips smack as they lifted, his cheeks swelling. She imagined him, blood running down his face onto his sweating neck.

Smiling at her idiotic attempt to save the day.

Smiling at tricking her into thinking she wasn't alone down there.

That was what she was. Alone. Dead soon. She'd be dead soon.

She wanted it now. Anything but going back into that room. Death instead of darkness. A good trade.

She let herself go. Her eyes closing, slow laughter, the feeling of being under water.

So close.

The silence shifted around her as she came swimming back to the surface of consciousness.

When she opened her eyes, she was back in the darkness. Her escape attempt already a fading memory, even though she didn't feel she'd been unconcious long.

Down there.

She wasn't dead, but she may as well have been. Nothing to do but wait. So, that's how she'd spent her time in the days and weeks which followed her attempt at escape.

Waiting.

Waiting for another chance.

She'd been in there too long. She'd lost count of the amount of times she'd slept since her time outside the room. In those minutes, hours, days following her escape, she barely moved from her bed. She couldn't have, even if she'd wanted to. She rubbed her wrists as she remembered the shackles which had kept her in place after her failed attempt to get out.

The empty feeling in the pit of her stomach as no food was delivered. Hunger making her weak, the lack of water finishing the job.

As she lay on the thin mattress, her voice sounding worse and worse as she sang to herself, the voice had spoken to her once more. Coming through the walls again. Telling her why she was there.

He went on for so long, her attention slipping constantly as various images of food and drink fought for space in her mind. She heard him talk about experiments and death. She didn't understand any of it. She hadn't seen one beaker full of bubbling potions since she'd been in that hell hole.

Some time later, the door was changed. The hatch was smaller now. No chance of getting out that way again.

After that, he didn't talk to her again. Just dropped food and water through the now smaller-sized hatch, without pause.

She'd all but given up. She was just waiting to die. She didn't want to live like this any more. She wasn't living during all the days and nights down there. She was existing. That was all.

It was February when she was taken and put in this place. Over eleven months had passed since then.

She didn't know that though. She didn't know she'd been in the darkness that long. Almost a year. Time meant nothing. Her unravelling mind was just trying to keep track of what she was supposed to be doing. Eat, drink, sleep. Sing if she fancied it.

Talk to people who weren't there.

If someone had told her she'd been down there that long, she'd laugh and think they were crazy.

It had to be at least ten years. Twenty, more likely. That's what she would say. When she got out.

If she got out.

24

Thursday 31st January 2013 – Day Five

The early evening had become darker as they waited for the arrest warrant, the streetlights providing slight illumination to the scene of twelve officers waiting a few seconds for a door to open.

Scotland Road runs from the city centre, the turn-off for the Wallasey tunnel indicating the beginning of the long stretch that works its way from there towards Everton. In stark contrast to the concrete paradise of the Liverpool One shopping centre, Scottie Road is the beginning of the other face of Liverpool. Graffiti marked, shuttered shops. Burnt-out pubs and fire-scorched grass verges. The odd garage, which at first seems to be abandoned, before you look closer and see the boarded-up front is for security rather than to indicate closure.

A rundown set of flats, above three different businesses: a bookies, newsagent, and launderette. Access from a shared side door, which looked new, thick and hopeful.

It was a long way from the house Murphy had visited Rob in a year earlier. He wondered how far he had fallen. Whether that fall now extended to a moral one as well as a financial one.

Whether Jemma Barnes had been his first.

They were about to raise the enforcer to knock the door down, when Rob Barker exited the newsagents a couple of doors down from the flat entrance.

Took one look at the officers, turned, and ran.

Murphy was closest.

Rob pulled away quickly, as Murphy sprinted to catch up. Turning left onto Hopwood Street, Murphy had already fallen at least a hundred yards behind him. Railings on the main road prevented the cars from following them, but Murphy could hear a few officers trying to catch them up as they ran down the side street, passing bemused hooded kids on bikes, and one stout woman in a dressing gown.

Rob ran straight on ahead, Murphy turned right.

He knew the area better. He was counting on that.

He sidestepped a purple wheelie bin as he ran down an alley, his shoes echoing around him as he upped the pace down the cobbles. He reached the end of the alleyway within seconds, turning left onto Bangor Street, deep into the housing estate which ran behind the main stretch of Scotland Road.

Then he came to a stop, waiting.

Rob appeared around the corner, panting, out of breath, but still moving forward. Murphy stepped back, trying to melt into the brick of one of the buildings that lined the main road.

Rob closed the gap, the effort of the run becoming clearer on his face as he passed a streetlight.

Twenty yards, ten yards, five . . .

Murphy stepped out, extended his arm, and dropped Rob to the floor.

Murphy stood next to a handcuffed and scared Rob Barker. He looked different close up. He could see the effect of the last year written all over his face.

He hadn't spoken.

'You know why we're arresting you Rob?'

He received a blank look in return.

'Course you do. Where did you keep them?'

Rob shook his head in response, finding the concrete path of sudden interest.

Murphy helped him into the van which would take him down to the station. Processed and locked up overnight. They'd start questioning him the next day. Early. Let him stew for a few hours, and see if he'd talk then.

'You do not have to say anything, but it may harm your defence if you do not mention when questioned something which you later rely on in court. Anything you do say may be given in evidence. Do you understand Rob?'

A nod. About as much as they'd got so far.

Murphy looked towards Rossi, who was sat to his right. Allowed her to begin.

'Do you understand why you're here Rob?'

Rob didn't look up at them. 'Yes.'

'Why are you here?'

'You think I'm him.'

'Who, Rob?'

'The man you're looking for. The man who took Jemma.'

Rossi looked down towards her notes. Murphy continued to stare at the crown of Rob's head.

'Jemma was your girlfriend.'

'Is.'

'Sorry?'

'She *is* my girlfriend. We never split up.'

Rossi looked towards Murphy. Carry on, he thought, trying to indicate with his eyes.

'Of course. She's been missing almost a year now. That's

216

not why we're here now though Rob. We're speaking to you about the three people who have been murdered in the last week, okay? What do you know about them?'

Silence crowded into the room for ten seconds, then twenty. They waited.

His voice was quieter. 'I think he took them too.'

'Who, Rob?'

'The man who took Jemma.'

'Do you know who that is Rob?'

Rob looked up at them then. Bloodshot eyes, dark rings underneath. His eyes found Murphy's, staring through him. One word passed his lips at first.

'No.'

A pause, lick of his lips, then, 'I don't want to speak any more. I'd like a solicitor in here now please.'

'It doesn't make sense. Why was he picked up on the cameras if he wasn't involved . . . why else would he be there?'

Murphy was standing in the small kitchen area off the major incident room, facing the sink. Rossi stood with arms folded, leaning against the counter to his right, the kettle boiling behind her.

'He looked lost,' she replied.

'He looked guilty.'

She shrugged at him, pursed her lips. 'Reckon we can hold him?'

'You're joking, aren't you. We've got nothing on him. They're tearing his flat apart looking for something, anything. They've not found a thing. Just unpaid bills and stained dishes. Fuck all.'

He didn't realise what he'd done until Rossi jumped beside him. The mug he'd been rinsing under the tap was reduced to just the handle .

'Sorry,' he said, taking the broken pieces out of the sink carefully. 'Don't know what came over me.'

'It's okay. We're all stressed out.'

Murphy smiled, dropped the broken mug into the bin under the counter top. 'Shall we try again?'

Murphy sighed and sat back in his chair, folded his arms and rested them on his disappearing gut.

'No comment.'

That's all they had received for the past hour and a half. The time was growing short, it had been almost twenty hours since they'd arrested Rob Barker.

Rossi was relentless. He admired that, but even she was waning in the face of the stonewalling. Murphy knew he was hiding something, but the more time went on, he looked more scared than guilty.

'Why did you run from us Rob?'

'No comment.'

'When you said you think someone is holding Jemma, and it's the same person who we are looking for, how did you come to that conclusion?'

'No comment.'

'If you believe that Rob, why do you not want to help us?'

'No comment.'

The solicitor who had been provided to Rob wore a shit-eating grin which grated with Murphy no end. He was young, power suit, power tie. Nothing like the guys Jess worked with and had introduced him to over the past few years. They'd looked harried, harassed. This man looked fresh faced and confident, not ground down from defending scallies who'd shoplifted a frozen turkey at Christmas, or a packet of razorblades to sell at the local pub.

He was enjoying it.

218

'Rob. Listen to me,' Murphy said, holding up a hand to Rossi, indicating for her to stop. 'If you're not the person we're looking for. If you didn't kill three people, three people who are connected to the university where you work, but know who that person is, now is the time to tell us. Because I'm not buying it. It's too coincidental. You're near a murder scene, minutes before Colin Woodland was placed there. Why? What possible explanation is there for you being at that place, at that time?'

Rob looked up at him, something etched across his face. Murphy knew it. 'No comment,' he whispered.

'I think my client has made his position quite clear, detectives,' the cocky lawyer said. 'If you have nothing else, I think it's time to bring this charade to an end. Don't you?'

Murphy stared at him, wanting to dive across the desk and force feed him his stupid royal blue tie.

'Interview terminated at four-seventeen p.m.'

'We can't keep him any longer. You've got nothing David.'

Murphy sat forward in his chair opposite DCI Stephens, running his fingers over his face and hair. 'I know. I don't think he's our man anyway.'

'Why do you say that?'

'He's scared of something. I don't know what it is, but he's scared.'

Stephens sucked her teeth. 'He remains a person of interest, but for now he's out on bail.'

Murphy nodded. 'Look, we could do with some help with deciphering the psychology shite that keeps popping up in these letters.'

'You know the score David. I can't bring anyone in to help right now. Do you know how much a psychologist would cost? Sorry, for now you're on your own with it.'

He'd known the answer before she said anything. Had to try though. He let the silence grow in the room.

Stephens pursed her lips. 'How about that professor you saw a few days ago? Do you think he'd be willing to help out?'

'I'm sure he could be persuaded.'

Murphy met Rossi outside Stephens' office. She looked tired, the day catching up on her.

'Well?'

'He's got to be released.'

'Shit. I thought we'd get him eventually. That bastard solicitor.'

Murphy half smiled. 'Just the way it goes sometimes. You think he did it?'

Rossi pondered on the question. 'I think he seems as likely as anyone. You don't?'

Murphy indicated with his head for Rossi to follow him over to the kitchen. Once in there, he spoke quietly. 'No. I think he's scared of something. I just don't know what. We need to find out more about the girlfriend. It's been almost a year, and she's still gone. I think we need to find out why.'

He'd managed to convince Stephens to allow them to show the professor the letters, and Rossi had set up a meeting at the university.

'We'll have to wait until Monday,' she'd said, tucking her hair behind her ear, 'but hopefully it'll make a difference.'

It didn't seem enough. They were reacting constantly, being led by the killer's actions. If he decided to go to ground, do a Jack the Ripper and never come out again, they'd be

220

screwed. Murphy leaned back on the toilet cistern, escaping into the bathroom for a bit of peace. He pulled his phone out, opening his eyes to see what he was doing. The lights causing his head to pound once more.

What time do you finish?

He sent the message, hoping Jess was finishing early.

The phone buzzed in his hand.

Half an hour. Meet you at yours?

He was typing out a reply, when the bathroom door opened with a bang.

'Did you see him before? Looked like he'd been crying or something?'

'Don't think he was, his eyes were all red though, maybe he's drinking. Going full cliché on us.'

Murphy tried to place the voices. He thought one of them belonged to a young DC, Alex something. Wore too much gel in his hair, looked like he was auditioning to be a Next model most days.

'Maybe. Can't believe he's still here. Thought he'd of been bombed out by now. Three dead in a week? That guy they arrested as well, no way he did it.' Smythe, Murphy thought, that's the other guy's name.

He knew they were talking about him. He'd noticed the looks from other officers around the station. It was as if they searching for something in his eye, a weakness which would confirm their suspicions. It had been that way since he'd married Sarah, the way in which they'd met causing problems with fellow officers from the start. It only intensified after his parents were murdered. Now, a week and three bodies later, with Murphy seemingly getting nowhere, the rumours would start. He knew this, had seen it happen previously to other detectives. They'd been forced out eventually, moved quietly to small areas where the crime rate wasn't so high as it was in a city of the size of Liverpool. Less pressure, less stress. That's how it worked. Murphy had just never thought it would be him on the receiving end.

He's got fuck all. I heard Rossi will be given lead on the case once he fucks off with stress or whatever.'

'Great. Another bird giving out orders. Haven't we got it bad enough, with a DCI doing that? Should give it to Brannon. Anyone with eyes can see Murphy's not up for it. You know they used to call him Bear years ago? 'Cause of his size and that. Fucking Koala Bear more like it.'

Murphy finished sending the message and stood up, listening as they laughed together outside. He flushed the toilet, without needing to and banged the stall door open. As he stepped out, the younger one looked over his shoulder and snapped his head back, nudging the other man with his elbow. The sniggering stopped as he walked out, both of the men standing at the urinals, frozen. Murphy took his time washing his hands, watching in the mirror as they stood silently. He turned the tap off and dried his hands.

As he got to the door he turned to the two men, still staring straight ahead. 'I interrupt something?'

'No, sir.' Alex replied.

'Good. The pair of you should see a doctor. Can't be healthy to have to piss for that length of time.'

He walked out, leaving the two men nervously pulling up their zips. Spotting Rossi at her desk, he walked over towards her. 'I'm getting off Laura. You should too. We're not going to get any further tonight.'

'Okay. Just finishing off my notes. A call came through for you by the way.' She leaned closer. 'Sarah,' she whispered, not wanting anyone else to hear. 'She sounded upset.'

Murphy sighed heavily. 'I'll deal with it.'

He walked away, grabbing his coat from the back of his

chair as he left. It was the last thing Murphy needed right now, Sarah back on the scene. His head wasn't in the best place as it was. With her back in his life, things could only get worse.

Experiment Six

He watched it again.

The detective's sweating, round, bearded face filled the screen. He smiled as DI Murphy rose up from the desk, shouting at someone unseen in the room.

The footage had been released in the last couple of hours. As soon as they'd found Experiment Five. Seemed it had been kept under wraps, but the discovery of a third body in a week had been cause enough to release a video of the main investigator snapping at a press conference. Backed up by the front page of the *Liverpool News*, and it was only a matter of time before the media turned on the police. And Detective Murphy in particular.

It was on YouTube at the moment, but he had no doubt Sky News would be showing it soon enough. He'd found it via a link on Twitter, searching for news about the discovery of his latest experiment.

He felt secure, safe. For the moment. They didn't have a clue. No idea of what they were dealing with. He'd been careful, overly so in some ways, yet it was paying off. The risks of delivering his subjects greatly outweighed by the thought of his work being discussed by so many.

His initial doubts were gradually fading. He shifted in the chair, his back rigid against the hard metal.

They'd understand eventually, not yet, but soon enough. For now he was prepared to take his time, prepare for his next one.

On the screen in front of him, Experiment Two screamed soundlessly. He rarely turned the sound up on her screen any longer; the sounds she generated annoyed him.

She sat with her back against the wall. He leaned forward towards the bank of desks the monitors were resting on, pressing a button on a keyboard.

The camera moved in, her profile filling the screen.

He grinned.

She was crying.

It was time to feed her.

He reached the top of the steps, before turning back.

There was little light in the basement, but he could see the door he'd just left behind, and the door opposite, which led to the other room down there. Soon to be filled once more.

He closed the door which led down to the basement, locked it.

Safety first. Just one of the many mottos he'd now procured for himself.

He walked down a dark corridor, passing the kitchen to his left, before entering his study.

The room was vast, the desk, which now acted as the hub of his activity, placed squarely in the room. The floor-to-ceiling windows, which had once streamed sunlight into the space, were now covered completely.

He sat in the hard chair which faced the desk. The screens which took up the length of the desk sat exactly forty inches from the edge, giving him enough space to not only watch

225

the girl and the outside for any unwanted visitors, but also perform the hard work of notation.

He began by reviewing his notes from experiment four. A total mess. He had to learn.

Make sure he didn't make the same mistake. Lose his self control again. Experiment Five had gone successfully, but he was now obsessed with making up for number four.

Experiment Six would be tricky. He needed him though. The police were closing in on the wrong person, and he needed to fix that. Make sure they didn't lose sight of the bigger cause here.

It was time for the Unit 731 experiment.

25

Thursday 31st January 2013 – Day Five
Rob

The radio came on, the same Scottish ex-footballer talking, the same time in the morning as it always had been.

Rob was already awake though. He lay in bed, on one side as usual, staring at the bedroom ceiling. Light traffic sounds came in from outside, the single-glazed windows shut but still allowing outside sound to enter. Rob continued to stare, lost to his surroundings.

Dreaming whilst awake.

It wasn't the same bedroom as before. It wasn't the same house as before. Things had changed since she had gone.

Five minutes passed, then ten. Rob lifted himself out of bed, out of necessity rather than desire. He glanced at the clock, the digital display flashing 7.12 a.m. back at him. He was going to miss the bus if he didn't get a move on. He went through the motions, showered and walked through the flat to the kitchen. He opened the window and lit a cigarette. He wasn't supposed to smoke, according to the tenancy agreement, so this was his compromise. Cold air drifted in through the window, winter still keeping a firm hold on the weather.

Eleven months. She'd been gone for that long he had to check her picture to remember what she looked like. Every time he did so, a sharp pang of guilt hit him.

You forget things so easily. Faces, events, places.

And he hadn't heard from her mum, Carla, or any of her other mates in all that time. He knew they suspected him after the first few weeks. When she hadn't turned up.

He didn't blame them really.

When he had a car, he'd drive past her mother's house park up and wait. Make sure Jemma hadn't come home and no one had told him. Just to see if anything had changed.

When he had to get rid of the car, he took to walking past. Standing off to the side, the pain in his calves and thighs a burden he was willing to put up with.

He marked the day on the calendar. Another one passed. He checked the time again.

'Plenty of time,' he said out loud, his voice gravelled and croaked. He'd found himself talking out loud more often now. Talking to an empty flat wasn't something he would have imagined doing not so long ago, but he couldn't keep every thought locked inside his head any longer. Too crowded in there.

He booted up the laptop. It was the only expensive item he owned now. He must be the only person without a flatscreen TV around there. There was a Brighthouse store down the road, where most people picked up the latest gadgets and paid four or five times the list price, just by virtue of paying on a weekly basis. He owned an old, heavy Sony television, which had needed both him and Dan to lift up the stairs to the flat.

Dan. The only one who stuck by him. Helped him out sometimes, talked things over.

He needed the laptop though. Not only for work, but because it was his only connection . . . to her.

It was on the list.

He clicked to connect to the internet. His homepage was set to what he needed. The page loaded, and he logged in. The screen changed, a list of topics appeared.

Billy Nolan – 16/01/2011.
Donna Bowen – 08/09/2010.
Michelle Short – 29/12/2011.
Karen Smith – 16/03/2007.
Kieron Hurst – 18/06/2011.

And on and on. Hundreds of names, the dates they had gone missing next to them. They barely registered to Rob now, but when he'd first signed up to the forum, he'd spent hours going through all the different threads. Over 250,000 people go missing each year, he'd discovered. Most are found within seventy-two hours, but many are never seen again.

Eleven months.

He found the thread he was looking for, a few posts down.

Jemma Barnes – 18/02/2012.

A new reply was waiting, which set Rob's heart thudding in his chest. It was always this way, the hope of some kind of response, someone who knew.

He clicked, and waited as the new page loaded. He couldn't help but feel anticipation, excitement even. Something, anything, to take him away from reality. Give him purpose.

I really hope you receive good news soon. My son went missing fifteen years ago. Not a day goes by when I don't think of him. He will be thirty-two this year. You and your partner will be in my prayers tonight.

Rob had been holding his breath, and now let it out in a

heavy exhale. He appreciated the thought, yet always felt the same way when he received these kind of replies.

Disappointment, annoyance, empathy.

He typed out a quick reply, his stock answer of thanks for the support etc. He was about to log off and pack up the computer when he noticed a new message in his inbox. It wasn't rare for people to send him private messages, but he hadn't received one in a while. They were usually well-wishers, pleas for help also dropped in. He never knew what to reply to those. He could barely help himself, never mind others.

He opened it.

Robert Barker,

How long has it been now? Eleven months? Yes, eleven months. How has that time treated you? I ask, when I know the answer.

Not well.

You're smoking again, spending hours in that cheap flat you had to rent when you could no longer pay the mortgage on the house. Such a large mortgage it was, yet with two incomes coming in, I suppose it was manageable. And it was all in your name . . . silly boy.

A family live there now, they seem respectable. Two well turned-out children, polite, and well spoken. The mother works part time in an office, whilst Dad has an important job as a sales director of a large shipping company. He works long hours, but every weekend he makes sure he's free to spend time with his family.

It's amazing what people will tell you when they suspect nothing. Maybe I could go back. Cut out his still-beating heart and show it to his lovely wife and kids. I can do that, you know.

Such a shame you had to sell it. And to not make

230

more than a couple of thousand on it, a damn shame.
That's the economy for you I suppose. I guess you and
Jemma didn't buy into the whole buy low, sell high
ethos did you?

You've lost weight as well, and you look tired
Robert. Sleep not coming easily to you? I guess the
bed feels emptier now. It's nice to see you haven't
replaced her yet Robert.

They told you she'd done this before, didn't they?
Of course they did. She has, just to clear that up.
Many times. Only this time she didn't leave willingly.
She's alive.

You bought her a charm bracelet once. The dolphin
charm is her favourite.

She has a small birthmark on her lower back.
She wasn't afraid of the dark.
She is now.
Believe me?

Jemma is an integral part of what I am doing, my
most valued work. It wouldn't do for her to be found.
Not yet. She will be returned to you, soon in fact. First,
you must do something for me. I want you to go to the
Albert Dock at precisely three a.m. tonight. Wait
at the corner of the car park entrance, opposite the
bars and clubs that are now there.

Suffice it to say, I'd suggest you keep this to
yourself. If the police are involved, I will not hesitate to
start again, with someone new. Jemma will be an
unfortunate setback, but she is dispensable.

If you've been reading the papers recently, you will
know what I am capable of.

Rob sat back in his chair. They knew too much. That was
his immediate thought when he finished reading. The person

who wrote this knew too much. He'd had a couple of cranks in the past, but not one this detailed.

He should call the police. He knew he should. He still had the detective's card somewhere. He grabbed his wallet from the mantelpiece, going through the various credit cards that no longer worked, the driving licence he didn't need any more, before finding the card the big detective had given him almost a year ago. Murphy.

But what if the man holding her found out? He'd been given a chance. He could have Jemma back. Nothing could get in the way of that. His life wasn't complete without her. He was going through the motions, he knew that. Not living, just existing. If he could have her back, it would be okay again. Everything could be as it was.

Rob stood, the message still on the screen. He was being played with, he could feel it.

He curled his open palms into fists, anger rippling through. He closed his eyes, forcing himself to count to ten. A sense of reality began to come back to him. He checked the time and saw he was going to be late for work. He couldn't afford to miss another day's work – too much time had been lost going on time-wasting trips around the country. Disappointment had been a constant companion on so many of those journeys. Now he had something tangible. Maybe.

He read the message again, the sense of hope being replaced by the stark reality of what the truth might be. Whoever had her was gloating over that fact. Rob didn't often have ideas as basic as black or white, good or evil. But reading the message again, he began to realise what he was dealing with. Someone who had no regard for life. For Jemma's life. Only someone evil could act that way.

Someone who would hold a person against her will for almost a year.

Rob shut the laptop down, placing it behind the desk.

He'd be late for work, but that seemed inconsequential to him at the moment. He just had to get through the day, then see what the night would bring. He could be walking into anything, but he'd be there.

It was a crank, it had to be. Why wait until now to show his hand? He couldn't let himself get excited about this, he decided.

Where had she been, that was one of his overriding thoughts. Where was she now, was another. Was she okay, is she still my Jemma?

All those questions could wait.

Jemma could be alive. In danger.

Waiting for him.

And that's all that mattered.

26

Thursday 31st January 2013 – Day Five
Rob

Rob managed to only be twenty minutes late for work, out of breath after power walking up the hill.

With all that had happened in the last few months, his job was the only constant still left in his life. He'd worked in the same building for almost six years, just an admin job, but the pay was enough to support him. Plus he was still hoping to learn by osmosis, being around educated people daily. Even if most of them didn't really pay much attention to the 'little people'.

He passed the café on the left as he pressed the button to call the lift. A minute or so later, he was entering the room where he spent most of his days. 'Morning Liz, sorry I'm late,' Rob said, hanging his coat up. The office was small, just two desks and a counter to one end where students would invariably show up, asking questions. Boxes of files everywhere; it was a health and safety nightmare. Drab beige walls, a couple of colour prints of green flowery fields on the walls. The only window in the room overlooked the Tesco over the road behind the building. They mainly dealt with student enquiries, unless it was deadline day for essay hand-ins. Then it got busy, especially five minutes before the shutter came down. Queues out the door then, as students tried desperately to get their work in on time. Rob never understood why they left it so late, but then he'd never been to university, so he kept quiet about it. He'd mentioned it to Dan once, but he'd just laughed at him.

Rob worked through the morning, answering phone calls, dealing with a student from down south who wanted to get involved with more groups. By lunchtime he was starting to flag, the morning's adrenaline rush wearing off. Doubts had started to creep in, as the words of the message he'd received played on his mind throughout the morning. Was he being played? Was it someone after money maybe?

'Rob, you ready?' Dan had stuck his head around the door, interrupting Rob's thoughts.

'Yeah, coming,' Rob replied, grabbing his coat off the rack and waving a quick 'see you in a bit' sign to Liz . As soon as he hit fresh air, he lit up a cigarette. Dan was talking about a lecture he'd given that morning, his voice still betraying his private school roots. 'So there I am Rob, instilling these young minds with the basics of statistics, something integral to the study of psychology, only to have three students having their own private conversation during the most important part of the lecture.' Dan was walking quickly, Rob struggling to smoke and walk as fast as him. 'So of course, I had to pause and remonstrate with them. It might only be a couple of days into the second semester, but it is important to make it clear to these children that talking during lectures is intolerable.'

Rob laughed, enjoying another of Dan's rants against the 'children' as he called them. Ridiculous really, considering Dan was only a few years older than them himself.

'So, the usual, Rob?'

'Yeah. Is there anything else?'

The 'usual' was a pint and a sandwich in the oldest pub in the immediate area. A small, old-fashioned public house, which seemed to be the only pub in the area not offering two-for-one deals in order to lure in the students.

A pint of lager each in front of them and sandwiches ordered, Rob and Dan sat at a table. 'So, what did you say then Dan?'

Dan smiled shiftily. 'I just made them aware of the fact it wasn't just their time they were wasting, but everyone around them. Plus, it costs an awful lot of money to come to this university and I'm sure their parents wouldn't appreciate them wasting their time.'

'And?'

Dan laughed. 'You know me too well Rob.'

'I do. So what did you say?'

'Finally, I simply stated that if they wished to carry out a conversation during my lectures, kindly fuck off out of the room first. That raised a few chuckles in the room, I can tell you.'

Rob shook his head, smiling. 'I expect that won't go down too well.'

'You're probably right. I expect Garner will have me in his office this afternoon.' Dan said with a sigh, before taking a swig of his pint.

'Your pinkie's showing Dan.'

Dan almost choked on his drink, it was an easy joke, one he used to say a lot until Jemma left. Rob enjoyed ribbing Dan about his auspicious background.

'Haven't heard that one from you in a while Rob, what's with the good mood?'

'Nothing.' Rob replied.

'Pull the other one Rob. Something's going on. You've been moping about the place since Jemma left . . .'

'She didn't leave,' Rob said, punctuating his words with a slam of his pint down on the table.

'Well, that is what her mother told you. We've been through this numerous times. Don't you think it's time you listened?'

'No. She's out there somewhere and she needs me.'

Dan sat back with a heavy sigh. 'Look Rob, if you need anything let me know. I'm here for you.'

'I'm fine. I just have another lead is all.' Rob decided not to say any more than the minimum. 'Possible sighting of Jemma.'

'Oh right. Well, sincerely Rob, I hope it comes to something. I really do.'

The sandwiches arrived and they ate in silence, an uneasy atmosphere between them. When they were finished, Rob went outside for a smoke, his apprehension about that evening becoming nervousness. He'd overlooked something, lost in the thoughts of having Jemma back. He didn't really know anything. He'd spent eleven months taking days off every other week, travelling across the country trying to find her, with no luck. Now, a message on the internet of all places had lifted him out of the dark mood. It couldn't be as simple as that.

He entered the pub again, seeing Dan writing something on a notepad. Dan looked up and caught Rob's eye, stopped writing. 'Just got the call from Garner,' Dan said as Rob sat back down. 'Office at two. As I suspected.'

Rob smiled. 'Not the first time, and I reckon not the last. Share a packet of crisps before we go back?'

'No, I best not. I have papers to grade before seeing him.'

'Okay. I'll get a paper on the way back and read for a bit.'

Rob stared at the front page of the local paper. So this was him. This was the man who had Jemma.

A killer.

The *Liverpool News* already had a nickname for him. 'The Uni Ripper'. Two students, both at his university.

He'd obviously heard about it. He just hadn't thought about it all that much. Too consumed in himself. His own problems.

Which raised the question if the person who had contacted him was the same person who had killed two women, then why was Jemma still alive?

Rob checked the time on his phone display. Two thirty a.m. Still half an hour early. He'd walked into town, down Scotland Road, an hour earlier.

The only sound encroaching on the silence was sporadic traffic from the main road which ran alongside the entrance to the Albert Dock. The water which separated the dock's bars and the main road, Salthouse Dock, was moving silently in the biting wind.

Rob felt alone.

He made his way over to the corner he'd been directed to in the email, and leaned against a small concrete post, the streetlights illuminating him.

Droplets of rain began to fall, soft on the ground in front of him. Rob checked the time again; only five minutes to go. Too late to back out now. He glanced around, aware he was at a disadvantage if he was rushed from behind, open ground all around him.

Three a.m., and nothing happened.

He waited, feeling more foolish by the second for thinking anything would. He thought he could feel eyes watching him, the trees seemingly taking on form, hidden shapes lurking behind them.

'Are you watching me? Come out, face me.'

There was no answer. Rob sighed, stood up preparing to

leave, berating himself for having wasted a night on a stupid prank.

His phone vibrated in his pocket. He'd turned it to silent, fearing noise from an unexpected call would scare someone away. It didn't matter now he supposed, pulling the phone from his pocket. Unknown number on the display.

'Hello.'

There was static on the line, muffled traffic in the background. 'Hello Robert. Leaving so soon?' The voice was distorted, the pitch shifting around meaning he couldn't work out what the real voice was.

Rob stopped in his tracks, looking around for any sign of the caller. 'Where are you, where's Jemma?'

A low laugh came down the phone, Rob gripped the phone tighter. 'Where is she?' he said, his teeth grinding around the words.

'All in good time,' the voice replied. 'First, I'm so glad you came tonight. Alone as I asked. It pleases me you can take instruction.'

'How did you get my number?' Rob asked, scanning his surroundings for some sign of the caller.

'Oh, I have my ways and means of getting what I require. Right now, I believe I have something you need.'

'Just tell me what the fuck you want.'

'Now now, keep that temper under control Robert. It won't help you. For now, just walk back towards town. Near the Liver Building, there's wooden benches in front. Underneath the third bench on the left, there's something there I'm sure you'll be happy to see. I'll be in touch soon.'

The phone went dead, Rob looked at it, before turning and hurrying towards the Liver Building. The main road to his right was quiet, just the odd taxi passing.

When he got to the bench, he reached underneath, sweeping

his hand across the wood. His fingers brushed against something, and he pulled it out and walked away.

He came to a stop beneath a streetlight and inspected what he'd pulled out from underneath the bench.

An envelope.

He knew he should go the police now; they could fingerprint it, he thought, CSI it or something. But the overwhelming feeling of what it could contain took over. He lightly opened the end, and pulled out the contents. One sheet of paper.

The sheet of paper contained one sentence, written in sloping handwriting.

Harlow was the first, I'm just taking it further.

Rob looked around, noticing a few cars on the road. A black hackney cab or three driving down the main road.

'Who's Harlow?' He whispered quietly into the wind.

Rob gave the taxi driver a five-pound note. 'Keep the change,' he said, exiting the car. The rain was now pouring down, a large puddle forming in the gutter outside his flat. He strode over to the front door, which led into the communal hallway, opened it as quickly as he could and closed it quietly behind him. He stood still for a second, his heart hammering in his chest, as he realised the full scope of what had happened that night.

In the past, if he felt threatened, he knew what to do. Get the first hit in. Sort out the rest later. At this moment however, he was at a loss.

Once inside, his wet coat hung on the back of his desk chair, Rob typed *Harlow* into his computer, and waited for the results. A couple of seconds later and he was going through Wikipedia, looking at the different uses of the word.

One stood out instantly. Harry Harlow, American Psychologist.

He clicked on the article and read.

Ten minutes later, he was sure what had happened to Jemma.

Rob went back to his homepage, opening the mail box. He clicked on the message he'd received earlier that day, ignoring the words and hitting reply.

I know what you're doing. Harry Harlow, American psychologist. You're replicating him in some way, and you're using Jemma.
What do you want?

Rob waited thirty minutes before getting a reply. Pacing around the flat, his fists clenched, attempting to will the man into existence in front of him, so he had something tangible to release his anger on. All that appeared was his own reflection as he passed the mirror above the small mantelpiece. He just wanted a minute alone with the bastard, that'd be perfect.

That didn't take long at all! My, my, I may have under-estimated you. The cat is out the bag I guess. The infamous Harry Harlow, an incredibly intelligent man. Of course, what he carried out back then would never pass an ethics board today. Even if it was just monkeys. No, sadly, that sort of groundbreaking research wouldn't happen these days.
Not officially, anyway.
I've been carrying out my own research, with little progress. Of course, I've learnt a few things, but it's not as exciting as I thought it would be. The only one of any interest seems to involve your precious Jemma.
It's coming to the end of her time with me. Now, I don't see many options open here. If I let her go,

241

*I may be under threat . . . even if there's little chance
she could tell anyone a thing that would lead to me.
I don't care for loose ends.*

*You showed courage earlier. It'll be fascinating to
see how far that takes you. Once again, contact
anyone about this, and she dies.*

*And not a quick death Robert. I'll make sure it's
slow. That I take pictures of every second of her
agony. Share them with her mother and friends, so
they know exactly what you were responsible for doing.
Once again, I'll know if you tell the police anything.*

Rob began typing a reply, before stopping himself. He had
to keep control. Let himself be led back to her, and then
make his move.

He needed to get fit and strong again.

He needed to be ready.

He was awake for the next few hours, reading as much
as he could on the experiments carried out by the psychologist. He couldn't make sense of most of it.

But he knew who could help him.

He crossed to the laptop, the screen coming back to life
once he'd pressed a button. He typed out a reply to the last
message.

I'll wait.

The next day the police came.

His first instinct was to run, scared something would
happen to Jemma if he was seen with them.

So he had. Within seconds, his decision to start smoking
again caught up with him. That, and a clothesline from a
large detective.

He wanted so much to tell them everything.

242

But those last words he'd been sent played over and over in his mind.

So he stayed quiet. Answered 'no comment' as the solicitor had informed him to do.

Hoped to be released before anything happened to her.

27

Monday 4th February 2013 – Day Nine

They'd lost time interviewing Rob Barker; the weekend was soon over. Nine days in already and still they were no closer. Interviews with staff at the university were giving them nothing.

'You coming sir?'

They were back at the university, Rossi eager to move on. Murphy had slowed down as they passed a small pub on the corner, recognising the man sitting inside. Rob Barker. Talking to a tall, well dressed man. He'd caught his eye, and Rob averted his gaze quickly.

He still wasn't sure about him.

He was tired, unbroken sleep a distant memory at that moment. Images of darkness creeping into his vision at every turn.

'Yeah, Barker is in there. Either a victory drink or consolation. Hard to tell.' Murphy replied,

Rossi looked through the pub window. 'Guy he's sitting with seems nice.'

Murphy rolled his eyes at her. 'Can you wait until this is over before going out with our suspect's friends please.'

She stuck a tongue out at him.

'You're getting too comfortable around me,' Murphy continued, 'I might have to get rid.'

'Yeah, right,' Rossi replied, stretching her legs to catch up with him as he walked off. 'You'd sooner have me than any other DS back there.'

Murphy sighed. 'True.'

They passed the library once more, a lot more activity around the area than the last time they were there.

The university felt different to Murphy the second time around. Instead of the endless maze of funny little corridors, it began to feel more like a coffin, a cocoon of madness. The passages smaller, the walls closer. His eyes were playing tricks on him . . .

Dozens of clever and bright men and women locked away in small offices, thinking up new ways to test society. It was at that moment Murphy began to become sure the killer was among them. He'd always known that on some level. It was proving it which would be harder.

'Do you think he's doing it on purpose?' Rossi said as they waited for the lift.

'Who's doing what?'

'The killer. We're dealing with a supposedly highly intelligent guy, who thinks everything through. Is it really likely he would lead us straight to his place of work?'

'Possibly. He wants us to know what he was doing, maybe to be in awe of his work.' Murphy stepped back to allow Rossi into the lift first.

'Hmm,' she said, pressing the second floor button. 'Just seems a bit neat, that's all.'

The professor was waiting in his office, opening the door with a solemn look on his face. 'Detectives, I wish it was we were meeting in better circumstances.'

'Likewise,' Rossi replied. 'Can we use the meeting room again?'

'Of course. Follow me.'

They followed the professor as he led them around the corridors. As they passed an open office, Murphy took a look inside, seeing a spiky haired, young-looking guy in front of a computer. He recognised him as the lecturer who had brought them to Garner's office the first time they'd been there. The man wasn't what he fixed upon however; rather, the copious amounts of alcohol surrounding him. Boxes of bottled lager, large bottles of vodka and other spirits. Murphy caught up to the professor as they walked, touching him lightly on the arm. The professor jumped slightly, stopping in the middle of the corridor, looking between the two detectives.

'Sorry professor.' Murphy said. 'I didn't mean to make you jump. I just wanted to ask about the office we just passed.'

'No bother,' Garner said walking on again. 'Just the old heart isn't what it once was. That would be Tom Davies, a lecturer here. He does a lot of work looking at the affects of alcohol in society. He's published some very good work.'

'Really? People drink too much, get drunk . . . what else is there to know?'

'You'd be surprised what we can learn with a bit of initiative' Garner replied, showing those nicotine stained teeth once more. 'Here we are.'

They'd reached the conference room and sat in the same seats as they had the last time they were there, Rossi taking the opportunity to produce the folder containing copies of the letters they'd received up to that point. 'This is the correspondence we've received so far,' she said, placing the letters in order in front of the professor. 'If you could shed some light on them, we'd be grateful.'

Murphy watched as Garner took out a pair of small reading glasses, perching them on the end of his nose. He began reading, occasionally making small noises in the back of his throat. Murphy looked around the room, his eyes settling on a particular piece of artwork which was on the wall behind Garner. A blurred colourful piece, if Murphy squinted his eyes, he thought he could see a face in the pattern. He looked away when the face began to take form.

'Interesting,' Garner said, as he finished reading. 'I have a couple of questions if that's okay?'

'Of course.' Murphy replied, cutting in on Rossi. He was determined to play more of a role this time. 'We'll do our best to answer.'

'Okay. What was the cause of death for each victim?' Garner said.

'First victim – asphyxiation. Second – numerous stab wounds, one to her throat being the fatal one, we think. Third – stab wound to the heart.'

As Murphy spoke, he watched as Garner touched each letter in turn as he listed the causes of death.

'Okay, and each letter was found on the body, yes?'

Murphy nodded in confirmation.

'And was this directly on the body, or in their pockets or something similar?' Garner said, removing his glasses and looking up at Murphy.

'Two in the clothing the victim was wearing,' Murphy replied, attempting to keep his face from betraying any emotion. 'The first one was attached directly to the skin.'

Garner nodded, placing his glasses back on. 'Okay, I will go through each letter and share my initial thoughts. I'm sure you'll have made the same conclusions from them as I have.'

Murphy pulled his chair closer, as he watched Rossi hold her pen steady at her notebook.

'Firstly, the numbering is troublesome. He begins with Experiment Three. Two possibilities arise from this. One, he simply does not want you to discover the first two experiments. They didn't result in death, so are inconsequential. Or, two, they are still ongoing. As they haven't ended, he's not ready to share. Onto the letters. The first letter is his attempt at gaining instant attention. He also wants you to realise his intentions. What's interesting is that he goes straight into talking about the experiment *before* talking about death. It's as if he wants to explain himself to you first, why he's done what he has done. It's his first contact, which makes this important. He's not sure of himself, tentative maybe. So he wants to convey what he is doing straight away. He also talks about how she "wanted to die" and doesn't actually state how he killed her. He's absolving himself of liability for her murder within a few paragraphs. I'd suggest this means this is quite probably his first murder, and he wrote that letter once the adrenaline of committing the act had worn off.'

Garner paused for a moment, allowing Rossi to catch up with her note taking. 'Moving on,' Garner said, his voice unchanged. 'He then goes on to discuss why he's doing what he is doing. He makes grand announcements about death, grief, and how we in society deal with it. He's more confident here. He's been thinking about this for a long time. I'd suggest it is someone who has had to deal with death at a young age, possibly up to late teens. That event may have affected him immeasurably, meaning his view on death is warped.'

'Warped?' Murphy said.

'Yes.' Garner replied. 'I'd say he views death as he says, as something natural. What he wants is for people to see what he's doing the same way. A natural act, for which he shouldn't be punished. To me that suggests, at least in this first letter, that he is still looking to shift blame from himself to society; *we're* forcing him to act in this way. The tone changes with the second letter however. He's more confident now, and violent. That's the difference. He feels more powerful perhaps. He still wants you to know what he's doing; even straight out telling you where to look. It also displays his

248

anger, his quick temper. He killed the girl because she was a nuisance to him. Now it's been just over a week and three murders have occurred. From what little I know about serial murderers, they usually escalate and become more and more violent. Not so here. The third victim in that case should have been maimed in an even worse manner than the second. He spells out the reason . . . control. He needs to be in control of every part of this. Including you Detective Murphy.'

Garner stopped, looking down. 'The third letter seems to be another blame shifting exercise. He discusses other instances of the bystander theory in practice, showing he is not breaking new ground.' Garner shook his head slowly, Murphy surprised to see him become more emotional as his eyes turned filmy as if he were on the brink of tears. 'I'm sorry, this is a little overwhelming. You think you've seen it all . . .'

Murphy looked to Rossi and nodded.

'Do you have tea or coffee around here? I could get us a cup before going on.' Rossi said, placing her notebook down on the table.

'Yes, we have a little kitchen area opposite,' Garner said, indicating the door behind him. 'That would be nice, thank you.'

Rossi left and Garner removed his glasses, rubbing his eyes with the thumb and forefinger of his left hand. Murphy studied him for a few seconds before averting his gaze when he looked up at him. 'You know he's focused on you now Detective?' Garner said.

Murphy sighed, turning his attention back to him. 'Yes, I guessed as much.' Just what he didn't need; becoming even closer to this than he already was.

'He sees in you as something, someone to control. He's using your tragic loss in an attempt to unsettle and destabilise you and the investigation as a whole. It is down to your own level of acceptance of that loss, as to whether it will affect what happens.'

'Unless of course we get lucky and he makes a mistake,' Murphy said with a forced smile.

'I suppose that's usually the case with serial killers.' Garner replied. 'He is an intelligent man however, so don't rely on that too much. He felt himself losing control with the second unfortunate victim, so rectified that with the third victim. He now has someone to fixate on, to test himself against. And I sincerely doubt that you're up to it. You may need to take a step back.'

Murphy dropped the smile, leaned across the table. 'With all respect professor, you have no idea what I need to do. You may be a clever man, but I know how to do my job. So, I appreciate you helping us here, which you are doing, but rest assured I'm up to it.'

Garner sat back in his chair with an exhale of breath. Laced his thin fingers together over his chest. 'Good. I'm glad that's how you feel,' Garner said. 'Your eyes say different.' Murphy attempted to interrupt, but Garner waved him off before carrying on. 'I was a clinical psychologist out in the field before moving into lecturing on the subject. I know something of this kind of thing. More than most, I would say. I counselled many, many people who were dealing with grief. I can see you're not sleeping. I can see this case, as it probably should, is weighing heavily on your shoulders. But I also see how you move, how you react whenever the subject of death is discussed. I also know what happened to you, as many people within the city do, so I know what it is I see when you deign to look me in the eye. I see great loss, grief. And you haven't dealt with it all. Believe me when I say this, talking to someone would be good. I've dealt with grief so often More often than I ever wished to. Everyone reacts differently, but I'm positive bottling things up is not the right path.'

Murphy held Garner's stare, attempting to show strength. 'I dealt with things fine. Let's drop this, okay?'

'I'm simply telling you what I sense as a professional. Feel free to ignore me.' He leaned back, his fingers tapping together. 'Or perhaps, when you're in a less confrontational mood, we could talk more about it.'

Rossi came back in with a tray carrying three cups. 'Made coffee for us all, found milk in the fridge, hope you don't mind. Couldn't find sugar though.'

'That's fine,' Garner said. 'Thank you.'

Rossi placed the cup in front of Garner, walking around to hand Murphy another. They settled back down, an uneasy silence descending on the room.

'You've given us some great information about who the man may be, what he is. Is there anything else you can tell us, professor?' Rossi said.

'Well, please don't misinterpret what I'm saying. I'm not attempting to profile the murderer, that's fool's science. Widely discredited. You will have noticed I haven't given you an age or occupation, because that would be guesswork. What I am merely pointing out is some possibilities behind his compulsions; what is driving him. This links into the psychology part of it, which is perhaps where the interest may lie.'

28

Monday 4th February 2013 – Day Nine
Rob

'What did you want to see me for?'

Rob and Dan were sitting in the pub again, the weather keeping a few of the older blokes away, so they had the place almost to themselves.

'I was arrested on Friday.'

Dan reacted exactly as Rob had expected him to. Quietly, a raised eyebrow only. 'Really.'

'Yes. They think I had something to do with the murders that have been happening around here.'

'Yes. Terrible business. I've started parking the Audi closer to the building. Gets spooky in the evening. I'm guessing their evidence didn't hold up?'

'I'm here aren't I?' replied Rob.

Dan smiled, his thin lips spread wide across his face. 'Yes you are.'

'Well, you're the most intelligent bloke I know. And I need that intelligence,' Rob replied, knowing the best way to get information from Dan was to appeal to his ego. 'I have a few questions about something in your area of expertise.'

Dan smoothed down his shirt. 'Okay, I'm intrigued. What do you need to know?'

'What do you know about Harry Harlow?'

Dan looked at him quizzically, although Rob could see a spark appearing in his eyes. 'The psychologist?'

'Yes.' Rob replied. 'He did something with monkeys I think?'

'Well yes, but so much more. He studied isolation in rhesus monkeys. His most widely known study was on baby monkeys removed from their mothers. There were two groups, both placed in a cage. In one group they were provided with a surrogate model made of wire, which gave food, and a separate surrogate made of cloth which gave comfort. In the other group, the roles were reversed. Harlow found the monkeys would cling to the cloth model, whether or not it provided food. Thus showing comfort over sustenance is of importance to newborns.'

Rob was nodding along, not really following what Dan was saying. He had read this last night, yet it still didn't make sense. What he was really interested was his other experiments. 'What else did he do?' Rob said, taking a swig of his pint.

'Well, perhaps his most infamous work,' Dan replied, leaning forward and lowering his voice, 'was in social isolation and depression. He would isolate monkeys for up to twelve months in what he called the Well of Despair. Deprived them of social interaction completely. The results can be guessed at; shock, blank staring, self harm. After being isolated for a year, the monkeys would barely move. When you look back at it now, it's staggering to think they could get away with that kind of thing. It's completely unethical now and it was widely criticised even back then.'

'What do you think would happen to someone if they were in that position?'

Dan studied him, that spark in his eyes still there. 'A human?'

'Yes.' Rob couldn't meet his eyes, afraid of what questions he might ask.

'Well, you're probably looking at similar results. The only difference really is the monkeys used by Harlow were infants. If you took an adult with a full history of social interaction, there's a chance they could recover. I'd imagine they'd show signs of a major depressive episode, something which wouldn't be an easy thing to get over. It's not something anyone could guess at, though. Why are you asking me about this Rob?'

Rob finished off his pint, looked around at the bar. 'Food's taking its time.'

'You're stalling. What's going on?'

Rob sighed heavily. 'I'm just following a trail is all.'

Dan sat back in his chair, 'Wait, you think this is what's happened to Jemma?'

'No.' Rob replied. 'Well, maybe. I don't know Dan.'

'It's pretty outlandish mate. How did you get to this?'

Rob didn't know how to answer without revealing too much. Jemma was in enough danger as it was without him adding to it. 'At this point I'm willing to consider anything.'

'Well, forgive me for this Rob, but don't you think it's getting to be too much?'

'What do you mean?' Rob replied, biting the inside of his lip.

'It's just that you've been running round the country on fool's errands to no avail, now you're talking about Jemma being part of some crazy experiment. I implore you to think of other options.'

Rob was drinking, but stopped and slammed his glass down on the table, the beer in the glass sloshing upwards. 'What other options do I have Dan? I've lost the house, the car. Her mum and friends think she's gone off for a nice fucking holiday, or failing that, that I killed her.'

'You can let me help.'

Rob turned away. 'You can't help me Dan.'

'Yes I can Rob. More than you realise.'

'What do you mean?'

Dan leaned over the table. 'I don't know if you've noticed Rob, but I'm a very wealthy man. Why not let me hire someone? There are people who can help in these matters.'

Rob snorted, looking at the ceiling. 'A private detective you mean? I can't imagine there's an abundance of them in Liverpool mate.'

'I was thinking more of a high-ranking defence lawyer, given recent events, but yes, a private detective may be a better idea. I bet I could find one. A good one as well. I don't mind paying at all, if it'll stop you running around like a headless chicken on silly adventures, getting yourself into trouble.'

Rob dropped his head to look at Dan, who was leaning across the table with a look of pity on his face. 'I don't need charity Dan.'

'It's not charity Rob,' Dan replied haughtily. 'It's a man helping his friend when he's in trouble. Recognise that.'

'I don't even know if I could pay you back any time soon . . .'

'Don't worry about that,' Dan interrupted. 'It's not as if I'd miss it.'

'I don't know Dan. I'm not used to this type of thing.'

'I understand Rob.' Dan said leaning back in his chair. 'So take advantage. You wouldn't allow me to intervene with the house or car. Allow me to help with this.'

Rob thought on it. He was worried about screwing everything up, allowing someone to start poking their nose in. But if he turned down the help, it looked odd, as if he wasn't determined to find her.

'I'll think about it. Give me a day,' Rob said, finally. Not saying yes, not saying no. Safest bet at that moment.

'Very good,' Dan replied, turning as the food was brought to the table by the barmaid. 'And excellent timing my lovely.'

Dan studied him as Rob accepted the plate, causing Rob to avert his gaze, knowing there were further questions Dan wanted to ask. He stayed silent, and internally breathed a sigh of relief as Dan started eating.

He didn't think he would have held out much longer before spilling everything, hoping for an easy answer. Truth was, Rob knew there was no easy answers. He just had to wait.

29

Monday 4th February 2013 – Day Nine

Murphy sipped from his cup of dank tasting coffee, as they waited for Garner to talk further. The warmth from the cup was helping to override the cold feeling he'd had since the professor had begun speaking.

'These experiments all have one thing in common . . . ethics. Or rather, a possible lack of them.' Garner continued, once he'd taken a sip of his drink.

'Ethics? He's killing people, there's no possible about it.' Murphy said, placing his cup down on the table.

'You misunderstand me Detective,' Garner replied, turning his gaze back to him. 'I'm talking solely about the experiments he is supposedly replicating. They are an almost Psych 101 entry into ethics in psychology.'

'How so?' Rossi said from the right of Murphy, her drink forgotten as she sat poised with her pen.

'Well, let's take it from the beginning with MK Ultra, in particular, the specific experiment he talks about doing, Operation Midnight Climax, using LSD on the poor girl before killing her. One of the most important aspects of ethical treatment of participants is to not do anything which may harm them, unless of course the benefit is outweighed by the cost. That they consent to being involved in any research, and have the opportunity to withdraw at any time.'

'And the people involved in that research were not aware they were being experimented on, were they?' Murphy said.

'That's correct,' Garner replied. 'Which means they didn't consent to it. Something which categorises most experiments talked about when discussing unethical research. Similarly, the Unit 731 experiments were carried out on prisoners. However, without knowing which experiment in particular he was planning to carry out on your second victim, it's difficult to say for certain what ethics were involved.

'The third experiment, the unfortunate man left near the Albert Dock, isn't what I'd call an unethical experiment. It's more a theory than an experiment. I guess you could say he was revealing more about society's lack of ethical responsibility with that one. That's a hypothesis however. The letter begins with a whole monologue about grief. The experiment, such as it is, is secondary.'

'You think he's not interested in psychology experiments anymore?' Murphy said, feeling a dark cloud form above them, as he began to understand where the conversation was leading towards.

'No. I think it started that way, but now it's just about one thing . . . death. The experiments are all about death, he's fascinated by it. This is his way of investigating it further.'

'Do you think he's killed more, outside of what we know about?'

'It wouldn't surprise me if he has. But I think those were for him alone. They didn't form part of the controlled actions he's presented to you.'

'So, there could be more. Jesus . . .' Murphy swept a hand over his face as the worries he'd had over the past few days were voiced by someone else.

'He's not been scared to reveal victims so far though, why wouldn't he announce others?' Rossi said.

'It goes back to control.'

Murphy swore under his breath, 'Sorry professor. If he has killed others we don't know about, these would be prior to these three. Why is he announcing *these* victims?'

'He isn't finished, perhaps?' Garner replied, taking a sip of his coffee. 'He talks about a grand gesture in the third letter, which suggests he's been working on something from the beginning. Which would lend weight to it being another experiment. I mean, you haven't been made aware of experiments one and two at the moment. He's only allowing you to see what he wants you to.'

There was a knock at the door, their three heads swivelling as it opened. The spiky haired man Murphy had spied as they passed his office in the corridor stepped into the room apologetically. 'Sorry to interrupt professor,' the man said. 'Dan said you were in here. Just wanted to remind you of the seminar you have at two o'clock.'

'Ah, yes. Thank you Tom. Detectives, this is Tom, one of the senior lecturers at the university. He's doing some incredible research at the moment, as I said earlier. Very interesting.'

Murphy looked over. 'We won't keep him much longer Tom.' Murphy said.

'Not to worry,' Tom replied, looking only at Murphy. 'I'll leave you to it.'

He left the room, Garner turning back around to face Murphy and Rossi. 'Sorry about that, he's an eager one him, very intelligent though. He'll go very far.'

'Where were we?' Murphy asked, hoping to get back on course.

'I believe I was trying to guess at his actions now. And that's important, this is all guesswork.'

'I think you're underestimating yourself professor,' Rossi

said, smiling. 'You're giving us much more information than we've had previously.'

Murphy caught Rossi's eye, hoping to tell her to shut up. He didn't enjoy hearing how little they knew about so many murders occurring under his watch.

'I doubt that,' Garner replied, Murphy aware of his watchful eyes. 'I imagine I'm only giving you information you already know, or what you will have guessed. I think there *is* something I can give you, however.'

'What's that?' Murphy said.

'What I think he's doing now, what he is leading you towards.'

Murphy felt his mood darken as the professor leant forward. 'Go on,' Murphy said.

'I believe there is an experiment he has been carrying out from the beginning. It'll have more in common with his original experimental aims. Yet, it will be much bigger, much more hard hitting. What it is in particular, I couldn't say. Everything I've read here though suggests he won't stop until he's ready to unveil what it is. So I wish you luck detectives.' Garner held Murphy's stare. 'And you, Detective Murphy. Take care of yourself. I have a feeling you're a part of this now. I hope you don't also become a target.'

'He has a point Bear. You're involved in this now, you have to face up to that.'

Murphy was sitting on his sofa at home, the remnants of a Chinese takeaway congealing on the coffee table in front of him. Jess was standing at the back door, shouting through to him from the kitchen as she smoked. Murphy began picking up the cartons, placing them back in the carrier bag they'd been delivered in. 'I don't have to face anything Jess. Of course I'm involved in it – I'm the one trying to catch the bastard.'

'Yeah, but he's made this much more personal than you're

260

used to. You have to think about what that means,' Jess continued, turning as Murphy entered the kitchen.

Murphy's face darkened as he remembered what the letter said. Being reminded about his parents' murder wasn't something he relished, especially from someone who was currently the city's most wanted. 'I'm okay about it. Really. I'm enjoying being back in the driving seat, honest. And Laura is coming on leaps and bounds,' Murphy replied, trying on a smile, before deciding it didn't lighten the situation.

'That's good and all, but it doesn't change the fact this nutter has zeroed in on you.'

'I know that Jess,' Murphy said, jamming the bag of rubbish in the bin. 'But I'm not going to let him get to me.'

'You mean he hasn't already?'

'What's that supposed to mean?' Murphy replied, his voice rising slightly. 'I'm not doing anything differently than I have before.'

'I know you, Bear,' Jess said, squatting down to stub her cigarette out on the back step, before turning around and closing the back door behind her. 'You're not the same. Which, as I've said continually, is not exactly fucking surprising.'

'I need this Jess. I need to be sitting across from this bastard in an interview room, explaining how he'll be spending the rest of his pitiful little life in a cell.'

'I get that. I do. But what if that's not how it plays out? What if he tops himself first, or you don't find him. What then?'

'That's not going to happen,' Murphy said, turning away from her and walking into the living room. He heard Jess running the tap in the sink, filling a glass.

'What does Laura think?' Jess said, entering the room holding the glass of water. Murphy sat on the sofa, waiting for her to return to the chair closest to the radiator – her favoured position when she visited. She was always cold, he thought. He'd never seen her wear anything with sleeves outside of work however. He'd bought her a jumper for Christmas a couple of years back, and she'd asked if he kept the receipt. False economy he thought.

'She thinks our best bet is to release more details to the press. I'm not in agreement on that though. The last thing we need to do is have them more on our backs than they already are.'

'You're not exactly getting anywhere fast at the moment though are you?'

'No,' Murphy said with a sigh. 'But we're not exactly overcome with options here. This guy is so careful, he keeps these people for days, so we have no idea how the circumstances of them being taken happens. We have nothing to go on evidence wise, forensics have turned up nothing. We're up shit creek without a fucking boat, never mind a paddle. So we do leg work. We interview more people, we do more media asking for people to come forward. And end up with nothing in return, most probably.'

Murphy sat back, rubbing his eyes with the palms of his hands, his headache starting to get worse. 'Worst of all, I've got to deal with Sarah suddenly calling me at work, calling my friends.' Murphy said, gesturing towards Jess. 'It's the last thing I need.'

Jess stood, joining Murphy on the sofa. He turned to look at her.

'She has things to say. Yeah, it might not be the best time, but maybe you should listen to her.'

'Why should I, Jess?'

'Because it wasn't her fault.' Jess replied, her hand draped on one of his shoulders.

'If we hadn't . . .'

'Like that mattered,' Jess interrupted. 'You did, that's all there is to it. Yes it turned into a fucked-up situation, but that wasn't her fault. More importantly, it wasn't your fault.'

262

'I know.'

'You don't, not yet. But you will. I just worry that's all.' Jess said, 'How long have we known each other?'

'Whenever I ask you that, all you say is too fucking long,' Murphy said, finding it easier to smile at that. 'Almost twenty years, that's how long.'

Jess smiled back at him. 'Jesus, we're getting old. Well, you are anyway.'

'Piss off.'

'Love you too.' Jess said, standing up. 'I best be getting off. Peter will be wondering where I am.'

'Of course.' Murphy replied, standing up to show her out.

As Jess got to the door, she turned and hugged Murphy, wrapping her arms tightly around his shoulders. 'Take care of yourself, Bear. Don't do anything stupid. I don't like many people, but you're all right,' she said.

'I will and I won't.' Murphy said, patting her on the back. He watched her drive off, shutting the door behind him after she'd pulled out of the cul de sac. Cold air had entered the house, causing him to shiver as he walked back in. He locked the front door, the outside world now shut firmly behind him. He went back into the living room, pulling out the photo album he kept at the side of the couch, out of sight.

Leafed through the pages. The happiest day of his life.

The day he married Sarah. He picked up his phone, scrolled through to her number, then hesitated.

His finger hovered over the call button for a few seconds, before he threw the phone to one side.

Not tonight.

30

Monday 4th February 2013 – Day Nine
Rob

They'd left the pub in silence. Rob's mind elsewhere, his heart racing, as the appearance of the detectives who'd questioned him that weekend, just walking past the pub, causing instant panic. Dark clouds formed slowly overhead, the sky blackening around him. He entered the psychology building, Dan giving him a pat on the shoulder as he walked away in the opposite direction.

He cried off work early, but with no intentions of actually going home. He pulled his coat a little tighter, putting his head down against the driving rain as he walked the ten minutes towards town and Liverpool Central train station. It was downhill all the way, the pavements busy with students of various fashion tastes. Skinny jeans and tight, revealing shirts . . . and that was just the lads. He waited only a few minutes for a train, a cold breeze blowing through the underground platform. It was becoming busier, the shift workers filling the space.

An hour later, with the rain pelting down, he stood outside a terraced house in a quiet street. A hanging basket of dead flowers hung outside. He rang the doorbell and stepped back, waiting for the door to open.

'Hello Rob,' Jemma's mum said as she stepped into the doorway, arms folded. 'What are you doing here?'

'I just wanted to talk, Helen,' Rob replied, wiping rain off his forehead. 'Nothing else.'

Helen stared at him for a few seconds before shaking her head slightly and stepping to one side, letting him into the house.

'Wait there, I'll get you a towel,' she said, closing the door behind her and stepping past him. Rob stood in the hallway, watching as she walked up the stairs. He looked around for anything that may have changed. The same photos adorned the walls, Jemma as a baby, her brother coming later when she was a few years older. Same wallpaper on the walls, same everything. He didn't know what he was expecting, it being only been six months since he'd last been there. Rob just expected there to have been changes here, as there had been in his own life.

'Here you are, dry yourself off a bit.' Helen handed him the towel as she came back down. 'Take your shoes off as well. Remember the rules.'

Rob nodded, *rain outside – shoes off inside.* He slipped his shoes off and removed his coat, placing it on the banister as Helen walked through to the kitchen. He followed, sneaking a peek into the darkened living room. No change there either, from what he could see.

'I've put the kettle on,' Helen said, sitting on a stool at the breakfast bar. The kitchen was larger than most in the area, Helen's ex-husband having built an extension a few years before. Every appliance was stainless steel, and expensive. Helen had remortgaged a year or so before, when the ex-husband left. Rob had tried to talk Jemma into talking to her mother about that, put her off doing it, but Jemma wouldn't hear of it. She was happy to see her mum doing something for herself for once.

'Thanks,' Rob said, sitting down opposite her. 'I won't keep you long.'

'That's okay. You seem calm for now. You start shouting and you're out though. Okay?' Helen locked eyes with Rob, daring him to disagree. He turned away in embarrassment, nodding his head. 'Good,' Helen continued. 'I'm not having that in this house again.'

An uneasy silence fell, broken only by the water in the kettle bubbling up to a boil. Helen stood up and made tea, placing the cup down in front of Rob.

'Why are you here, Rob?' Helen asked, sitting back down.

'It's been a while. I thought I'd check in.'

'Well, it's all the same here,' Helen said, her fingers lightly tapping the breakfast bar surface. 'I've not heard from her. If that's what you're thinking.'

'I know. You would have told me if she had done.' Rob looked up at her, hoping to see agreement on that point. Helen averted her eyes. The ticking clock reminding him of the last time they'd spoken in a kitchen. A very different time.

It had been a few months or so after Jemma had disappeared. He'd been a frequent visitor to Helen's house, growing more and more annoyed about her lack of concern.

Then she did become worried.

Rob knew things had changed. Helen looked at him with different eyes. They screamed suspicion at him.

One day she had flat out asked him if he had anything to do with Jemma going missing. Turns out Helen had heard about the ex. The one who had accused Rob of hitting her and then moving from the area when her lies had become known.

He still got the odd letter from her. Evil rants about him.

266

Drunken ramblings from a bar in a Spanish resort she'd always talked about wanting to move to, he guessed.

When Jemma disappeared, he assumed the same thing had happened. That he'd driven another one away.

At first.

Helen hadn't listened to him when he explained about the ex. It ended with them screaming at each other in the kitchen and Rob storming out.

'Yes, I imagine so,' Helen said, checking the time.

'Good. So you've heard nothing?' Rob asked.

'No,' Helen replied, sighing. 'Nothing at all.'

'Have the police been in touch?'

Helen stopped tapping her fingers, bunching her hands together. 'Nothing. She's over eighteen so they've just stuck her on some list. They don't care really. Her history . . .' She waved her hands instead of finishing the sentence.

Rob shifted on his seat. 'I'm sure they've looked as best as they can.'

Helen nodded, took a hankie out of her sleeve and dried her eyes. 'I just want my baby girl back. She wouldn't just go like this. Not for this long. I need to say something to you. I've been wanting to get this off my chest for a long time.'

Rob braced himself, bit on his bottom lip and didn't say anything.

'I never really thought you did anything Rob. People were saying things, how it's always the partner, that sort of thing. I should have thought more about it. You would never have harmed her.'

Rob felt a knot form at the back of his throat. 'Thank you.' He was aching to tell Helen of what little he knew. He didn't want to be there, he realised at that point. He couldn't work out what he'd expected to find. He wanted to say

267

something, but was afraid. He couldn't jeopardise what little hope he had.

'I think I may have a lead,' Rob said, treading carefully. 'Dan, my friend from work, he's helped me out a bit. We may be onto something.' He found the lies coming easily. Half truths, better than nothing. 'I just thought I'd let you know.' He picked up the cup, drinking a little.

'What is this new lead?' Helen asked, leaning forward earnestly.

'I'm not totally sure yet.' Rob replied. 'It may be dangerous though.' He realised why he'd gone there now. He was scared of what was happening to Jemma, scared of what might happen to him. He wanted to say much more, but didn't want to burden Helen. He wanted someone to know what he was about to do, but without putting them in any kind of danger. 'I just wanted to let you know, in case you had changed your mind. About me, I mean.'

Helen looked at him questioningly. 'What's this about, Rob?' she asked.

'I can't really say. But I'll let you know the second I hear anything.'

Helen kept staring at him, making him shift uneasily as he tried to keep the guilt off his face. After a moment or three, she shrugged and drank her tea. She sat the cup back down, appearing to have made a decision. 'Okay, I'm not totally sure of what you're doing Rob, but I won't ask any more. I just have one thing to say.'

'Okay,' Rob replied. 'What is it?'

'If she's not in any danger, I want you to leave her alone. I don't care if you can't accept that you two were over to her, I want you to promise me that. If she's making a new life for herself, then let her be. I can accept that, as long as I know she's safe. I want you to do the same.'

Rob digested what she'd said, knowing almost certainly

it wasn't a promise he would have to keep. 'Okay, I promise,' he said without hesitation.

'And if she's in trouble.' Helen continued. 'You bring her back to me. To us all.'

Rob didn't have to worry about that one. 'I promise.'

He left shortly after, nothing further to say. The rain had eased off as he shoved his hands in his pockets and trudged towards the station again. As he got closer, his phone began ringing in his inside pocket. He opened his coat slightly to retrieve it, his heart beginning to quicken as he noticed the Unknown Caller sign on the screen.

'Hello.'

'Robert. How are we, this fine night?'

The voice was distorted again, the tone changing every other word. Rob felt his other hand forming into a fist. 'What do you want? Where are you?'

'Not important,' the voice answered. 'I just wanted to make sure you were keeping to your side of the bargain. You haven't told anyone of our little chats have you?'

Rob bit down on his lip. 'Of course not.'

'I'm glad to hear that. Now, I'd like you to keep tomorrow free, if you would. I think you'll need to be totally alert for the day.'

'What do you mean?'

A low chuckle came through the phone, the voice changing from a low-pitched guttural sound to a high-pitched laugh, sending shivers down Rob's spine. 'Let's just say, it's finally coming to an end for you Rob. It'll all be over soon. I'm sure you'll be happy to hear that.'

'Let's do this now then. Why wait? Tell me where you are.' The phone was already dead; Rob stood talking to himself. He looked around, hoping to see the car he'd seen near the Albert Dock again, but the street was quiet.

'Fuck!' Rob shouted out, feeling desolate. He wasn't the one in control, he never had been. He was following orders, and that meant waiting. If he wanted to see Jemma again, he'd have to do as he was told.

No matter what.

31

Tuesday 5th February 2013 – Day Ten

He's dreaming, he knows that. He can understand the unreality of it all, the broken images, the distorted scenery, the blurriness of his surroundings.

It feels real. The anxious, nausea inducing feeling in the pit of his stomach is real. Even in its dream state.

He's entering his parents' house again, the silence overpowering him once more. There's something else though, a different quality to it. He moves towards the kitchen, finding it empty, before turning back to the living room. He can't t open the door. It's jammed shut. He uses his bulk, throwing his shoulder at the door. His movements are in slow motion as he feels no give to the door. He steps back, examining the door again.

It opened outwards independently as he stands there. He can see his parents, the same as always. The words on the wall aren't there yet.

Now he knows what that difference is. The silence, not as silent as usual.

It's because he's not alone.

The man is still there. Standing in the centre of the room. The man is breathing heavily, tired from the exertion.

He stands in the doorway, looking directly at the man.

He can't move, yet he wants to. He can feel the anger coursing through him, wanting so much to cross that room in two long strides and pick the man up by his puny little tattooed neck. Watch the last flicker of life leave his eyes. Yet, he can't move. His legs stuck in the same position. He looks down at them, willing them to move, but they won't comply. He bunches his fists, banging them against his thighs.

Then, he's not himself any longer. He's someone else. He's three and half feet shorter, no longer towering over the man as before. . He turns his hands over, staring at the hairless small stubby appendages. And he's scared. He's shaking, and can't move his legs. He can't run away, he can't hide.

He raises his head, slowly, afraid of what he'll see.

The man is using his fingers to write on the wall, stopping every few seconds to procure more blood from the open neck wound on Murphy's father. He's whistling as he goes about his work. Happy, smiling.

And Murphy can't do anything but stand there and watch, as the man uses his father's blood to send a message to him. To make sure he knows who is to blame.

The man finishes, his white t-shirt now drenched in splashes of blood. He stands back and admires his creation.

And he begins to laugh, quietly at first. Then more louder, a crescendo of laughter erupting from him. He whispers, his voice slurred.

'You can't save them.'

There's another noise.

Bang.

The man turns, the laughter subsiding, changing to a sadistic grin.

Bang.

He looks down at the carving knife in his hand, and moves purposefully towards Murphy.

Bang. Bang. Bang.

Murphy woke up slowly, breathing rapidly as the vision of his dream followed him to full consciousness. The noise was there too. It took a few seconds for Murphy to realise the noise was real.

He stepped out of bed and walked over to the window, closing it over where it had slipped its latch. He ran a hand over his face and checked the time. Four in the morning. Just a few hours sleep then. Great.

There was no point in going back to bed, so he slipped on some jogging bottoms and padded down the stairs.

He slumped onto the sofa, moved the photograph album back to beside the couch. He pulled the throw which adorned the back of the couch around his bare shoulders.

He stared through the television, thinking, going over and over in his head what he thought he might have missed.

Ten days, three bodies.

There was something there, on the fringes of his conscious, waiting to be discovered. The answer – how to stop all of this. But every time he tried to access that information, it would merge with everything else.

He thought about ringing Sarah.

He stayed there until the sun began to rise, failing to think of anything other than the images of death which replayed over and over in his head.

32

Tuesday 5th February 2013 – Day Ten
Rob

Rob dialled and waited, picking at a loose thread on his shirt.

'Hi Liz, it's Rob.'

'Hi Rob,' Liz replied, sounding resigned. 'I'm guessing you're not coming in?'

'Think I'm coming down with something. Like you said yesterday, you know?'

Rob heard a sigh over the line. 'Okay. Do you think you'll be back tomorrow? Only it's coming up to a deadline for first years, and you know how busy we get.'

'I'll do my best Liz. I'm sorry for leaving you in the lurch.'

'It's okay I suppose. Just rest up today. Get some Lemsip or something down you. And get your arse in tomorrow.'

Rob smiled. 'Okay boss. Speak to you later.'

Rob stared at the phone, feeling guilty for lying to Liz. He could have told her everything and not worried about her saying a word to anyone, but he couldn't put her in that position.

It was coming up to eight-thirty a.m. and he was at a loss at what to do. He had no choice but to wait. He smoked, watched TV, researched what being on bail meant on the internet. It was strange to think he was suddenly a 'person of interest'. The past year, no one had been interested in him.

He busied himself tidying up after the police search. Papers had been strewn around, cupboards emptied and not refilled. It took up an hour or two.

He made notes. About Harlow, and what he had learned. Jemma, kept away from normal existence, like she was a lab rat.

Rob could kill him. He had no doubt about that. Grab him by the throat and squeeze until his eyeballs popped out.

He phoned Dan, just to hear a friendly voice, but only spoke to him for a few minutes as he was off to a lecture.

By the afternoon, he was pacing the living room. A stupid American sitcom which had already been shown that day on the same channel, was playing in the background, but Rob barely noticed it. He wrung his hands together and stopped pacing when he reached the window, once more sweeping back the net curtains to look outside. Traffic greeted him from the road, but no mysterious figures. Watching him, waiting.

'Ring, you fucker. Ring,' Rob said, his voice raised over the sound of the television. His tension had grown throughout the day, as he felt it slip away with no contact.

He slumped down on the sofa. Useless. That's what he was . . . useless. The canned laughter from the TV mocked him. He tried watching but couldn't even keep up with the simple storyline being played out.

Just over an hour later his phone started ringing.

'Hello Rob.'

'What took so long?'

'I'm sorry, have you been waiting?'

'Yes. You know I have.' Rob stood up, wanting to say much more but holding back. 'What happens now?'

'No small talk? No, how has your day been or anything?'

Rob gritted his teeth, his grip on the phone tightening. 'Just tell me what I need to do.'

'Very well, I can imagine this is a stressful time for you. Newsham Park. One a.m. tonight. There's a duck pond with a bench, near the top right corner if you face it with the hospital to your back. Do you know it?'

'Yeah.'

'Good. Wait there. As before, come alone. The first sense I receive that you're not, she dies without you even knowing about it. The first sense I receive that you have told anyone, the same.'

'Wait, let's do it sooner. I've been waiting here all day. I'm ready.'

The line went silent. 'Bastard!' Rob threw the phone at the sofa, looking around the room for something to take out his anger on. He was panting, his fists balled up. He closed his eyes. He pictured Jemma in his head, the thought of her coming home, lying in bed next to her. He opened his eyes again, feeling calmer. He retrieved his phone, making sure he hadn't damaged it, before walking through to the kitchen to smoke. He looked at the clock on the wall, nine hours to wait.

'You can do this.'

Rob walked slowly around the lake for the seventh time since he'd arrived at the park. He'd got there early, waiting around for whatever was to come. He checked his phone again; five minutes to one a.m. He completed the final circuit, and sat down on the bench.

Rob looked up towards the sky. It was a clear night in the park, and even with the light pollution from the surrounding houses, he could see stars twinkling in the sky. He didn't know any of the constellations, or names for the stars which seemed to be bunched together. It was calm, a serene sight. Any other night, he would have felt at peace there. That night however, he was on edge, anticipation running through his veins.

He watched as the time clicked over to one a.m. without fanfare.

The phone rang a minute later, surprising Rob from his star gazing. He quickly answered it, putting the phone to his ear.

'You're here. How delightful. And alone again, a trusting sort aren't you?' The voice held the same quality as the other calls, the voice raising up and down with changing pitch. Rob wouldn't have been able to place that voice in a line-up.

'I'm here. What happens now?' Rob asked.

'Stand up.'

Rob stood carefully, looking around as he did so. 'Okay, I'm standing.'

'Now walk towards the exit, on Newsham Drive. I'll call you back when you reach it.'

The phone went dead, and Rob began walking quickly. It took a minute or two to reach the still pond to his to his left. He slowed down, wary of what hid in the shadows. He listened carefully, but heard only his footsteps on the path. The exit was closer, the road beyond it was quiet. He looked towards the road, but couldn't see clearly enough through the high railings to glimpse anything.

He reached the exit to the park, and stood six foot away from the permanently open gates. He was still holding his phone in his right hand as it vibrated.

'Good. That's very good.' The voice was quieter, as if he was whispering.

'I'm here.' Rob replied. 'Are you going to tell me where Jemma is?'

'All in good time.' The voice came through. 'Stay there and don't move.'

Rob stared at the phone, as once more the line went dead. He shivered a little, as the hairs on the back of his neck stood on end. It was quiet, the road empty of passing traffic. To his left he heard a noise, the bushes moving slightly. He turned towards the noise, preparing himself, but there was nothing there he could see.

He heard a rush of footsteps behind him, and then there was a blinding pain as something hit him in the back of the head. Then he was falling, the world going full black.

He came to with a sound he couldn't place. He was moving around, but was still groggy. He remembered what happened slowly, the pain in his head a reminder. He tried to move his hands to rub against the pain, but couldn't.

He was tied up, and from what he could see he guessed he was in the boot of a car, the small cramped space meaning he was lying in the foetal position, his hands palms together as if he was praying. The ties holding them wouldn't buckle.

This wasn't what was supposed to happen. He thought he had more time, to become strong again. He'd only had a few days.

Not enough time.

The car came to a stop some time later, the sound of tarmac covered roads having changed to gravel moments before. He heard the sound of something mechanical, guessing it was a garage door. He braced himself, waiting for the moment the boot opened, determined to surprise whoever had brought him there, not to go down without a fight. He couldn't move his arms, but his legs were free.

The car moved forward once more, coming to a stop after only a few seconds. He heard the car door open, footsteps echoing through the enclosed space. He turned as much as

278

he could, so his feet were facing the back of the car, ready to kick out as soon as he had the chance. The boot opened, bright light momentarily causing Rob to close his eyes. He opened them as soon as he could and noticed the space above him was empty. He blinked against the harsh light after the time spent in darkness, and waited, the only sound being his breath coming in short bursts.

His vision went dark, yet his eyes were open. The figure in front of him, dressed all in black, hood covering his face completely, blocking out the light. Rob got ready, but stopped when he saw what was being pointed at him.

The figure raised the hand that wasn't holding a sawn-off shotgun up to his mouth, and the distorted voice came back.

'You'd be dead before you even reached me,' the figure said. 'Lift yourself out of there. Slowly.'

Rob didn't think he could move; paralysed, fear crawling around his skin. His eyes never left the gun as he slid his legs out of the boot of the car. He stood up slowly, as the figure in black backed away, beckoning towards a door to the left corner of what Rob determined was a garage. He moved slowly, looking down at his cable-tied hands in front of him. He reached the door and turned towards the man who was standing behind him. He indicated with the shotgun to open it, but Rob held up his tied hands. 'How am I supposed to do that?'

The man moved quickly, pushing Rob through the door, causing him to almost lose his balance. The room beyond the door was dark, and Rob stiffened as he felt a barrel pushed into his back. He allowed himself to be guided along, his eyes becoming accustomed to the dark seeing a door in front of him. The voice came out of it. 'It will open.'

Rob pushed against the door, using his tied hands. There was a little more light there, small pale spots of illumination coming from the ceiling. He could see steps leading downwards in front of him, and feeling that now familiar weight pushing at his back, he headed down the steps.

He was led into a small recess, a door on each side. The one on the left of Rob was open, and it was that one he was pushed into. That time, he did lose his balance, falling to the floor. As he turned around, trying to get to his feet quickly, the door closed.

He rose to his feet. 'What's going on? Where's Jemma?' Rob said, his voice loud in the small space.

He stood in the darkness, the silence overbearing. He ran his hands over one wall, pacing out to the opposite side.

Realisation creeping over him all the time.

'This is where she was held, isn't it?'

No answer came.

PART THREE

There's nothing bad about it at all except the thing that comes before it . . . the fear of it.

Seneca

It is the great unknowable. One of the last mysteries of the common man. Whilst science still searches for new questions and new solutions for many different things, it still cannot ever answer the one question which plagues us all.

Religion tries to provide an answer, yet even the most pious of believers still does not know for certain what lays beyond life.

No one can ever tell us what the experience of dying is. How it feels, how it affects you. The experience is beyond explanation. No amount of experimentation can answer the unanswerable.

However, this will not end the questions. Man cannot comprehend something over which we have no control.

We are faced with a choice. Do we continue with our present set of ethical guidelines which forbids most forms of experimentation which could perhaps increase our understanding, or do we go back, to when the Harlows and Milgrams of the psychology world were performing incredible work which told us so much.

In one way, we will all receive the answers we require. It is just presently impossible to acquire that knowledge whilst still alive.

Taken from 'Life, Death, and Grief.' Published in Psychological Society Review, 2008, Issue 72.

33

Tuesday 5th February 2013 – Day Ten

Murphy arrived at the station early, the team who had been working overnight unable to give him any good news. He sat at his desk and pulled up the list of university employees that had been singled out for attention. Nothing stood out really, just a couple of cautions, a few speeding fines, and some drunk and disorderlys. No violent behaviour, no bright, flashing siren saying 'this is the murderer!'. No easy way out.

Another press conference was scheduled for that morning. He looked down at the suit he was wearing. Licked a finger and rubbed off a bit of mayo that had stained the lapel.

DCI Stephens breezed into the room, heading straight towards her office with only a pause to beckon Murphy to follow her. He chucked the pen he'd been holding on the desk and stood up.

The door was shut five seconds before he reached it. Couldn't leave it open could she . . . He knocked on the door and waited.

'Come in,' he heard from behind the door.

Murphy entered and closed the door behind him. 'Ah, David, sit down.'

He sat opposite her and tried to find a comfortable position on the small chair Stephens provided for her guests.

'Did you want to see me?' Murphy said.

'Yes. I need to know you're going to be okay this time, with the press.'

'Of course I am . . .'

'Wait, let me finish.' DCI Stephens interrupted. 'This case has already made us look like fools. We're getting desperate now, the super wants my head on a platter next to the salmon sandwiches at the next gala dinner. If we have a repeat of what happened last time we went in front of press, we're all screwed. What I need is your head clear and focussed.'

'I understand,' Murphy said. 'I'm okay, I can do this.'

'Very well,' Stephens replied. 'Inform me of any significant developments.'

'Thank you,' Murphy said, rising from the chair. 'I assume you'll be giving the same speech to everyone else on the team?' Sarcasm, that'll work, Murphy thought. Stupid.

Stephens sighed. 'You know why I'm saying this to you. Given what's happened in your personal life recently. I've made arrangements for you to see someone in the past and you've not turned up. You're good at your job but you need to talk things over with someone. Don't become a cliché. I think it'd be best for all concerned if you didn't keep things bottled up.'

Murphy leaned over the desk, his size looming over the DCI. 'Are you unhappy with my work?'

'No,' Stephens said. 'You've done well of late, but they weren't murder cases. You changed when this started. I just wanted you to be aware of your responsibilities, that's all.'

'I'm very aware of my *responsibilities*.' Murphy said, backing away from the desk. 'You have nothing to worry about.'

284

'Good. That's all I need to hear. So you'll keep the next appointment?'

'Of course, if that'll make you happy. Just send the details my way.'

'Very good. That'll be all David.'

Murphy gave DCI Stephens one last look, and then turned and left the room. He tried to shake off the anger he could feel building inside him. The noise of the room began to gently build to his ears, as he calmed himself. It wouldn't do to let his emotions take over now.

'Again, we'd urge anyone with any information to come forward, especially anyone who was in the Albert Dock area on Friday night between two and five a.m. I'm going to hand over to Nathan Dunning, the husband of the second victim, Stephanie.'

Murphy stared out into the crowd of reporters as Nathan Dunning spoke. Nathan held it together for a solid minute, before the tears started. Murphy almost rolled his eyes, but thought better of it.

He couldn't stand it. The nakedness of it. Baring their entire being for people to chew over and make fun of. He knew, right then, there'd be someone sitting in front of their TV saying the husband did it. He'd been one of them at first, but it had been quickly dismissed when it was discovered he had an alibi for each of the murders.

Nathan finished with a choked plea for help, before he had to stop. Flashes illuminated the podium, the shutter clicks fighting against his sobs to fill the silence. Murphy leaned forward. 'Stephanie Dunning leaves behind two sons. Anyone with any information should come forward now.'

He stopped, hoping that would be it, that he could get out of there without anything happening. No more videos showing up showing him shouting at idiot journalists.

'We'll take a few questions.' Stephens said from beside Murphy.

Damn.

The first few went well. Just questions about the investigation which were easily answered. Stephens did most of the talking. Murphy sought out the podgy local journo, finding him quickly, his smirking red face seemingly waiting for his gaze. He smiled at Murphy, a hand raised in the air holding a bic pen.

'Russell Graves, *Liverpool News*. Given the recent footage that was released over the weekend, is your confidence in Detective Murphy still unwavering?'

Murphy sat back. Lips sealed. Bit the inside of his cheek as Stephens answered.

'Detective Murphy was responding to a particularly personal form of questioning which had no business being brought up. He has shown his tenacity over the past week to bring the person or persons responsible for these heinous acts off our streets.'

'Yeah,' Graves said, pushing his bottle-thick glasses up his acne-scarred nose, 'but he hasn't done so. The people of Liverpool deserve better than someone who can't control himself, don't you agree?'

'There is no one better to handle this investigation. That'll be it for today.'

Murphy stood, his fists clenched, nails digging into his palms. He dared not release them, fearing blood would trickle down his hands.

'You handled that well,' Stephens said as they left room.

'I wanted to rip the smug bastard's nose clean off his face. Decided to wait until this is over instead.'

'I'll take that as a joke David.'

Murphy grunted. 'We're going back through the CCTV. All the normal cars came back clean, none of them could have been our guy. Going to check through the taxis, just to be certain.'

'Okay. Did we get anything substantial on the psychology front?'

'Not really,' Murphy replied, scratching his beard as they waited for the lift. 'We know what he's doing, but no individual suspects as yet.'

'The answer is at the university. It's just finding it. If we don't get anything in the next twenty-four hours, we're going to have to start processing everyone.'

Eight taxis. Two black hacks, and six private hire. Rossi was already going through the black hacks, so Murphy started on the private hire cars. Running the registration through the council records, making sure they were all registered as taxis. Rossi was clicking her pen against her teeth.

'Do you have to do that?' Murphy said, pointing towards her pen.

She put a hand over the mouthpiece of the phone. 'It's just a pen. Listen, first one checked out, second one is proving more difficult. Been on hold for ages.'

'A murdering taxi driver. Wouldn't be the first one.'

'Don't you think our guy is a bit more intelligent than just a taxi driver?'

'Stranger things have happened. They must have some smarts. They always seem to know every road in the city. That must take some time to learn.'

Rossi rolled her eyes and went back to waiting.

A few minutes later, the pen stopped clicking. Murphy watched as her face changed, tried to read what she was hearing.

'And when was this . . . right . . . okay . . . so it was never stopped? . . . yeah that does seem like a mistake.'

287

Murphy left his seat moving over to Rossi's desk. Made a 'what's going on?' gesture with both hands.

'Thank you . . . no, that's great, thanks.' She put the phone down and swung her chair towards Murphy.

'Well?'

'The second hackney. It's a registered cab, but the driver is not the owner of it any longer.'

'What do you mean?'

'He sold it. Bought another one and drives that. The registration should have been moved to that new one and the old one ended. Seems that never happened. Think it will now.'

'So he sold it to who?'

Rossi pushed hair behind her ear. Murphy sighed, decided to ask Jess to pick up some hair clips for him so he could pass them on. 'Don't know yet. But we've got the name of the driver.'

'Well, let's get going then.'

Experiment Six

Rob was sitting down, his back against a wall, trying to work out how long he'd been in the room. Resting, before going back to work.

The floor was concrete, rough to the touch. He leaned forward on his knees, his hands thrust out in front of him, and began to move his hands back and forth against the ground, scratching at the ties which bound his hands. He didn't know how long he'd been going at it for, only that he hadn't exactly got very far with breaking free of his restraints. His hands were still as bound as they had been hours before.

Rob yawned, stood up and stretched as much as was possible. The lack of light was bothering him. It seemed empty, just a hard rough floor, and ridges where the door was set in place. He went around the room again, trying to feel for any exposed brick, a nail, something he could use. The walls were smooth though, as far as he could reach around them. He got to the door, and began banging on it, using his weight to try and force it, but feeling no give in it whatsoever. He kicked out at the bottom of it in frustration, using the sole of his foot. The light trainers he was wearing weren't up to the task, however.

He stopped, dropping to the floor again. He began scraping the cable ties against the rough surface once again.

'Come on, come on,' he said aloud, his voice echoing in the darkness. 'Break, you bastard.'

A voice came from within the walls.

'Robert.' It was a whisper, hissing on the last letter of his name. 'It's pointless.'

Rob stood up, the voice setting his heart off at a fast pace. 'Where are you?'

'Everywhere,' the voice answered. 'There's no point trying to free those hands. You won't be here long enough to make any advantage count.'

'No harm in trying. Where's Jemma?' Rob asked, looking around in the dark, trying to locate a specific point the voice was coming from.

'All in good time.' The voice responded. 'First we're going to have a little talk.'

'Oh yeah,' Rob replied, walking around the room. 'How about we talk about Jemma, about what you've done with her for the last eleven months?'

'I think I'll choose the subject.'

'Touchy. Why don't you come in here, speak to me face to face. Without the gun, just two men . . . talking.' Rob said, testing his own bravery. His voice faltered over the sentence however.

There was laughter, starting out low before becoming high pitched.

'Do I know you?' Rob said, sensing a familiarity to the voice he couldn't quite place.

The laughter stopped. The voice changed again. 'You don't know me Rob. Not me.'

The voice was different, Rob struggling to make sense of the familiarity he had when the voice changed so often. 'Why don't we start off with introductions then?'

'I don't think so.'

'Well, what then? You've locked me in a room, now you want to what? Leave me here to rot? Talk? Get it over with you fucking psycho.'

'Temper, temper. Remember what I said. You wouldn't want anything to happen to your dear Jemma now would you?'

'Let me see her,' Rob said, his teeth coming together, grinding down at the end of his sentence.

'I don't think you're in a position to make any demands now, do you? No, I think you need to listen and answer. Like a good boy.'

'Fine. Go on.' Rob stood with his back against the wall, willing the door to open so he could rush at it. He may have had his hands tied, but the anger he was feeling would mean he would fight his way out of the room with everything he had.

'Good. Much better. Now, you went to the park tonight on the basis you would see Jemma again, correct?' The voice asked.

'You know that,' Rob replied.

'Of course. You also didn't contact anyone about the communication we've had.'

'Again, you know I didn't. Do you really think I'd have been sat here for hours if I'd told anyone?'

'Perhaps. That's a chance I have to take.'

Rob could hear the voice louder in certain parts of the room as he walked around. 'Speakers in the walls,' he said. 'Nice touch. This whole thing must be expensive.'

The voice chuckled quietly. 'Anything and everything can be provided for people with the means to pay for it Robert.'

'I guess so. Have you got Jemma in a room like this?' Rob asked, thinking about the other door he'd seen earlier when he'd been led down into the basement.

'My turn for questions. We'll get to yours.'

Rob sighed heavily. 'Okay,' he replied.

'Now, you lost everything when Jemma disappeared. How did that feel?'

Rob stopped walking, finding a spot in the wall where the voice was strongest. He leaned back against the wall, his back aching from the hours he'd spent without proper support. 'It felt like shit.' He bit back a question. 'I wanted to know why.'

'And you always believed she had been taken. Even though those around you believed differently?'

'Yes.'

'Interesting. That feeling you've been having the last eleven months, has it been getting easier to deal with, before my intervention of course?'

Rob looked up, raising his tied hands to his eyes, rubbing at them. He thought back to the morning he'd received the first message. 'It's as hard after eleven months, as it was after eleven minutes. Happy?'

'Come now, you went to work, you went out with friends to pubs, how hard were you finding it, honestly?'

'It was devastating, is that what you want to hear? You have no idea what you've done.'

'I'm starting to understand. You were putting on a front, yes?'

Rob slid down the wall, unable to stand any longer. 'I had to. I'd lost everything. I had to keep going. For her.'

'For her. Yes, her. What if I told you Robert, I have no idea where Jemma is?'

Rob's head snapped up. 'What?'

'What if I told you Jemma could be anywhere, and that I've never had the pleasure of meeting her? How would that make you feel?'

'I don't believe you.'

'Of course you don't. You won't let yourself believe that.

292

Otherwise, all you've done is exchange conversations with a stranger, someone who has ended the lives of people. For no reason whatsoever. Jemma would still be as lost as she always was.'

'You're lying . . .'

'Am I Robert, how can you be sure? You have no idea of what is really going on here. You came here because I wanted you to. You went to the park because I told you to. When you think about it Robert, you've not done an awful lot to find Jemma. You've waited around hoping for someone else to do the work for you, playing the pity card over and over. You posted something on a missing persons website, well let's throw you a parade. It means nothing. You let your house go, your car. Your life crumbled around you, because you didn't know how to cope without her. Pathetic.'

'No. That's not what happened. I tried.'

'Please spare me. You drove around, hoping to catch sight of her. Have you spoken to the police recently Robert? Asked them anything? I don't think so.'

Rob lowered his head. As much as he wanted to disagree with what the voice was saying, he knew it would be useless. 'Why bring me here if you don't have Jemma?' Rob asked.

'I have a theory of why you haven't done more Robert.'

'Yeah,' Rob said with a heavy sigh. 'What's that then?'

'I think you know she's already gone. You were grieving. You couldn't move on, you couldn't accept the fact that she was never coming back to you.'

Rob choked back a sob, the voice saying the words he didn't want to hear.

'I think after that first week, you knew,' the voice continued. 'Since then, you've been coasting along, without much effort, hoping she'd turn up again and all would be well again.'

'I went to that park didn't I? That was something,' Rob said, a single tear falling down his cheek.

'Only because I told you to. You couldn't allow yourself not to, because not doing so would accept the inevitable. She wasn't coming back.'

'No.' Rob stood up, crossing the darkness towards the door. 'No, no, no.' He punctuated every word with a foot to the door.

Lights blared, blinding him. He lifted his arms up to shield his eyes, slowly putting them down after a few seconds, squinting his eyes against the brightness. The hiss had disappeared.

Rob stepped back from the door, his eyes becoming more accustomed to the light. He waited. Finally he heard movement, slight, in the distance. The door opened inwards, he remembered that from earlier, so he made sure he was sufficiently distanced from it, ready. He heard the lock turning, the door opening slowly as if by itself. He waited for it to open wide enough for him to spring forward.

Emptiness. Nothing was there. His brain had enough time to process this, even as he moved forward, a guttural cry escaping from him. He stopped, sensing a trap.

Then he heard something. Coming from the room opposite. Singing.

'Frère Jacques, frère Jacques. Dormez-vous? Dormez-vous? Sonnez les matines. Sonnez les matines. Din, dan, don. Din, dan, don.'

He recognised the voice.

It was her. It was Jemma.

He stood paralysed for a moment, not knowing what to do. He looked out the door, seeing the other door opposite, and moved fast, covering the distance in seconds. All the time, he could hear the song being repeated softly from beyond the door opposite his.

Rob began throwing his weight at the door, using his feet, his tied and bound hands to try and force it open. Sweat poured down his face, his eyes stinging as the salt reached them, as he used every last ounce of effort he had to get into the room.

'Jemma. Jemma can you hear me?' Rob shouted. 'Jemma, it's me.'

Behind him the singing stopped. He paused, trying to hear anything beyond the door, but failing to.

'Jemma . . .'

A movement to his side entered his vision, but he reacted too slowly, weight hitting him in the back, forcing him to the floor before he had the chance to raise his hands and break his fall properly. His face smashed against the hard floor, instant pain hitting him. Rob could feel his vision going dark, growing smaller around him. He shook his head, lifting it from the ground. He felt weight on his back, something slip round his neck.

'Silly, silly boy,' a voice said in his ear. 'Far too easy. I just wanted you to hear her one last time.'

He felt his breath being cut off, something constricting his neck.

'You'll stop breathing soon, not soon enough sadly, but soon. She's in there Rob, through that door. She's been there for almost a year, with nothing but food and water for company. And the voices in her head of course. You should see her now, you wouldn't recognise her. Astounding.'

Rob's hands were trapped beneath him, he tried to buck around, remove the weight that was pressed against. He lifted his legs up, but couldn't shift it.

'And you couldn't save her Rob. She'll be there for a little longer, and then I'll be done with her. Your small efforts were wasted.'

Rob could feel himself fading. He tried to move, but all his strength was gone.

'You never deserved her Rob, you never appreciated her. You sapped her life, you were a drain. She's going to be my masterpiece. A living death. Once I'm done with her, she'll be unrecognisable, a zombified version of her previous self.'

The darkness enveloped him.

'Now, number six. Let's see what you're made of.'

Rob came around slowly. His eyes opening and closing. Darkness replacing darkness. His mind wasn't so fast. He couldn't work out where he was. He thought he could hear an alarm sounding and was confused, as they didn't have an alarm. He woke up to the radio, always had. He tried to turn over, to tell Jemma to turn it off. Annoyed his sleep had been interrupted.

He couldn't move.

'Hello Robert.'

The voice came from above him. Rob tried to focus his eyes, but they wouldn't respond, there was just darkness. He blinked. And again. Nothing.

'Can you feel what's in your hands?'

There was something resting on his palms. He tried moving his fingers to feel what it was, but nothing happened.

'Can't have you staring at me throughout this Robert.'

His mind couldn't keep up. He looked to his left, where the voice was coming from, but nothing happened.

'We're going to do a little experiment. Do you mind?'

Rob tried to answer but his mouth wouldn't open. He blinked, trying to clear his vision. Told his body to sit up, but it didn't respond.

'How long do you think it'll take Rob? If I cut your foot off, how long would you last?'

The words didn't make sense. He was at home surely. Was the radio on? What was he tuned into? Some weird station, that seemed to know his name.

'How about a leg? Or an arm.'

Rob tried to move his head. Clear it. He didn't understand why it wouldn't do as it was told.

296

'Let's try a few fingers first.'

Silence. He couldn't even hear his own breathing. He was in a park. Someone had Jemma. But she was lying next to him wasn't she?

Pain exploded in his right side. He screamed, filling whatever was in his mouth, cutting off the noise.

He didn't understand.

Why couldn't he feel his hand anymore?

He could smell burning, coming from below.

'Just cauterising the wounds. Don't want you bleeding out just yet.'

The voice. He knew the voice.

'This little piggy went to market . . .'

He heard a snap.

It came to him. His fingers first. Now his toes.

Soon, he couldn't feel his feet. Then his legs.

By the time the feeling in his arms left him, he'd closed his eyes.

Just darkness. Only that, nothing more.

34

He pulled the axe from the neck. The head toppled off the table and came to a rest near the wall. A pointless effort, the body having expired long before.

He exhaled, spat on the floor as he got his breath back. Hard work.

The blood. Everywhere. He'd started on the fingers, removing them with a pair of pruners bought from B&Q.

The axe took care of the larger limbs.

He'd tried to stem the bleeding as best as he could, cauterising the wounds to try and make it last as long as possible. It was difficult on his own.

It was different this time.

He could feel it entering every pore of his body, as if the life he'd just ended was now looking for a new body to meld with. He felt energised, his heart beating fast, his hands shaking. He looked down at them, still holding the small axe he'd used. He threw it aside, blood splattering against more blood. His hands were turning dark. He rubbed them, smearing the dark red stains further.

He smiled. Then laughed as he realised the girl had started singing again. She couldn't process what had happened not six foot away from her door. The eleven months she'd spent in there destroying her mind. She stopped after another verse, no sound following. He looked around, the sudden quiet unsettling him.

'You're okay, you're okay.' His voice echoed around him, strengthening him, supporting him.

He rose to his feet, wiping his hands down his front. Looking down at the body, he couldn't place what he was feeling. Was it guilt?

Did he have a conscience still?

It was different this time.

He had barely known most of the people he'd terminated before. He knew this one.

Known this one.

Was this what he was supposed to do? Was this the reason for him?

He shook it off quickly, looking for the feeling of excitement he'd had previously.

Finding it.

He climbed the steps behind him, feeling the adrenaline fade from his body. The effort he'd just given catching up to him.

He didn't have much time. He needed to get going.

He'd already prepared the things he would need. The bags, the twine to tie them shut. He went back down the steps, carrying what he needed.

The eyes though, the eyes were looking at him. Resting on the table where he left them after removing them from Rob's hands. Staring up at him, judging him.

'Stop it,' he whispered. 'Stop looking at me.'

He couldn't take the stare. The eyes accusatory, damning him without trial.

It had to stop.

He puffed out a breath, breathing in and releasing it slowly.

He laid out a few bin bags next to the body, then rolled it over so it was lying on them. He then covered the top with more bags, taking the roll of tape and sticking the bags to each other. He'd learned early on this method made it easier to transport. 'Practise makes perfect,' he said under his breath, smiling once more.

It took him longer than he thought it would, but eventually he had all the body parts on the ground floor. He sat with his back against the wall, breathing heavily, sweating even more. He was exhausted from the night's activities.

He would change his plans. He'd originally thought he'd leave the body to be found that night, but to do so could be risky. He'd come too far to make a mistake now. He needed to rest, work out what was next. Move on.

First he'd check in with the little lady. See how she was doing.

He moved slowly through to the room. His sanctuary. He sat in the chair facing the two monitors, eased himself back slowly. The bottle of water was where he'd left it, he unscrewed the cap and knocked it back, finishing the bottle.

Singing, still singing. He watched for a few minutes, before leaving the room.

'*Frère Jacques, frère Jacques. Dormez-vous? Dormez-vous? Sonnez les matines. Sonnez les matines. Din, dan, don. Din, dan, don.*'

Jemma sang. Blocking out the noises. She couldn't understand them, it'd been too long. She wouldn't let herself believe.

She'd known that voice once. She was sure of it. But it couldn't be him, not down here.

Rob. That was his name. Her partner, her lover, her other half.

He couldn't be down here. It had been too long. It must

300

be at least five years since she'd last seen him. Surely. He'd have moved on. Moved to the countryside or something. Got married. Forgotten her. Maybe he was a dad now. A little boy he'd call John, after his own dad.

She was alone now. He was long gone.

Jemma wondered what the boy would look like. The dimples in his cheeks, and the cleft in his chin, both being passed down. The blue eyes and dark thick hair. Curls when it grew a bit longer.

That's what will have happened, Jemma thought. Rob wouldn't be down there.

Not in the darkness.

Please God, not down there with her.

35

Tuesday 5th February 2013 – Day Ten

The Strand shopping centre in Bootle was a few minutes' walk away from the small cul de sac of Georgia Close where George Duffy lived. His cab was parked on the short driveway of the semi detached house, the window frames and door painted blue, new builds with light red paving stones leading up to the front.

'No record?' Murphy said as they pushed open the low steel gate which lay at the front of the property, sidestepped an overflowing green bin and approached the door.

'Nope. Been a driver for the last fifteen years,' Rossi replied.

They knocked and waited. Knocked again, louder. Eventually, they heard the sound of a key turning and the door was opened.

Duffy was in his late fifties. Bald, with a grey goatee beard, dark eyes and a weary expression plastered on his face. A paunch protruded over black jogging pants, which were the only thing he was wearing.

'Yeah?'

Murphy introduced himself and Rossi, showing ID and being invited in. Duffy tidied up as they walked inside, picking up discarded magazines and underwear and putting them away. The smell of grease and cigar smoke was harder to mask.

'It's about the taxi isn't it? I knew that was gonna come back to haunt me.'

'We just have a few questions Mr Duffy.'

'He didn't seem right from the off. Wanted everything done off the books but when someone's offering you thirty-five grand in cash, you don't ask questions do ya?'

Duffy pointed to a black leather settee, as he plonked himself down on a matching armchair. A fifty-inch flatscreen was screwed into the wall above the fireplace, dominating the room.

Murphy lowered himself down, Rossi moved a dirty plate from the other side and did the same. 'So you sold it?'

'Yeah,' Duffy replied, scratching an armpit. 'Picked a guy up from town one night and got talking. He took a card off me and called the next day.'

'When was this?'

'About a year ago. January I think. Yeah, not long after Christmas. Didn't think he was serious at first. Said he wanted the cab and was willing to pay in cash. Offered thirty grand and I bumped him up to thirty-five. Bought that one outside for fifteen and still had a nice amount left.'

'It didn't seem odd to you?'

'Course it did. What's he done then? I'm guessing it's some kind of fraud. Look, I just sold it on, nothing wrong with that.'

Murphy sighed. 'It's a bit more serious than that. Did you get a name from him at least?'

'Said it was Steve something. Can't remember now. It was ages ago.'

'What did he look like?'

'I can't really remember now. About your age maybe, looked well off. Clean cut, trendy maybe. I don't know.'

Rossi took over then, trying to get more from him, but that was all Duffy had.

Murphy walked into the hallway as Rossi went over and over the description, seeing if he could remember any more. He called through to the station, putting out an alert for the cabs license plate. Automatic number plate recognition, or ANPR, would do the rest. As soon as the cab passed a camera, they'd have it.

It was all too late.

Murphy stood inside the white tent, staring at the lifeless form of a man. He was lying on his back, arms and legs outstretched, just like the last four victims.

Yet, he was different.

'Reminds me of that song, *the head bone is connected to the, shoulder bone . . .*' Houghton paused from his examination to say.

The body wasn't whole. Not by any stretch. The toes were cut from both feet. The feet away from the calf, the calf cut away from the thigh and top part of each leg. And on and on. Only the torso was unmarked.

It was a human jigsaw puzzle, the pieces put back together again. Only the small gaps between the pieces marking a difference.

'More like Humpty Dumpty,' Murphy replied. 'What is this?'

Dr Houghton sighed, lifting himself up. 'I don't know. He wasn't killed here, I can tell you that much. No blood. And believe me, there would be a lot of it. Anything that could be removed, has been. Almost clean cuts in some places, skewed in others. I'm going to make a guess at a heavy implement, such as an axe. Something different on the smaller parts, pruners or something.'

'Letter?'

'Of course.'

The eyes had been removed. Dark holes where they once sat. The perfect O of the mouth matching the black of the eye sockets.

Murphy remained passive, trying to stay focused. Images interspersed in his head, his mum replacing the man on the floor. Intangible shifts of light, playing with his vision, as tiredness threatened to overcome him. He watched as the SOCOs went to work, bagging and tagging various body parts.

And he knew that face. They all did. Even with the damage that had been done to it, they recognised it, having only seen him a few days earlier.

Rob Barker.

Another link to the university.

And he'd let him go to his death. He'd screwed up again, and someone else had died. Murphy felt his legs threaten to buckle, fingers tapping against his thigh. Anxiety coursing through him.

This was too much.

Dr Houghton, the pathologist, was speaking to him, his features covered by the surgical mask. Murphy hadn't been listening, lost in his thoughts. 'What was that doctor?'

'I said, it's shock due to blood loss most likely. He's been dead at least eighteen hours.'

'Looks like some kind of thin rope, or wire was used on his neck as well though. Choked him to death, first maybe. Hard to tell. The eyes . . .' the pathologist paused, steeling himself. 'The eyes were removed whilst he was still alive. And we can't find them. Maybe whoever did this kept them?'

Murphy nodded. 'Anything else?' he asked.

'We're bagging the letter now so you can read it sooner. I'm guessing we're on more of a time limit here.'

'Thanks doctor.'

Murphy had to leave, he could feel himself swaying on his feet. It was too much. He pushed his way out, moving away from the tent. From death. Lights blinded him as he came outside, the images of his parents' living room flashing in front of his eyes.

'You alright sir?'

Rossi was at his side. 'Yeah,' Murphy replied. 'It's a bad one.'

'I guessed as much. We've got a witness. Saw a black hackney. Driving away from the scene.'

'Good. Just give me a minute Laura. Just need to catch my breath.'

'Of course.' Rossi moved away, leaving Murphy alone. He stared out on to the main road. It was a deserted side road, off the busy dual carriageway of Scotland Road. Yet there was lights only a few yards away, a busy road, houses. He turned around, looking towards the main road. Boarded-up shops and off-licences hanging on in there, selling six cans for a fiver.

He was taunting them. Taunting him. Whoever he was. He wanted Murphy to know he was in control.

Murphy began to remove the gloves he'd had to put on before seeing the scene, snapping them off, and throwing them to the floor. Anger building in his chest.

He was escalating.

Murphy knew what he had to do. Pretend the last year hadn't happened. Be calm, assured.

Murphy beckoned Rossi back over. She hurried back, a concerned look in her eyes.

'He's getting careless Laura,' Murphy said when Rossi got to him. 'I think we'll have him soon enough. He hasn't realised we know about the cab. He'll still be driving it.' Murphy looked around, there were no windows overlooking the small grassy area where the body had been found. 'Who found him?'

'The woman over there.' Rossi replied, pointing to a

middle-aged woman. 'She'd brought her dog out with her whilst she was walking up to the offy about five minutes up the road. Walked up here to let the dog do his business. Stumbled across the victim's . . . parts.'

'Okay. It can't have been long after he was dropped here. See if she remembers the black hack as well.'

'Will do.' Rossi replied.

Rossi walked off in the direction of the woman. Murphy moved towards a small wall which surrounded the grass and sat down on it. Pain fired across his forehead. He closed his eyes, instantly trying to force out the images which appeared as soon his eyelids shut.

They wouldn't go.

He held his head in his hands, rubbing his temples slowly. A position he was becoming used to assuming.

'Sir?'

Murphy lifted his head to see a SOCO stood over him. 'Yes?'

'Dr Houghton asked me to bring this over. I'm supposed to stay with you whilst you read it. If that's okay?'

'Of course.' Murphy took the plastic bag containing the letter from the SOCO. Moved closer to the light to read it.

EXPERIMENT SIX

Detective Murphy,

He was too close, he wouldn't stop looking. He had to go. Just like with the others.

Do you remember the Unit 731 experiments? I had to try that out.

I removed his body parts one by one, over a lengthy period of time. Waited to see the light go out.

307

I dislike the name the papers have given me. Maybe you could talk to someone about that David?

Do you know how it feels to end someone's life? To be the cause of it? It's unlike anything you can imagine. So much more than I expected it to be. When you kill animals in experimental situations, rats, dogs, etc. you think you can treat human subjects with the same apathy. It doesn't work like that though. It takes you over, a hunger for more.

But, then you have to factor in your own survival. It's still a gamble. One that I am willing to take.

Yet, none of the experiments really matter.

Except for one.

One experiment I started this whole process with. An ongoing investigation, which is almost at its end.

And I'm torn as what to do when it's finished. Should I terminate the project, just as I have with so many before? Or do I reveal the results of my hard work?

For all to see. A masterpiece.

Decisions, decisions.

What would you do Detective Murphy? Would you give up on the whole thing, just in case it leads to *my* end? Or would you take the chance to show the world what can be done?

It's a tough one. I'll be chewing it over in the coming days.

In the meantime, I'll let your fruitless investigation go on.

I am so enjoying the game. I hope you are too Detective. Experiment Six was so much fun to act out. That's four bodies you've found now.

Of course, that's only the ones I have let you find.

Do you know how many people go missing every year, every day? Thousands. Never to be seen again.

Still, I do have that nagging worry over what to do about the experiment.

Not long left now. And then onto pastures new I guess.

In the end, all that matters, is that what I do lives on forever. No one will ever forget what happened in this city, by my hands.

Murphy handed the bag containing the letter back to the SOCO, looked for a uniformed officer. He beckoned to a young woman who was manning the police cordon, and she hurried over.

'Yes sir?'

'I need you to check that everyone is on the lookout for that cab.'

'Okay.' She took her radio off her shoulder and talked to control. Murphy waited as she explained what she needed.

'Thanks,' Murphy said, moving away from the officer. He went over to where Rossi was studiously taking notes from the witness. As he reached her, she was thanking the woman for her time, and telling her what to expect next. Murphy waited for her to finish her spiel, before taking her by the arm and leading her away.

'Laura. We need to find this guy now. We don't have much time. He's planning something.'

'The letter?' Rossi asked.

'Yeah. He talks about an experiment and having to make a decision over someone's life. We need to find him before that happens.'

Rossi nodded, as Murphy rubbed at his temples again. 'First though, we check out the victim's house. See if anything can help us there,' Murphy continued.

'We were only in there a few days ago. Didn't find anything.' Rossi replied.

'We don't know what he's been doing in the past few days. He was close to something. We need to find out what.' Murphy reached into his inside pocket, took out some paracetemol, and dry swallowed two. 'We best get the next one right. Everyone we suspect seems to end up dead within a couple of days.'

Rossi attempted a smile, but Murphy knew it was for show. She was feeling the pressure almost as much as he was.

The wind whipped around the green, rippling the tent which surrounded the body parts in the distance. Haunted faces of various officers stood around the scene, Murphy looking around for inspiration.

It would take a long time to forget this one.

Experiment Two

She was thirsty. Cold as well. She hadn't eaten for a while, just to see what would happen. It was okay though, her dad was with her. He'd turned up some time ago, she could hear his voice talking to her from the corner. She hadn't been able to see him though, it was too dark. Plus every time she ran towards the voice, he'd disappear. Playing probably, she thought. He always had a strange sense of humour.

It was nice to not be alone any more. She'd been alone for so long.

The walls didn't talk to her any more. Every now and again she'd wake up after eating to find things had changed, the air in the room smelled differently. Expensive aftershave, a musky scent lingering in the air.

And then the silence. Stretched out for so long. She slept often, her dreams becoming more vivid as time had gone by.

She dreamt of Rob.

She'd heard him recently. She thought he'd been here, but he couldn't be. Not here. Not down in the darkness.

'My name is Jemma. Jemma Barnes.'

She repeated it to herself often. She was scared of forgetting. She couldn't remember so much now. Her thoughts ran into each other, not making any sense. She heard noises coming from the walls one second, then she'd listen more carefully and not hear anything.

He hadn't touched her. Not there.

She'd know. 'I'd know,' she said towards the dim noise she could constantly hear. It sounded louder sometimes. Things kept changing around her, she was sure of it. 'Don't think you'd get away with it.'

She paced out the room again. 'One, two, three, five, six.' She'd forgotten again.

'Four!'

She sat down heavily on the floor, pain shooting up her back. She enjoyed it now. The pain she could inflict on herself. She could bang her head against the wall until something cracked. Or she knocked herself out. 'Make it permanent.' She laughed, the sound echoing in the room. It didn't sound like her.

'Who's there?'

There was no answer.

He'd been here. Rob had been down there with her. She'd heard him through the walls.

'No. No he wasn't. My name is Jemma Barnes.' Her throat was sore. She shouldn't shout. She needed water.

She scrabbled across the floor to find what should be there. She couldn't find it.

'Where is it? Come on, I know it's here.'

Her fingers brushed against something solid. She brought it up to her face, the coolness now gone. She unscrewed the cap and poured the contents down her throat. The water was warm, but no less soothing.

She found the food next. She remembered food. She hadn't eaten for four days. That was her best guess.

'Four,' she muttered to herself. She took the food and turned to face the opposite way whilst still sitting. She got to her feet, walked slowly forwards, stopping when he right foot hit the toilet. She squatted down and put the food in the bowl.

It had come to her when she'd heard Rob.

'Not him. It wasn't him.'

She felt guilty. She was worried, about the conversations she'd had with her mum and friends. About Rob.

A drama queen, that's what she was. Needed a little more excitement so she'd exaggerated things with them, made them believe her and Rob were having problems. One argument became so many more.

She needed to get out. She wanted to make sure. That it wasn't him. She could take being locked away in the darkness. The man had told her she'd be let out eventually. She just had to be patient. But then she'd heard his voice, his pain, and she was no longer certain.

So she'd began looking for a way out again. She spent so much time trying to force her way out the solid door, open the hatch from the inside so she could crawl out. She'd ran her hands down her sides, feeling the rib bones poking out from beneath the thin t-shirt she'd been wearing recently. Sometimes the man had put her in a jumper, they always smelled the same.

Sweet, like lavender.

It had come to her quite soon after she'd lost half her right index fingernail, trying to create an opening where one wasn't to be found.

She could block the toilet somehow. He'd have to come down there, and she would claw her way out. With all nine fingernails. A kick to the bollocks, and he'd go down quick enough. Whatever it took to get out of the room.

She'd kept some toilet roll to one side, just in case, and then stuck the rest of the roll down the toilet. Then she'd put food wrappers down there.

313

Then the next time the hatch opened, she'd drunk the water and not eaten. Putting the sandwiches and chocolate down the bowl.

That time was the eighth.

The man hadn't been down there. She hadn't gone to sleep without wanting to. She was hungry, she worried about not having any strength to fight him.

She moved over to the mattress in the other corner, sat with her back against the wall. She could see Rob's face in the darkness, a blurred memory now. She couldn't remember if he'd had stubble or a full beard when she last saw him.

'It doesn't matter, I'll be home soon,' she whispered to him.

Her dad sang to her.

'*Frère Jacques, frère Jacques. Dormez-vous? Dormez-vous? Sonnez les matines. Sonnez les matines. Din, dan, don. Din, dan, don.*'

She smiled. Then lay down her head on the mattress, and closed her eyes, letting her dad's voice sing her to sleep.

She hadn't wanted to sleep.

36

Wednesday 6th February
2013 – Day Eleven

They showed ID to the uniform standing at the door and climbed the stairs up to Rob Barker's flat. Nicotine-stained ceilings in the communal hallway, black mould patches in the corners, the wallpaper peeling away from the damp.

Murphy wanted to smoke. A nice pack of twenty L&B would do nicely. Smoke them down to the filter and then light another one as he was putting out the last.

The craving never leaves you.

'When did he move here?' Murphy said, as they entered the flat.

'He had to give up the house three months ago,' Rossi replied, looking through the notes she'd scribbled down on the way over. 'It was in his name and when his partner didn't come back, he couldn't afford to keep it. Mortgage was too high.'

They walked up the small, narrow staircase, a small wattage bare bulb hanging in the entrance providing the only light. The flat smelled musty, the smell of dirty dishes and damp clothes emanating from inside.

'Do we know when the last sighting of him was?' Murphy asked as they reached the top of the stairs.

'He called in sick to work two days ago. That's the last we know at this moment.' Rossi replied.

They were wearing gloves, SOCOs coming up the stairs behind them. They went left at the top of the stairs, entering a small living room which was slightly lit by the rising sun streaming through the uncurtained window. Someone behind Murphy, switched a light on bathing the room in starker light.

Murphy was taken aback by the sparseness of the room, just a small sofa and TV taking up most of the space. There was a desk in the opposite corner to the TV, which Murphy thought he'd have a lot of trouble sitting at, given its size. A door to the right of the desk was open, and Murphy could see a small kitchen leading off it. Murphy and Rossi stood aside as the SOCOs took their time taking photographs and labelling anything of interest. Only a few days since they'd done something similar. There was no evidence the killing had taken place at the flat, but with four bodies in total and DCI Stephen's orders still ringing in their ears, they were looking for any clue they could find.

They were allowed to start looking around after a while, Murphy already having taken stock of the room from his position near the doorway.

'Laptop on the desk.' Rossi said as Murphy approached it. 'Is it on?'

Murphy stopped in front of the desk, bending slightly to miss the ceiling which dipped at that point. He lifted the lid and was surprised to see it running. It was plugged in, the lead running alongside the laptop. 'It's on. No password either. Take a look Laura.'

Rossi moved over, sitting in the small chair as Murphy took the piles of paper stacked next to it on the desk. Murphy walked over to the sofa and began going through the pieces. A couple of pages down, Murphy read a few hurried notes, and set the page aside.

'His homepage is a missing persons site. He's automatically logged in. Just having a look around it.'

Murphy grunted in reply, reading through another page. It seemed to match the page he'd set aside, notes and notes about someone called Harlow. Monkey experiments, isolation, and other words had been underlined. He set it on top of the other page, going through the other pages which were more scrawled notes than the carefully made ones on the first pages.

'Have you heard of a "Harlow"?' Murphy asked as he reached the end.

'Isn't there a Sergeant Harlow, works over the water?'

'Probably, but I'm talking about someone else. There's a lot of notes here about a Dr Harlow, stuff with monkeys and experiments. Given what's been said in the letters, this has probably got something to do it.'

'There was a psychologist called Harlow. I remember from the psych class I did in first year,' Rossi said, looking up from the laptop for the first time. 'He did some weird experiments with monkey or somethings. That's about all I can remember.'

'Right. We need to look into that.' Murphy stood up, and went through to the bedroom. The door was open, a couple of people milling about inside talking quietly. As Murphy entered, they stopped talking and went back to looking through what little was in there. 'Just looking,' Murphy said as he entered, taking up the rest of the available space in the room. Most of the room was taken up by the bed, neatly made against the wall. A small bedside table next to it held just a clock radio on top. And something underneath.

Murphy walked over and lifted the radio up, freeing what was underneath.

'It's him,' Murphy muttered to himself.

'What was that, sir?'

'This is a letter from him. The killer.' Murphy read the short message, recognising the mixed handwriting scrawled across the page.

'*Harlow was the first, I'm just taking it further,*' Murphy read aloud.

He moved quickly back through to the living room.

'Laura. The killer was in contact with Rob.'

'I know.' Rossi replied.

'How? I've just found this in the bedroom.' Murphy said, holding the letter up.

'Because he contacted him through the missing person site first.'

Murphy stopped dead. 'When?'

'A week ago,' Rossi said, writing notes in her book. 'First message is to tell him Jemma, his partner, was still alive and set up a meeting at the Albert Dock. Victim was at work after that day, so explains why he was there. Turns out there was another message later that night, which seems to be carrying on from something that may have happened that night. Something about Harlow again. It links in with his latest letter as well.'

'How so?' Murphy sat down on the sofa, the pages he'd collected still in his hand.

'He talks about how Jemma is the focus of his research. One he's been working on for so long.'

'His experiment is Jemma?'

'Or that's how he got him to comply. He could have just used that to get to him.' Rossi replied, sitting back running her hand over her head, smoothing her hair back down. 'She went missing . . .' she checked her notes, '. . . almost a year ago.'

'It would fit,' Murphy said, the gravity of the situation weighing down on him as he worked through what that meant. 'Holding someone for a year?'

318

'Harlow. One of his experiments was with isolation.'

'We need to know what the full story is with this Harlow.'

'I think you're probably holding most of the answers in your hand.'

'He's only been active in the past week though. Would he keep someone prisoner for a year and then start killing people?'

Murphy wasn't sure. He looked down at the pages of notes. 'I don't think I'm going to make much sense of these Laura. Probably best if you go through them back at the station.'

'No sign of it yet? Right. No, that'll be it for now. Call the second he shows.'

Rossi was sitting across from him, staring dead eyed at the computer screen in front of her, making notes every now and again. She'd been sitting there for an hour or so, Murphy occasionally asking how she was getting on, receiving grunts in reply. A meeting was scheduled at six p.m. as usual, and Murphy was attempting to put his thoughts in order for it.

He watched as DCI Stephens entered the incident room, talking to a couple of DCs on the way in before reaching her office. He knew he couldn't put off the inevitable any longer, and crossed the room towards the office. He knocked confidently, waiting to be allowed in.

'How are we getting on David?'

Murphy sat down in the chair opposite her. Stephens was looking harassed, yet still maintaining an air of authority. Even if the dark circles under her eyes betrayed her calm exterior.

'We have a lead on what may have happened to the victim's partner. But we can't locate the cab yet.'

'Sorry, why are we concerned with the victim's partner at this moment, rather than the murderer?'

Murphy brought her up to speed with the early morning's

events, the DCI's expression remaining neutral until he began talking about the possibility someone may have been kidnapped a year earlier.

'Jemma had a history of running off. Looked like a simple case of someone packing off to sunnier climes. I don't think anyone thought she was in danger, apart from the mother and partner.'

'And she is in danger?'

'I think so. Rossi is currently looking into it further, but given that he started with these psychology experiments, and that his latest letter confirms there's an ongoing one, I think we should face the fact he may have been holding Jemma Barnes for almost a year.'

DCI Stephens leaned back in her chair, removed her glasses and shook her head. Murphy shifted in the small seat, the atmosphere in the room changing as the weight of what may have been going on without their knowledge became apparent.

'When the papers find out about this . . . we're royally fucked.'

Murphy raised his eyebrows; it was the first time he'd heard the usually mild-mannered DCI swear. 'I think that's the least of our problems, with respect.'

'Of course. We need to find her as soon as possible.'

'We're working on it.'

'Okay. You and Rossi talk to any family members, and also Jemma Barnes's mother.'

Murphy nodded, stood up to leave.

'Wait,' DCI Stephens said before he had chance to leave. 'Have you seen the counsellor yet?'

Murphy sighed turning back around to face her. 'I haven't had a chance with everything that's been going on.'

'How are you feeling?' DCI Stephens said, a concerned look on her face which reminded Murphy of his mother after he'd got himself in trouble.

320

'I haven't had time to worry about it.' He sat back down. He didn't know if it was tiredness or something else, but he suddenly had an overwhelming feeling to release so much of what he was feeling.

Instead he blurted out, 'I'm going to speak to Sarah, see if we can meet up.' It surprised him. He hadn't thought of doing that.

'That'll be good,' DCI Stephens replied.

'I need to see her.' Murphy hadn't said that out loud before, but now the words were out there, he realised how true they were. He did need to see her. 'I just don't know what I'm going to say yet.'

'Well, my door's always open David. But if any of this is affects your work, I won't hesitate to remove you from the case. It's too big for any mistakes to happen.'

Murphy winced, but forced himself to bite his lip. 'I'm focused only on bringing him in. Whoever he is.'

'Good. Get back out there.'

Murphy left the office, the DCI's words burning in his ears. The truth was, he didn't know if he could focus. Everywhere he looked he seemed to be surrounded by darkness. He was trapped, closed in from the outside.

He was tired. Tired of it all.

He had to do this. He had to find him.

Experiment Two

Jemma was sitting in a restaurant. The Italian place on the corner of Ranelagh Street, opposite Central station. It was warm outside, and they had a table in the window, causing Rob to shield his eyes with the menu.

'Let's get a different table.'

Rob laid the menu down. 'No. This is where you like to sit, so we're staying. What's a bit of burned retina between lovers.'

Jemma rolled her eyes at him. 'Lovers? Ugh. Don't say that.'

'Isn't that what we are?'

'Well . . . yeah. But it just sounds like a bad romance book.'

He laughed. Jemma smiled back.

'Okay. I won't say it again. What are you getting?'

Jemma looked at the menu again. 'Bruscetta and the cacciatore.'

'Good choice. I'm going for the lasagne.'

Jemma chuckled to herself. 'Of course you are. That's what you always get. Why not try something different?'

Rob shook his head. 'I know what I like. Why take a chance and get something I don't like?'

'Because you might end up finding something new.'

'Nah. I'll stick with what I know. The grass isn't always greener you know. That's why I keep you around.'

Jemma threw a breadstick at him, laughing loud enough to earn stares from some of the people sat at the closest tables.

'Fucker.'

'Mind your language Jemma Barnes. This is a posh place you know.'

Jemma gave him a sombre expression. 'Posh? I wouldn't go that far.'

'I would. Have you seen all these knives and forks? They should come with labels so I know which one to use.'

Jemma laughed again. 'Just work from the outside in.'

'My, my. You really are losing it Jemma.'

The restaurant began to fade, growing darker and darker. She felt the walls closing in around her, as her face fell and reality became clearer.

'Where do you think you are?'

The voice wasn't coming from Rob. It surrounded her.

'No. This isn't real. Let me go back.'

'Jemma. I'm afraid you're mistaken. This is your reality now. But don't worry, it's coming to an end.'

Jemma looked around, the darkness now all around her. The smells of the Italian food being replaced by sweat and waste.

'Let me go back.'

'It'll all be over soon. Don't worry.'

Jemma rocked herself, sitting against the wall closest to the door. Her arms tucked around her knees as she brought them up to her chest. She preferred it when the walls didn't speak to her.

'Not real. This isn't real.'

37

Wednesday 13th February 2013 – Day Eighteen One Week Later

Dark grey clouds hung low in the sky over Anfield Cemetery, seemingly unmoving, waiting until their work was done. Rain fell in short bursts. Mourners entered the small chapel on the site, black umbrellas being held by a few. Others allowed the light drizzle to dampen their heads.

Murphy and Rossi kept a distance from the few family members and friends that were slowly filing past them. Murphy watched as Rob's father was led to the front by another family member, the coffin containing his son in front of him.

'His dad looks ill.' Rossi said behind a gloved hand to Murphy.

'His mum died a few years back. Apparently the father didn't take it so well. He's not been well for some time. They weren't really on speaking terms since his mum died,' Murphy replied.

'Are you sure you want to stay?' Rossi asked, soft eyes tracking his.

'Yes,' Murphy said firmly.

Rossi nodded once, then pointed to a couple of chairs on the back row. They sat down, listened to the eulogies, scanning the small gathering for anyone who didn't fit.

Murphy was doing okay until they played the final song, the coffin going behind the curtain. 'You'll Never Walk Alone' was piped in through the speakers, a standard at so many funerals in the North West. The famous football anthem bringing tears to the eyes of most of those gathered around him.

Murphy felt a pat on his back, turned to see Rossi motioning her head towards the exit. It was at that point he noticed the dampness under his eyes, the lump at the back of his throat. He nodded at Rossi and followed her out.

The low winter sun had broken through the clouds, the smell of damp grass surrounding them as they moved to the side of the building, still able to see the exit.

'You okay sir?' Rossi said, once they'd moved away.

'Yeah fine. Just that song.'

'I know. I'm guessing it was played?'

Murphy sighed, looked around at the gravestones which were close to the crematorium building. 'At the funeral. *Carousel*. It was Mum's favourite musical. It had nothing to do with Liverpool really. Although Dad was a season-ticket holder for a long time. Spent ages trying to get me to go with him, but I was never that interested in football as a kid.'

'They had a good turn out that day. I remember it was packed in there.'

'They made a lot of friends. That was the type of people they were,' Murphy said, leaning against the stone wall for support.

'Have you been back since?' Rossi asked, standing next to Murphy against the wall. She adjusted her jacket to try and keep some more of the cold out.

'No. I get the odd letter from one of the old dears who live on the same road, but I can't go back there.'

They heard gentle murmurings as people started to file outside. They recognised some faces from the week's

325

investigation following Rob's death. Others they could tell were family members.

'Jemma's mum,' Rossi said, indicating with her head to the small figure emerging from the doorway. 'Wonder how she's doing?'

'Can't be good.' Murphy watched as she dabbed at her eyes. 'She blames herself. Doesn't matter what anyone will say to her, she'll carry that for a while.'

Murphy pictured her crying across from him. Quietly weeping into an old tissue. Rob had been to see her recently, she'd told them, talking about finding her daughter. Now, it looked like he'd instead been targeted, led to his death.

Rossi went quiet, taking the opportunity to scan the remaining faces. It was something they'd done for all the murder victims in the previous week, attending their funerals to see if anyone turned up who shouldn't have. At some point, a murderer must have attended the funeral of a victim, but Murphy had never found it useful.

'The best friend. What was his name?' Murphy asked.

Rossi took her notebook out, flicking to the page she needed. 'How do you always know where the right page is?'

Rossi smiled tightly. 'Just something I've learned over time. Here it is, Daniel Jones, goes by Dan. He's a senior lecturer at the university. He was the victim's best friend for the last five years.'

'We saw him didn't we, at the uni?'

'Yes, a few days ago. He didn't have much to say though. Shock I suppose.'

'I don't know. He was making eyes at you.'

'*Levati delle palle* . . . sir.'

Murphy smiled. 'I do love how swear words sound in Italian. 'We need to get back to it. Follow ups with the uni staff?'

'Good idea. I doubt we'll find anything, but at this point it can't hurt.'

Murphy paused as he scanned the few remaining people. 'There's no one here, we may as well get going.'

They started to walk off, towards the main road outside the cemetery where they'd parked up earlier. Murphy heard hurried footsteps behind them, and as he turned, the man rushing over towards them almost bumped into him.

'Sorry detective. I just wanted to speak to you before you left.'

'Hi Dan,' Murphy said, 'Everything okay?'

'As okay as they can be.' The clipped tones belied his upbringing. Murphy guessed Dan was a product of somewhere a lot nicer than the area he himself had grown up in. Murphy watched as his eyes caught Rossi's, who pretended to look away. He gave it a couple of minutes once the case was over before they were jumping on each other.

'I was just wondering if there's been any movement on the case?' Dan continued, finally bringing his attention back to Murphy.

'We're doing all we can,' Murphy replied, placing a comforting hand on Dan's shoulder. He attempted to soften his accent a little, feeling suddenly embarrassed about his roots on a council estate. Stupid when he thought about it, but he couldn't help it. 'How are the family holding up?'

'His father keeps having to be reminded he's gone. Dementia I assume. Rob didn't talk about him much, so I had no idea. Jemma's mother is taking it hard, as I'm sure you're aware. She thought so much of him. We all did.'

Murphy listened, trying to portray the right emotion on his face. He always found it difficult with the non-family members of victims, half knowing that their lives would move on far quicker than the actual people closest in blood ties to the victim.

327

'How is everyone at the university?' Rossi asked, joining the conversation.

'They've been coping.' Dan pointed to a woman walking by herself, studying the gravestones as she passed them. 'Elizabeth worked with him closely, so she has had some time off. First time I've seen her is today. I've not had a chance to talk to her as yet.'

'Well, we best get back,' Murphy said, half turning.

'Wait, there's a reason I wanted to speak to you. I was wondering if you could meet me at the pub, The Oxford, near the psychology building in an hour?'

'Why not now?' Murphy replied.

'Just want to finish up here. Not entirely sure it's even urgent, but I did want to speak to you to make sure.'

Murphy looked at Rossi, who shrugged in response. 'Okay, we'll be there.'

'Good,' Dan replied, his eyes moving around the cemetery. 'It's sad really. To think this is how it all ends.' He paused, looking for the words. 'It's so inevitable. All of us being drawn to here.'

Murphy followed Dan's gaze across the headstones in the distance. Hundreds, thousands maybe, all lives now gone. 'We'll see you there Dan,' Rossi said, snapping Murphy back to attention. 'You're best getting back.'

'Of course. Thank you,' Dan said, nodding and turning away.

Murphy watched him walk back over to where everyone was standing. Something gnawed at the back of his mind as he looked at the faces in the small group of people. He'd been feeling it all week. 'What are we missing Laura? There's something there, some link we can't see.'

They turned to walk away. 'I know. I've never experienced anything like this in an investigation,' Rossi replied, slowing her pace as two women walked by silently carrying a small bunch of tired looking flowers. 'We have a serial, with four victims. He leaves letters at each victim. All of them dumped. Every victim is linked to the university. We have no DNA, one hackney we can't find. CCTV has been no help, and the papers, with their "oh so helpful" nickname of the Uni fucking Ripper, think we're all clueless. All in all, it's as my Dad would say . . . *stronzo*.'

They'd reached the car as Rossi finished talking, Murphy waiting for her to end before getting in. 'But other than that, we're doing okay yeah?' Murphy said.

'Oh. We're doing a great job,' Rossi replied, getting in the car. 'What else can we do?'

Murphy had no easy answer.

'We keep working. That's all we can do.'

Rossi sighed heavily next to him. 'Work on what exactly?'

'Get those notes in order. See if anything has come back on the CCTV from the tunnels, and over the water. That cab has gone somewhere, and I don't think it's far. Most importantly, we don't give up.'

38

He needed to move on. Keep going.

He wasn't finished yet.

Laid low for a week. Since experiment six. He'd been sure the cab had been spotted. Waiting for a knock at the door since he'd placed those parts together on the quiet grassy area off the busy main road, convinced he would have been spotted.

Waiting to be stopped.

Busied himself preparing for number seven. Trying to choose a specific experiment to use. It was becoming more difficult. He thought about creating new experiments, testing his new-found abilities.

That wasn't what it was about.

So he waited. For inspiration. Or something else.

The first few days, he'd done little but sit there, shaking, nervously living in a bubble, waiting for it to burst. He imagined himself making one last stand, using the shotgun to take out a police officer or two, before turning it on himself.

He thought about that. If he'd be able to do so. Leaving Experiment Two to be found days, maybe months later. Emaciated. Hunger finally killing her.

Maybe that's how it should be. For her to go quietly, alone, with no one with her.

Three hundred and sixty days. And she seemed better than he had anticipated. Still able to form sentences, talk to him if he chose to speak to her. She knew who she was, and where she was most of the time.

By now he'd imagined her to be completely gone.

He'd pondered on that for a couple of days. Came to the conclusion it was an age thing. She had too much history behind her to lose it completely. Maybe a year wasn't long enough. Maybe he should go for two.

Next time, he could use a child. See if that made a difference.

He backed the hackney out of his garage at home, and headed for the university.

There was someone new he had his eye on.

39

Wednesday 13th February 2013 – Day Eighteen

It wasn't what he was expecting.

Murphy had entered, waited to be assaulted with cocktail offers and a games console on one wall. Maybe a shots menu, advertising slippery wotsits and all that shite. Bass driven music in the background.

Instead he found an old style boozer. Old guys with the racing pages open in front of them, tiny red pens in hand as they marked off their runners. A stout bald guy behind the bar, polishing glasses with a teatowel.

Murphy had almost walked out to check he had the right place. Worried he'd walked off campus and ten miles down the road to Speke.

'What . . . I don't understand.'

Rossi grinned next to him. 'I knew you'd be shocked. No idea, honest. Only came here a few times when I was studying. It's like the uni was built around it, and no one told the old fellas.'

'Right.'

Dan was waiting in a corner table, a pint in front of him. They headed towards him, Murphy looking at the pictures on the wall, the obligatory dogs playing snooker next to old football teams. 'Can I get you anything?' Dan asked once he'd finished a hefty gulp.

'No, we're okay,' Murphy replied, eager to get back. 'What did you want to talk to us about?'

'We used to come here for dinner, Rob and I. Most days. No one believed we got on so well, being so different, but we just did. He laughed at my "posh" ways, and I took the mickey out of him about his council estate background.' Dan caught Rossi's facial expression change to one of distaste and threw up his hands. 'Not out of spite, of course. It was just a bit of banter. You can't help where you're raised.'

Murphy shrugged.

Dan looked off into the distance. Murphy leaned on the table with one hand. 'You said you had something to tell us.'

'Yes,' Dan said after a pause. His eyes returned to them. 'On the Monday we met here, he seemed . . . different. Agitated. Wanted to know about some strange things.'

'Like what?' Rossi said, speaking for the first time.

'Psychology stuff. Wanted to know about Harry Harlow.'

Murphy sat back. 'Yes, we found some things in Rob's flat about him. It's an area of interest.'

'I didn't understand the connection. Until I thought about it more closely this past week. Rob still thought Jemma had been . . . well, kidnapped, I suppose is the right term. Rob was clinging onto that hope, that she hadn't just left him.'

'You weren't convinced?'

Dan took another swig. 'No. To be honest, it's not the first time he's been left behind. Happened a while ago, an ex upped and left one day. I get the impression he could be a bit stagnant. Too lackadaisical. He didn't enjoy anything out of his comfort zone.'

Murphy shrugged. 'Well, we spoke to Jemma's mother this week, and she confirmed Jemma had run away numerous times in the past. Although she was quite sure it wasn't the same this time around. There's nothing to suggest this could be any different though.'

'I suppose not. I just thought it best to inform you of it.'

'No, that's good, thanks.'

Dan lifted his glass, swirled the last quarter of his pint around the glass. 'It's too short.'

'What is?'

'Life. Just too damn short.'

Rossi cut in. 'The Harlow aspect is intriguing, however. It would fit in with the pattern. Unfortunately, we haven't really been able to find any information about his work.'

Dan finished his pint off. 'I have a few books which may be of use. You're more than welcome to borrow them.'

Rossi looked towards Murphy. He shrugged, what harm could it do?

'You could come now for them?' Dan said.

'You go Laura, I've got a call to make.'

Rossi and Dan walked towards the psychology building, Dan chatting away as she listened half-heartedly. He was good looking, in a posh boy type of way, she thought. Clean cut and well spoken. Someone to take home and introduce to your parents without worry.

Rossi chanced another look at him as they reached the psych building. Not bad. Not wearing a ring either.

'Lift or stairs?'

'Stairs,' Rossi replied, not wanting to be stuck in a confined space with him. With her recent dry spell, she was liable to jump him there and then. And she was pretty certain that wouldn't go down well with Murphy.

'Do you think it's someone here behind this whole thing?'

Rossi thought for a moment, deciding on the best way to answer. 'It's certainly all focused at the uni. Students, staff . . . probably not a coincidence.'

'I suppose.' Dan rounded the first floor, moving ahead of Rossi. 'Hard to imagine anyone here would be involved though.'

Rossi didn't say anything. She'd heard much the same thing over her years. People never believed anyone they knew could do anything that evil. Most prefer staying blind to what happens right under their noses.

Dan held the door open for her as they entered his office. Small, but practical, she thought. A single bookcase next to a desk which was free from clutter. It was the antithesis of Professor Garner's office, which still stuck in her mind. The smell of the memory clinging to the back of her throat.

Dan moved over to the bookcase, indicating for her to sit down in the only other chair in the room other than the one at his desk. She continued standing, leaning against the wall near the door.

'I have a couple of old works somewhere which have more about Harlow's work in them. Really, it's all online now I guess, but you don't really get a feel for his work without reading what was written at the time.'

'I know what you mean,' Rossi replied. 'When I did sociology, there was endless amounts of work on Marx. At first I used all the new textbooks, the Giddens, Keating, that sort of thing. It wasn't until I actually sat down and read his own words that it started to sink in for me.'

Dan was squatting at the bottom of the bookcase, pulling out each book in turn and then placing them back. 'Where did you go to uni?'

'Here. Graduated about ten years ago now.'

'And you joined the police?'

'Yeah. Seemed a natural progression at the time.'

Dan flicked through a book before placing it on the floor next to him. 'I understand that. I considered going out into the field, but a lecturer position opened up here after I'd

335

finished my PHD, so I just stayed. Took the easy option I suppose.'

A head poked through the door, close enough for Rossi to smell the aftershave of it's owner. 'Dan, do you have a second?'

'What is it, Tom? I'm busy here with the detective.'

Rossi moved into the line of sight of Tom Davies.

'Oh, sorry. It's just I was wondering if you'd seen Richard today?'

Dan sighed, Rossi biting back a smile. She guessed this posturing was for her benefit. 'No. Sorry. Have you checked if he's smoking outside. That's usually where he's to be found.'

'Erm, no. I'll do that now.' A quick glance at Rossi, his gaze averted as soon as she met his, and Tom shuffled his way out the doorway. His quick footsteps echoed away down the quiet corridor.

'They make a strange pair those two. Must be forty or fifty years between them, but they're always discussing something.' Dan stood up, handing three weighty books over to Rossi. 'Here we are. This should give you a bit more to go on. Not sure it'll help much though.'

'Thanks.' Rossi said, swiping dust off the top book's cover. 'We'll take what we can at the moment.'

'Glad to help.' Dan moved behind his desk, sitting down and leaning back. 'I think we should go out some time. Dinner maybe?'

Rossi looked up, taking a step forward from the wall. 'What?'

'I think we're a good match. Young still, both professional, both attractive, although you're far more attractive than myself of course. However, with the job you do, I'm assuming you're single, yes?'

Rossi tucked a strand of hair behind her ear. Wondered

what the hell to say. 'I'm not sure this is appropriate. Where has this come from?'

'Oh, it most certainly isn't appropriate. But with what happened with Rob, it's given me a fresh outlook on life. I've vowed to take more chances. Shouldn't we all?'

Rossi met his gaze. It'd been a while since she'd been surprised by anything. 'I guess we should. Still, this isn't exactly the best time.'

'Ah. You're still suspicious of everyone at the uni. I understand. I'll tell you what, when this is over, and you've caught your man, I'll be in touch. Sound fair?'

Rossi didn't reply, still standing with her mouth slightly open. 'Well. We'll see.'

'I guess we will, detective.'

Rossi backed out the room without saying a word. Closed the door behind her, stunned into silence. It'd been a while since she'd been propositioned whilst working, and they usually had fewer teeth and more weight on them.

She turned and walked back into his office without knocking. Dan was still in the same position as before.

'Listen, just so you know, I'm not that easy. You can't just demand a date and expect one.' She raised a hand to cut him off as he began to speak. 'I'll be in touch if I decide I want to find out what a bit of posh tastes like.'

She walked out, without waiting for a response. Shook off the encounter, putting her business head back on as she entered the stairwell.

'*Pazzo*.' She muttered under her breath. 'Bloody crazy.'

Murphy waited for Rossi and Dan to walk back towards the psychology building. He stood on the corner where the pub was situated, his thoughts mingling together in his head, like moths in the darkness, searching for light. He thought back to that day. His parents' house, months earlier. Yet that day was still as fresh in his memory. His thoughts went from that moment to the days before. The phonecalls late at night, the visits to her work. All the signs he'd missed.

He took out his phone, scrolled through to her number. It was the wrong time, his attention shouldn't be on this. Yet he couldn't stop himself.

He'd put it off too long.

'Hello Sarah, it's David.'

'I know. Your number came up. You okay?'

Murphy sighed, the voice on the other end of the phone feeling so familiar, yet so distant. A hazy memory of something that had once been so vivid. 'I guess. Working on a big case, should really be concentrating on that to be honest.'

'I saw you on TV. Those reporters are like vultures.'

'They're just doing their job Sarah.'

He heard a huff on the line. 'I know that. But it doesn't change anything. How have you been?'

'You know. Getting on with it.'

'I'd really like to see you David.'

Murphy closed his eyes, rubbed at them with his free hand. 'I know. I think I'm ready to see you too.'

'Really?' Sarah replied, her voice barely containing her surprise. 'What's changed your mind?'

Murphy walked down the short road, looking around as he spoke. 'Nothing Sarah. I'm still not there. But I'm willing to speak, if you are?'

'Of course I am. I've been waiting ever since . . . ever since that day.'

'Yeah. I know.'

'So do you want to come around here, I could make us something to eat maybe?'

Murphy stopped at an alleyway, glanced down it. 'That'd be good. Nothing big, don't go to any trouble.'

'I won't. When do you want to do it?'

338

Murphy heard a noise down the alley and turned towards it. Someone opening a door and getting into a car.

'Soon, I'll check . . .'

Not a car. A black hackney cab. His eyes immediately went to the licence plate.

'Shit . . .'

'What, David? What's happening?'

Murphy was stood in the alleyway exit, the cab facing him. The engine came on, and the driver finally looked up at him.

'I've got to go Sarah.'

He ended the call, shoving the phone in his pocket. Began walking towards the cab slowly.

The cab moved forwards, speeding up. Murphy shoved himself to the side of the a wall just as it was about to bear down on him.

He wasn't going to stop.

Murphy started running.

The man behind the wheel, Murphy recognised him instantly. The office with its boxes of alcohol. The short spiky haired guy in it.

Tom Davies.

40

Wednesday 13th February 2013 – Day Eighteen

Murphy ran, going through his pocket for the car keys, thankful for the fact they'd parked closer to the pub that day than the other times they'd been to the university. He reached the car, just as the cab driven by Tom Davies drove around the corner onto the main road.

Murphy got in the car, switching the engine on as soon as he sat down in the driver's seat. He reversed out, getting to the corner within seconds and seeing the cab in the distance. He took his phone out again, taking his eyes off the road to dial Rossi's number.

'Laura?' Murphy turned onto the main road heading towards the city centre, the road thankfully quiet as he put his foot down on the accelerator to catch up. 'I've got him.'

'What do you mean? Who?' Laura replied, her confusion apparent over the static.

'The killer. It's Tom.'

'What? You're not making any sense sir.'

The phone buzzed in his ear, as he reached the bottom of the hill, turning right onto Renshaw Street. He went through a red light, horns blaring from his left as he cut into front of slow-moving traffic. 'Tom Davies. He's the killer. I'm in the car, he took off in a black cab, *the* cab, without me having the chance to do anything.' Murphy made a sharp left turn into Ranelagh Street, the car ahead moving fast past Liverpool Central train station on the left-hand side.

'Shit. Are you sure?'

'Unless he has some other reason to run from us, I'm pretty damn sure.'

'Okay . . .'

'Think about it Laura. It fits. He works at the uni, he's intelligent, fit enough to do everything he's done, single. And he's currently doing sixty down Ranelagh Street in the fucking hackney that we've been trying to find for a week.'

Rossi said something Murphy couldn't hear. His phone buzzed again, his battery giving up the ghost. 'Fuck,' Murphy shouted, his voice echoing around the car. He saw the car in front moving into Paradise Street before turning right onto the A5036, Strand Street at the bottom. He followed, shifting down as he turned the corner. 'You still there Laura? He's going home I think.'

'Yeah, I'll call it in, get some cars to take over from you.'

'Okay. I'm on Strand, just going past the Albert Dock heading towards the Liver Buildings.'

'Stay on the phone, I'm getting security at the uni to phone through to the station.'

Murphy cut across two lanes of traffic, following the car up ahead which seemed to be pulling away. 'Laura, my shitty battery is dying. He's pulling off right going towards Bootle. I'll stay on him. Find out where he lives . . .' Three sharp noises in his ear signalled the end of the conversation. He looked quickly at the phone, seeing only a blank screen. He threw the phone down in the passenger seat hard. It bounced into the foot well. He increased his speed, trying to catch up with the increasingly blurred car a few hundred yards ahead.

The road they were on was a straight run up towards the north of the city, the River Mersey running alongside it on the left. Within minutes, they were passing Bootle on the right, Murphy gaining on Tom with every mile they passed. He looked down at the speedometer, pushing a hundred m.p.h, the right hand lane quickly clearing as they sped along.

Murphy began trying to work out where they were heading. The A road led up towards the leafier suburbs of the city, where money was more abundant than in the estates at the other end. Fifteen miles from the city centre lay the town of Formby, where houses regularly changed hands for more than seven figures.

Close proximity to the victims, psychology, experiments. He slammed the steering wheel in frustration. 'How did we miss it?'

They were heading towards Crosby. Passing Bootle in a blink of an eye, the River Mersey still to their left, only yards away. He was only a few car lengths behind, the speed of the cab decreasing. Murphy frowned, what had began as a chase, now almost seemed as if it had turned into a procession. He was being led somewhere.

Murphy checked the clock. They'd been driving now for almost ten minutes. He checked the mirrors again, no signs of any pursuing marked cars. He fingers turned white as he gripped the wheel, the thought of what possibly lay ahead making his heart thud against his chest.

Murphy stepped down on the accelerator again, more determined. Within a minute he was pulling alongside the cab, trying to get Tom's attention, without avail. He was staring straight ahead, giving no notice to the frenetic arm waving Murphy was employing as a tactic.

Tom slowed the cab, the road turning to two lanes, Murphy suddenly on the wrong side of the road. He moved across the lane, finding himself now in front of Tom's car.

He began to slow the car, hoping Tom would have to do the same in his car. It was a police pursuit procedure he'd done a few times before, but usually another two cars would be involved, boxing the suspect's car in. He shifted down into third gear as he slowed down to under forty. Tom was now matching his speed, just behind him. The road was getting busier and they passed a primary school as they headed towards Victoria Park. Murphy had one eye on the mirror, watching for any swift movements. There were numerous roads Tom could turn off into, yet he seemed to be content to follow Murphy. Again, Murphy's hands tightened on the steering wheel, wondering what he was driving towards.

He was crossing a junction, looking for the road sign just in case. 'Fir Road.' A huge pharmacy on the corner.

Murphy looked back in the mirror for the car behind him. Tom Davies sat rigidly upright, his hands in the perfect position on the wheel. When he looked back in front, he had to brake sharply as a motorbike pulled out from the road he'd just passed, cutting across him. He came to a stop, banging the wheel in frustration, and looked up to see the motorbike ride off into the distance.

'Bastard!'

Murphy looked in the mirror. Tom was gone.

'What the . . .'

He turned the car around in the road, horns blaring from two cars in opposite directions which had to slam on the brakes to avoid hitting him. He barely registered the noise, turning the car around in the road and pointing it back towards where he'd just driven.

He turned right into Fir Road, on instinct, thinking there wasn't enough time for Tom to have gone any other way.

The road was thinner here, terraced houses replacing the fast moving A roads he'd been travelling on for the last ten minutes.

343

Murphy saw the cab in the distance, under a hundred yards away. He shifted gear and accelerated to catch up. The cab turned right, and Murphy followed closely behind. Cars were parked on either side of the street. The cab slowed and turned into a driveway.

By the time Murphy reached the cab, it was in an open garage, the driver's door still open. He strained forward, attempting to see any sign of its missing occupant, but couldn't see anything around. He put his key back in the ignition, clicked it forward, and lowered the window. Once it was halfway down, he stopped, listening for any sounds, removing his seatbelt softly.

He reached down into the foot well and retrieved his phone. He pressed the power button on the side. 'Please, just a little more.' He wanted just enough time to send one text message, the quickest way to communicate where he was to others. The screen loaded up slowly, and a couple of button clicks later he was typing out a message to Laura.

Fir Rd, Crsby.

Murphy clicked send, and hoped the battery would last long enough for it to go through. 'Shit.'

The screen went blank before he knew if it had gone through or not.

He sat back in the seat, running his fingers through his hair and down his face. The image of the young woman, missing for almost a year, came to the forefront of his mind. Pain shot across his forehead, the cusp of something worse on the horizon.

'Two choices.' Murphy said aloud, his voice wavering in the quiet of his car. 'Either you stay here and hope that message went through. You'll be relatively safe, but he could be killing her now and escaping out the back.'

He breathed deeply.

'Or, you try and stop whatever he's doing in there.'

Murphy took in a deep lungful of air. Closed his eyes for a couple of seconds, then opened them, retrieving his baton from down the side of his seat.

Opened the car door and stepped out.

41

Wednesday 13th February 2013 – Day Eighteen

Murphy approached the house, waiting for the door to open, and for Tom to burst out and jump him.

He reached the door, noticing it was open a crack as he got there. He nudged it open wider with his foot, before stepping back. He couldn't see in properly; not enough light entering from the outside. He paused for a few moments, his back against the wall on the outside.

The only sound Murphy could hear was his own breathing. He tried to control it, holding his breath in, letting it out in one long silent exhale. His hand clasped the baton, extended out to its full length. He willed himself to move, to think about the young woman who he was sure was in danger at the moment, but all six foot four inches and sixteen stone of him felt paralysed.

'Come on . . . come on.' His whisper broke the silence. His legs started to work and he concentrated on putting one foot in front of the other. Within four steps he was at the threshold. He stopped for a second, before sidling around the doorframe into the house.

He held the baton upright to his side, ready to bring it forward with force at the slightest movement. He shuffled forward, keeping each foot firmly planted. The house was deathly silent, dust motes hanging in the air as what little sunlight there was shone through the uncovered window to the side of the room.

There was a staircase in front of him. A door to his right. He nudged it open with his foot.

'Police.'

His voice sounded different as it echoed back in the darkened room. He shuffled forwards, his back against the wall as the door remained open to his other side. He held the baton up, ready.

'Tom?'

The air changed to his left, the open doorway empty. Senses on fire, Murphy's eyes flitted back and forth as he walked into the room, his footsteps soft on the carpet. He scanned the room, looking for anything out of place, where someone could be hiding. Flowery paper on the walls, sparsely furnished, a small two-seater couch pointed towards a flatscreen TV.

Movement behind him, Murphy turned quickly, just as Tom swung something towards his head.

Too busy looking at the wallpaper. Idiot.

Muphy tried to block with his left arm, already swinging the baton with his right, when pain exploded in his arm.

A crowbar smashed into his arm, all of Tom's force behind it. His own baton missed by some margin. Murphy went to one knee, shifted to his right in anticipation of another strike, and tried to swing again. He aimed for the legs, but Tom side stepped and moved forward as Murphy went momentarily to the floor.

Tom was still standing, and as Murphy looked up, he saw him draw the crowbar up over his head, holding it with both hands. Murphy moved at the last second, getting up from the floor as he did so, the crowbar whistling past his right ear. Tom followed the crowbar, his torso exposed. Murphy didn't pause, throwing a right hook he'd learned twenty years previously in a boxing gym into Tom's side, hoping to bust a rib or three.

Tom buckled from the punch. Went to one knee, and stopped breathing. Murphy had done exactly as he'd intended, knocking the wind completely out of him. The crowbar dropped behind Murphy's head, and he pressed home the advantage.

Murphy stood, moving towards the crowbar, placing a foot over it. Tom was clutching his stomach.

Tom wasn't in range for a punch this time. Murphy settled for an old fashioned, face to the floor, arms up his back, kneeling with all his significant weight on Tom.

It all happened within a minute, Murphy surprised to find himself breathing at a normal enough rhythm. Wasn't as out of shape as he'd believed.

'You're screwed Tom. We've got you.'

'He's under control.' An officer in heavy uniform poked his head around the door to Murphy's right, giving him the nod.

Rossi and around fifty coppers had turned up five minutes after Murphy had pinned Tom to the floor. Five minutes where he'd concentrated only on not letting him go.

He motioned to Rossi to move with him, before going back inside and entering the room. He could see the psychologist on the floor.

'What's going on? I don't understand. Someone has to tell me what's happening. Where are you going to take me?' Tom Davies said from the floor, his voice squealing and high pitched. Murphy winced as Tom let out a yell, as one of the officers subduing him knelt on him a little more.

'Thomas Davies?' Murphy asked.

The man being held down attempted to lift his head, but the gloved hand pressing it down wouldn't allow it.

'I'm arresting you on suspicion of the murder of Donna McMahon, Stephanie Dunning, Colin Woodland, and Robert Barker.' The names came easily to Murphy, burned on his memory. 'You do not have to say anything . . .' as he reeled off the rest of the caution, Murphy watched as Tom's expression turned to one of horror.

'No, no. This can't be happening. I haven't finished,' he said from the floor.

Murphy looked over at Rossi, who had her notepad out, writing down every word. Murphy turned and nodded at the officers holding Tom. They lifted him to his feet, pulling him out of the room. Murphy watched from the doorway as they placed him in a van, parked on the kerb. He looked over to the houses opposite, a wry smile on his face as he saw the curtains twitching. Human theatre. Never fails to attract attention.

'Are we staying behind for a while sir?' Rossi said, standing behind him.

'No, we'll let the SOCOs do their stuff. We'll go down the station, let him stew for a bit and then start. If anything turns up we'll hear about it,' Murphy replied, stepping out of the house.   They had him.

He scratched at his beard, wondering if anyone else was sharing his fears of the scene not being right, seeing only pats on the back for a job well done.

Murphy couldn't share in it. The gnawing feeling of being controlled playing on his mind.

'I wasn't finished.'

Murphy sat impassively opposite Tom Davies, as he cried the same words repeatedly to himself.

His blonde spiky hair now looked untidy rather than stylish, as Tom's hands repeatedly passed through it.

'We can sort this out quickly Tom,' Murphy said, trying to

use a soothing voice, but it coming out rougher than he'd wanted. 'We just need to go over a few things, that's all. Now, are you sure you don't want anyone representing you for this?'

'No,' Tom replied, sniffing loudly in the interview room. 'I'm okay.'

'Okay. Can you tell us what you do for a living.'

'I'm a senior lecturer in behavioural psychology at the City of Liverpool University.' Tom sighed, his head in his hands.

'And how long have you been there?'

'I finished my PHD eight years ago. I've been in the department ever since.'

'Why did you choose psychology?'

Tom shrugged, 'it's the best subject to do what I wanted to.'

'Which is?'

'Experiment. Find out more about things.'

'What kind of things?'

'Life, how we interact, the way people work.'

Murphy looked over at Rossi who was making notes. 'Can you tell us how this started?'

Tom sniffed. 'How what started?'

Murphy slid a photograph across the table. Tom looked at it quickly. 'Number three.'

'Donna McMahon.'

Tom pursed his lips. 'I forget their names.'

'Okay. Do you remember them all Tom? How you left them?'

Tom put his head back in his hands. 'Of course I do. They were magnificent.' His head came back up. 'Did you read the letters?'

'Yes we did. Take us through each of them.'

Tom looked between Murphy and Rossi, his eyes settling on Murphy, 'Number three, LSD experiments. To see what would happen to someone with no inhibitions.'

'How did you find her?'

350

'She was working at the library one night. She seemed . . . interesting. Young, a bit naïve of course, but there was something about her. Intriguing. You can learn so much about someone by just watching them. She never knew I studied her for weeks. One night, I took the cab. Picked her up just outside campus.'

'What happened?'

'I got the dose wrong the first time. Just made her ill. By the fourth day she was flying. I watched her constantly, listened to her. She wanted to die. Wanted to meet God and shake him by the hand for creating such beauty. She could see things we'll never experience.

'I just helped her on the path to what she desired.'

Murphy swallowed, his mouth watering. He produced another photograph. Tom's face changed from the obvious delight he'd had talking about Donna McMahon to one of disgust.

'Number four.'

'Stephanie Dunning.' Rossi said, her voice steady and controlled.

'Number four, it didn't work. Couldn't get her to stay still. She scratched at me, spat, kicked, fought the whole time. I needed to sedate her so I could properly prepare her for what I wanted to do. She just screamed about her children, her husband. She had to go.'

'Did you pick her up at the university as well?'

'Yes. Same method. They are so trusting sometimes.'

'What about him,' Murphy said, pointing at the photograph of Colin Woodland he'd taken out. 'Tell me about Colin.'

'Number five, bystander theory. How long did it take for someone to find him? I never did find out.'

'Just under twelve hours.'

He smiled at that. Murphy had to grip the table edge.

351

'Awful. To think of all the people that walked past him. Two bodies found in the previous week, and they still left him there.'

'How did you get him?'

'I'd seen him at the library a few times. I knew it was only a matter of time before he said something about me spending time in the evenings there. He had eyes like a hawk for the women. I followed him as he walked from the university. He never took a cab or a bus, so I took him off a side street. They really should check the amounts of streetlights they have out there. Anyone could be out there in the darkness. He became number five. I found his heart. Watched as I made it stop.'

'And finally . . . Robert Barker.'

'Ah, Number six, Unit 731 experiment. I was finally able to perform this one.'

'You chose him.'

'Yes. Wasn't difficult. I wanted to see how much he'd been affected by the last year. He was broken before I got to him. I anticipated he'd accept death easier. More willing to give up and accept his fate. He fought only when he thought he could rescue his girlfriend. Even then, he was easy to dispose of.'

'You cut him up.'

'That was my favourite. Intermittent blood loss. Cut off a hand, a foot, a leg . . . see how long you can keep them alive. Didn't take that long.'

'What happened to numbers one and two, Tom?' Murphy said.

'Not ready yet.'

'Who's not ready?'

He got silence in return.

'Are experiment one and two still alive Tom?'

Tom raised his right hand in mid-air, waved it back and

forth. 'Maybe. Maybe not. Experiment two looks highly doubtful though. It's been a while.'

'What do you mean by that?'

'You'll see.'

Murphy sighed, ran a hand over his beard. 'Did you murder four people Tom?'

Tom ran a hand through his hair again. 'Yes. Did you understand why?'

'Why don't you tell me.'

Tom smiled slightly. Murphy gripped the table harder. 'To see what happened.'

'Is one of the experiments Jemma Barnes?'

The smile vanished, replaced with a frown. 'I know the name . . .'

Rossi interrupted, 'she was Rob Barker's partner. The one you cut up into pieces.'

'Of course.'

'Well? Is she experiment two Tom?' Murphy said.

'Rob and I knew each other in passing. He was Dan's friend though. Had no time for me really. I'd go to the pub whilst they were at lunch. Sit away from them, where they couldn't see me watching. They never invited me. He was always complaining about something or other. He was one of those people who never embrace life. He'd tell Dan everything, and I would sit and listen.'

'Did you take Jemma? Are you holding her still?'

Tom paused. Stared at Murphy in the silence, only the scratching of Rossi's pen on her notepad breaking it. 'I have no idea what you're talking about.'

'I think you do,' Murphy said, standing up. 'And you're going to tell us exactly where she is.'

'She ran off. I heard Rob and Dan talking about it loads. Constantly moaning about it. It was obvious she'd done one. I would have as well.'

'You might as well tell us Tom. It's over.'

'Let's talk about how you killed your parents instead. I'd love to know more about that.'

Murphy looked towards Rossi, who had put her notepad down. Looked down at his hands, clenched together as he leaned on the table which separated him from Tom. 'I didn't kill my parents.' Stared at Tom, hoping to kill the conversation before it went any further.

'Oh, I know you weren't holding the hammer, but it was your fault, was it not?' Tom replied, a sarcastic tone to his voice.

'I can't control what other people do,' Murphy said, looking past Tom at the concrete wall behind him.

'No one can, but we can lead them to do things, don't you agree?'

Murphy shifted on the chair. 'I certainly didn't lead him to kill my parents,' Murphy replied after a few moments. 'He was just a pathetic little man who couldn't take rejection. So he took something else instead.'

'Not so pathetic that he can destroy your life though?' Tom grinned, his teeth brilliant white.

Murphy's shoulders slumped a little more. 'This has nothing to do with what we're here for, Tom.'

'I disagree. Don't you see? There's only one type of person who could understand what I've done here. I think they are easily explainable to someone like you, David. You've experienced death, unexpected, unimaginable. Whilst not by your hand, you carry that feeling of guilt with you forever. *You* should understand what I've done in the last week.'

Murphy lifted his head up to find Tom staring at him, a questioning gaze fixed upon his face. 'I never will. You killed people. Good people, innocent.'

Tom laughed, his cackles filling the room with noise.

'Innocent?' he said, once his laughter died down a little. 'Don't give me that. Not one person is innocent. And that's a pointless way to think anyway. What makes them any better than anyone else? What makes them any more worthy of our regret or remorse than the thousands of people who die every day?'

'Because you stole their lives.'

Tom eyes danced. 'And you don't hear the same thing said about anyone who is deemed to have died sooner than they supposedly should have?' His voice became mocking. 'Oh poor Jeff, he was only fifty. Had so much more to give before the bus hit him.'

'People mourn, are you suggesting they shouldn't?'

'That's exactly what I'm saying. It's completely natural to die, it's a fact of life. We live to die. Why do we treat death the way we do?' Tom paused, looking around the room as if it held the answers. 'You know who the worst are? The religious ones. All sad at their funerals, when they're supposed to believe in a heaven, a better place than here. His voice raised at the end, saliva flew from his mouth and landed on Murphy's shoulder.

'So, you're just making us see that death is natural, by killing people?'

'Can you think of a better way David? What does it all mean to you?'

Murphy sighed, his arms beginning to ache as they bore his weight. 'I think it's all been meaningless. People know they're going to die, they just don't want to face it. We're taught to fear it, because if you're so preoccupied with death you forget to live.' He ignored the snort which came from Tom before continuing. 'You think anyone will care that you've had this huge philosophical reason why you've killed four people? They won't. They'll call you evil and be done with it. You think you're original? Professor

355

Garner told us Freud's view on death. *It's the aim of all life.* You're just trying to prove him right, to yourself more than us.'

Tom stared at him, his face blank, devoid of any emotion. 'Professor Garner says a lot of things.'

Silence filled the room, as both men stared at each.

'Well, that's okay I guess. I don't expect everyone to think as I do.'

'Who died, Tom?'

Tom looked away. 'What's that?' he replied, his voice wavering almost imperceptibly. Murphy noticed it.

'Who died? Someone you were close to, I imagine.'

Tom shrugged his shoulders. 'No one.'

'Oh, come on. We know that's the case. Parents? Girlfriend? Sibling? I don't know . . . maybe it was your favourite dog when you were growing up. I don't care really. I can see it was someone though. Best get it out early. I know you'll go for a psycho defence.'

'And you think that explains why I'm like this? Is that it?'

It was Murphy's turn to snort. 'Oh, nothing like that. You're this way because you choose to be. I'm just interested, that's all. You're obviously a psychopath, all that shite they spout about your types. "Didn't get enough cuddles as a kid so he started pulling the wings off flies".'

Tom lifted a cuffed hand to his face, drumming fingers on his clean-shaven cheek, before slapping his hand on the table. 'No one, David. No one of importance anyway. I'm sorry to disappoint. This was only about experiment-ation. I wanted to find out the answer to death. Why we treat it the way society does. But I think I'd still be this way even if I'd lost my parents at an early age or watched a sibling die. They're fine by the way. Mum and Dad live in the lakes, early retirement. Grandparents died at a good age, leaving a nice pot of money behind for the four of

356

us. The fourth is my older sister. She's an accountant in Manchester.'

Murphy sat down in his chair. 'Why then?'

'I'm just not wired like all of you. I believe in progress, in learning more about ourselves through testing us to our limits. This is the ultimate experimentation of modern man. And I'm privileged to be . . . leading it.'

Murphy sensed something unsaid. 'Leading it?'

A slight shift, almost unseen if Murphy hadn't been paying attention. 'Yes. The leader of the experimentation.'

'No help from others then?'

'Of course not.'

Murphy unclasped his hands, picked up his pen and chewed the cap. 'I think you're more like us than you realise.'

Tom scoffed, back on an even keel. 'I don't know of many people who kill four people in the space of a couple of weeks.'

'Away from that.' Murphy said. 'You're like everyone. You fear death as much as anyone else. I know you do. You just think you can control it. You think if you show how worthless it all is, it'll make you feel better about your own fear. So you kill. You wanted to kill people for your own sick gratification. You couldn't deal with just killing them though, you had to dress it up as something else. All this bollocks about experimenting, it was all designed to clear your conscience.' Murphy could feel sweat rolling down the back of his neck, worried that he'd gone too far and maybe goaded Tom into silence. They still needed the information on the other two experiments.

Tom just stared at him. The blank emotionless expression returned. 'Interesting theory,' he said after what seemed like minutes had passed. 'I guess I'll have to give that some thought.'

'Is this just a game to you?' Murphy said.

'Oh no, David. This is important work. Much needed in these times.'

'You know you'll spend the rest of your life in prison, don't you? No way of doing your little experiments in there.'

'We'll see.' Tom leaned forward, his eyes never leaving Murphy's. 'Despite what you say, I don't fear death.'

'Tell me about Experiment One and Two Tom. Where are they?'

Tom rolled his eyes. 'You tell me something first. Did you get to your parents before they died David? What was it like at the end?'

'Shut your mouth.'

'Did you see their last breath? Tell me about it, I'd like to hear. Did they bleed to death?'

Too many questions. Murphy felt himself rise up off his chair. 'Don't . . .'

Tom was shouting now. 'Do you think they died at the same time David? Looked into each other's eyes and cursed the day they ever brought you into the world, just so you could be the reason to end theirs? You and your junkie whore of a wife?'

Murphy had him by the throat against the wall in one single swift movement. Tom's handcuffed hands tried to push back at him, but he was too strong. 'I said keep your fucking mouth shut, you psycho.'

Rossi came around, tried to pull him off Tom. He wasn't letting go.

'I'll choke the life out of you, see what happens at the end for you, hey? Would you like that?'

'Let go of him, sir . . . sir, let go.'

Rossi's hands left his shoulders, and he heard the door open in the background. His eyes never left Tom's.

'Me . . .' The voice came out as a whisper.

'What?' Murphy loosened his grip a little.

'It was me. *I* was experiment one. I was the first.' It came out in choked gasps.

Then, there were hands on Murphy's shoulders.

He was already letting go of Tom.

Experiment Two

She breathed in, the singing continuing from the corner. She resisted the urge to ask for quiet, knowing it was important she didn't. She was Jemma. She could do this. It didn't matter something was crawling across her bare foot. That the walls were closing in on her again.

Always there, crushing her, squeezing the life out of her.

She was going to be out of there soon. She knew it. This would work. She just had to be very quiet, ignore the voice whispering in her ear, ignore the pain in her chest.

She shivered, tucking into herself slowly to feel more warmth, hoping the slight movements wouldn't be picked up by the man.

Why had she got in that taxi . . . it'd had been dark, but she should have guessed something wasn't right. He never turned to look at her, speak to her.

'She'd just fallen asleep, like a bleeding idiot.'

She laughed at the sound of her rasping voice. She didn't even sound like herself anymore.

Stupid. That's what she was. Too trusting. And where had that trust landed her? Stuck in the darkness, with only a dead man singing, things crawling around her, moving walls, and a hunger only overridden by the need for water which had now crept up on her.

And it wasn't the first time she'd made a mistake.

She'd been nineteen, her mates from school now all at university or in full-time jobs. She didn't go out all that much, working odd days here and there for a little bit of extra money. Shops mostly, sometimes pubs, but she tried to avoid them as much as possible.

Her mum was on her case constantly. Worried she'd disappear again or something.

That was what she did though, anything to get away from reality. Just take off, stay with her aunty on the east coast, friends she'd met online down south. Anywhere other than Liverpool.

She'd hated living there. Her more successful, happier friends, seeming to rub her nose in the bad choices she'd made.

She missed her dad.

And then she'd met her first proper love. She thought things could be better, she could be settled. They made plans to live together, a future.

She was happy.

Her mum was happy.

Then a few of the girls she was still mates with suggested going out round the uni bars. Told her it was a cheap night out, and loads of fun. That she shouldn't miss out on the lifestyle just because she wasn't still a student.

She'd got drunk, dancing on tables, getting free drinks handed over. It'd been a great night. Until those lads turned up, trying to pair off with each of them. She'd been seeing someone for over a year before that night. She was drunk, it was a mistake, but he didn't see it that way. It was over and she vowed never to lose control again.

And yet here she was, after another night out had ended with her making a bad choice.

No, that wasn't her fault. She was blaming the victim, something she always hated others doing. Blaming herself for what someone else had chosen to do. He had no right.

No right.

Her fists were clenched together, her bitten short, sharp nails digging into the flesh of her palms. She made herself relax.

It wouldn't be long now, she thought. He'd come in the room, and she'd show him what she could with those nails. Teeth, head, legs, everything.

She was getting out of there.

42

Thursday 14th February
2013 – Day Nineteen

He sat opposite DCI Stephens, resigned to what was going to happen.

He'd lost control. Exactly what Tom had wanted to happen. And Murphy had played right into his hands.

'What the hell where you doing in there? Do you think you're Gene frigging Hunt or something?' Stephens' voice echoed in the small office.

Murphy shrugged. 'You heard what he said. He's a psycho.'

'Yes, but at the moment we only have his word for what happened. If your actions have jeopardised that . . .'

'Don't worry,' Murphy said with a wave of one hand, 'he's too proud of what he's done.'

'You don't speak to him again. For God's sake David, if he makes a complaint he could retract the entire confession. I don't know what you were thinking. I never should have put you on this case. It's too soon.'

Murphy stood up. 'If it wasn't for me, we'd never have found him. Gratitude would be nice.'

Stephens sneered, 'thank you David. Now get out of here. Cross your fingers that this doesn't come back on us.'

Murphy left the station, got in his car and drove away. His hands gripped the steering wheel, knuckles white against the black.

Stupid. That's what he was. He shouldn't be anywhere near that place.

He knew where he had to go.

Murphy pulled the car to a stop outside the house and walked up the path towards the door, his heart rate increasing with each step. It reminded him of the day he got married for the second time; the same feeling he'd had waiting at the registry office. He was sweating underneath the thick coat he was wearing, despite the cold. He stopped halfway up, took a deep breath in and let it out, noticing his breath was now visible. 'You can do this,' Murphy muttered to himself. Steeling himself, he carried on walking. 'It's stupid, you've walked up this path so many times. It's no different.' It *was* different though, he knew that. It had been so long, and now nothing was the same. And he didn't know if it ever could be again.

He rang the doorbell, hearing the soft chimes from within. The door opened, revealing her.

'Hello David.'

Murphy smiled. 'Hello Sarah.'

It had been awkward at the door, neither of them knowing how to greet each other. They settled for a quick kiss on the cheek, Sarah bringing a hand to her lips as they touched his beard, Murphy smiling in return. She hadn't changed much at all, he thought. She would have been tall in any other setting, but Murphy still had six inches on her, meaning she had to reach up to kiss his cheek, her blonde hair tied back neatly in a loose braid. Her deep blue eyes boring into him as he crossed the doorway.

He couldn't help but stare as she walked ahead of him into the room which led off the hallway.

Then they were standing on opposite sides of the living room, Murphy looking around the room at all the familiarity which surrounded him.

'Tea?' Sarah said. Her voice cutting through the silence which had hung in the room since they'd entered.

'Please,' Murphy answered, wishing she'd offered something a bit stronger. Murphy walked around the living room after Sarah moved into the kitchen. The ornaments on the mantelpiece, the rug on the floor . . . even the position of the bloody coasters on the coffee table. All the same. It was as if the last eighteen months hadn't happened, that Sarah had lived in a bubble, not existing whilst Murphy was away.

He turned and faced the wall he'd been avoiding since entering the room. Photographs tastefully placed on the wall by Sarah years earlier. His attention moved to one photo only. His parents on holiday, around two years before they died.

'It's been bugging me for ages. Where was that taken?' Sarah asked from the doorway, the kettle boiling behind her in the kitchen.

'Kos, that Greek island.' Murphy replied, his hand touching the photograph. 'June 2009. We paid for it if you remember, a fortieth wedding anniversary present.'

'That's right. They look so happy.'

'They were. They hadn't been before, and mum wanted to see the active volcano there, it was off the island at a place called Nistros, or Nisyros . . . something like that.'

Sarah turned, hearing the kettle click off, not before Murphy noticed her bottom lip trembling slightly. He sighed, and moved away from the photograph, taking a seat in his chair. 'My chair . . .' he muttered under his breath, snorting.

It hadn't been his chair in a long time. Perfectly in line with the TV in the corner, so he had an uninterrupted view. He wondered if anyone else had sat here in the time he'd been away.

'Still two sugars?' Murphy heard being shouted from the kitchen.

'Yeah.'

Sarah came in carrying a tray with two cups and a plate of biscuits on it. 'Chocolate bourbons still your favourite?' she asked, sitting on the sofa.

Murphy smiled. 'Still my weakness,' he replied. 'You never liked them. Which means these are either going to be very stale, or you've bought them specially.'

Sarah raised her eyebrows in reply, a look Murphy was intimately aware of.

An awkward silence fell over them once more, Murphy concentrating on dipping his biscuits in his tea. It had never been this way before; in the past they had so much to say to one another. Now, there seemed to be nothing.

'I saw the news. You got the Uni Ripper.' Sarah said, breaking the silence, forming quote marks with her fingers around the words 'Uni Ripper'.

Murphy winced at the name. 'Yeah, but we don't really call him that at the station.'

'Sorry. Did he own up to it?'

Murphy sighed, sitting back in the chair . . . his chair . . . sipped on his tea, which seemed to be more biscuit than liquid after five or six dips. 'Yeah,' he said finally. 'It was hard, he's very clever, didn't leave us anything to go on. We got lucky in the end really.'

She set her cup back down on the table. 'Was this the first one since . . . since then?'

'Yes.' Murphy said without emotion. 'They've been keeping me away from these sorts of cases. Turns out this one wasn't as straightforward as they thought it was going to be. Not an *ease your way back in* kind of case.'

'How has it been?'

'You know. It's difficult sometimes, but I'm getting through it.' Murphy found the lie easy to articulate. 'How have you been?'

Sarah's voice dropped along with her head, her chin tucking into her chest. 'In limbo, David. Waiting for you.'

'Maybe you shouldn't have,' he replied, more severely than he'd meant it to sound.

She snapped her head back up at him. 'What was I supposed to do, move on, forget about my husband? I couldn't just do that David. Is that what you've done?'

'Of course not,' Murphy said, beginning to regret going there. 'It's just, I don't think anything has changed.'

Sarah pulled strands of her hair forward and began sucking on them. Murphy recognised the movement, her nervous energy breaking out into familiar self-comforting measures. Murphy sat forward, wanting to be away from there. Anywhere else but sitting with someone he once felt so deeply for.

'You still blame me,' Sarah said, her voice barely audible.

'It's not that. I just can't do this yet.'

'It's been almost a year. If you were going to be able to, don't you think you'd be there by now?'

Murphy stood up, paced the floor of the living room in front of the fireplace. 'I don't know what you want me to say, Sarah.'

'What about me? Have you thought about me at all? Or can you just not admit to me you think it's over? That it's my fault they died.'

'I can't do this.'

Sarah crossed the room, banging into the coffee table as she moved quickly, but not missing a step. She came up to

367

Murphy, causing him to take a step back. 'We're already doing it David. You're here, so why not get it off your chest? It's my fault, it was because of me, because of where I'd come from. I'm the reason they're dead. Admit that's what you think.'

Murphy turned away, his fists clenched, biting his lip. 'It's not like that.'

'Then what is it like then?'

'If I hadn't met you I wouldn't have fallen in love with you and they'd still be alive. It's not your fault. It's mine.' He turned back around, feeling the tears falling down his face. Sarah's lips were trembling.

'Get out.'

'What?'

'I said get out of here. I don't want you here.'

Murphy felt a flicker of saliva hit his face, as Sarah shouted at him. 'Wait. I want to talk to you, I *need* to talk to you.'

'You wished you'd never met me?' Murphy reached out a hand to touch her arm. 'No . . . no. I don't want to hear it.' She shrugged off his hand, stepping back and crossing her arms. 'That's enough. Please, just leave.'

'I'm sorry Sarah. I didn't mean it that way.'

'Of course you did. If we hadn't got together, your mum and dad would still be alive. It's true. It's my fault I was with *him* before us. That I didn't see it coming.'

'How were you supposed to know? I should have seen what he was capable of.'

'Because he gave me a few beatings? That's ridiculous David. I knew what he was like. You didn't. How could you know?'

Murphy sat down heavily on the chair. 'That's my job Sarah. I'm supposed to see these things coming. I didn't, and now they're dead.'

'He was still obsessed with me,' Sarah said, kneeling down next to Murphy. 'I thought he'd get the hint that I'd moved on. But he just kept coming around and I should have told you that.'

'It doesn't matter now. It's done.'

'It does matter. We're never going to move on with our lives if we never talk about it.'

Murphy sighed, rubbed at his beard. 'What is talking about it going to change?'

Sarah placed a hand on Murphy's knee. 'It's a first step. Don't you still love me?'

Murphy stared into Sarah's eyes, feeling the same way he always had. He loved her, he just couldn't look at her face after it had happened. See his own guilt reflecting back at him. He reached over, stroked her face. She closed her eyes, nestling into his palm. He leaned forward, his lips parted.

It was soft, at first, then it became more urgent. He needed her. He gripped her tightly, hands over her back, in her hair.

Murphy pulled away. 'Wait. There's something I want to say.'

She looked at him, head tilted, her upper lip and cheek already turning red from his beard rubbing against her. 'What?'

'It's my problem. I'm going to talk to someone. Not the shitty counsellor they want me to see at work, someone who I think can help me.'

'Okay. I think that's for the best. Now, let's get something to eat. I'm starving.'

Murphy smiled, 'that sounds great.'

43

Friday 15th February
2013 – Day Twenty

Rossi grumbled to herself as Stephens spoke to them in her office. A sweat-stained Brannon beamed beside her.

Bet he couldn't believe his luck.

He'd take the credit for this. She knew it. The man who finalised the interview with Tom Davies. He'd be promoted off the back of it, no doubt.

Testa Di Cazzo.

She'd been trying to call Murphy since what had happened the previous day. He hadn't answered. Probably sulking.

She thought of the posh boy at the university. Wondered how long she should give it before ringing him. Another day maybe.

'Now, he's had overnight to calm down, and hopefully he's going to keep quiet about what happened with Murphy. All I want you two to do is finish off the statement and that's it. Okay?'

Brannon got in before her. 'No problem. I'll make sure it's sorted.'

They didn't switch on the recorder at first. They waited.

'About yesterday Tom, you understand you goaded detective Murphy into doing what he did?' Brannon said, leaning over the desk. His shirt tail was hanging out the back of his trousers. It was a mass of creases. Rossi shifted her gaze.

'Oh yes. Don't worry, it'll be our little secret,' Tom replied, a smile on his face that turned Rossi's stomach.

'We just want to get your entire statement down, okay Tom?'

'Certainly.'

Rossi switched on the recorder, and began writing up Tom's statement. Listening as he talked about each murder again, in flat tones, precise. Listing everything he'd done.

She wouldn't forget this for a long time. It was going to be a week of Mamma Rossi's food before she even went to her own home again.

'Well, thanks for that Tom. The next bit is obviously a formality. It seems you're aware of how this goes.' Brannon looked down at his notes and cleared his throat. Rossi rolled her eyes. 'Thomas Davies, you are being charged for the murder of Donna McMahon, Stephanie Dunning . . . erm . . .' he checked his notes, 'Colin Woodland and Robert Barker. Do you understand those charges?'

'Yes. Can I say something else?'

'Of course, Tom.'

'I want to tell you about Experiment Two. I think it's only right that I do.'

Brannon sat up in his chair. 'Yes, yes of course.'

'There's a house in Aintree. On Lancing Drive. It was my aunt's house, but she moved into a nursing home a couple of years back. I've been renting it out. I made use of the tenant. You'll find number two in there.'

'Who is it Tom?' Rossi asked.

'You'll see.'

Rossi had to summon all the strength she had to not take Brannon's egg-stained tie off from his neck and shove it down his crowing mouth. He was holding court in the incident room, boasting how his softly, softly approach had meant he'd finally got some more information from Tom Davies.

'It's all about knowing them, how they work,' he said, as Rossi checked the drawers of her desk for something to eat.

'You've got to know what you're dealing with. It's all psychology, you know.'

She found half a Bounty at the back of the middle drawer and shoved it in her mouth. It was soft, the coconut tasting a bit funny, but it stopped her from shouting out.

Her phone rang on her desk.

'Rossi.'

'It's me.'

She leaned forward, swallowed the chocolate down. 'I've been trying to call you. Are you all right?'

'I'm fine,' Murphy replied. 'Listen, I need you to get an address for me.'

'Okay.'

'You need to keep this quiet though.'

'Sure, no problem.' She listened as Murphy gave her a name and she pulled up the information on her computer. 'Why do you need that?'

'I think he can help me.'

'Good thinking.'

'I'm guessing Brannon finished off the interview with you?.'

Rossi looked up. Brannon was still holding court. 'Yeah. Soft shite thinks he's cracked the case. Tom told us where we could find number two.'

A sharp intake of breath came over the earpiece. 'Well, that's something. He told me he was number one.'

'He experimented on himself?'

'Turned himself into a killer I guess. Listen, I've got to go. Hopefully I'll be back in soon enough. Let me know how you get on.'

Rossi ended the call. Turned in her chair and patted her

knees, standing up. 'Right. Shall we stop gassing and get over there?'

Murphy put the phone back in his pocket and entered Victoria Road into his sat nav. Pulled away from the kerb by Sarah's house. Or was it their house again now? He wasn't sure. Too early to say.

Twenty minutes later he turned onto Victoria Road in Formby. This was where people with money lived. It didn't surprise him this was where he'd had to go.

The road was less wide, a more old English village setting replacing the fast moving A roads. He came to a level crossing and passed over it, searching the road ahead for the right house.

A small lane was to the right, wrought-iron gates opening inwards, and he turned the car towards it. The road underneath turning to gravel. He pulled the car to a stop as the house revealed itself.

Tall dark windows adorned the front of a large building which Murphy thought looked more like an old hotel rather than a home. Pillars surrounded the front door, the marble colour blending perfectly with the red brick façade. A silver Mercedes was parked at an angle on the large patch of gravel which lay in front of the house.

Murphy parked up and left the car.

Jemma was curled on the mattress, trying to ignore the pains in her stomach. Her dry mouth.

Failing.

It had been days. Weeks maybe. She tried to remember how long someone could go without water. It was either four days or fourteen. She couldn't quite reach that fact in her head. It was drowned out.

Ha. Drowned. She'd give anything to be plunged into water. She'd gulp it in, not caring if it filled her lungs.

No voices. No voices in the walls.

Then, there was.

'Jemma.'

It was different. It wasn't the same.

'Jemma, can you hear me?'

'Yes. Am I going now?'

The walls went silent. She sat up, waiting for something else. Nothing came for a few minutes.

Then she heard footsteps coming down from outside the room. She stood up, her legs wobbling underneath her. The footsteps stopped, and the hatch opened. She scrambled across as something was dropped through.

'I'm sorry it took so long. There's been some slight mishaps the last few days. It's okay though. I know what to do.'

She tore off the cap on the bottle of water, guzzled down as much as she could.

'I'm not happy though. So there's going to be a slight change of plan. You're going to be here a little longer . . .'

Jemma's head shot up, 'no, please let me out.'

'You be quiet now.'

They gathered on Lancing Drive, ready to enter the property. The road was quiet, just the odd curtain twitching and some neighbours brave enough to stand on their front step.

It had been raining overnight, the grass at the front of the property still tinged with early morning dew. A low sun in the sky, not bringing warmth with it. Rossi had her hands in her coat pockets and stood as close to Brannon as she could deal with.

'Do we knock first?' he asked her.

'There's a doorbell, why don't you check that first,' she replied, rolling her eyes.

'Seriously?'

'All we have is his word,' Rossi said, turning to look at

the other officers stood on the path, 'it could be just another game.'

Brannon shrugged and pressed the bell.

'You said I could go though. You said.'

'Not just yet. We're not finished. Another few months, maybe a year. Then you can go.'

'No.' Jemma shouted, moving close to the hatch. It was too small, she couldn't get through there again. It was letterbox sized now, just big enough to put a bottle of water and some food through it. She thought she could see his mouth behind it. 'No, I have to go now.'

'I'm sorry Jemma. Plans change. I'm afraid it has to be this way. The experiment must be completed.'

'What experiment? I'm not an experiment. I don't agree to this, just let me go.'

There was a noise in the background. Then, silence. It came again.

A doorbell.

'You've tried twice now Brannon. Let's just get in. There's obviously no one in there.' Rossi said, leaning against the wall next to the front door.

Brannon looked around, let out a cheesy breath. 'Can you see any movement through the window?'

Rossi motioned to a uniform to take a look.

'Nothing,' he said in a stage whisper, 'looks dead in there.'

Rossi asked him to check in with the team at the rear of the property, receiving the same response.

'Step aside Brannon. Let them break it down.'

'Okay.'

He climbed the steps of basement with some effort. Paused at the top to catch his breath, before moving through the house. He walked past the monitoring room and checked the front of the house via the camera pointed to the entrance.

'Oh dear.'

He grabbed what he needed and moved towards the hallway. Breathed in and out a few times and then opened the door.

'Sorry it took me so long. How can I help you Detective?'

Murphy pushed the doorbell again. Felt stupid for not calling ahead.

What a wasted journey.

He was about to turn back to his car, when the door opened.

'Sorry it took me so long. How can I help you Detective?'

He turned around to see Professor Garner's now familiar yellow teeth smiling back at him.

'Please, do come in. I assume you're here about Tom.'

'Thanks,' Murphy said entering the house. 'Not about Tom. This is a bit more of a personal visit.'

'Oh . . . Intriguing,' Garner said, shutting the door behind him.

Experiment One

It began with an academic paper.

Life, Death, and Grief.

It was his idea to bring Tom on board to co-write it with him, knowing if he was left alone to create it, he might reveal more about himself than he wished to.

They bonded, of a sort. They spoke often about society, life, people.

Death.

Garner had already began thinking of something to do in his old age. No longer able to do the things he'd done as a younger man.

He'd always so enjoyed the hunt. Discovering so much about death, by inflicting it on others.

Then, he was too old, too infirm. His heart wouldn't take the strain any longer. He needed it still however, that feeling of power.

He began thinking of ways he could achieve it.

It came to him when he was researching one day.

Stanley Milgram.

Tom had already shown he had the capability inside him. He just needed the push.

He needed someone in authority to tell him what he should do. Garner was in that position.

Garner took it slowly, spent many months preparing him for the change.

He took the best of the Milgram experiments and added his own flair to it.

He started off without murder. Just the kidnapping of a young girl. Of Tom's choice. He provided the money to buy the taxi, told him how to pick someone up. Taught him how to use the lock, so once someone was in the back, they wouldn't be able to get out.

He was with him the whole way.

He watched the first few weeks as often as possible, waiting for Experiment Two to break. Instead, they almost lost her. Garner had acted fast, playing on what he thought would work best to get her back down into the basement. Her own compassion for her fellow kind.

A girl screaming in a room just like hers.

He'd watched via the monitors as she'd gone back down the steps, willing Tom to come back to consciousness. And breathing a huge sigh of relief when he had.

Garner had to rein him in. Work on him for a long period of time, eleven months in total, to get him ready for the next step. Destroy his old belief system, make him a murderer.

The result surprised even him.

It was as if Tom had been waiting his entire life to end people's lives. Like he'd been born to do it. Garner had just brought it out of him, given birth to his lust for death.

Tom took to it all, eager to please, to carry out Garner's will. There had been moments when Garner could scarcely believe his luck in discovering someone like Tom Davies.

Experiment Two was isolation. When he'd asked in the beginning, Garner had told him they'd release her after a year.

Just to see how close mentally they could bring her to complete shut down.

A living death.

Tom was a good pupil, but he wasn't as good as Garner was. He'd taught him so much, even given him his own signature victim posing, based on Vitruvian Man. Added weight to what Garner was instilling in Tom daily. He'd enjoyed playing with the detectives at the university, giving them just enough information. The rush of being right there, under their noses without them realising.

Forty years undetected, and now he had to clean up Tom's mess.

Next time, he'd choose someone prepared to make no mistakes at all.

44

Friday 15th February
2013 – Day Twenty

EXPERIMENT

I spent three days checking on the man you found this letter attached to before leaving him here. He was an incredibly interesting subject. I'll be watching out for reports of his cause of death. As it was, I was most fascinated when I tied him by his feet and hung him upside down for

From what little information there is, I suspect it will have been a stroke which caused his death. The blood pooling in his brain as gravity took its hold. Once the blood pressure increased, risk of stroke was inevitable.

I wasn't sure if he would in fact die from the procedure. There is no data I can find on this phenomena, this may be the first in the country in fact. I am sure

*you are honoured to be a part of this
exploration.*
   It's an experiment in

Rossi placed the letter back down, trying to work out why
it was so incomplete. Brannon was standing off to her side,
one hand to his mouth as he tried to block out the smell.
Dust in the air was sticking to back of Rossi's throat, the
smell overpowering.

'Jesus Christ.'

Rossi turned towards the voice, biting back an admon-
ishment.

They'd put the door in within seconds, the smell informing
them instantly what they were going to find.

'How long?' Rossi asked Dr Houghton, the grey haired
pathologist looking a tad disturbed by the scene. Something
she hadn't seen previously.

'Not sure. A week, maybe two.' Dr Morris replied. He
crouched down in front of the body. 'So this is number two?'

'Yeah, this makes five in total. He reckons he's number
one himself.' Rossi replied, looking over the pathologist's
shoulder. She shooed a fly away from her face.

'I'd make a joke about him hanging around until we found
him, but that seems a tad distasteful, even for me.'

'Quite.'

The kitchen was decorated in an country-cottage style.
Aga oven, a white fireclay sink with ornate taps over it. A
large American-style fridge freezer, with what appeared to
be an ice maker on one side. The ceilings had been stripped
back, wooden beams the most eye-catching feature of the
room.

Well, usually.

A man was silently swaying in the dust by his feet. Hung

381

upside down and left to die. Flies had rested on a wound to the back of his head. The smell was overpowering.

Rossi regretted eating that half a Bounty.

'And I'm guessing there's little evidence left behind?'

Dr Houghton snorted. 'A wallet. Bank cards and a provisional license in the name of Keith Henderson. But other than that, no. Nothing of use so far. He's good, Laura. Very good. Let's hope I can get something useful from the autopsy. Help you along a bit. Even with a confession, unless he pleads guilty it'd be good to have more.'

Rossi nodded at the pathologist, turning away from the sight of the body. Letters piled up by the door confirmed Keith Henderson as the tenant living there. 'Brannon, let's leave them to it for now.' She followed him out the room, taking one last look over her shoulder at the body as they began the process of cutting him down. She shuddered internally, the thought of the man who did this being across a table from her only a few hours before.

'You alright?' she said, pulling Brannon to a stop in the hallway of the semi detached house. He was looking a wrong shade of green.

'Yeah.' Brannon replied. 'But this . . . this is crazy. What the hell is that in there?'

'That, is what me and Murphy have been dealing with for the past few weeks. Still pissed off he chose me?'

Brannon attempted a smile. 'I guess not, Laura. What's the plan then?'

'We let them do their job,' Rossi said, indicating the room they'd just exited. 'Whilst they're doing that, we go speak to the neighbours. See if they can be of any use.'

'Was there a letter? Like with the others?'

Rossi nodded, 'wasn't complete though. Most of the information was missing. Including what number it was.'

'Hmm.'

Rossi turned away from the entrance to the kitchen, heading for the front door. Brannon followed behind her as they exited the house and took in lungfuls of clean air. There were two uniforms stationed at the bottom of the path, standing guard at the gate. Rossi looked over to the other side of the road, noting local reporters already in attendance. She rolled her eyes, as she looked out for that bastard from the local paper. She looked towards the sky, expecting to see a news helicopter already there, but was greeted by dark clouds instead.

Rossi took the lead, walking towards the house which shared a wall with the victim's. As they walked up the path, an unkempt and messy front patch of garden with over-growing weeds to the right-hand side, she began to form a picture in her mind. An overwhelming sense of seclusion seeming to emanate from the bricks themselves, cutting it off from its surroundings. The house didn't fit with the rest of the street, every other house gleaming from the outside, prim and proper as a house could be.

Rossi nodded towards the uniform at the open door, and stepped over the threshold.

Cats. That was all she could smell. Seeping from the woodwork, the worn down carpets, the essence of the house was cat.

She hated cats. Evil little things.

She gagged upon entering, earning a sympathetic look from the uniform standing by the door. She rolled her eyes toward him, earning a brief smile.

'Think I'd rather be back next doo,.' she whispered to Brannon behind her, covering a cough with her hand.

'What's the problem?' Brannon replied.

Rossi sighed. He was probably used to this type of smell. 'Come on, let's get this over with.' They moved into the living room, where the sole occupant was holding court in an over-stuffed chair, which might have been considered antique over a century ago. Another PC was stood in there, and looked relieved to be excused when they entered.

'Mrs Andrews, is it?' Rossi asked.

'Yes. Please, sit down. Can I get you a cup of tea?' she asked, holding a used tissue in one hand.

'No that's okay,' Rossi replied. 'We won't take up too much of your time.'

'Well I don't know much. Just that the smell . . .' she stopped, dabbing at her eyes with the tissue. Rossi noticed no tears were falling. 'It's been getting stronger.'

'I'm surprised you noticed it,' Rossi said under her breath, earning her a stern look from Brannon.

'When was the last time you saw Keith, or Mr Henderson, Mrs Andrews?' Brannon asked, turning back to the woman.

'Couple of weeks ago now.'

'Can you remember exactly?'

Mrs Andrews' brow furrowed as she tried to remember. 'It'll come to me.'

'Did you speak to him often?

'Not really. He kept himself to himself, like everyone round here. Not like it used to be. Used to be able to talk to your neighbours and that, know how everyone was getting on and that. Not now though.'

Rossi nodded, hoping to show she was interested, when really all she wanted to do was shout at her. Talking about knowing the neighbour's personal lives when one of them lay dead next door. 'Have you noticed anything unusual in the last week then, anyone hanging around who you didn't recognise?'

'Well . . . there was a car?' Mrs Andrews replied, sitting forward and digging around in the sides of the chair looking for something. 'It was parked outside for hours about two nights ago.'

'Do you remember anything about it, colour, registration, something?' Rossi asked.

'I wrote it down, just in case. Can never be too careful. Could be burglars or anything. Here it is.' She pulled a small notebook out.

'Silver Mercedes, here's the registration number.' She carefully ripped off just that information and Brannon stepped forward to take it off her.

'Thanks very much,' Rossi said. 'That's incredibly helpful.'

'I just hope you catch whoever did it. Won't be able to sleep at night for thinking about what happened. Just glad I've got my babies to look after me.' She indicated the cats currently perched on any available surface.

'Yes, well, if that'll be everything . . .?' Rossi said quickly, not wanting to get into a conversation about her 'babies'.

'No. It's a terrible thing. House prices will go down now as well. That's all we need.'

They stood to leave, and almost got to the front door before Mrs Andrews shouted them back.

'It was last Tuesday. I spoke to him in the afternoon. I remember because that was Bertie's birthday.'

'Last Tuesday, nine days ago?'

'That's right.'

'Who's Bertie?' Brannon asked, Rossi already knowing the answer.

'That's the grumpy one on the windowsill.'

Rossi leaned against her car, tucking the same strands of hair which always fell across her face, behind her ear. It was a comfort gesture.

'It doesn't make sense,' she said, Brannon looking up from his phone towards her.

'What doesn't?'

She suffered his slowness in silence. 'If she saw him only nine days ago, how is he number two?'

He looked back at his phone. 'I don't follow.' She glanced

down at it, seeing a Facebook page on the screen. Typical. Lazy bastard couldn't be arsed to give his full attention for more than a few minutes.

'He was already on number five by then. Why would he go back and start two?'

Brannon shrugged. 'You think too much, Laura. That's your problem. Between you and Murphy losing his mind, no wonder it took you both so long to catch him.'

Rossi clenched a fist. 'Listen, think about it. Everything has been in order. Why change now?'

'I don't know, and I don't much care. It's done now. Let it go.'

Rossi fumed quietly. She missed Murphy, his openness to the pattern and his knowledge.

'We've got a name back from the car,' Brannon said eventually, 'Richard Garner. Mean anything to you?'

Rossi swallowed. 'Yes.'

Experiment One was Tom Davies. This was supposed to be number two. Yet, it wasn't right.

Unless, this was a distraction.

'If Tom Davies was Experiment One, does that mean he began the whole thing, or was someone else behind it?' Rossi spoke softly, thoughts spooling out of her head. 'Murphy was right. Jemma is Experiment Two.'

'Jemma who?' Brannon asked, staring at her with a confused expression.

She ignored it, 'and now with Tom inside, he has to return and finish off the experiment. *Stronzo* . . .'

'What? Can you speak in English at least?'

'Murphy.'

'What about him?'

Rossi circled the car to the driver's side. Motioned towards the uniforms stood outside the house.

'He's in trouble.'

386

45

Friday 15th February
2013 – Day Twenty

Murphy entered the house in front of Garner, unable to help himself from staring at the décor inside, open-mouthed. The grand staircase facing him, the antique furniture. He wasn't sure he'd ever been in a house so nice.

'Come through to the sitting roo,.' Garner said from beside him.

'Thanks,' Murphy replied, still staring at the artwork on one wall. Looked original.

They entered the sitting room as Garner had called it, Murphy expecting just a normal living room. Instead it was lavish, leather armchairs and an open fireplace. Bookcases filled the walls, filled with thick books which looked off-coloured. He paused looking at the titles, as Garner stood by an armchair.

'Please, sit. A drink perhaps?'

'Yeah, sure,' Murphy said, his attention still on the furniture, the grandness of it.

'Whisky okay? I know it's early, but I find it always takes the edge off a difficult situation.'

Murphy thought for a second. 'Just a small one. You have a remarkable home.'

'Thank you. Years of hard work. Oh, and of course it's a family deal, I was left the house by my parents. Professors aren't paid all that well, detective.' Garner said, handing a thick glass filled halfway with whisky, ice floating on top.

'Please, call me Murphy.'

They sat opposite each other, a small dark wood table between them. Murphy took a sip of the whisky. Smooth, a small kick as it hit the back of his throat.

'What can I do for you then, Mr Murphy.'

Murphy searched for the right words. 'Well, the case is over. I'm sure you've heard.'

'Yes. I was astonished, as you might have guessed.' A crooked hand around his glass, his other resting on the cane at his side. 'I suppose you never really know anyone.'

'Definitely. This case has been difficult for me, on a personal level. When we spoke the second time, I think you picked up on that.'

'Yes,' Garner replied, bringing the glass to his thin lips. 'Was this the first one since your parent's death?'

Murphy nodded, took a larger swig of his whisky.

'Well, it's to be expected that you'd find it a struggle. I'm not sure why you're here however.'

'When we spoke, professor . . .'

'Please, call me Richard.'

'Sorry, Richard. When we spoke, it seemed that you knew more about the whole process than I do. That you had some experience in counselling?'

'Well yes, that was my previous job. I've also written many papers about the grieving process. I'd be willing to share some of them with you.'

'That'd be good. But I need to talk to someone about things. I don't want to go to one of those counselling places. They're not for me. I need to speak to someone who understands it better. I thought you might be able to help.'

Garner studied him over his glasses. 'I'd be more than willing to talk to you. You understand I'm not a clinician any longer, though? I'm not sure how much I can help you, that's all.'

Murphy drained the last of his glass. Warmth filled his insides. 'I'm just trying to understand it all better.'

'Tell me what happened, with your parents?'

Murphy took in a breath. 'My wife . . . she has a dark past. The ex-boyfriend being the main part of that. He did four years for assaulting her, almost killed her. When he came out, he was angry. Felt it was my fault. When he found out we were married, he flipped I guess. Tried to get Sarah back, but she wasn't having any of it. He started following her, trying to pressure her into coming back to him. She never told me. When that didn't work, he targeted me instead. He found out where my parents lived, and killed them both. A neighbour had a CCTV camera in his front window, he had problems with kids hanging around his house. Caught him on that, plus the prints and blood in the house he'd left behind. He pleaded guilty and was sentenced three months ago. Life, minimum of twenty-seven years.'

'Do you feel like justice has been done?'

'Yes. No,' Murphy sighed, leaned forward with his hands over his face. 'I don't know. I've been running around the past few weeks, trying to work out how someone could do what Tom did. All the time, I was just thinking about myself. About my situation. If I could just come to terms with things, move on, I think I'd cope better.'

'Indeed. Death is inevitable, yet we're always surprised when it happens, when it touches our lives.'

Something stirred in Murphy. 'I've heard that before.'

'You read our paper?'

Murphy looked at him, confused, 'which paper?'

'The one I wrote with Tom. I should have known then. It

389

was titled "Life, Death, and Grief". He was only interested in the death part of it. Fascinated him. Tell me Mr Murphy did you tell anyone you were coming to see me?'

Murphy shook his head. 'This was just something I needed to do, you know.'

'Quite. Refill?' Garner shook his empty glass at him, standing up easily, before seemingly catching himself and grabbing his cane. Murphy handed the glass over to him.

'Tell me Mr Murphy, did you ever discover why Tom started at number three?'

Murphy's head span for a second, the momentary head rush you get from standing up too quickly. 'We thought he may have been involved with someone who went missing a year ago. He didn't acknowledge that though. He called himself Experiment One.'

'Interesting.'

'It doesn't make sense.' The room was becoming fuzzy around him. Murphy shook his head to try and clear it, confused. Alcohol never affected him this quickly.

'Have you ever heard of a psychologist named Stanley Milgram, Mr Murphy?'

Murphy rolled his head back up from where it had dropped onto his chest. 'I don't feel too good. How strong is this stuff?'

'Milgram was a psychologist, American of course. His most famous work is on obedience to authority. What could you make someone do, just by giving orders . . . far enough to kill for you, for example?'

'I don't understand . . .' Murphy rubbed at his eyes, trying to focus properly. The professor became blurry in front of him.

'Milgram tested forty people in his experiment. Each person took the role of teacher, sat in front of a board. Another person would be a *learner* and they would have to recite words, in a basic memory task. However, the learner was an actor – a fact unknown to each of the teachers. Each answer they would get wrong, the teacher would give them an electric shock, increasing in voltage at every point. Now, of course as the shocks got higher in strength they began to protest, they didn't want to continue. You know what kept them going? Someone telling them they must go on. That's all. A verbal prod in the right direction.' He paused, as Murphy rubbed at his eyes.

'How many of the forty teachers do you think gave them the highest voltage shock of four hundred and fifty, David?'

Murphy shook his head. 'I don't know. One . . . three . . . five?' He giggled to himself. Was he drunk? How much had he to drink?

'Twenty-six of them, Mr Murphy. Almost two thirds of the people willingly gave another human being a fatal electric shock, just by being told to do so. Isn't that incredible?'

'They must have known it wasn't real.' His voice sounded alien to him. Slurred. His arm came up to his face, but it took too much time. Far too slow.

'That's the beauty of it Mr Murphy. They had no idea. They thought the whole thing was real. They just went along with it. It gets better. When the teacher wasn't the one to administer the shock, when they could absolve themselves of responsibility and only watched as someone else seemingly electrocuted the learners, the level of obedience rose. Out of forty people, thirty-seven ordered the highest shock possible. That is the power of obedience. An incredible experiment, I'm sure you'll agree. How obedient do you think you are David? Do you listen to authority well?'

'I do my best.' Murphy sniggered at the thought of DCI Stephens trying to control him. 'I should have killed him.'

'Of course you do. You're in the police, you must have a lot of bosses, and I can't imagine it's all like the TV shows and films with the rogue detectives and such like. You'd be out of a job in no time.'

'Should have strangled him to death.'

'Quite.'

Murphy tried to stand, flopping back down into his seat. 'What's happening to me?'

'The whisky has gone to your head I see. Come with me. We'll get you sorted out.'

Murphy stood up again, his legs supporting him in an odd fashion. Garner held out an arm for him and Murphy grabbed hold of it. It felt thick, like a tree trunk. So confused.

'Just down here.'

The doorway led to a darkened hallway, another shaft of daylight shining through from a smaller window at the end.

'Keep walking towards the end, the door on the bottom left is open. Can you see it?'

Murphy wasn't sure what he could see. He continued to shuffle forwards, the smell of tobacco and whisky walking alongside him. They got to the doorway, pausing for a second before turning and entering it. It was darker inside the room than the hallway. He thought the windows were at the far end of the room, the black cloth hanging from the ceiling covering that area giving him a clue. Only a soft glow from a few floor lamps gave off any light. His attention was drawn to desks in the middle of the room, and the banks of monitors placed upon them. The images were blurry from a distance. He was only able to tell they were CCTV type video images on six different small screens.

A large metal chair was placed directly facing the screens. Murphy walked towards it, shuffled, sitting down as soon as he reached it. He could see the screens, his eyes scanned across them as he saw his car parked up, the dirty lane he'd driven up to reach the house.

'That's my car,' he said, pointing at the screen.

'That's right. I'll have to get rid of that somehow.'

'What's happening to me?'

Garner walked around the chair to face him, his cane left behind. 'I'm afraid you were mistaken coming here.'

'You . . . put . . . something . . .'

'Yes. Terribly 007, don't you think?'

'I don't understand.'

Garner lifted his hand, pointing at the last screen. 'Do you see her?'

Murphy swept his head across to look. Squinted his eyes to focus.

Night vision gave out a weird green glow. A woman, by a door.

His head cleared for a brief moment.

Jemma Barnes.

'I'm carrying on the experiment Mr Murphy. It needs to continue.'

Murphy tried to lift himself up, 'I've got to get to her . . .'

'Don't let me stop you.'

Murphy got to his feet, swayed, but moved forward out of the room. He opened the door in front of him, a large kitchen appeared. A door was open, stairs leading down. 'She's down there.'

Garner appeared beside him. 'Yes. Go to her.'

Murphy shuffled forward, holding one hand against the wall to support himself. Nothing made sense. It was like a dream become real. He reached the door, opened it out. A staircase was below him.

'Here, let me help you.' Murphy turned, Garner stood a few feet to the side of him. The cane held in his hands aloft.

Murphy was flying.

Moving forwards, slowly, hung in mid-air. Then the stairs rushed up towards him.

He didn't feel the pain.

Just the darkness which took over him, sending him into unconsciousness.

Helpless.

Experiment Two

She waited, expecting him to come back at any moment.

The hatch remained open as the voice which had spoken to her earlier had left it. Careless.

She waited longer. Stood still for what seemed like hours . . . days?

She strained to hear anything. Thought she could hear voices, but wasn't sure if they were coming from outside the room, or from the corner.

Something stirred inside her head. An idea?

Jemma remembered the one time she'd heard the door open. A bolt moving across.

She looked at the hatch. Rolled up her sleeve and edged her arm through the opening. Her skinny arm, all bone and barely-there flesh, fit through easily. She swept her hand across up and down the side, searching for it.

Her hand bumped against metal. She scrabbled across, reaching for it, for the bolt.

Found it.

She released it, pulled it across towards her. Heard it clunk back out of its locked state.

Jemma drew her arm back through the hatch opening, scraping it along the wood, causing her to flinch in pain.

She dared not believe.

Jemma gripped the hatch opening with both hands and pulled. The door opened easily.

She was out.

Shit. She was out. That easily.

Jemma crept from the room, into the basement she'd once escaped out into. She closed her eyes, picturing the way it had looked. The room opposite hers now silent, the door closed. The stairs to her left, the light coming through there now.

Then something . . . someone appeared at the top.

It fell forwards. Bone on concrete, crushing against it.

She fell against the wall, her breathing rapid, loud.

She had to be quiet.

Jemma waited. Heard footsteps come down. Held her breath, as she waited to be found. Out of her room. She shouldn't be out of there. That was her home now.

No. She had to get out.

She heard a voice, old, soft. Phlegmy.

'Tom was my experiment, Mr Murphy. I wanted to see how obedient he would be, how pliant. I wanted to make him my own personal project. He went further than I ever could have imagined. In that room there, is Tom's first experiment. She's mine now though. I want to break her. Like Tom couldn't.'

Jemma willed herself to move, to run past them, up the stairs.

Out.

'I never thought I'd be in a position to do this again, but you came right to my door. Made it so simple for me. But I see now that it's too dangerous.'

Jemma put one foot forward, praying he wouldn't hear her.

'I'm going to take care of you, and then leave. I'm a very wealthy man, Mr Murphy. I can disappear any time I like. It will be fun to start again.'

Jemma kept moving towards the open space where she hoped to find the stairs out of there. Whoever had come down them face first had fallen to the side, four or five feet away from the staircase. She could see by the light coming from the top, a man crouched over him, talking to him.

He felt the pain. His head was muddy, like he was trying to think through treacle.

He felt the pain though.

Then, he could hear him. Talking.

He opened his eyes, tried to focus. The lack of light made it difficult.

Murphy knew what was coming. Didn't think it'd end like this. He tried to move, but couldn't, pain firing across every inch of him.

He felt the hand over his mouth, his nose being clenched tight. He tried to move. He tried. He tried.

He was slipping away.

Sarah. Mum, Dad.

He'd told Rossi. But he knew it wasn't enough. It was too late. Then, movement. He'd almost missed it, but there was a shadow. He looked past the professor, focusing.

It was Jemma.

He willed her to run. To go, not look back.

Murphy would be okay dying down there, if it meant someone else got to live.

She paused at the top of the stairs.

She should just go. Run. She'd made this mistake before.

She was going. Leaving whoever was down there.

They probably didn't exist. They weren't real. Outside was real. Daylight was real. She remembered it.

Rob was real.

Rob was dead. She finally accepted all she had heard down there.

She could hear gasping from below. She turned away from it.

It was too late. She had to leave.

Then she saw the cane leaning against the doorway. Heavy.

He couldn't breathe.

He was going. Fading.

He never got the chance. To fix things. To make up for what he did to Sarah.

Murphy's foot moved. Reflex.

Jemma Barnes was really down there, a whole year. He couldn't imagine it. He was almost thankful for the fact the professor was ending this quickly.

Then, he heard a loud crash and both hands, the one over his mouth, the other over his nose, went slack.

He sucked in air, as the professor slumped over him.

Murphy looked up, someone standing, holding the professor's cane to her side, panting heavily.

Jemma looked down at him, kicked the professor's limp body away from Murphy.

Then, the cane came down again, Murphy flinching as he heard skull crunching, something wet sprayed across his face.

Blood.

He became aware of screams, Jemma, taking out one year of frustration on what Murphy hoped was a now-lifeless body.

Let her have it. Let her have her own form of justice.

He welcomed the darkness as its waves crashed over him.

* * *

She breathed heavily, throwing the cane to one side as she'd finished. It was done. She could leave, escape. In the dim light she could make out the two bodies at her feet. One old man, no longer breathing.

The other man, lying there, shallow breaths. Eyes closed.

She didn't know if he was one of them; she didn't even know how many were involved. There could be more waiting up the stairs.

She wrung her hands, pulling on the end of her short hair, throwing the strands which came away to the floor.

No more. No more. No more.

She was talking out loud, without realising.

Looked at the cane where she'd thrown it to the floor. Back towards the other, still breathing, man.

Cocked her head to one side. Thinking, thinking, thinking.

Turned and ran.

Epilogue

The rain stopped falling as the clouds parted, allowing a dull sun to shine down. She stepped out of the car, her mum rushing around to the side of the car to lend her a hand. She brushed her off, wanting to do it alone.

'Stay here.'

She had to do it alone.

She walked slowly up the path towards the building at the centre. She paused every few steps, pretending to read gravestones as she did, in order to not worry her mum.

She reached the centre display. The dim sunlight glinting off the gold plaques for those cremated instead of buried.

She walked slowly around it, looking at each one in turn.

She knelt down when she found the one she was looking for.

'Hi Rob, it's me. I'm sorry it's taken me so long to visit. I've been asking to leave for so long, but they wouldn't let me go until they were happy with my progress. I'm doing better now, I'm eating properly, I can be out in the daylight again.' She smiled, it not reaching her eyes.

'I miss you so much Rob. Towards the end, I started to forget your face. I'm sorry. I'm so sorry Rob.'

She wiped the tears from her eyes.

'I bought you something. I was going to keep it, but this way, I'll always have a reason to come here.'

She dug into the earth behind the stone, making a small hole. She put her hand in her coat pocket, removing the bracelet. She traced a finger round the dolphin charm. She took out a small plastic pouch and placed the bracelet inside, sealing it closed.

'I can't wear this without you around. So I'm leaving it here for you to look after for me, okay?'

She dropped the bracelet into the small hole, moving the soil back over the top of it.

'He took you away from me Rob, but there's something he can't take.'

She traced a finger around his name on the plaque, the letters raised in black. Rob had been cremated, she'd been told. A plaque on a stone structure filled with grass and flowers in the warmer months, rather than a grave to visit.

'You taught me not to run. You showed me there was a place for me here. I'll never forget that.' Her touched her fingers to her lips and then to the plaque.

'I love you.'

She stood up, dull pain in her legs, less sharp than it once was, getting better every day.

She walked back to the waiting car, the smell of damp, recently cut grass swarming around her.

Jemma reached the car, noting the concern on her mum's face. She pulled her into an embrace, tucking her head into her mum's shoulder.

'I'm okay Mum, really.'

Jemma broke the clinch, wiping her eyes again. She saw him, standing with folded arms about a hundred yards away. His size gave him away.

She walked towards him, meeting him halfway as he did the same.

Uncomfortable silence. She broke it.

'You don't have to say it.'

'I think I do.'

She smiled softly. 'If you hadn't turned up, I wouldn't have been able to get out.'

'And if you hadn't come back, I'd be dead.'

'How are you?'

'Good thanks. Broken arm and a couple of broken ribs. Don't think my back will be right for a while. Good job I had all this weight to cushion the fall. You?'

'Can't complain. It'll be a while before I'm back out in town, but little steps and that.'

'You need anything, you contact me. Any time.'

He handed her a card. She pocketed it without a word.

They looked at each other. Something passed between them. He withdrew a hand from his pocket, placed it on her shoulder. Gave a soft squeeze.

She smiled more strongly at him. Then turned back towards her mum.

She reached the car. Her mum raised her eyebrows. Jemma responded by pulling her into an embrace, hugging her tightly.

She broke it off, wiping her face. 'Okay. I'm ready.'

Murphy leaned forward, shifting the phone to his other ear as he grabbed his coffee from the centre console. Only one a day now, otherwise he'd be up late. He was sleeping better now, and didn't want to disturb that.

'Sad. At least they'll get closure now. The families I mean.'

'True. We're still checking on his movements though, see if there are any more possible victims. I think he's been doing this for a long time.'

'How is she doing?'

'About as well as can be expected. It's going to take a long time for her to be normal again, if ever. A year, Jess. Can you imagine it?'

'I'd rather not, Bear.' Jess paused. 'How are things going?'

'Can't complain. Start back soon. Once I'm out of this sling. Looking forward to it.'

Jess laughed. 'It won't last. Are you ready?'

'Yes. Bring it on. Like the kids would say.'

Jess snorted. 'No kids say that. Not for years.'

Murphy rolled his eyes. 'I was being sarcastic.'

'Course you were.'

'I've got to go.'

Jess sighed. 'I'm already being shunted out of the way for her again. I knew this would happen.'

Murphy laughed. 'Of course not. Just, I wouldn't make the trip over any time soon. And maybe ring ahead from now on?'

Murphy sat on Rossi's car bonnet, placing his phone back in his pocket. The rain began to fall gently, as they watched Jemma leave.

Rossi stood off to his side, her face creased into a frown.

Murphy looked up at her. 'How has she been . . . really?'

Rossi sighed. 'Malnourished, light sensitive, confused, disorientated. As well as can be expected. It's going to take a lot longer than a week or so before she's back to normal. She'll be going through counselling for years probably.'

Murphy looked away towards the cemetery, pleased to feel its hold over him not as strong as before. 'How much do you reckon he was worth?'

'As in money?'

Murphy nodded at her.

'Good few million I reckon. Lot of it will be tied up in property. Why?'

Murphy turned back to Rossi, 'just makes you think doesn't it? You can be screwed up, no matter what your background.'

'I'm sorry I didn't get there in time. She shouldn't have had to do that.'

'I think she'll be all right.'

No charges were going to be filed against her. Murphy had put in a word. Embellished the life or death situation in her favour a little.

'Hmm. I keep thinking, why?' Rossi continued.

'Who knows,' Murphy replied. 'Maybe he's a tortured genius. Wanting to use humans for experimentation. Wasn't that long ago people accepted it. Or maybe he was just a nutcase. Not our job to analyse. We solved it all, end of story for us.'

Rossi came around and sat next to Murphy on the car. 'And you?'

'I'm good. Much better now. This is a new beginning, Laura. Me and you, we're going to do some good work together.'

He looked towards her, smiling as he saw her expression relax. 'Did you ring that bloke from the university?'

Rossi turned away from him. 'Early days. Think he might be a bit too posh for me.'

'Give it a chance Laura. He seemed alright to me.'

She nodded, standing up off the bonnet. 'Want me to drive you over the water? I don't mind driving. Even if it is technically woollyback country,' she said, smiling.

Murphy scratched at his beard. Looked to the sky, letting the rain hit his face a little more.

'No. It's okay. I'm not going there.' Murphy replied. 'I'm going home.'

Luca Veste talks serial killers

There's something about the serial killer - that rare breed in reality which nevertheless has filled the pages of many crime novels in the past thirty years - which has captivated crime fiction readers. Even going back as far as Agatha Christie, the serial killer has stalked the pages of many a thriller or police procedural, utilising numerous methods and reasons for their murderous intentions. However, how do our favourite fictional serial killers measure up to what we know about the reality of those who would be categorised as such outside of the pages of a novel . . . and what's really under the surface of the modern serial killer?

The popularisation of serial killers within crime fiction can be traced back to the creation of Hannibal Lecter by Thomas Harris in 1981. Even though serial killers had been utilised in crime fiction previous to this, it was Lecter and his effervescent allure and charisma, combined with his capacity for extreme violence, which captivated so many readers and has led to a plethora of serial killer novels. Much like the case of the real-life serial murderer 'Jack the Ripper', and the attempts to unmask his identity, the serial killer has become the story, rather than the victims, with his (or her – however this is much less the case in reality than in fiction) crimes, emotions, reasons, being much more of interest than the victims. There's design, formula, with (invariably) someone in authority pitting their wits against the killer.

But what motivates a serial killer to commit his crimes? As can be seen with the continuing interest in the Jack the Ripper case, attention on serial killers is by no means a new phenomenon. The growing attention given to the murder of multiple victims by a single person, gave rise to the term 'Serial Killer', during the late 1960s. The term which is usually attributed as being coined by FBI Agent Robert Ressler, was in fact first used by John Brophy in his 1966 book 'The Meaning of Murder'. Robert Ressler is however widely credited as being at the forefront of the explosion of concern for the seemingly growing trend of mass murders. It was at that point, profiling of serial killers began to gain some traction; predominately through the work of Ressler and John Douglas and the interviews they carried out with thirty-six mass murderers in various prisons. This in turn led to Holmes and De Burger in 1988, and then further in 1996, classifying serial killers into four different types; namely 'Visionary', 'Mission-Oriented', 'Hedonistic', and 'Power/Control Oriented'. In turn, each type has certain characteristics which mark them out as different to each other. The Visionary type, is one who commits their crimes whilst being told or commanded to do so by voices or visions. The Mission-Oriented type believe they have a certain goal which they must reach, or problem to solve. This could take the form of eliminating a certain group from their surroundings, such as prostitutes or children. Victims are often unknown to the killer, yet fit into the category they wish to remove from their society. The Hedonistic type, which contains many strands, uses the umbrella term to describe a killer who commits their crimes for pleasure. Lastly, the power/control oriented killer type shares many aspects the hedonistic killer. However the difference is at the epicentre of their motives, which is to exert complete control or power over another human being. The act of murder provides the finality of a series of acts leading up to that moment, all providing pleasure to this type of killer. In more recent times, more strands have been added to these four different types, but the various aspects of each still remain.

Back to the release of Thomas Harris's 'Red Dragon, this epitomised the growing public interest/concern into serial murderers. The novel was released at just the right time, capturing the imagination of the public in a much similar way as Jack the Ripper had done over ninety years previous. Of course the difference here, is one is fictional and one is not. Does the mythologizing of the Jack the Ripper case say something about how a public interest in murder, and in particular the randomness of some serial murder, manifest itself in the fiction they read? In crime fiction, arguably the most popular choice for writers when creating serial killer characters tend to fall into a mix of categories with the hedonistic type and power/control orientated types. In British crime fiction, from the excellent creation of 'Stuart Nicklin' in Mark Billingham's 'Scaredy Cat' and 'Death Message' to Val McDermid's 'Jacko Vance' the most popular serial killer creations have their basis on those types first indicated by those criminologists in the 1980s. However, over time more strands are being explored within the serial killer novel. When done well, this can work, with the likes of Dexter Morgan from the Jeff Lindsay novels and his 'code' - only killing those who have done wrong - and also, with writers such as Lauren Beukes, Steve Mosby, and John Connolly utilising other genres in their work, this helps to keep the serial killer genre fresh and exciting. There's also characters such as Lee Child's 'Reacher', who is for all intents and purposes a serial killer, but is never treated as such by readers in the main.

The appetite for serial killer novels is arguably rooted in a deeper sense of security in the fictional. It's long been suggested that readers use fiction to live out their own fears vicariously, knowing in the vast majority of cases the "hero" will prosper. The motivating factors of fictional serial killers are laid bare, in a final act of good vs evil, before all is made right in the world. Most are often resolved to a satisfactory conclusion, providing a sense of balance to what is often not the case in reality, with serial killers often not providing explanations for their actions leaving psychologists and criminologists to provide answers based on the best evidence available. For example, the most prolific serial murderer in the U.K. is Harold Shipman, with over two hundred victims linked to him. However, was Shipman a power/control orientated type, or did he murder for financial gain (which would place them in the hedonistic type), or did he hear voices, such as a visionary type would? It's impossible to know now. Do our fictional serial killers ever match up to the nightmare of the very real serial killers of Henry Lee Lucas, John Wayne Gacy, or Dennis Nilsen? Or is there protection found between the pages of a novel - the reader safe in the knowledge that it will *probably* never happen to them . . .?